NOW SHE IS WITCH

Also by Kirsty Logan

The Rental Heart and Other Fairytales
The Gracekeepers
A Portable Shelter
The Gloaming
Things We Say in the Dark

Now She is Witch

KIRSTY LOGAN

Harvill *Secker*

LONDON

1 3 5 7 9 10 8 6 4 2

Harvill Secker, an imprint of Vintage, is part of the Penguin Random
House group of companies whose addresses can be found at
global.penguinrandomhouse.com

Penguin
Random House
UK

First published by Harvill Secker in 2023

A CIP catalogue record for this book is available from the British Library

penguin.co.uk/vintage

ISBN 9781787303423 (hardback)
ISBN 9781787303430 (trade paperback)

Typeset in 10.3/16.5 pt Ashbury by Jouve (UK), Milton Keynes
Printed and bound in Great Britain by Clays Ltd, Elcograf S.p.A.

The authorised representative in the EEA is Penguin Random House Ireland,
Morrison Chambers, 32 Nassau Street, Dublin D02 YH68

Penguin Random House is committed to a sustainable future
for our business, our readers and our planet. This book is made
from Forest Stewardship Council® certified paper.

To Great Aunt Edith – I hope I'm like you when I grow up.

'The dead are not separate from the living.
The darkness is not separate from the light.
They are intertwined.'

– HANNE ØRSTAVIK

'they are the damsel they are the horse
they are riding themselves they are saving themselves'

– REBECCA TAMÁS

Before

my mother tells me a story –

  our house in the forest is tiny & ramshackle & the winter wind slips freezing through the cracks & my belly is never full & my hands always ache but i dont care when there is a story –

  especially when it is this story which is the scariest & best –

  it is about the north witches –

  they are terrible my mother says –

  they are rotten & filthy to the core & burned black inside from the raging fires of their power –

  the north witches my mother says burn so fierce that in the land where they live they created a volcano which is earth & fire & liquid all at once & not one thing at all –

  a volcano surrounded by black earth & a sea lapping at black sand –

  the north witches my mother says can transform into ravens & wolves & suchlike other wicked creatures –

  the north witches my mother says are lit by a sun that stays in the sky all night in the summer & hides entirely in the winter –

  the north witches my mother says dont need the light at all –

  not from the sun and not from god –

they take out their eyes & polish them & then they can see in the dark –

so you can know them from the unholy gleam of their eyes –

when they come for you in the night –

& what we do –

thats my mother & i –

what we do isnt the same as what those witches do –

we sell our poppets & our poisons & we promise curses but its different –

because most of it is use less & a fancy show & no thing else –

we live in a house barely bigger than our out stretched arms & we are all ways hungry how could a curse from our mouths do any thing –

the only power is in the plants & poisons because their power comes from god & not from us –

but the north witches can make things happen with only them selves –

they are neither one thing nor the other making them unnatural dangerous –

which is why my mother says i am to stay well clear –

which i think will be very easy –

its not exactly like theyre knocking on our door now is it –

you must stay away from the north witches my mother says –

& its no good i am already asleep –

i am deep inside a dream –

about a white sea that never rests licking over the sand as black as night –

about blue glaciers cast up glassy and gleaming on the shore –

about a volcano so powerful so restless its steam billowing into the wild sea from a crevice in the folded rocks –

about light & dark together in one woman –

a woman neither one thing nor another –

free to spill out & glow & burn so she scorches every thing even the
land she stands on –

a woman with fire inside and power in every word she speaks –

& i want –

i want –

but theres no use in a girl wanting –

PART 1

1

Now She is Outcast

Full night. Bitter bone cold. Winter solstice, the longest night of the year. Lux had started on her mother's grave long before daylight, clearing the nettles from the centre of the poison garden until she reached bare dirt. But the ground was hard as gritted teeth, and she'd had to smash the ice on the well and raise buckets of water and build a fire and heat the water over the stove and pour it on the frozen ground before she could even start to dig. Her hands were swollen and lumpy with nettle stings, made worse by the grazes on her palms, but she was so cold she couldn't feel it. She hadn't noticed the meagre light failing, and had kept working into the darkness; the shortest day was over, and now stars swayed in her eyes.

She was making the grave in the poison garden so it would stay hidden; no one would venture into the murk behind the house, particularly if they knew it was full of things that could kill them. Since she'd been away, the nettles had grown shoulder-high, but she could see that some of the garden still grew beneath. The dried-up tongue of the foxglove, the curled purple ear of the wolfsbane.

There wasn't much else. She'd found the empty house in a sorry state. Everything movable was gone; everything attached was broken. The two wooden chairs that flanked the fireplace, the broom and bucket that hung on the wall, the dented copper pot – all gone. Half the roof was pulled down. Someone – or many someones – had pissed in the corners, and the damp and reek had spread over much of the floor. The straw that had been ripped from the mattress stuck, wilted, in the piss. It was fair enough that the people from the village had thieved from her, considering all the things she'd taken from them over the years. At least the things she took had tasted nice. And she'd never pissed in their houses. Though she probably would have, given the chance, and spat in them too.

There were some things left – things no one had dared to touch. Scraps of sacking and carved bone buttons used to make poppets in the shape of a person. Tiny bottles filled with piss and spit and some herbs. Shrivelled flowers, looking like pretty bits of nothing, though Lux knew each small bloom was enough to kill a man – or sicken him, if that's what you preferred. And right there, hidden in the shadows in the corner where she used to sleep: a tiny jar of oil with a handful of plump black pearls. Lux's blood leapt to see the nightshade.

One drop beautifies a woman's eyes, making their centres black and round as the moon. Two drops reddens the lips and gives a woman a slow, fainting grace. Three or more – then her beauty is set in stone forever, and she will never age another day, and she's fit only for the grave. A full necklace of nightshade would go far; there was never a lack of women who wanted to be beautiful, nor who wanted someone dead.

She'd immediately found a needle and thread and stitched the nightshade pearls into a necklace. If people were glad to hear she'd returned, she would have something to sell to them. If they weren't glad, she would have something to threaten them with.

That was what her mother had taught her: they won't love you, so you will have to make them fear you.

Lux dropped to her knees, feeling her bones judder, feeling her breath hitch. She'd wanted to make a grave as big as her mother's body, even though she didn't have her body to bury. Her mother's black teeth, her cracking bones, her milky eyes. The time she rested her hand on Lux's head. The lullaby she once sang, late-night and half drunk, voice soft and wavering. Now all that remained was a scrap of bright red ribbon, the thing her mother had most cherished, the thing no one had seen fit to destroy or steal from their empty house. But the ground was so hard and every scoop of dirt took so long that after a whole day's work, she'd barely managed a grave big enough for the ribbon.

Lux put the ribbon in the meagre grave and curled her body around it. The nettles met like a roof over her head; down here it was dark as pitch, dark as ravens, dark as a Bible. She was starting to shiver. The black woollen dress and thin cloak they'd made her wear to leave the sanctuary were filthy and sweat-sodden now. They had been fine when she was moving through the forest or digging, but now that she was still, the cold seeped into her bones.

She stayed there, watching as the moon grew loose and milky behind clouds, then shone bright and clear again. She stayed until her shivering stopped and she felt only numb. She stayed until her mother came to her, stroking her fingers along Lux's forehead and around her skull and down the nape of her neck, then back, and again, and again; soothing her, smoothing out the fears, singing a lullaby so soft that it was barely more than breath. Mother, she said, and in the dream she hadn't come home too late.

Lux jerked awake. Soil dirty and morning cold and nettle itching and a voice was calling out to her, and it was a woman.

Lux flexed her hands and feet, feeling life pinpricking back into her body. Frost glinted on every surface: the nettles, the moss-padded logs that made up the outer walls, the looming trees circling the clearing. She had slept until dawn, the winter light pale and unsure, knowing it only had a few hours to stay. She wrapped her cloak around her arms, pushed through the nettles, and peered around the side of the house.

She met a hooded face, peering right back at her, close as a kiss, and in surprise she let out a cry. She couldn't see the stranger's face; the hood cast its own shadow.

The stranger lifted a hand to Lux's face – then seemed to think better, and snatched it back. Lux thought the stranger had moved to hit her. But then she thought that the stranger had reached out softly, to touch her cheek.

The stranger stepped back to make space between them. To cover her confusion, Lux ripped a fistful of dock leaves and rubbed them on her swollen hands. The soothe was instant. Habit took over; Lux strode to the house.

She stood in the doorway, pulled to her full height, hands pressed to the frame to keep them steady. She was so tired, and the cold went right through her bones and out the other side, and the grazes on her palms burned, and the nettle stings throbbed, and she was so hungry that she felt like bending over and retching, and she hadn't slept in a bed for weeks, and she wanted everyone and everything to go away so she could bury her mother's bit of stupid ribbon in peace.

She blinked her eyes clear and swallowed the lump in her throat. She knew that she was dirt-smeared, exhausted, stinking of her labours; knew that juice from the nightshade berries would have streaked like blood down her throat. But she also knew that she needed this stranger's coins. She could do it. She could be what this stranger wanted her to be.

'I have what you need,' Lux said. 'Tell me what you want, and I will use all of my powers to help you achieve it.' She had never felt so powerless in her life, but the stranger didn't have to know that. She felt the nightshade berries around her neck, and tried to take strength from them.

'You,' came the reply. Under the hood, the stranger spoke from her own personal shadow; Lux could see nothing of her face, but her voice sounded like a woman's. The words came out strangely, slowly, as if she'd forgotten how to use her tongue. 'What I want is you.'

Lux felt a shiver of irritation. Why was nothing ever straightforward? Why couldn't she just help this woman get rid of her baby or her husband or her neighbour or whoever was burdening her simple little life? Why did there have to be a guessing game when everyone knew the purpose of this house in the forest and the things that grew there?

The brief winter day would soon fade and there was still so much to do to make the house habitable. Sweeping, and scrubbing, and afterwards fresh clean hay spread all over the floor. She could sneak to the village and steal it from the cowshed. She could take some other things while she was at it, food and clothes, perhaps something soft to sit on; there was sure to be someone sick or sleeping or distracted. Those who had the least often couldn't stop others from taking it. Things too big to steal could be fixed. The furniture could be mended or remade. The roof could be patched; spoons and bowls could be carved again. She could make things as they were before. She could be what they wanted. Give them poppets and possets in return for peace. She could be less troublesome than her mother. She could forget that they had accused her of witchcraft and that the lord had sent her to die. She would keep their secrets and not ask for anything in return. She could play nice, take her mother's place, walk the line between useful and dangerous until they decided that she knew too much and sent her to die too. A fire rose in her, rage and shame and revenge and injustice all tangled together and burning her, lighting her way to –

She tamped it down. She blinked her eyes clear. She bit down on what wanted to come out of her mouth: a sigh, or a shriek.

'Well,' she said, 'here I am. Tell me what you want from me.'

'To help me seek revenge.'

'I am not in the business of revenge,' said Lux carefully. 'I am a mere healer. I can sell you a salve made from herbs that have healing powers. But I will warn you that if you use more than I tell you to, and it causes harm, or even death – that's not my business, but yours. Do you understand?'

'*You* don't understand.' The woman's words still sounded strange and slow, like her tongue was swollen. 'I want you to help me get revenge on a man. The man who calls women witches so he has an excuse to kill them.'

The world shivered around Lux. She reached out her hand and pressed it to the door frame to keep from drowning. She hadn't been there when her mother had died; she was in the sanctuary; held down in her bed, shrieking and sweating, the exorcist's cool hand pressed to her burning forehead, and the devil inside her, making her do things, making her say...

'I can –' Lux's voice faltered, and she swallowed before trying again. 'I can sell you a salve that will... that will...'

'No,' said the stranger. 'I want you to help me poison the lord. He is at the stronghold north of here.'

Lux reached for her nightshade necklace, grounding herself. 'This is nightshade,' she said. 'I will sell you three berries. But listen carefully. One drop will make you beautiful – two, if you're careful, or you don't mind being asleep while beautiful. But you must not use all three on a person, particularly not all at once, because they will surely die.'

'That is not what I want.'

'That is what you can have.'

Lux thought then of a story her mother used to tell her: a warning about north witches, who had fire inside and power in every word they spoke. Witches who didn't need the light at all, as they polished their eyes to let them see in the dark.

She looked more closely at the stranger. Her face was still hidden in the shadows beneath her hood – but as she tilted her head, Lux was sure she caught a flash of light.

'Who are you?' asked Lux.

'My name is Else.'

'I'm Lux.'

'Lux,' repeated Else, and though Lux couldn't see her face, from her voice it was clear that she was smiling.

Else still had her hood up, so it was hard to be sure, but Lux thought there was something around her mouth: little pocks or scars. Perhaps she'd had the sickness as a child, black roses blooming across her forehead, leaving their marks as they withered and faded. Perhaps her nostrils had been slit or her cheek branded – punishments for thieving or sexual deviancy. Diseased or criminal, and which was preferable?

'Perhaps I will buy your pearls,' said Else. 'But I wish to see their power. Such a display is always convincing, I find.'

Else plucked one plump black pearl from Lux's nightshade necklace. She raised it to her scar-circled lips, smiled, and pushed it into her mouth. Lux started forward, fingers flinching out, wanting to grab the berry from Else's tongue.

Else reached for two more pearls and ate those too.

'Stop!' cried Lux, grabbing at her necklace, 'that's too many!', pulling away from Else, 'it will kill you!', shoving Else's hands away from her, but it was too late. Else had another pearl in her hand. Then it was in her mouth. Then it was gone.

Else swallowed daintily. She held out her hand for another berry.

Lux had been handling poisons her whole life – could wade into the poison garden and come out with nothing more than a few nettle stings – and still, she couldn't eat that many nightshade berries with no effect. It took ten or so berries to kill, but four would certainly make an attempt at it: the heart will race, the speech will stumble, the body will convulse. And yet Else was fine. This was a power that Lux had never seen before.

'Show me your eyes,' said Lux.

Else reached for her hood, but hesitated, pulling it back into place, keeping her face in shadow. She reached out a hand towards Lux's face – but this time, she didn't pull it back. Softly, she rested her hand on Lux's cheek.

A flame rose up in Lux then. It wasn't enough to burn. Not yet. Without thinking, Lux leaned in to Else's hand. Else's skin was cold and soft, gentle as dawn.

At the first howl, Lux felt she was waking from a dream. Her heart stuttered as another cry joined, then another. Not beasts, but men: the ululating calls of a hunt.

Without thinking, Lux pulled Else into the house and shut the door.

Silence. Footsteps, breathing. Then: a single knock on the door of the house.

'Miss Lux?' A male voice, deep but not so deep: a boy, not a man. 'Are you there? I've come for a charm.'

Lux couldn't be sure, but she thought she could hear him swallow a laugh. She knew that voice. It was one of the boys from the village. She went to open the door, but Else held up a hand in warning.

'Miss Lux? Please let me in. I have coins.'

'You won't need to pay for her charms,' called another boy. 'Not a girl like that.'

The boy at the door had dropped his pretence. 'Open the door, Lux! I'm cold out here!'

Another boy joined in. 'We know you're in there! My sister was at the sanctuary, she knows you were kicked out.'

Another boy – or the same one, it was hard to tell, the way their voices merged, laughter and shouts – added: 'Your mother's not here to protect you now! You know what they say about a girl alone.' He stretched out that final word in mockery, turning it into a wolf's howl.

One of them banged hard on the door. 'It's only me. Little old me. Don't you want to let me inside?'

'And me!' called the other boy.

'I want to come inside too!' called another.

'How many can fit inside you at once, Miss Lux?'

'Let us in and you can show us. We heard what you did.'

'Are you frozen inside from the devil's cold prick?'

'We'll warm you up!'

'We heard you begged for the devil to ride you all night!'

'Witch bitch! Bitch witch!'

Together, Lux and Else barred the door and pressed their backs against it. Lux wished that she still had the heavy wooden table, or an intact chair, or the wooden bed frame - anything that could be put against the door. But everything was stolen or broken.

They began to chant: witch, bitch, witch, bitch. Another voice joined, and Lux almost cried out: a girl's voice, one she thought she knew, but couldn't place. So this was the sister from the sanctuary.

Lux looked frantically around the house. They could hide in the roof beams. They could lie in the nettles. They could run into the trees. Lux felt sick and scared and angry and not ready, not ready to fight, not ready to give up.

Then she realised: she could see, despite the darkness of the house. There was light from outside, flickering and gold, and had the boys really come for her with burning torches? She felt a bright high laugh rise in her throat. This was it, then. The villagers were marching with burning torches to burn the witch, just like the stories, and how ridiculous it was that she was going to die like –

And then, without warning, the boys were upon them. Fists battered the door. Fists and feet, a barrage of sound, in rhythm with their chanting. Lux was pushed forward by the force of the blows. She pressed her heels into the dirt and stood her ground.

Else, too, was jolted off balance. Her hood tipped back, revealing her close-cropped hair, her gleaming eyes, her face. A face Lux hadn't seen before, but one that felt familiar. Fear rose up in her - and love, and sadness, and the ache for comfort, and she didn't have time to think about that more because the boys had kicked right through the door now, the splintering of it, the sudden lack of anything at her back.

She fell to her knees. The ground juddered her bones. Else dragged her to the back wall of the house where they both crouched in the dark, eyes gleaming like trapped animals. The fire from their torches dazzled Lux's eyes and she couldn't see anything, she couldn't feel anything, her heart was going to choke her and she couldn't breathe. She couldn't breathe. She reached for Else's hand, and her skin was cold and dry, and that helped. She thought of nothing except getting to the next breath.

'Come here, Lux,' said one of the boys, outlined in the doorway. 'Come here, little pretty bit.'

Lux did no such thing. 'No thank you,' she said, and she heard how her voice shook.

'We won't hurt you,' said another boy, his voice calm, reasonable.

'Unless you like it,' said another. 'And I think you will.'

Their faces were smiling and open. Their voices were steady. There was no shrieking now, no calls of the hunt. They didn't want to spook the animal. Lux felt her heart beat high and hard.

'No,' she said again, 'thank you.'

The winter sun was pale, and the torches were bright against it, but she thought she caught a movement in the darkness beneath the trees. Was it the girl from the sanctuary? Surely she would speak out. She wouldn't let the boys hurt Lux.

But nothing emerged from the trees. No one was coming to help.

The first boy made a sad face. 'You made us do this,' he said. 'We cannot suffer a witch to live.'

'If you think I'm a witch,' said Lux, 'then why aren't you afraid I'll hex you? If you really think I can do harm, then shouldn't you be more cautious?'

The boy frowned and said nothing. Lux saw then that it was just an excuse. Because a dirty, stinking girl in the forest, a girl all alone, a girl with nothing and no one, could only be who they wanted her to be. Whore. Admirer. Servant. Pretty bit. And if she wouldn't be those things, then there was only one other choice.

'This is your fault,' said the boy. Slowly, deliberately, he put his burning torch on the ground and kicked it into the house.

The flames shuddered, and for a moment it seemed they might go out. Then the logs of the walls caught, the flames licking up, flickering across the remains of the roof.

Lux and Else had no choice: they ran out of the door, away from the flames, into the hands of the boys. Lux scrambled around for a weapon that she knew wasn't there. She had nothing to fight with, but she'd fight with it anyway. A boy reached for her, for the softness of her throat, but she jerked back, and his hand caught her nightshade necklace. It snapped, the berries falling to the ground. The boy snarled and leapt to grab her.

And then - hot breath - black fur - jaws snap - sharp teeth - red tongue - high scream - blood spat - bare meat - and a stench, a hunting smell, the bitter reek of fear.

Everything so fast, all at once.

And then -

The boys were gone and the stench was gone and the heat and the fur and Else was beside her, breath coming fast and hard. In front of them, a trail of blood leading to the trees, the retreating sounds of a group of hurt boys running home through the forest. And behind them, a house on fire.

Lux rushed to the well, then realised that the bucket was still in the house. She couldn't get any water because the bucket was on fire. She didn't know whether to laugh or cry. She knew a single bucket of water wouldn't save the house, but at least it was something. At least she could have tried to salvage *something*. She stood there, watching as everything she had ever had burned to nothing.

She felt a presence at her side. For a second she flinched, thinking the wolf was back: jaws, tongue, meat, blood. But she saw the black hood and felt the cool skin, and realised it was Else. She resisted the urge to reach out and take Else's hand. She was a witch, she commanded a wolf to appear and disappear at her will, she knew the devil by moonlight, she sacrificed babies, she drank blood. She was everything that Lux had been taught to fear. But right now, she was all that Lux had. She stepped closer to the flames. They were warm, and she was cold.

She stayed there for a long time, feeling the day turn to night around her, feeling her home burn to nothing.

She kept her eyes shut. The dying flames ached against her lids. She imagined the boys making their way back to their village at the edge of the forest. They'd come here for her because she'd been exiled from the sanctuary, or because her mother couldn't protect her any more, or because of whatever story one of their sisters had told – or just because they could. She knew they would not think of her again, until their cocks hardened and they wanted somewhere to warm them. They would not know whether they hated or desired her, or whether there was a differ-ence between the two. She thought of the berries and firewood and rabbits they would take from the forest; how they'd say that their injuries from the hunt, the blood on their hands and the scratches on their bodies, were worth it; how they would present the wounds so proudly along with the spoils of the hunt, held up triumphant and justified, as if getting things to keep their families fed and warm was all they had been doing, all they had ever wanted to do. Their houses, fire-warmed and food-filled and populated by people who loved them. Men they wanted to emulate; mothers who fed them and loved them, and would only let them go when it was into the arms of another woman who would feed them and love them and give them sons, who would grow up to go into the forest and find a girl in a house all alone, and bang on her door until it opened.

Lux wished, in that moment, that she really was a witch. She wished she could command a wolf and burn the earth black. She wished she knew a curse that worked, so she could use it against everyone who had turned on her mother.

'I'll go north with you,' said Lux. 'If you tell me who you –'

Lux heard the whisper of fabric and knew that Else had pulled back her hood. She opened her eyes and looked at Else in the fireglow. Again, that churn inside her: a face she knew and did not know. She saw a woman a few years older than herself. Pale skin, dark hair, hollowed cheeks. Eyes with a gleam in them like a flame caught at the bottom of a well. Lips full and red – but the shape of the mouth was strange and twisted around the edges, where pocks marred the skin, the scars evenly spaced like stitch marks, narrow and deep.

Lux wanted to reach out to touch Else's hair, but instead she reached to her own. She knew it was dark, because she could see the length of it, but she didn't know the colour of her own eyes or the shape of her own cheeks. There had been only dull metal and no glass in the house, no mirrors at the sanctuary. She'd only ever seen her face reflected in a bucket of water, and that was unsettled and wavering, never steady.

Else pulled her hood back up. Lux felt Else place something into her hands. She didn't have to look to see that it was the cold slither of a ribbon, all she had left of her mother. Lux tied the ribbon around her upper arm, where no one would be able to see it. She pushed her way through the nettles and collected what she could from the poison garden. There was nothing else. Lux's nightshade berries had been trampled into the ground, utterly ruined. Anything left in the house would soon be ashes. She had only the clothes on her back and two mangy furs. She thought about giving one of the furs to Else, but despite the thinness of her cloak, she didn't seem cold. There had been not a shiver in her limbs, not a chatter of her teeth. The night was cold and the fire was dying; Lux kept the furs for herself.

'We go now,' said Else. 'There's safety in the dark.'

There was only one path leading away from the house, and that went to the village. Else and Lux didn't go that way. They went the other way: into the forest, where it was winter, and it was dark, and there was no path to follow.

2

Now She is Prey

There in the forest, the trees stole the stars. It was so dark that Lux had to blink hard to check that her eyes weren't shut. She took two steps and immediately tripped over a tree root. She got back up and kicked the root. She edged out her foot, wary of another fall. Then – Else's hand on her elbow, pulling her close, guiding her.

'I can see,' said Else. 'Let me help you.'

Else led them through the night, walking in tandem, arms woven tight. Lux's body was warm beneath the furs, but the winter air chilled her face, keeping her awake. She was utterly turned around. She felt she could fall up into the black sky or down into a black grave with every step. But she didn't, because Else warned Lux of each low branch that tried to tangle in her hair, each high root that wanted to smack her shins, each tangle of thorns that threatened to tear her skin.

'How can you see?' Lux couldn't resist whispering. It was the dark, and the quiet, and the thought of the villagers who might be coming after her. 'Is it witchery?'

Lux couldn't see Else's face, but she could hear the smile in her voice. 'No.'

'Then what –'

'Something else.'

It felt like they walked for years, though Lux knew that wasn't possible. Her head was light from thirst, her belly twisting with hunger. Beneath the shadows of the trees, she saw the silvery gleam of witches' eyes following their progress. So many of them – more and more each time she looked, going back and back into the forest, layered like stars in the sky. Lux felt a pull towards them. Her feet were already moving before her thoughts had caught up with them – but then, holding her back was Else's hand on her arm, keeping her steady.

As they walked through the dark forest, Else sometimes hummed a song. It was so quiet that Lux had to hold her breath to hear. It felt private, like Lux was intruding on a secret. What intrigued her most was that she thought she recognised the song. It was not one she had heard a villager sing, and it was not the only lullaby she could remember her mother singing. Yet she knew it, somehow.

Another sound in the night: the low hush and high spill of a burn. Lux felt the ground begin to lower beneath her, as if she was being led down a slope. Then Else was pulling her down, and her hands touched water so cold it instantly numbed her skin. She knelt to the black burn, pulling up handfuls of icy water to her mouth.

'Careful,' said Else. 'It's cold. Your belly will push it back out.'

Lux wanted to drink the whole burn, but forced herself to step back. She counted to ten then went for another mouthful.

She was about to stand up when the moon emerged from behind a cloud, and she noticed something on her sleeve. She straightened her arm out to look properly: a tongue-sized stain, red-brown and damp. Blood. From a boy, or several boys. Blood drawn by a witch's wolf.

She scrubbed at it in the numbing water. But the stain only darkened. She scrubbed harder, suddenly frantic. She wanted to tear off her clothing and throw it in the water to clean it, but knew she would freeze if she did. She jarred at a hand on her shoulder: Else, of course.

The pressure of her hand increased, and Lux gave in to it, leaning back on her heels by the water. Else smiled, the pocks around her mouth pinching. She stood up, and Lux followed. But her steps were unsteady, and she stumbled into a tree, knocking it with her shoulder. Snow shivered over her. She realised the snow must have fallen as they walked, but the trees were too dense to let it fall through. The ground beneath them was black and loamy, sucking at their feet. Lux focused on her steps, letting Else guide her.

They walked for so long that Lux felt she had fallen into a trance. She was in a part of the forest she'd never seen. Before the sanctuary, she had never been more than half a day's walk from her house. She'd seen the closest village, and parts of the forest, and three hills, and the base of a cliff, and a small lake. Before the sanctuary, she had never slept anywhere but her own bed. She had heard tales of these parts of the forest, from pedlars and merchants passing through. Not tales told to her, of course; but little ears can hear much, and Lux had spent a lot of time pretending to sleep while her mother shared a drink with a stranger through the bright summer nights.

She had heard of wondrous things: dozens of women and men all dancing together in rooms with polished floors, the men in suits made of ten pieces of red velvet, the women in green dresses embroidered with a whole garden of flowers in thread coloured gold. Churches with windows made of coloured glass, each window telling a different story, each colour bright and gleaming with sun. Creatures that live in the sea, half-woman and half-fish, and perhaps wholly something else again.

She had heard, too, of terrible things, of people being witch-struck, witch-cursed. Powers stranger and harder to understand than her own cures and poisons. They said that the further north you went, the stranger things became. A large black dog had appeared to a girl while she was churning butter, and scared her half to death, though the dog was no ordinary dog: it had the face of an ape, and two horns like a goat, and wore a silver whistle on a chain around its neck, and carried in its mouth the key to the door of the milk house, and he dropped the key on the girl's lap and declared that he would have some butter, if it pleased her.

A boy found a peg in a neighbour's wall and twisted it, and milk flowed out, but he couldn't turn it shut again, and he ran around the house filling every bowl and pan he could find, and all the local farmers were deprived of their cows' daily produce. A woman woke at midnight to see two marvellously big and ugly cats debating at her fireside; a dew of blood appeared overnight on all the fields round about; a whole village found small cakes of feathers left by witches on sleeping people's pillows, the feathers bound together so tight they were impossible to pull apart, so that they had to throw the cakes into the sea to be rid of them.

But how did they bind the feather-cakes so tight?

'A good question,' said Else, and only then did Lux realise she'd spoken out loud.

Else tilted her head and Lux could just see the shape of her smile. And perhaps Else answered the question, or perhaps she didn't, but all Lux knew was that she was too weak to keep walking and her feet were going out from under her and Else was catching her.

'Food!' cried Else. 'I forgot about food. I'm sorry. You must be hungry.'

She lay Lux down on a fall of dead leaves and wrapped her furs tightly around her, and Lux began to protest, but she could feel the words catching in her throat, could see the sounds of the words in her mind, the colours and sounds of them twisting like coloured ribbons, and the next thing she knew she was opening her eyes to a pale greyish dawn and Else had lit a fire and was holding a dead rabbit.

The rabbit looked fresh: its fur as soft as sleep, its eyes black and bright. The only marks on it were the tooth punctures at its throat. Lux reached for it. It was years since she'd touched rabbit fur. As a child, a rabbit – Best Rabbit – had been her only friend. How she'd wailed when her mother threw Best Rabbit's body onto the fire. Lux's stomach clenched with desire.

Lux could already taste the meat on her tongue. She could already feel the softness of rabbit-fur layered under her clothes. She hadn't thought of Best Rabbit for years; now he was all she could think about.

23

She could feel him stroking her forehead with his big grey paw. The taste of his soft white tail in her mouth. The way he would lie on her chest and count her breaths. She wanted – but there's no use in a girl wanting.

Else laid the rabbit on the ground and pulled a knife from her belt.

'Don't you sleep?' asked Lux. 'Don't you eat? Let me guess: you're all wood inside. You're made of trees and branches and twigs and suchlike. You're a wolf. You're a raven.'

'No,' said Else, but she smiled as she said it. 'I'm not wood inside.'

Lux glanced up at Else, at her strange pricked smile, and felt something inside her settle; her heart a small panicked creature backed into a corner, finally calming. There was the fire, and there was the meat, and she didn't have to fear. She wasn't yet sure what she would do when they got to the stronghold – she knew she wasn't going to kill some man, anyway, no matter what Else wanted. But she'd use Else for what she could, and then shake her off. At the stronghold there would be things to eat, and places to sleep, and a chance for something new. Surely they would need someone to grow useful things, to cook and bake, to clean, to sew and weave and dye. Lux could chop vegetables and stir a pot. Cleaning was easy enough. And as for the rest – if it was needed, she'd pick it up along the way. No one would know who she was. She wouldn't have to be a dirty, stinking girl in the forest, a girl all alone, a girl with nothing and no one.

Else lifted her knife and in a series of swift chops cut off the feet, tail and head of the rabbit.

'Why is the forest so empty?' said Lux. 'We've been walking for so long, but we haven't seen anyone.'

This was not quite true. Lux had caught glimpses of something bright and moving in the shadowy distance; had heard the slightest sound of a high ringing bell when the wind blew the right way. But as soon as she turned to peer at the flash of colour, or cocked her head to hear better, it seemed to move away. Whatever it was must be travelling in the same direction, as the glimpses continued, never growing closer or further.

She caught Else turning to follow the sound of the bell with her silver-gleam eyes. She looked concerned. Perhaps Lux was imagining it, but Else seemed to be leading her away from the bright thing in the distance.

Lux pulled the furs from her head and tucked them under her chin. 'Have you been leading us away from people? There should be people here in the forest. Villagers collecting firewood, foraging for mushrooms and herbs. Men with bows shooting for rabbits and voles. Travelling women collecting up hair and teeth to sell.'

Lux couldn't help a shiver at the memory. The women used to knock on their door sometimes: their wide white smiles, their sacks of hair on their backs, their scissors as sharp as anything, offering good coins for a girl's hair, the longer the better. Lux sold her hair several times – or rather, her mother sold it, as soon as it grew back long enough. Children's hair was even more valuable, soft as it was, and many a fancy lady in a keep or a stronghold wore a mix of several children's hair on their heads. The women also carried a pair of pliers to pull teeth out, the metal blood-stained and creaking with rust – though they only wanted adult teeth, not small baby ones, and they had to be good teeth, mind, not rotten ones that might at first look fine in a rich person's mouth but would stink their breath before long. Luckily Lux's mother never sold her teeth; she knew they wouldn't grow back.

'Even off the paths, there should be poachers,' said Lux. 'Smugglers. Criminals hiding out. People with secrets and suchlike.'

Lux had travelled the forest only days ago – weeks? She'd lost sense of the days and nights already, walking in the dark beneath the trees. Back then, she had met a few people who had shared food with her. But for much of it she had been alone, on her hands and knees, laden down by dozens of wooden crucifixes.

Else lifted her knife; from belly to throat, she sliced the rabbit open, peeling off the fur and turning it inside out so the skin and the body were separate. 'I don't know why it's so quiet,' she said.

Perhaps it was safer for a woman not to know things. Lux had always thought the opposite: her mother had kept them alive for years by knowing things that other people didn't want her to know. She knew which men lived every day in hidden pain. She knew which mothers' milk wouldn't come in. She knew who cried when they shouldn't, or laughed at what they shouldn't. She knew who was sickening, and whether that sickness was God-given or from their poison garden. She knew who wanted rid of a child, and why – because it wasn't their husband's, or because they already had enough mouths to feed, or because they feared dying in the birth. Being the keeper of all those secrets had served her well – until it hadn't.

With great care, Else sliced open the rabbit's belly, careful not to puncture its stomach. She reached in with two fingers and pulled out the innards.

Hungry and impatient, Lux fidgeted. Her fingers caught a loose hair that had fallen from her head, and she leaned forward to throw it on the fire. In the firelight she noticed Else watching her.

'So the witches can't get it,' said Lux, 'and make a poppet of me and then use it to do terrible things to me.'

'So it's witches, then. That's who causes terrible things.'

'I don't know. That's what I heard.'

'I suppose you believe everything you hear.'

Lux stayed silent, irritated by Else's question that wasn't a question, because it seemed that Else never asked questions.

'When the witches make poppets,' said Else lightly, using her knife to cut the rabbit meat into chunks, 'I suppose they are like the ones you had in your house.'

'No!' Lux pulled out another of her hairs, but she didn't throw this one on the fire; she wrapped it around her fingertip, watching the trapped skin pale. 'It's different when the witches do it, because they have power and they can make things happen. The ones I made are different. They don't do anything. They're just a story.'

26

Else threaded the rabbit meat on a stick, then leaned forward and set-tled it over the fire. 'And people believe it, even though you know it's not true. Just as you believe that you must burn things to stop witches.'

'That's also different,' said Lux. 'The north land – it's not like here. It's the mouth of hell. It's rotten with witches. Filthy with them. They're why the sand and soil in the north is so black: from their sin. And there are no trees there because wood is too sacred, wood is what the saviour's cross is made from, and so the witches can't touch it. Back before I was born, there was a land bridge between the islands and the witches were more of a danger then as they could pass freely, walking back and forth whenever they wanted. But then God raised the waters and covered the land bridge, and now it's safer, as witches fear water because it cleanses and it can be blessed. They stay in the rotten, dangerous north where they belong.'

Lux's voice had grown louder as she spoke, and the silence after seemed to echo. She wanted to kick out the fire so that Else could not look at her by its light. Instead she reached for the rabbit meat and took a bite. It was charred hard on the outside and squishy-raw on the inside; she chewed and swallowed fast. It burned her tongue and then all the way down her throat. She knew she should leave it on the fire longer so it could cook through. But she reached instantly for another piece, and burned her tongue again.

'Let me tell you a different story,' said Else, her voice soft. 'And then you can decide for yourself. This is why people here fear the north. No matter how much people may try to control the land, still it resists. There is a volcano that bides its time, and then one day explodes without warn-ing. White steam billowing into the wild sea from a crevice in the black rocks, the rocks in folds like pleats of velvet. And a white sea that never rests, licking over the sand as black as night. The glaciers blue like you've never seen, floating out to sea, so big you could ride on them like a boat. The people there may not be good as you have learned to think of good and wicked, but they are good in a way that's right to them. I'm not going to tell you everything is perfect there. But I will tell you that they don't condemn one another as witches.'

This was the longest thing that Lux had heard Else say, and she was left speechless in the wake of it. When she'd first met Else, her words had been strange and slow, as if her lips were frozen numb, as if she'd forgotten how to use her tongue. Now it seemed to be loosening.

Else sat back and chewed a hank of meat; she had waited for it to cook through and then to cool, and did not flinch from its burning as Lux had.

'How do you know so much about the north?' asked Lux. 'Have you –'

But her blood dropped at a sudden sound: the blast of a hunting horn, off in the trees. Else's hand shot out and grabbed Lux's wrist. Lux, shocked, cried out. Else loosened her grip but did not let go. Lux felt a heart beat in the ground under her body: horses' hooves, fast approaching.

'The men are hunting,' said Lux. 'If we stay quiet, won't they just pass us by?'

'Or it's not an animal they're hunting, but us. Those boys will have told stories about you. That you're a witch, that you hurt them. That you have a wolf.'

Is this what they'd done to her mother? Hunted her down like an animal? Chased her through the forest until her feet were ragged, until she left a trail of her own blood, until her eyes showed white in fear? Lux felt the flame rise up in her again.

The horn sounded again, shockingly close. There was no time to argue. Else piled rocks on the fire to try to hide its glow while Lux snatched up their cloaks and furs. The daylight was still new, and everything had an unreal silvery tint to it. They slithered down the bank, away from the hunt.

Lux took Else's hand and together they leapt the burn. The water here was slow and narrow, but they still landed on the slick rocks in the shallows, slipping to their knees in the water. It was so cold that it stole Lux's breath and for a second all she could do was gulp at air like a fish. Else's hood had slipped back, and she did not pull it up. Quick, quick, they were up and running, feet bloody from burst blisters and already numb with cold.

Lux heard again the ringing of a bell – it could not be from the hunt, then, as the bell was ahead of them, and much louder than before. Over the sound of her own beating heart and their noisy passage through the forest, she could hear other noises. Music, singing, laughter. Between the trees she saw flashes of colour and movement. Else did not seem to see as well in this light, even dim as it was, so Lux kept a hold of her as they ran. She headed towards the colours and sound.

Suddenly, shockingly, the dense trees ended. A clearing opened up, circled by houses that seemed abandoned: doorless, windowless, holes in the roofs where the thatch had fallen. Here the snow hadn't been caught by the tree canopy, but covered the ground, gleaming spectral in the weak sun. In the centre of the clearing stretched a silver birch, its branches hung with coloured ribbons, surrounded by a group of strange animals that had stopped the moment that Lux and Else burst into the clearing. No, not animals – people costumed like animals. Some wore antlers on their heads, wrapped in ribbons with the ends left to flit in the wind. Others wore wings, cut clean from a white bird and shrugged on over the shoulders with straps. Some were dressed head to toe in suits of fur. Lux hoped that these strange animals would understand how it felt to be hunted.

'Please,' she said.

Without waiting for a response, she and Else ran to join them just as the first horse emerged into the clearing. It was the biggest, most beautiful and most terrifying creature that Lux had ever seen. Pure white from head to hoof, its haunch was as high as her head. Its mane and rump were protected by gleaming armour. If it chose, it could stamp right over her. Lux tried not to flinch at the thought of her bones crunching. The horse had been ridden too hard; its eyes rolled and its mouth was flecked with spittle. More followed, less grand but equally exhausted. The armour showed this was no ordinary hunt, but the hunt for the Unmaking, which Lux's mother had told her about: a captive bear would be released into the forest, then hunted down and killed. It would then be split apart and served at a great feast at the stronghold, the parts of it portioned out based on everyone's importance. Lux felt her heart slow as she realised that the hunt was not for her. She was so entranced by the huge horses in their finery that she didn't notice the men astride them until one spoke.

'Take off your costumes and show yourselves. The lord's men command it.'

Lux felt heat beside her, and realised that three of the dancing people had sidled round to stand with her and Else. The three strangers looked so similar to one another that they must be related – except that one wore a crown of flowers, one was dressed all in black, and one all in white. Lux tried to blend in, tried to breathe without moving, tried not to call any attention to herself. Her guts felt loose with fear. A dozen horses and a dozen men, and all of them armed with swords and arrows and spiked metal horrors.

No one spoke. One of the men on horses unsheathed his sword and cut the ribbons holding the swan wings on a woman's back. She didn't cry out, didn't protest, didn't move; merely fixed the man with her steady gaze as the wings tumbled to the snow, twisted and bent. Annoyed by her silence, the man raised his sword again –

Then someone stepped forward from the huddle around the beribboned tree. He was the tallest man that Lux had ever seen, with the darkest skin she had ever seen. He was as thin as a skeleton: if he lay on his side during rain, a tiny puddle would form in the hollow of his cheek.

'We have done nothing wrong.' It seemed that the tall man was finished, but then – after a weighted pause – he added: 'Sir.' He had a foreign accent, and seemed to be playing it up, putting strange intonations on his words.

The man on the horse, who was also heavily armoured, peered down at the tall man. 'Then you will show yourselves.'

A pause; then the tall man nodded around the snowy clearing at the others. They shucked off their costumes, and now they looked just like anyone else. They must have been cold without furs or cloaks, but no one shivered.

Lux glanced around. In the centre of the clearing was a wicker basket, opened, its contents spilling out: bones and swan wings and fistfuls of dried petals; sheep skulls and apples and dead leaves; a whole pig and strange stitched shoes and a metal thing that seemed about to fall apart; bricks and spun wool and an enormous ring of keys; onions and rope and salt and a wheel and dishes and candlesticks and a pitchfork and a horseshoe and material red and green and brown and black and white and purple. The ribbons on the tree hadn't been fastened at the bottom, and had begun to unwrap themselves from the trunk, the ends twisting in the wind.

'Where are you from?' said the man on the horse.

'Here and there.' A pause. 'Sir.'

'Not here. Not with skin like that.'

'Not originally, sir.'

'You're a slave? A trader?'

'Not any more, sir.'

The man on the horse seemed to be losing patience. 'Are you all mummers?'

'Of a sort. Sir.'

'Poachers, then.'

'Oh no, sir. We would never, sir. The punishment for poaching the lord's prey is death, sir. We do not want to be prey. Or dead. *Ssssir.*' This last he hissed, snake-like.

The man on the horse rested a hand on his sword's pommel in a clear threat. His eyes were small and gleamed rodenty. 'You are upsetting the hunt,' the man said grandly. 'You will cease your revelries and stay silent so that we can better track our prey.'

'Are you asking?' A long pause, in which Lux forgot to breathe. Then, finally: '*Sir.*'

'You are on the lord's land. You will heed his words.'

'And where is he, sir?'

'That is not your concern. I am here on his behalf.'

The tall man eyed the man on the horse. 'You do look about half of him, sir.'

The man on the horse narrowed his eyes. 'Are you going to the stronghold?'

'Yes, sir. To perform for the lord. We tell the stories he wants us to tell, and in return he feeds us and keeps us warm. He likes us most especially.' Before the man on the horse could reply, the tall man added: 'But whatever you're hunting, there is no lord in the forest. *Sir.*'

The man on the horse smiled. He toyed again with his sword, considering. 'I suggest,' he said, his voice soft as falling snow, 'that you put on a better show for the lord than you have today. Otherwise you may find him less merciful than I.' Then he leaned forward and spat in the face of the tall man, who made no move to wipe it.

Instead his face split into a grin and he ran to the ribbon-laced tree with a strange high-kneed gait. He sang a jaunty song without any words. When he reached the tree, he spun round it three times, then touched his toes and pulled his furs down to expose his arse.

Lux's heart climbed her throat. The man must be insane. Surely he was about to die. If the man on the horse was angry enough, they were all about to die. Lux made her hands into fists, cracking the scabs on her palms. She was glad of that; the sudden pain stopped her from running away.

Silence in the clearing.

The white horse sneezed.

The man on the horse took his hand off his sword's pommel. 'Mere jesters,' he said dismissively. 'Fools, touched in the head. They know nothing.' He turned and rode out of the clearing. After a moment, his armoured riders followed.

Lux turned to the side and vomited on the ground. Bile and chewed-up rabbit steamed in the air. A dog dressed in a red-and-brown costume pattered over and sniffed at the pile. The fur-clad person standing closest to Lux bent down and picked up the dog, stroking its ears.

'I'm Ash,' the person said. 'And you'll need some food in you to make up for that. Come on.'

The winter sun had brought more heat than it should, and although it was now fading the mummers were making the most of it. Lux realised now that they were well into their cups when she and Else crashed into their clearing, and they had only swum deeper since then. Several fires had been lit around the edges, and the warm gold light had already overtaken the last of the daylight. The mummers had chosen the most intact of the empty houses, spread a length of canvas across the sunken-in roof, and built a fire in the hearth.

Something was about to happen with the ribbons hanging from the tree, and Lux watched over the lip of her cup. The mead was sweet and good. She'd been fed, too: the potage was salty and hot and dense with meat. Her full belly should be making her tired, but she had never felt more awake. There was so much to see and so much to hear. She only wished she could taste and touch it all too – but perhaps later.

The lowest branches of the tree were the height of Lux's house, and many coloured ribbons hung from its branches and reached to the ground. A red bright as blood, a brown deep as earth, a green like summer grass, a purple that made her mouth water. Lux was dizzy thinking that someone must have climbed up the tree to attach the ribbons so high. She squeezed her upper arm against her side, reassuring herself that her scrap of red ribbon was still there. How pathetic it would look, so grubby and small, next to this bright finery. The mummers had put their costumes back on, transforming back into strange animals.

Lux counted thirteen, including Ash, but not including the cow that pulled the cart, or the gang of costumed dogs that ran around the clearing, pissing on the tree trunks and begging for food. She couldn't be sure how many dogs there were as each time she counted she ended up with one more, as if they were whelping in the bracken.

The mummers circled the tree, taking the end of a ribbon in each hand – all except for Ash, who lurked by the fire with Lux and Else, and the tall man. He stood apart, his eyes cast in shadow, his cup clutched in his huge bony hands.

'That's Mister Gaunt,' said Ash in an undertone. 'He decides what stories we tell. Our current show is about a lot of things, but our part – that's me and Pock and Posy – is all about the sickness.'

'What sickness?' said Lux. Ash frowned at her, confused, so Lux added: 'I've been away. We didn't get much news where I was. They said it wasn't good for girls to know things, as our brains were too small and couldn't hold it. No point putting more things in when they'd only leak out.'

'You must have been far away, by the sounds of things. Before I was born – before you were born, I'd think – there was a sickness. It spread fast and far, and many died.'

'I know about that sickness,' said Lux. 'But that's long gone. Why do a show about it?'

'Because it came back. It took a lot of people first time round, and it took even more on its second try. It's fading now, but it hasn't gone. People still fear it. Whole villages empty, farms gone to rot and ruin, entire family lines gone forever. One day fine, the next day dead. But me and Posy and Pock – we had it, but we didn't die.'

'Why not?'

'The grace of God.'

'Because you're so good and holy and pure etcetera?' asked Lux.

In response, Ash winked; Lux felt a heat rise in her cheeks. 'Anyway,' went on Ash, 'that's how we got our names. I'm Ash because that's what comes after Pock and Posy. Pock is all in black, to show dying. First you see the black pocks on your skin – that's when you know death is coming for you. Then it's time for you to collect up some posies, to hide the stink of your dying body – so Posy's crowned with flowers. Ah, but no use in that. The only thing that's coming is ashes and dust. And that's why I'm all in white, to show death.' Ash's voice was cheerful, as if passing comment on the weather. Perhaps coming so close to death, then stepping clean out of its jaws, made the whole world seem lighter. 'Why are you called Lux?'

'It's my name.'

'But why?'

'I don't know,' said Lux. 'I didn't choose it. How do people get the sickness?'

'Well,' said Ash, 'I have an idea about that. Do you want to hear it?' Lux didn't have a chance to reply before Ash continued. 'See, I think it's bad air. Miasma, you know? Pock reckons it's the movement of the planets, some kind of curse from the heavens. Posy reckons it's pointy shoes.'

'Pointy shoes?'

'Heard some holy man talking about it. In the cities, you know some people wear the points so long they have to be tied to their shins with fine silver chains so they don't trip on them? It's deviant, the holy man said. That folks who wear pointy shoes have long hair like women and wear their shirts too tight and engage in unholy filth, and that's what's brought the sickness on us all. Then again, the man was whipping his own back with a scourge at the time, so I'm not sure he can be trusted.'

'So if I don't wear pointy shoes, I won't get the sickness?'

'If you trust that man. Which I don't. I still reckon it's the bad air. None of the mummers have died of it, see? And we're outside most of the time. There's an upside to not having a home, as it turns out. And anyway,' said Ash, 'the holy folk say it's witches.'

'I thought the holy folk said it was shoes.'

'It was.'

'And then it was air?'

'And then witches.' Ash shrugged. 'All I know is, witches get sent to the drowning posts where the land bridge used to be between the south and north lands. They get tied to the posts and left there. If they're witches, they'll go to the north land where they belong. If they're innocent, they'll float to the south land.'

'And what usually happens? North or south?'

'As I've heard it, they just stay tied to the posts, and the tide rises, and they drown.'

'They don't all drown,' said Lux. 'Some burn. I've seen it.'

And would she have watched her mother die too, if she'd been there? Sent to the posts. Sent to drown. Her mother, alone and helpless as the tide rose to her chest, to her chin, over her mouth, over –

But Lux had known nothing of it; she'd been praying on her knees and screaming on her back and watching as the bees went mad in their hives and letting the words of God fill her mouth until she choked on them –

No. Lux closed her eyes and took a breath.

She opened her eyes and watched as each mummer lifted the end of a ribbon in each hand, and lined up in two circles: one inner, closer to the tree; one outer, at the furthest reach of their ribbons. A bell rang, and the dance began. A series of bells kept time, and a stringed instrument that Lux had never heard before played a high, sweet melody. A song began: wordless, it seemed, though all the mummers kept the tune. They danced in circles: the inner circle one way, the outer circle the other. The outer circle held their hands high, lifting them over the heads of the inner circle as they danced. With each pass this switched, so that the ribbons became entwined around the tree, and each step took them closer to the trunk. Lux watched, the cup in her hands forgotten. The ribbons wrapped around the tree trunk, the colours overlapping, an intricate braid appearing. With each circle around the tree, the music faster, the song louder, the dance wilder, the dancers closer. Finally they all came together at the trunk, a mass of bodies. The music reached its peak and all the mummers fell on one another. Lux almost dropped her cup as she thought they were fighting – but they were embracing, heads tipped back in laughter, teeth exposed and throats making animal growls as they pretended to eat one another. There were calls for more drink, more fire, more heat in their aching bones.

Lux was starting to know the mummers' faces, if not their names. There was the brown-haired woman with the scar across her cheek. The one with a milk-white eye. The one wearing a string of red beads. The one who limped. The man with hair bristling from his nose and one eye stitched shut. The fair, scowling one she had thought was a child but realised was a man, only he was the height of her belly. The woman with a body as tall and broad as two men tied together. The man with no hair and only one ear. And the one with a smile as wide as a crescent moon, full of teeth only a little rotted.

Lux still felt apart from them all, but she liked watching them from a distance. The community, the camaraderie. It made her think of the other girls at the sanctuary; the times they'd all sat together in a circle, doing their chores and sharing their secrets, all working as one. She'd felt a part of something. Accepted.

Then she remembered why the boys had come for her. The names they called her. The girl who'd hung back, doing nothing as the boys howled and banged on her door.

Perhaps she never had been a part of anything after all. Perhaps she'd always just be watching from the shadows.

She watched as Ash stretched out closer to the fire. She drained her cup and looked again at Ash's face in the firelight.

Hair cut short, pale like wheat. A spray of golden dots, like a scatter of pollen, across a long nose and high cheeks. A small mouth with full lips, swollen like a flower. A pointed chin that Lux suddenly wanted to take in her hand and turn towards her so she could suck those lips into her mouth, bite into them a little, to see if they tasted like rose petals.

She did not do that. She stayed quiet and put down her empty cup. Though Ash had instantly welcomed Lux, the others did not seem so sure. At first they had eyed her warily, watching her hands. Lux didn't blame them. From what Ash said, they were probably wondering if she was a witch, or a spy, or a thief. Women without men were bound to be objects of suspicion. They hadn't been thrilled at the appearance of Lux and Else, but they had fed them, and shielded them from the men on horses, and that was worth something.

Else had not spoken to Lux since they'd entered the clearing. She sat far from the fire, her hood up, her bowl held close to her face. Either she was sipping it very slowly, or was just using it to hide her face. None of the mummers had spoken to her, but Lux was sure a few of them had cast sly glances her way. Perhaps they were afraid of her. Lux didn't know any more if that was a good or bad thing. Ash disappeared, and returned with Lux's cup refilled. Lux slid her body closer to Ash's and took the full cup. She drank deep before she dared to speak.

'Ash,' she said, 'are you a girl or a boy?'

'No,' Ash replied with a smile, then kissed her, very gently, at the corner of her mouth.

They all slept like dogs. Piles of bodies and furs rolled up together in a single house, packed wall to wall. It was the best way through the cold night: layers of skin and fur in the steamy, sweating darkness. Every breath in was farts and dog fur and a bready, yeasty smell that could have been sour ale or could have been bodies. Over and over Lux tensed and came suddenly awake, half sitting up, sure that she could feel the wolf's warm breath on her face. But each time, there was nothing there.

When Lux was younger, her mother had told her that the mark of a good husband was one who let you sleep on the side of the bed that was not pressed up against the wall. If he made you sleep against the wall, you would have no place to escape to, and so he could have you any time he wanted. If not, perhaps it would be your choice whether he took you. Of course, by the time you were in a bed with him, it was already too late to change your mind – whether you were beside the wall or not, you had to take what you were given. Lux still couldn't decide whether it was better to know what was coming, if you couldn't do anything about it anyway.

Sometime in the night, Ash's hand slipped from one fur to another. Lux knew that she had nothing to steal, so she let Ash search all her pockets. Ash's hand began to retreat, and Lux snaked out her own hand. She held Ash's hand tight in her own. Breath held, eyes blinking against the dark. Then she slipped both their hands down, down warmer. The night was long and boring, and she couldn't sleep anyway. She clenched her legs tight, feeling the bones of Ash's hand grind. Lux felt a sudden desire to bite the fleshy lobe of Ash's ear. Or the apple-curve of the cheek just below the eye. Or the soft skin under the jaw: gently, a nip of incisors, like a puppy trying to play and accidentally drawing blood. But she stopped herself, afraid of how Ash might respond.

She slipped her own hand beneath Ash's clothes. Around them was movement: snorts and sniffs and rolls. In the centre Ash and Lux were still, hands kept pressed to one another's warmest places. They fell asleep like that, and dreamt of deer antlers wrapped in layers of unravelling ribbons.

By the dawn light, as the mummers packed their cart, Lux lurked at the edge of the trees. She did not know what their payment would be in exchange for the night's food and shelter. A woman's body had many uses, but Lux couldn't see what use her particular body was in this situation. There was no land to work. There was no house to clean. There was no food to cook. There was always the other use, but any of them could have taken her at any time in the night, and had not. Lux knew she had another use, but she didn't dare tell the mummers about the plants she'd taken from her garden. She thought of her mother; of how easy it was for trust to turn to suspicion. There had been changes since she'd been sent to the sanctuary. She'd survived up until now, but there was much she didn't understand about this world; its sickness and its suspicions.

So she didn't ask whether they could join the mummers. As soon as they had packed up, she fell into step beside Ash. Her belly ached empty when she thought of not going with them. It wasn't that she was hungry – at least, not for food. She was hungry for stories. For experience. For colours and songs. For antlers and ribbons and swan wings. There was no use in a girl wanting – but still. She wanted.

She peered back over her shoulder, sure that she would see Else standing there in the clearing, circled by the houses of the dead, her wolf by her side, her hood pulled back, her bare head high, watching them all leave.

But Else was right behind her. Hood up. Head down. Lux's shadow, her safety, all the power she didn't have – there with her, matching her step for step.

3

Now She is Maiden

Travelling with the mummers was not like travelling with Else. Then, they had moved silently in the dark and kept off the paths, stayed sleek and sharp like night foxes. Lux's world had shrunk to the lull of the stream and the feel of Else's hand in her own. It had felt like moving through a dream.

But now, she was awake. The mummers walked in daylight, following the paths. When there was no sun, Mister Gaunt led with a burning torch to light the way. The river wended close, then away, following its own path. Above them the clouds were heavy, milk-thick, and it seemed like the sun never really rose. But for all that, it wasn't a sombre procession. The mummers were a rowdy bunch, and every step was taken to the rhythm of song. One person would start, and others would join, apparently making it up as they went along. Lux didn't dare to join in, though she enjoyed listening.

No one spoke to Lux. But she was used to that. Her ears were large, and through eavesdropping on what the mummers said to one another she learned the following things:

They were following the river to reach the lake.
The lake was frozen.
When the lake was frozen, there was a frost fair.

People came from all over for the frost fair, and they had money and things to trade.

There was not enough meat.

There was never enough meat.

They wanted to eat a rabbit but could not catch one.

The only reason they did not eat the cow was that it pulled the cart and gave milk.

They did not trust Mister Gaunt.

Mister Gaunt was the only thing keeping them alive.

A bear may or may not have escaped from the hunt to run loose in the forest; if they stumbled on the bear then they may or may not try to capture it to perform in the show; if a bear were to be captured then it may or may not eat them all.

The forest is the forest is the forest, but also it looked different to Lux. She'd never been this far north. It was wild land: roots snaking grotesque over the ground ready to trip a traveller; strange eyes blinking from hollows above the flash of teeth; nothing flat or steady for miles.

A cry from the mummers snapped her awake: a house! Like the house Lux had grown up in, this one was made of rough logs with moss shoved in to fill the gaps, thatched with straw, and with two squinting little windows and a wooden door. But this house had shapes carved into the door, leaves and berries, mice and rabbits, pretty woodland things. The vegetable plot was busy and well tended, though it could do with weeding. There was a pen, for goats or chickens, and although nothing was in it now, it all looked neat and clean, the trough well scrubbed. It made it seem like someone cared about living there.

Mister Gaunt approached and pushed open the door – then quickly backed out again. The man pursuing Mister Gaunt out of the house was naked from the waist up, and seemed unaffected by the cold. His skin was sweaty as a tallow candle and he trembled uncontrollably. Black

42

roses bloomed underneath his arms. Dried blood crusted at the corners of his mouth.

'Back, devil!' shouted the man. Spittle shot from his mouth. His shout spread his lips wide, making the sores at the corners crack and weep fresh blood. He fell to his knees. His body looked so ravaged that Lux could not understand how he was still alive.

So this was the sickness. She hadn't known it would be so terrible; it was as if God was angry at this man in particular, and was punishing him. It seemed the witches sacrificed on the drowning posts weren't quite enough. God was still angry about something.

'We are leaving, sir,' said Mister Gaunt. 'God bless you and be with you.'

He rejoined the procession, all of whom were staring at the man. It seemed that he wanted to shout some more, but a hacking cough overtook him. He knelt there outside his silent house, spitting blood onto the frozen ground.

'Why did you bless him?' the woman with the scarred face asked Mister Gaunt.

'He won't be in this world long.' Mister Gaunt was back at the head of the procession, ready to lead them on. But the light was fading, and the man with the limp laid his hand on Mister Gaunt's arm. He spoke in an undertone, but Lux held her breath so she could hear.

'He will be dead soon,' said the man with the limp.

'Before next light, likely,' said Mister Gaunt.

'We can go back then.'

'No.'

'He's practically dead,' said the man with the limp, very reasonably. 'If we take shelter in his house, what can he do about it?'

'No.'

'Why? What was in there?'

'The rest of the family,' said Mister Gaunt.

'Alive?'

43

'No.'

'How long?'

'Long enough that we don't want to go in there.'

By the time the mummers found a house with no one in it, the glimmering light had faded to nothing, and Lux was so tired and hungry that everywhere she looked she saw a line of spectral rabbits, their silvery guts hanging out of their slit bellies, their black eyes gleaming as they danced and beckoned to her. She pinched herself awake. Around her the mummers were unpacking the cart, collecting firewood, bickering over who slept under which fur, making the dogs jump and beg, and portioning out the remaining mead. Lux knew what there was in the wood to eat: chestnuts and hazelnuts, blackberries, wild garlic, crab apples, mushrooms. A fair meal could be cobbled together from those; with time, she could make enough for everyone. But she didn't have the energy to search for them – or the nerve to wander off alone into the trees. As Lux was wondering if eating leaves would make her sick, Else appeared at her side. She nodded towards the deep shadows beneath the trees.

'Come,' Else said. 'We travel with the mummers and must earn our keep.'

'Come where?'

'You must trust me,' she said. 'Come.'

And Lux followed her into the dark.

It did not take long to find the wolf.

It took only a little longer to find the rabbit.

Twigs snapped and a salt-white tail bobbed fast in the gloom – but a rabbit is not faster than a wolf, or the world would be all rabbits and no wolves. Flash of teeth and snatch, snap of jaws. Papery sound of dead leaves kicked up. A high cry cut short.

Pile of soft grey, only a little blood-darkened, laid at their feet.

Out the wolf went again, and there they waited.

While they waited, Else told Lux stories. At first she still moved her tongue stiffly, as if she hadn't used it for a long time. But the dark made her bold, and soon she was telling Lux about the old times, not so long ago, when the world was not so simple. Wolves roamed free in this land then, as many wolves as people. There was a reason for that balance, for the wolves could change into people, and the people to wolves. The tail of a wolf has great power, and even a hair from a wolf can be used to strengthen a spell for freedom from chains.

She told of white hares who were the ghosts of girls who took their own lives after their men betrayed them; the hares came back to haunt the faithless lovers. A hare might not seem able to frighten, but – so Else said – anything that follows you wherever you go is a haunting. A hare's heart, then, can be used in spells to turn a reluctant lover into an honest husband.

The wolf did what wolves do; another rabbit joined the first, and another. One rabbit for every story that Else told Lux.

In return, Lux told Else of the use of mushrooms as portents. The bright red ones with clean-edged milky spots – sickness is coming. The pale brown ones with rounded tops and ridges beneath their skirts – a strong harvest, unless the top is circled with soft patches, and that is a cow with rotting feet. The yellow ones with eyelashes – a woman will come, but don't trust her. The ones long and white like dead man's fingers – the best of all, because it means a husband if you don't have one but want one, or children if you don't have them and want them. All the things she and her mother had promised they could know in exchange for a coin. Lux wasn't sure she believed in signs and portents, as much as she enjoyed the stories. In truth, she thought the best purpose of a mushroom was to fill your belly – though she was her mother's daughter, and also knew which ones could be eaten only once.

Else told of the north, how the light falls there, how the snow can blow a hundred different ways, and each way tells of something different. Each snow has a name, and sometimes it's not snow at all but ice or sleet or hail, but it's all made of the same thing, and it all goes back to the sea in the end.

Lux told of a man she had known at the sanctuary who could charm angry bees into peace just with the power of his touch, who could make daisies nod yes at the sight of his face, who caused gold dust to fall from the sky.

Else told of earthquakes, and volcanoes, and lightning storms, and how they were not God's anger or the sins of witches, but just a balance that the world seeks to strike, and that was surely the most unbelievable of all the stories, but by then the wolf was exhausted and the stack of rabbits was as high as their knees, one rabbit for each of the mummers, the bodies cloud-dark, cloud-soft.

Lux's head was full of stories: her own and Else's, merging. She'd heard stories at the sanctuary, but not like this. Not ones of magic and wonder and girls who could become hares or wolves; who could bend the world to their will even after death.

And no one had ever listened to her stories before. The bare truth of herself, shining in the dark.

It seemed they had been in the forest for days, but the fires had only begun to catch when Lux and Else returned to the house with a brace of rabbits slung over each of their shoulders, blood from each snapped throat painting a trail down their backs.

That night, Lux held Ash's hand hot and tight between her legs. The hand pressed, insistent, and she let it. She felt again the need to bite Ash's ear or cheek or jaw – and so, without thinking, she did. She leaned in close to Ash, as if for a kiss. Then a quick nip of her incisors, right on the fleshy lobe of Ash's ear. She heard Ash gasp and try to pull back, but she kept her legs together and her jaw tight, her body a trap. Not hard – she did not close her teeth tighter or bite down; she was not trying to rip through the flesh. She simply kept still, teeth gently catching the skin, bloodless. Ash kept still until she let go.

She waited for Ash to smack her, push her away, shout for the others. None of this happened. Instead Ash kept the hand right where it was. Lux could see nothing in the dark of the room, but could hear Ash shift position. She leaned forward and found, presented to her like an offering, the soft skin of Ash's throat. She licked the skin and heard Ash gasp again – but it was different. Not shock, but pleasure. Gently, she reached for Ash's throat. Gently, she bit.

After that, Lux slept. She dreamt that she danced with a man-sized rabbit in a hall dug down deep in the earth. She wore a gown made of rabbit fur, and a crown of wolf teeth so white it caught the light of every candle burning.

The next morning, Ash joined Lux by the fire as the rest of the mummers packed their furs and readied themselves to move on. It was not yet light, but they were close to the lake now. Soon they would reach the frost fair.

Lux busied herself in watching the mummers go about their business. She could help, but knew she would only be in the way. She already wore the fur and cloak that were now the only things she owned, so she had nothing to pack. Best to stay quiet and out of the way, here by the fire.

The contents of the mummers' cart fascinated her. Or, not quite – the contents of the wicker basket on the cart fascinated her. She wanted to see those swan wings again. Those twisted dangling ribbons. That fabric in every colour she'd ever seen, and some she had not. What it must be like to be able to see those things any time you wanted. To have more than only a scrap of a thing.

The mummer wearing a string of red beads had stripped the rest of the meat from the rabbits, and was wrapping it all in a piece of sackcloth to save for later. There would be enough for another meal at least – perhaps two if they could dig up some vegetables to bulk out the potage. Ash was not the only one who could be woman or man; this person had long hair like a woman, but a hard bristled jaw like a man. The red beads glowed even in the first of the light, and Lux thought longingly of her burst black pearls of nightshade. So beautiful and so useful. The mummer with the red beads picked up the rabbit innards and made as if to throw them in the river – but instead spoke words over them, and with a plop and slither dropped them again to the ground. Lux stared. The man with the wide smile joined, and together they peered at the mass of purple-red guts. They discussed something, nodding. Then something else, looking worried. She wondered what they saw there; if it was the same as her mushrooms.

'They wanted me to tell you,' said Ash, joining Lux beside the dying fire.

'Tell me?'

'The show later, at the frost fair. You're to be the maiden. Usually it's Coire, but let's be honest, she's getting on in years. She's better to be the mother now.' Ash nodded towards the woman with the scar.

'She has a child?' But there was no child here. It must have died, Lux realised. The sickness, perhaps.

'Ah, no.' Ash poked at the fire. 'That's not what I mean. It's part of the show. The year and the turn of the seasons. There's the maiden, see, and she's spring going into summer – bare bodies and flowers, youth and freshness, everything blooming. Then there's the mother, she's summer into autumn. Harvests and children, things all swelling and golden. Then there's the crone.' Here Ash nodded at the woman with the ice-white hair. 'That's Bealach. She's autumn into winter. Ripening, but then sickening, the leaves withering, everything bloody, ready for the chill of winter, the hardest part of the year.'

'Maiden, mother, crone,' she said. 'Then what?'

'Then we die.' Ash grinned. 'But mostly Mister Gaunt. He's perfect to play death.' Lux thought of the skeletal face and stretched-out body, the hands all bone and sinew. It was not hard to believe that he had gone to the world of the dead and come back again. 'Anyway, what I mean is you play the maiden. Then Coire can be the mother instead of having to change her clothes and play both. It looks better that way, see.'

Lux nodded, though she knew it wasn't a question. They sat compan-
ionably, watching the crack and spit of the fire. Perhaps she could be a
maiden. She certainly couldn't be a mother, as her blood never had come,
and she didn't have a husband. A crone wasn't appealing, either - her
mother had tried that, and had drowned for it. Maidens were quiet and
pretty. She could manage that.

But then - hadn't she been a maiden at the sanctuary? Hadn't she
been quiet then? And she hadn't done well. On her knees. Alone. Bloody.
Crawling home.

Still. Perhaps there was one more thing a woman could be.

'Have you seen what's north of here?' asked Lux.

'The lake? Yes, I've been there before. It's frozen now. That's why we're
going to -'

'The frost fair, I know. But after.'

'The city. With the cathedral and the stronghold. That's where we'll go
next.'

'Is that all?'

'Well, there's the north,' said Ash. 'Across the water where the land
bridge used to be. And there's the pines. Between the lake and the city is
a hill, the biggest you can possibly imagine. It's so high it almost reaches
the clouds. And the hill is completely covered with pine trees. They grow
as thick as the fur on a wolf's back. So close you can barely step between
them. When you walk beneath them it's dark and silent and all the same
for miles and miles. The pines swallow all the sound. You get lost and
turned around because it's all the same. The tops of the pines are so high
you can't see them, and they steal all the light. It's dark all the time, even
in high summer. The ground is thick with needles, so sharp you could
stitch with them, and they cut through your shoes and into your feet.
You could follow a trail of blood from a stranger's feet to find them, but
when you reached the end, there would be nothing there. The pines eat
them up.'

'If that's between here and the city, how will you get through it?'

49

'No one gets through it. We go around. There's a road, well travelled, with inns and stopping places. Lots of people. We can put on some shows on the way to pay for our supper. Tell fortunes, do tricks, make the dogs dance. Whatever brings in a coin.' Ash checked no one was watching, and picked up Lux's hand. 'You can play the maiden. Not just at the frost fair. Forever.'

It still wasn't a question, but this time Lux didn't nod. That was her choice: she could travel the daytime paths with the mummers, or she could go through the dark pines with Else. Maiden or witch. Dark or light.

'Do I have to tell it like that?' she asked.

'That's what the show is. That's what people want. Maidens arrayed in blooms, obedient and pleasant and pious.'

'But I've never known any maidens like that. They're not just one thing. It's more like...' Lux caught her breath against a rush of memory. All her time in her mother's house, all her time at the sanctuary, all at once. Stroking a rabbit softly to sleep even though she knew it was dead. Selling a woman mushrooms and knowing she'd use them to kill her husband. Wrapping a belt of rose thorns around her waist, relishing the pain of them as she prayed. Sitting in a circle with the other girls, laughing about the pricks they'd known and the pricks they'd imagined. Mixing her sweat and piss into loaves of bread. And the burning, the smell of his flesh as he...

Ash sighed and leaned away. 'Look, Lux. We do the shows so we can eat. We eat if people give us coins. They give us coins if the show is what they want to see. And the people, they don't want you.' Seeing Lux's expression, Ash hesitated. 'They'd want you if they knew you. Probably. But they want to be told what they already know.'

'Maidens who are pretty and biddable,' said Lux. 'Witches who eat babies and bring sicknesses. And is that what you think is true? Is that what you think maidens and witches are?'

'I think I want us all to eat,' said Ash, looking not at Lux but at the other mummers.

'You said they wanted you to tell me about being the maiden.'

'They're afraid of you. Because of the rabbits.'

'From last night? They ate them up fine enough.'

'And much appreciated. Don't misunderstand. But so many rabbits, and you were only gone a moment. You have no bow, no arrows, no knife. You didn't make any snares.'

'Say it, Ash. Say what you're thinking.'

'I'm not thinking anything. Only - how did you kill so many?'

'I didn't,' said Lux.

'Then who did?'

'A wolf -' Lux stopped herself. She had thought that fear was why the mummers didn't speak to Else - but she hadn't thought they'd be afraid of her too. She didn't know if their fear made her safer, or put her in danger. Her whole life, her mother had taught her that their only power was to make others fear what they could do - while secretly knowing that that was no power at all.

'A wolf what?' Ash looked around the clearing, but there was nothing to see. No bright eyes or slavering jaws in the shadows.

'A wolf - left them.'

'A wolf killed all those rabbits, but ate none of them, and then ran away, and left them for you to take, and didn't harm you?'

Lux opened her mouth to answer, but didn't know what to say.

'Ready up,' Mister Gaunt called over to them. He was looking at them oddly, and Lux felt that he could hear their conversation somehow, though they had spoken in murmurs, and he was much too far away.

She let go of Ash's hand. Ash tipped water on the fire. The smoke spiralled up to the first blinks of the greying dawn above the trees.

The light was still new-born when the trees opened up and the lake appeared. Lux stopped so suddenly that Else bumped into her back, though she barely noticed. The mummers continued around her; she was an obstacle, and they had work to do. But Lux stood and stared.

The lake stretched out, out, out, as huge and as white as a giant's fresh-washed bedsheet. It was so huge that the trees on the other side were dim and greyish, a mass of storm cloud. The lake was white like the sky, white like – Lux didn't know there could be so many different types of white. Much of it was thick and dense like chalk, the surface layered with cuts over and over, feathering up into dust. The centre shimmered like the inside of a shell, white and silvery and pinkish. The very edges were cloudy, layered white on white; if you fell on them, you would float.

Lux had expected the people to stay around the edges of the lake, as it was ringed with houses and gardens and vegetable patches; but they were all in the centre, on the ice, more people than Lux had ever seen in her life. People gliding along with what looked like carved bones attached to the bottoms of their shoes. Women stepping cautiously out, reaching for the hands of their beckoning men – and losing their feet from under them, skirts flipping up as they fell. But they didn't shout or cry; they tipped back their heads and laughed, and their men came to them and kissed the parts that had touched the ice to soothe them warm again.

All around the edge of the ice, fires burned. People huddled close to the flames to warm themselves after a turn around the lake. Others roasted mushrooms and chestnuts and skewered meat, all of which could be bought for a coin.

Small tents had been set up to one side of the lake, where there was an empty field. There people were doing all kinds of mysterious things: a woman with her face covered in tiny mirrors linked together like armour peered at the palms of hands and professed what she saw there; a preacher held painted boards showing biblical scenes both terrible and beautiful; three men shod horses and sharpened knives; a child rode a pig and sang songs for pennies; two women with identical faces hid behind screens then, popping out with matching smiles, invited others to tell them apart to win a prize.

Lux wanted to – she wanted to – she didn't know what she wanted to do first. All of it. Any of it.

But it didn't matter what she wanted. Ash pressed the maiden's clothes into her hands.

'Here,' said Ash. 'Go and change. Then I'll tell you how to be the maiden.'

Hidden from the audience under a tented contraption of cloths and sticks, the mummers waited at the edge of the frozen lake, huddled close, steaming breath mingling. They were in full costume, their true selves hidden.

A swan weeping golden tears, its huge wings folded around its human body. An angel with hair and skin and eyes and clothing so white it all seemed transparent, clearer than glass, bells stitched along the hems so every movement sounded in a high shiver. A deer, elegant and unreal, beautiful and terrifying, limbs spindly and eyes huge and antlers reaching to the sky. And Death, taller than any living man could ever be, with a face only bones and hands big enough to gather up every soul at once.

Lux hid at the back of the tent, pressed against the canvas, fidgeting in her red dress. She hadn't been able to close it properly and hoped her own clothes weren't visible underneath. Her cold fingers were too numb for the fastenings, and it didn't help that the healing grazes on her palms had scabbed over, making the skin tight and raw. She made her hands into fists and breathed on them, flexing the knuckles.

She had expected the show to be similar to the mummers playing with ribbons around the tree, haphazard and drunken, random-seeming, gleefully pulling props out of the basket and flinging them to one another to try on. But this was not play; this was work.

From outside, a slow, mournful drumbeat began to the rhythm of Lux's heart. A bell rang out, high and true. A count of three, and Death stepped out.

One by one, the creatures left. Each time a space appeared, Lux moved into it, bringing her closer to the mouth of the tent. It was so dark inside, and so bright out on the ice, that she could see little at first. But each step brought more sight.

A glimpse of Death raising his hands to the sky, a cluster of lost souls following. The quick flash of a frantic deer, chased across the colourless world by hunters with spears and swords. More instruments were added as more creatures emerged, until a cacophony of sound swelled up to the sky. The mummers were long gone – these were creatures from another world, another time, shifting shapes and changing form.

Lux's heart felt ready to burst out of her chest. Was this what she had been waiting for? Was this what she wanted? To take off the costume she had been given and put on a different one. Not the girl in the forest with her poppets and poisons, but someone else. Someone new.

Since the moment she had burst on the mummers while escaping the hunt – no, before that; from the moment Else had arrived at her door. From the moment she had dug the grave, had crawled from the sanctuary back to the house, had left the house for the sanctuary, had been born – this was it. Lux stepped forward, out of the musty shadows of the tent, and into the bright frozen day.

Afterwards, Lux sat on the shore watching the rest of the mummers' performance. It was swans and deer and angels and death. It was strange and magical. Anyone would be enchanted.

There was a loose thread on her red dress, and she pulled it, seeing the fabric bunch up at her sleeve. The ground was cold under her thighs. Her belly ached and she needed to piss.

Lux glanced up as Else sat down beside her. They both watched the mummers dance and Lux pulled harder on the thread. It came away in her hand, leaving an empty channel in the sleeve of the red dress.

'So that's the end of that,' said Lux.

Gently, Else took Lux's hand in her own. Her skin was as cold as the ground.

'I did want to be the maiden,' went on Lux. 'But it wasn't real. Maidens aren't like that. Pleasant and pious and powerless. I don't want that. I want –'

Lux stopped as something white and cold landed on their held hands. She glanced up at Else and saw that her cheeks were dusted with white.

'You want something else,' said Else softly.

Lux reached out with a fingertip; as soon as she touched the flakes, they melted on her skin. Snow fell, thick as feathers from a plucked goose. They tipped their heads back and let it cover them.

The show was over and the snow was over. Darkness bloomed. Lux and Ash sat by one of the many fires burning around the edge of the lake.

Ash plucked at the sleeve of Lux's red dress.

'You were good,' said Ash. 'You did just like I told you. I knew you'd be a good maiden.'

Lux said nothing, as it wasn't a question.

'Last night,' said Ash, voice dropping low. 'You bit me. Like a dog.'

Like a wolf, Lux started to say, but stopped herself.

'You could have hurt me,' said Ash.

'I thought you liked it,' said Lux. 'I did it so that you would like it.' It wasn't exactly true; she had done it because *she* had liked it.

'I've never known a woman do that.'

Lux felt a flame rise up in her. She was a woman, wasn't she? And she had done it. So it was a thing a woman did. She wanted to bite Ash again. She wanted to push Ash into a tumble across the snow. She wanted to kick out at the fire, make a dazzle of sparks, then stand up, quick, and run away into the trees, before anyone knew what was happening. 'I wasn't myself,' she said.

Ash grinned. 'So don't be yourself. Come with us, and you can be someone else. Every night, a new show. A new person.'

Lux couldn't help it. Her eyes searched for Else. There she was, not too far away – she was never too far away from Lux. In the light of the many fires, everything was lit gold. One of the children had enticed the mummers' red-jacketed dog onto the ice, and was trying to convince it to go further, holding a scrap of fat out of reach. The dog kept jumping up to get the fat, slipping on the ice, and retreating back to the shore. But it couldn't resist, and stepped back out onto the ice, and slipped again.

Else pulled her hood back to better watch the dog and the child play, a smile flickering across her face. Lux felt that familiar tumble of emotion to see it: the face of a stranger that was somehow familiar. From this distance, Lux couldn't see the marks around her mouth, the strange pocks she'd noticed in the firelight. Although Else was smiling, her eyes looked tired.

Lux could walk away from Else, be rid of her, stay with Ash, with the mummers. Be the maiden. Be the mother. Be the crone.

She thought then of the sanctuary, and the story she'd told there. The exact one that people wanted. She'd played her role perfectly. She'd said just what they wanted. She'd told them all about the devil, creeping into her, filling her up, so cold, so hard, making her say things, making her do things. She felt again the weight of those crucifixes, their wooden corners pressed into her softest parts, drawing blood. That endless journey home on her knees. Dread rose up in her, bitter on her tongue.

Then she turned to look at Ash. She saw the smile, the tease there. The eyes heavy with lust.

She felt a pulse of longing.

She and Ash were turned away from the others, making their own secret world.

It was different here. No crosses. No sin. No shame.

Only wanting.

Lux smiled. She held out her hand, and Ash took it.

A little way into the privacy of the forest, Ash laid furs down on the snow, black on white. Lux hesitated before stepping onto the blackness, sure it would swallow her up like a grave, that she'd drag Ash down with her. Then Ash kissed her, and she found steady ground.

They entangled there on the furs, sharing heat. Lux felt her blood throb in her head. Ash's breath came fast. They burrowed deeper into the pile of furs, heat rising around them.

'For you,' said Ash, the words a low murmur, coming between kisses, 'I would pull down the stars and make them into a crown.'

'For me?'

'And I would collect a hundred flower petals to make a dress for you to wear. I would feed you honey every day.'

'What else?'

'And I would get you ripe fruits and – and more honey. The ripest, biggest fruit. The sweetest, thickest honey. Anything you like. I would, for you. And only for you.'

The words had a practised air, the pauses and kisses perfectly timed. Lux did not care; Ash's lips were sweet, Ash's fingers were strong.

'What else would you do?' she asked. 'Tell me what else.'

'I would – I –' But it seemed that Ash had run out of sweetnesses. Still, kisses filled the gaps. And if God didn't like what they were doing, he would strike them down, and he had not.

'Would you give up God for me?' asked Lux. Her voice sounded strange in her ears. 'Would you give up your life after this? Would you stay with me here in this world and resign yourself to this life alone and nothing after? Would you sacrifice all your vows for me?'

'What vows?' Ash gave up on the kisses, pulling away to stare at Lux.

'Nothing,' said Lux. She shook her head; she was not at the sanctuary now. 'I was thinking about something else.'

'I want you to think,' said Ash, returning to Lux, stroking her hair back from her forehead and kissing along her hairline, 'about this.'

And Lux did. It was sweetness and warmth and the burst of summer fruits.

Ash kissed up her throat, dot-dot-dot, like a pause before speaking. Lux tipped her head back and opened her eyes wide to the dark – but it was not dark.

In the sky above them the northern lights pulsed. Pink, green, purple. Shapes stretching and contracting like the sky was breathing. Lux could have fallen up into it, swooning, but then Ash spoke:

'Can I?'

'Can you what?'

As a question, Ash slid closer to Lux and pressed a kiss to her lips. As an answer, Lux pulled Ash onto her. Overhead, the northern lights swayed and spun. A flow of slow purple from one side of the sky to the other.

Ash's lips were sweet as petals and Ash's tongue was soft as rabbits and Ash's skin was hot as new blood –

And Lux felt the words rise up in her like clouds, like smoke from a censer, like the sparks from a fast-burning fire –

Ave Maria gratia plena dominus tecum benedicta tu in in in

in mmmmmulieribus et benedictus frutas ventris t t t t t t t

tui amen amen amen amen

amen

a

m

e

n . . .

The moon was a bright white eye in a blackened sky. Lux and Ash lay on a pile of snow-scattered furs, limbs tangled. Lux kept her nose to the base of Ash's throat, to breathe in the scent there. Salt, summer, her own skin. She breathed in one more time to hold it inside her, then sat up and began to straighten her clothes.

'Where are you going?' Ash's voice was lazy, thick with sleep. 'Don't go back to the lake. Everyone will be drunk. We can sleep here.'

'What do I look like?' Lux asked.

'Oh,' said Ash, eyes still closed, 'you're very pretty. The prettiest girl I've seen in –'

'That's not what I mean. Just – I've never seen. Tell me.'

Ash's eyes opened. In the moonlight, Lux let Ash look at her.

'You're tall,' said Ash. 'Your hair is dark like burned bread. Your skin is the colour of the inside of a tree. Your eyes have a gleam in them, like you can see in the dark.'

'I can't see in the dark,' said Lux.

'Then you can't go in the dark. Through the pines. You have to come with us.' Ash, seeming to realise that something was wrong, sat up, fully awake. 'Lux? You know that, don't you? You have to come with us.'

'I'm not the maiden. And I don't have to go with you.'

She kissed Ash on those swollen petal lips and gave one last bite to that fleshy fruit of an earlobe. Then she got up and walked away without looking back. She left the bright red maiden's dress, spread out on the snow like spilled blood.

Lux found Else, golden by firelight, watching two of the mummers feed scraps to a yapping, flipping dog. She rested a hand on Else's shoulder. Startled, Else jumped up; but seeing who it was, she asked Lux, her voice soft: 'What do you want?'

Lux thought: I want to be strong. I want to shimmer with menace. I want to go north. I want revenge on the man who killed my mother. I want to want. I want to be the witch and the maiden and and and . . .

But she said: 'I want to go to the stronghold with you. Only with you.'

'All right,' said Else, and she smiled.

Together, they collected up the furs and cloaks they had arrived with. They walked away from the mummers, away from the lake, away from the people.

As soon as they stepped beneath the canopy of pines, the dark was absolute. Lux could feel it in front of her face, a velvet cloth stopping her breath. She reached out, helpless – and found Else's hands. Her heart calmed. Else stroked her thumb along the healing grazes on Lux's palms, so gently it might have been accidental.

Else took a breath to speak, and Lux expected a scolding, an instruction not to panic or wander away.

'It's easier to talk in the dark,' said Else, her voice soft. 'Easier to listen too. If you want to, you can tell me. I'll listen.'

There under the trees, it was black and silent and all the same. Lux blinked against the dark, held on to Else's hand, and walked with her deeper into nothing.

PART 2
Lux's Story

it is summer –

    & i am to get the water from the well –

    & mother is angry from a fox eating her best chicken so she does not ask me kindly about getting the water –

    but then she never does for that matter never is kind & never does ask just tells & not too nicely at that –

    i have out grown all of my dresses & have feet now too big for my shoes & dont have any thing to make new ones with so its bare feet for me & the soles of my feet already thick as tree bark –

    if i could i would take shoes from some one elses house & hide them in the nettles until they forgot about their loss & then i would suddenly reveal them & pretend to my mother that some one had given them to me –

    but i didnt think of it & now my mother knows i dont have shoes so that wont work as she would never forget me telling her what i lacked –

    not that she is against taking things but she is against being caught for it –

    though i have known fourteen summers now –

    meaning i am big enough that it would not be her fault & i would hang for it my self –

any way i am at the well fetching up the water –

i am sweating & my dress clings to me & my hands are slipping wet on the rope as i haul up the bucket it is not pleasant at all & i want to get inside or at least under the trees to be in the shade there so i suppose i am not best pleased & perhaps not best polite when my mother comes to me & says –

& by the way she doesnt even help me with the bucket though it is slipping & she can see fine well it is slipping & it is making it hard for me to pay attention to her & my hair is all stuck to my face from sweat & it is making me not pleased & i know it is not good to be not pleased at ones mother still i am telling you the truth so i will be truthful & i hope you will not judge me too harsh by what i do when my mother says –

& by the way i know what she is going to say because despite my many summers my blood has not come though i hope that summer it will as it always does seem like a summer thing & for a time i do think women bleed only in summer though i dont know if that is only because in summer it is hot & the summer skirts have not so thick a fabric as winter skirts so you can smell the blood more & also the boys do talk more about a girls blood in summer but again perhaps that is only because they can also smell it more & it makes them think of it –

& she says to me: do you have your blood –

& i say to her no which is true –

& by the way she knows this perfectly well –

& she says you will tell me the truth now girl you will tell me if you have known a boy from the village & you will tell me the name of the boy from the village & you will tell me if that is why you are not getting your blood –

but i havent known a boy from the village or from any village for that matter so i cant say a name of a boy that doesnt exist so i dont say any thing just try to hold the bucket without spilling the water though what i really want is for her to go back into the house –

but theres no use in a girl wanting –

& she says to me –

& it doesnt matter so much what she says because i know already that a girl who does not bleed is no use to anyone & i am of a marrying age now & there are men in the village & in nearby villages that are in want of a wife & i could & should be that wife to get me out of the house & off my mothers hands & stop being a burden but no body will want a wife with no blood because every man needs sons the more the better & no blood means no babies –

she wants for me to say the name of a boy so that he has to marry me because either i have known a boy & that is why no blood so then i can be a wife & useful even if its only a wife to a village boy young with no thing to his name & not a man with property & some things to his name that will then be my name –

or i have not known a boy & still no blood & that means something else perhaps the devil inside me or a sickness or i am not a proper woman & no body wants that least of all me –

because it is a careful line we walk my mother & i –

& we both know that a devil in a girl who is not a proper woman is only a sniff away from being a witch –

the true story is i am not a witch & my mother isnt a witch we only sell things that people think they can do witchery by though we never make any pacts with any devils so people are on to pebbles if they think theyve bought some strong witchery when usually theyve bought some sewn poppets or little bottles of piss and spit and perhaps some herbs –

though we do also sell herbs that can cause a person to die though they can cause them to not die too & you can call that witchery if you want but i call it nature –

but i know any thing that has the taint of witch on it is dangerous for me & for my mother –

& me not having my blood well that is dangerous –

but i would lie say a name lie quite happily & not worry because i understand that lying is not the worst thing that can happen & even if it means hell later well at least it doesnt mean hell now but i do not want to marry a boy from the village or a man from the village if im honest & i am trying so be honest when i tell you this so i still dont say a name –

& my mother says do you want to be a wife –

& i am so surprised by that as i dont think she has ever asked me before what i do or dont want that i dont answer her –

& the bucket is slipping from my hands & she asks me again what i want & i dont know so i dont say & its so hot my sweat oiling me under my dress what do you want & i dont know so i dont say & what do you want tell me girl tell me now it had better be more than this godforsaken place & i try to answer but the bucket slips & slams down hard on her foot & vomits water over us both & that is the end of that except i get a slap & also have to bring the water up from the well again –

now i am laden with crosses –

hundreds hundreds hundreds –

so much holiness enough for an army of unholies –

but these are for me only i have enough sin for a hundred hundred hundred girls & i keep it all crammed tight overflowing thronged & bursting all inside one girl –

crosses of wood dark & light & new & old & smooth & rough tied on with rope & string –

round my waist my thighs my arms my chest my belly my neck so tight my breaths come small & fast like a dog run too long –

im on my knees face down looking at the ground so heavy the crosses my legs tremble my arms tremble my belly wants to touch the ground lie flat from the weight of my sin of my lust of my possession of my bewitching but this weight is real & its the only thing that will get me rid of the weight of the other which cant be seen but is heavy in me hot & heavy –

i burn for Him still help me god i still burn –

i know i have been here more than one summer but its hard to count summers all the time here feels like summer the hot bright sun on my forehead the nodding daisies the weight of His hands on me the smell of the flowers sweet & sick the days endless counted out with prayer ave maria gratia plena dominus –

i wait for them to kick me like a dog to kick me out of the garden but they dont they stand & watch hands pressed together dresses pure white heads high holy waiting for me to crawl away & take my sins with me they dont want to look at me to dirty their eyes with my sin –

i have been stripped of my white dress i have failed to be pure i am not allowed it now i may only wear a black dress & cloak the dark colour will show my sin & also it will not show my blood –

& father fleck says –

he says to me eyes high but voice low only for me –

go home girl –

leave this place –

the holy life is too good for you –

you are too far gone & will taint the other girls –

you have shown lust & this is not the proper sort of love for all other love but the love of god is evil –

divest yourself of your sin –

let the holy light of god guide you through the dark –

& when you are home pray that your sin may be cleansed –

cleansed with your blood that will be drawn from you now –

by the blood on your knees & your hands may you be cleansed –

may you not become what your mother was & what the devil wants you to be –

but i know & i have been cleansed by Him over & over so i know i am clean & i know that crawling on my knees through the muck & the creatures & the shadows under trees will not get me cleaner than my love for Him because love is clean isnt love clean isnt it the cleanest the purest the holiest of holies doesnt love make our hearts shine gold & burst into flame doesnt it but not this love i suppose not love the way i am loving Him still now though i am in this world & He is in that other –

but i do as i am told as i always must do what i am told & i go –

& i never did get my womans blood but i bleed now from the sharp edges of the crosses –

& this is sin this is filth i am a pitcher of filth with a mouth full of blood & my blood drips into the ground my skin cut the sharp edges my blood –

on my knees & my hands i shake from the weight of the crosses thousands upon thousands & each time i move they clank & judder together the scrape of wood they scrape on my skin already raw & burning with my love for Him –

ave maria gratia plena dominus tecum –

& slow & aching hands & knees into the forest alone i leave the sanctuary finally after all the summers here trying to be good & clean trying to be pure for Him & for god & i go back to where i came from dirty bleeding i go –

i go –

i go home –

i first see Him in the rain & the daisies say yes –

i am at the window sighing & praying for i know not what plagues me –

its my sins i suppose with girls its always their sins what ever those sins might be well you know with a girl theres always a sin or two floating around –

i dont know the nature of my plague i know only that i am plagued –

the voices of my sisters in song only angers me & bores me which i know is not my own voice & my own thoughts because i have taken vows & that surely makes me holy in word & thought & deed –

my thoughts may not be holy & my words when i say them inside my own head are not at all holy –

but the vows will fix my sinful thoughts for me i think because god loves a sinner & i think often of sin & i hope that makes him love me more –

only one window looks out to the walls & the bridge & the river & the road & the woods beyond –

all the other windows look into the courtyard but one window a secret little small one thats up a tower & awkward you have to climb unladylike & tip your self so any one who might be coming up the stairs would see the unholy thing under your skirt & become unholy by the sight of it so theyd better not come up the stairs is all i will say –

& by the way the windows are set like that so that we dont look out of them & look always in wards in to our thoughts & not out wards to the world & its sinful etceteras so perhaps my vows would work better if i did not look out of the window so much i dont know –

outside the window the rain comes slow then quick quiet then loud thrumming spitting –

the daisies are out it is summer –

always it is summer –

the days long slow hazy endless –

tomorrow the same & yesterday & the next & before –

the air still holds the heat of the sun –

the rain falls hard & i put out my hand lean out of the window far so i might fall so i can touch the rain but i do not fall –

the daisies in the rain nod yes –

& i see Him walk by along the river & the rain does not bother Him at all His head high His eyes deep in thought of good pure holy glowing things & i want that to be me good pure holy glowing me & the good pure world i can show Him & the good pure light of my love for Him –

& the rain wet on my hands & i lean out so far my feet come up off the floor & i look down on Him passing & i nod yes i will have that one yes –

& He keeps walking –

& the rain falls –

& the daisies nod yes yes yes –

i first see Him soothing the bees –

some of the bees the ones in the sixth hive have gone mad & father fleck says they are possessed by demons –

which may be true because i suppose any thing might be true god has his ways & means –

all we know the girls & i –

thats me & jennet issobel grissel marion agnes gilleis lizabet alizon jehan hanna isidore oh & euphemia thats every one i think –

all we know is that the five hives of bees are fine & friends & so any one of us can go & collect the honey with the mask & every thing of course because they may be friends but they are still bees & bees have stings we must not forget the true nature of things suchlike as bees are full of stings & women are full of sins –

though mostly He collects the honey because the bees like Him best which makes me not surprised because i also like Him best –

He goes to collect the honey from the sixth hive & the bees all of a sudden possessed bewitched mad with sin & lust & anger the bees swarm at Him try to get inside His mask to sting Him –

& i cant help but think they only want to kiss Him & i understand i know bees i feel the same i want to swarm & kiss & bring honey to His lips –

but when He tells father fleck about the bees we –

thats me & jennet issobel grissel marion agnes gilleis lizabet alizon jehan hanna isidore oh & euphemia –

we all hear because girls have big ears & we are glad to hear because we are all too frightened to collect the honey because of the mad bees but father fleck needs the honey to sell to travellers & visitors who come passing by so the church can be kept up & so that we can etcetera have food to eat –

we hear many things we big eared girls such as it being a cruel year & a scant harvest & a hungry summer with many dead babies & animals –

any way father fleck says it is an unsatisfactory situation & the bees must be exorcised & father fleck tells Him to do it at once –

& He does the exorcisms mostly women of course but also chickens dogs goats frogs horses geese & once a caterpillar that kept eating the lettuces so of course bees are fine for Him –

we all have work to do we have to collect the eggs & milk the cows & suchlike but i get gilleis to do my chores because i did hers once when she had her blood & was dirty & didnt want to taint the food with her sins so i creep to the window & watch –

i watch as He in His layers of white wound round His body like Hes made of light –

i watch as He picks up the sixth beehive the hive full of mad bees & right away they swarm out & onto Him He is covered in a twitching raging black mass & the hum is so loud like a pain in my head but He is calm as if He is covered only in butterflies or feathers soft things stroking things singing Him soft songs –

& He carries the beehive away from the others –

far far away from the animals & from us –

He takes the beehive right over the bridge over the river all the way to where the trees start –

He sets the beehive down in the shadows there –

& He takes off His white things & He is far away & small now but i still watch as He lays His small far away hands on the hive & the small far away bees calm –

they do they calm for Him not mad not possessed but calm bees now good bees holy bees –

He walks away from the calm & holy bees & He does not see me watching Him He walks in beauty the sun golden on His hair His beauty is golden sun i swoon there watching Him the heat rises up in me my desire for Him burns like a hundred hundred stings all over my body –

i first see Him healing jennet who is struck by fever all of a sudden –

though of course it is not fever but demons who often pretend to be other things like fever or rabbits or small black flies & it is easy for a demon to get inside a woman because they are so leaky always bleeding & milky & weepy always some thing oozing from some where so very messy –

father fleck says the demon is named asmodeus & is residing in jennets belly & father fleck tells Him to exorcise jennet so she will be well & cleansed again –

two hours it takes & i am to fetch the water always cool always fresh constant in & out to fetch water & each time i go the well handle is still warm from my hand from the last time –

father fleck is there to bless the water & make it into holy water & then it can go inside jennet not all in her throat as she has already been sick a lot & theres no point putting the water in if it comes out that fast –

so it goes in all other places women as i say being leaky & oozy so things can go in & out of us very easily –

i heard of a girl who purged a live eel a foot and a half long & vomited fulsome stuff of all colours twice a day for fourteen days including hair wood pigeon dung parchment coal brass etcetera –

i heard of a girl who burned so with a fever she had a coldwater cloth on her fore head for many months to cool her brain & when it was taken away there was a bleached white patch there on her fore head which was a sign of the holy mother blessing her & i think she did die but at least she died blessed –

& now i am to help with jennets leakiness too though i dont mind as we do help each other with suchlike things if its needed & its only a case of buckets really a lot of buckets that i empty into the river after the holy water has come back out of jennet not quite so holy –

any way this goes on for a long time i think or so it seems & i am tired of running back & forth with buckets & i think i am actually asleep while walking & i come into the dormitory & there is no thing for me to take or bring for once & it doesnt seem as if jennet really knows what is happening so i dont look at her i look at Him doing the exorcism –

& its like ive never looked at a person before –

He is tired beautiful glowing head bowed as if in prayer but looking at the girl at jennet as her body arches & her breath comes fast fast fast & she lets out one final cry & i dont know what shes feeling in her body then but i suppose it must be god & He looks at her with total love as the demon leaves her body –

i see His hands resting soft on jennets face –

i see her eyes gazing up at Him –

i see her calm she breathes slow & she slips asleep –

& still He keeps His hand there & i think His palm is cool & good & it would feel –

& He is so beautiful –

& He is so golden so good –

& i want –

i want –
theres no use in a girl wanting –
but i want –

at the trial the evidence is pacts –

well not just pacts it is also the words of my sisters which mean not much & the words of the abbess which mean a little more & the words of father fleck which mean quite a lot –

i am mostly fainted through the trial by the way so i cant tell you all of it –

but the evidence is a lot about pacts –

these are things that appear in my sisters cells or that they have vomited up –

the pacts prove that covenants with satan have been made –

they say i vomited a pact up too i dont remember but there it is a piece of evidence labelled with marks that they say mean my name sitting on a tray –

it looks like a dirty black & red mass the size of a closed hand like chicken guts or some thing like that –

but they say that the demon told them through my mouth that the pact is not chicken guts it is a piece of the heart of a child sacrificed at a witches sabbat & mixed with that also the ashes of a eucharist & also some of His blood & semen –

i do not know where i got these things from but i suppose i did not get them satan did –

or He did at least thats what they say –

they say that i said so many things or rather that the demon inside me said them –

they say that i said He told me to steal a baby & put a nail in its navel so together we could suck its blood –

they say that i said He told me to desecrate graves & to take bones & scalps from them to be used to make pacts –

they say that i said He took me to dance naked with four black things going upright & also to lie down with the things & after wards let them take me as a bull takes a cow –

over & over at the trial they say it was not satan possessing me but Him because He is a witch & so a tool of satan & fit only to be tied to a stake & for a fire to be lit beneath Him & for Him to burn until –

for Him to burn until –

i can not say it –

only that He must burn & not drown so that His body will be destroyed & there is no hope for Him to ever be resurrected –

they also say that He left five roses on the sanctuary steps for me to find & this is how my lust for Him began He pricked Him self with the thorns & then when i was pricked on the thorns His blood went into me & i was bewitched in this way –

they say that is when satan came to me with his huge cold prick & from it liquid dripping cold & it was searing & thrilling for me although also wicked & filthmaking for me & he rode me & rode us all like a stal-lion among mares –

& i do not remember any of this but they say it so it must be –

my sisters scream & wail & fall to the floor their white dresses flapping around they look like panicked doves & its all very unseemly very unholy but then its not really them is it its satan possessing them –

their pacts are: a piece of paper stained with three drops of blood & containing eight orange seeds –

a bundle of five pieces of straw tied around spiders legs fish scales & snot –

a package containing worms cinders hair & nail clippings –

a glass vial containing urine & venom from a toad that had been hung upside down & the thing in the forehead of a new-foaled foal –

& some other things mostly pieces of animals & pieces of humans you need those you see to lay the curse on the human thats how it works –

& these things are all evidence that He has done all of the things that witches are wont to do like dance indecently & eat excessively & make love diabolically & commit atrocious acts of sodomy & blaspheme scandalously & run after all horrible dirty crudely unnatural desires & keep toads vipers lizards other sorts of poison as precious things & all sorts of uncontrolled characteristics of an execrable inconstancy that can be expiated only through the divine fire that justice placed in hell –

or thats what they say –

thats what they say about Him over & over –

& i do not know what His design was through all of these things as i do not know whose hair & nail clippings they were in the pacts & also i do not know what use it is to have a girl & by that i mean me what use is it to have me bewitched by you & it seems to me that only my sisters & me were harmed by any of this except of course for Him but i am sure His design was not all along to hurt Him self because what would be the point of that & also what would be the use of hurting us we are only some girls –

though this does not come up in the trial or perhaps it comes up when i am fainted which i mostly am –

father fleck & the others do not seem to care what His design is with all these pacts perhaps just general wickedness just general destruction of christian values just general pacts with evil things just general breaking down good family life & good men just general ruining girls who would have been useful wives & made useful sons but now are useless tainted desecrated pitchers full of filth with their mouths full of blood etcetera –

to father fleck & the others it seems it is enough to make covenants with satan & to know that it has happened & not to know or to ask what the point of any of it is –

i imagine my mother in her final desperate days –
    going from door to door in the village begging for a little meat –
    & being denied –
    begging for a scrap of firewood –
    & being denied –
    begging for a sip of water –
    a mouldy old onion –
    a crust of bread –
    begging just to sit by the fire for a moment & unfreeze her old bones –
    & being denied –
    & i think perhaps that was the moment she cursed them –
even though she knew her words couldnt hurt them unless they believed it did –
    there outside their doors in the dark while they sat warm in the firelight –
    she cursed them at the top of her lungs up and down from heaven to hell & every where in between –
    & it seems to me that she was still a woman when she was alone desperate starving abandoned by all the so called holy people sitting there by their warm fires eating their warm dinners talking louder so they do not have to hear her calling out for help agreeing with one

another that her misfortune shows she must have done some thing to incur gods wrath because he is all powerful and will reward those deserving of his grace –

    & it seems to me that she became no longer a woman –

    but some thing else –

    the moment she wanted some thing –

    & did not say please –

my mother & i go in to the forest & trap rabbits –

    tip toeing through the leaves talking in whispers –

    waiting watching for a long time forgetting to breathe –

    wire snares snapping tight around their throats –

    scrabble of leaves scuffing up legs twitching & then no thing –

    i carry the rabbits home in my arms following my mothers steps & they are so warm still so soft against my skin so heavy warm as blood –

    my mother is not looking at me she is looking ahead & i always walk behind her –

    so she does not see me press my face down into my armfuls of rabbit & breathe them in & feel them close & let them stroke my cheek so soft & tender –

    my mother wants to cook some of the rabbits into a stew & salt some of the rabbits for winter & use all of the skins of the rabbits to make warm clothes not for us to wear but to sell & i will do the stitching as my stitches are small & neat as i have small hands & clear eyes –

    & that is all fine of course but one rabbit is the best rabbit he is special because his eyes are still open round & black like tiny conkers –

    his tail also is special as it is huge & white & fluffy as if its made of autumn dandelions –

i hide the best rabbit so that my mother cant make him into stew or salt him or sell him –

best rabbit strokes my forehead with his big grey paw when i am sleepless –

best rabbit lets me put his dandelion tail in my mouth –

best rabbit lies on my chest & counts my breaths so black cats cant come in & steal them –

i feed best rabbit the sweetmeats of my food the little black pips from my apple like the black of his eyes & the burnt crisp parts at the edges of the squirrel & the sweet inner leaves of the cabbage –

the best bits for best rabbit –

& when i have my bath i wash him gently carefully i do not just drop him into the water –

i wash his ears separately & his dandelion tail & his black eyes not so shiny now but still open round & black & i scrub his tiny yellow teeth with a chewed stick of hawthorn before i kiss him –

& every night he sleeps beside me his body pressed tight to mine –

he is so good so soft so warm I push his body down down down so soft against me i love best rabbit & he loves me –

me & all the other girls thats jennet issobel grissel marion agnes gilleis lizabet alizon jehan hanna isidore oh & euphemia –

we do mostly separate chores things like sweeping tidying washing brewing baking weeding beekeeping candlemaking i wont list them all –

but some chores are all of us together –

& i do like those ones the best –

like this one which is twisting the cloth thats stitched in a loop end to end & soaked in hot urine & after that we sit in a circle on the grass in the afternoon sun & pass the cloth round & round pressing it all the time with our hands & this strengthens it or i think it does i just do it & we all just do it because we are told to & we have to wear thick brown aprons to protect our dresses which are white & always getting dirty with our chores & thats why we have to be doing laundry so often to stay clean & pure –

& we talk then all together about boys we have known –

most of us having known none at all but liking to talk about it any way –

except for grissel who does know a boy & gets herself with child or i suppose she doesnt do it all by herself but the baby is inside her not inside the boy so i suppose its her sin & not his –

grissel says she prays every night for the baby to not be there not for it to die as such but for it to not exist not be there inside her & then it is born too quick & she loves it but its too small & it dies which i think gris-sel is sad about but the baby is a sin & a manifestation of her sin & theres not much to be done about it as thats a womans burden so thats the end of that –

alizon has not known a boy the way that grissel has but she has seven brothers & sees their pricks all different times & states of being & tells about what they are like at all the different times & states like big & small & up & down & who knows a prick could be so many ways & she must be making it up but we squeal anyway & the air & our hands smell of old piss from the cloth & it makes us think more of pricks or at least it makes me think –

& i know i am unseemly & a sinner but a womans burden is such & it is a heavy one though on this day at this time it does not feel so heavy a womans burden actually feels not like a burden at all it feels like the heat of all my sisters bodies by mine & the feel of the grass under me & the sound of all my sisters laughter –

another thing we girls all do together is to prepare food which is a thing i dont mind doing because if the abbess isnt watching you can sneak small bites they have to be things you dont have to chew that you can let dissolve in your mouth like a tiny piece of cheese or bread or the abbess sees the jaws going & then its a good smack & the rest of the day crouching in the dark cupboard & no one wants that –

baking the bread is my favourite i am trusted to do it alone there is a lot of bread to bake but it is easy enough once you have made one loaf of bread you can make as many as you like & i like the rising of it the best –

to take simple things some flour some water some yeast & put them together & then it is magic –

or not magic for that would be against god & i have taken vows about god etcetera so its god making the bread rise –

though its not god putting the flour the water the yeast together its me –

but i suppose he must be doing some thing some where –

this day i make the bread every one is tired father fleck did a long matins to remind us of our sins etcetera so no one is looking at me there in the kitchen –

it is hot with the fire going & i wipe my forehead with the back of my hand & not thinking i keep kneading the dough the sweat from my hand is gone it is inside the dough now –

i lick my finger & dab it on the dough to try to lift out my sweat –

but that doesnt help now it has my sweat & my saliva in it both & i really dont want to throw away the dough & start again for that is a terrible waste & god would be angry & also i dont want to –

& i think of a thing that father fleck once told us which is that men desire women but its not their fault its because women are wicked –

& when a man sees a woman he must imagine the bile pus wax snot piss vomit inside her so that he will not desire her –

& i think well does that mean men should desire men because they dont have bile pus wax etcetera in them or perhaps just a different less repulsive kind –

or women should desire women because we have equal amounts of bile pus wax etcetera in us so it will balance out & men never need to be involved at all & we wont need to worry about who does or doesnt desire or whether its wicked –

& i think then of my mother –

not just because she had a lot of bile in her but because of the things she used to do suchlike as –

blessing crops & healing sick animals & helping a mothers milk come in after child birth & pulling the rot out of wounds & making monthly blood come regular & saying magical words & making poppets to protect or harm a person & putting charms on men to make them stay with women –

but there was one thing she wouldnt do no matter how many times she was asked –

& she was asked a lot –

& that was to put a love charm on a woman by a man –

& i think then as i stand kneading the bread about a charm she told me once –

it goes like this –

lead this woman to me & prevent her from eating & drinking until she comes to me & do not allow her to have experience with another man except me alone & drag her by her hair & by her guts until she does not stand aloof from me & until i hold her obedient for the whole time of my life & she will love me & desire me & tell me all that she is thinking particularly the parts she wishes to hide from me –

my mother said: that is no love charm –

my mother said: that is a curse –

my mother would do any thing for coins or for food but she would not bind a woman to a man any more than we are all already bound to men because even though she didnt think the curses worked what if they did & it was just not worth it to condemn a woman to that –

but i am thinking the charm & instead of this woman i say His name –

i go quick to the privy & do both my businesses & i take a bit of each –

just a tiny bit not that any one would ever notice –

& i go back & put them in the dough –

& i keep kneading until my sweat & saliva & piss & shit are fully mixed in & who would ever know well no one except god i suppose he knows every thing but he must be fine with this or he would have struck me down instantly & he did not i am still here kneading myself through the dough –

i put it aside to rise & it rises better than any bread i have ever made –

it looks beautiful truly a gift from god –

every one enjoys the bread when breaking their fast & as i watch there from the kitchen i am sure that He enjoys it most of all –

& god help me i like it –

i like that He has small pieces of me inside Him now –

that now He can never be completely free of me –

in the church where we spend much of our time -

more time than we spend in our beds any way which i am not best pleased about -

which is not a blessed thing to think i know but its hard to be holy when youre barely clinging to wakefulness & always slipping into dreams -

any way we are in church for matins and prime and terce and sext and none and vespers and compline and vigils -

strange to think how quick i am used to this new life different as it is to the one in the forest with my mother -

then our days were set by the sun & moon & the things we grew -

& now our days are set by god only -

or rather the men who god speaks through because of course he does not speak to us we are only girls -

but there in church with us is our lord -

on his cross he looks so tall up there even bigger than a real man -

though its hard to tell he is high up on the wall watching over us -

or that is what father fleck says but i dont think he is watching us -

because his eyes are raised up ecstatic to heaven -

& it makes me think of what grissel said about boys & how when they spend their eyes roll back like that -

& i look at our lord with his eyes rolled back

& i think about Him & whether i could make His eyes roll back –

this is not holy to think not holy at all but i am a wicked filthy thing & am doing my best despite my thoughts –

& there in church i am not watching our lord & i am not watching father fleck –

i am watching Him –

with His head bowed praying murmuring words to god –

& then His eyes open just a little –

& He looks over at me –

& in a gap between prayers He looks at me His eyes steady & He bites His lip –

i see His white teeth appear & dig into His bottom lip so hard it must bleed –

later when i am washing my self i find a bite mark –

high on my thigh a bite mark –

i can not know the pattern of His teeth but still i am sure they are His –

i am in a swoon at that it is a miracle it is a true holy miracle but jennet cries out –

she has a bite on her thigh how could it be so –

& one by one issobel grissel marion agnes gilleis lizabet alizon jehan hanna isidore oh & euphemia –

one by one we all call out –

we are bitten –

& i look at all the other girls bites & they do not look like bites to me but more like a bruise a pinch like the thumb & finger of a girl might make –

mine though is a bite a real bite i am sure of it –

but i do not say that –

i go to bed & lie awake & i think of Him there in church biting His lip –

& i put my fingers to the teeth marks high on my thigh –

& i touch them –

i am struck with fever of a sudden –

i arise to say orisons & i say the words of the prayer like im meant
though i am tormented by unseemly thoughts that are not my own –

i scream –

my head full of demons the hum of their torments so loud i cannot
hear my own prayers –

they call for Him to exorcise me to help me –

He comes to me then He comes to my bed –

He stands at the foot of it & He reads aloud from a book –

words i can not understand but i suppose the demon inside me can
understand because it takes me over once more –

the sound of His voice makes my body convulse –

i writhe i shriek i tear my dress i know not what i do –

to fight the demon He steps closer comes to the head of the bed i feel
His breath on my cheek as He says the words –

the demon speaks through me it says words they are sinful words terrible words sent by satan –

the things i say –

the things the devil says through me –

i say that father fleck is a strutting fatty coxcomb of a man fit only to rootle with the pigs & he laughs like a rooster when he should be praying he is pathetic & shameful -

i say that the other fathers are mandrake mymmerkins they are flimsy parasites held tight under father fleck's flabby thumb & they think not of god but only of their growling bellies & their underused pricks -

i say that the abbess is a scrawny mangy dog & most likely spreads her legs for father fleck & says her prayers backwards while he takes her like dogs do -

i say that i want to be a doxy & lie down with brigands to see how their pricks feel inside me -

i say that while i am with the men i will call on god to watch me -

i say that i am all ways hungry -

i say that i am all ways bored -

i say that i am trapped & hopeless & i want i want i want -

i know they are sinful words because He takes His hand off the holy book He is holding & puts His hand on mine -

my hand that is gripping my dress my body clutching at my self causing scratches -

the demon takes possession of my hand -

i do not know what i do with it for it is no longer my own hand -

He puts His hand on that hand -

His voice drops low -

the words must be pulling out the demon for some thing is coming -

out of me being pulled from me i writhe i call out for god to come to me to save me from this torment -

His words steady as a river flowing His hand cool on my own -

His sweet soft breath so close to me His mouth His lips -

& some thing is happening in me in my body i think it must be god it feels it feels it feels oh it feels -

His hands cool steady holding me anchoring me to this earth -

wild waves pull me under -

stars tilt above me -

the world spins & spins & spins –

avemariagratiaplenadominustecumbenedictatu –

inmulieribusetbenedictusfrutas –

ven

tris

tui

amen amen amen amen

amen

a

m

e

n

let me tell you about the food we produce here at the sanctuary –

first there are the cows which we must milk every day which give us milk that we drink or make into butter & cheese –

& then when the cows do not give milk any longer we can eat them well we dont eat them not the girls because god said we cant eat meat but the monks eat the cows god said that was fine –

there are the chickens which we must visit every day after matins & collect their eggs & this is a chore we fight over because we all like it the darkness inside the coop the huffling burbling sound the chickens make the eggs warm as blood but dry speckled bumps pleasant to rub your fingertips over even a nap is possible some times a very quick one the straw is soft the smell is sweet the chickens burble a lullaby –

& there is a river with fish such as tench dace roach bream etcetera for wednesdays & fridays & lent etcetera –

there are swans & geese which are fine for lent as birds are not meat for they go on the water so they are fish really –

there is a vegetable garden with peas beans carrots celery kale lettuce cabbage onions of course a lot of onions –

there are some smallish fields that grow barley for beer & oats for oatcakes –

& last of all there is a herb garden which doesnt have the herbs &
plants etcetera that i used to grow at home because these ones are for eating & fathers & girls dont need to poison any one apparently which must
be nice –

the moon is up & so are we –

the abbess ringing her handbell walking up & down the dormitory until we are all out of our beds heavy eyed sludgy limbed heat rising from our empty sheets –

we follow the light through the door down the night stairs & into the church for matins –

swinging of the censer the incense billowing out the smell rich smoky thick clouds creeping inside me with every breath –

i am still half in dreams –

of Him –

always of Him –

though if anyone asks i dream only of god –

i try to stay awake press my hands hard to the sides of my wooden seat perhaps there is a splinter that will help –

carved on my misericord is a shape i run my finger tips over it trying to know what it is –

it starts with a small round thing a head perhaps & below that two bumps a womans breasts it might be & then down swelling out to hips but some thing wrong some thing i can not understand not legs like a woman but some thing long flowing down then splitting at the bottom –

my finger tips look but can not see –

i keep them pressed to the misericord touching feeling not seeing –

we must not sit during matins or during prime or terce or sext or none or vespers or compline or vigils –

there is a lot of standing as you can see with services every few hours & all of them with no sitting –

thank god for a misericord which he must have made as he made all things & i know its just a small ledge & not much of any thing really when you think of the other things god has made like mountains oceans cows the sun but it means a lot to me as it means we can lean rather than standing straight up though we can not sit for some reason leaning is fine & holy & allowed for god but sitting is very different apparently & wicked & not allowed –

father fleck says that terrible sinful things are happening not here but out side our walls it is the end times so we must pray even harder for our selves & for every one else –

he says rains of frogs are falling & also rains of eels & worms all wriggling sorts of things not here but in other places & we must never go to those places this is the only place where we can be safe with god it is terrible indeed to be cast from the garden which to us means cast from the sanctuary –

he says that will not be the end of it because next what will happen is rainstorms of blood will fall from the sky & the stars will fall to the earth & the sun will turn black & then the dead will climb out of their graves for the final judgement by god –

well no time for us to worry about that now there are chores to be done & what are a handful of girls going to do about the end times any way –

matins is finished the sun is still asleep but we are not we have to do lots of things that the sun doesnt have to do like sweeping tidying washing brewing baking weeding beekeeping candlemaking oh & i have to get the bread started –

the abbess comes with her light to lead us out to wash & get ready to do our chores but i pretend i have dropped something –

i let the other girls go past me i kneel on the stone –

no candles near me the others take them when they go so it is hard to see –

i touch with my finger tips the shape i felt carved into the misericord –

the woman without legs –

why would she be carved in here –

why would they carve her lacking some thing so important –

& i like this thing & i want to take it & i give it a good shake to see if i can loosen it –

silly really as there is no where to hide any thing here so even if i could take it for my self i would have to burn it so as not to be caught –

but it is firmly attached & i can not move it –

& the abbess comes back for me bringing her light she is not pleased that i am slow –

& in that moment when she comes up behind me with her light the carved shape is revealed –

a woman without legs but a woman who doesnt need them because she has a tail like a fish –

a woman who can swim away can go any where has the whole sea all for her from one side of the world to the other & every thing in between all hers all open to her –

i never knew there could be such a thing & i want –

any way thats the end of that because the abbess smacks me round the head for being late & walks away with the light & i only get bread & water for the day & i dont get to sit on that misericord again –

my mother does not tell me why i am to stop living in the house in the
forest with her –

& instead i am to leave her & go to live at the sanctuary –

& be holy –

or as holy as i can be –

but i know its because i havent had my blood –

& some time i will have to marry a boy from the village & have his
children –

except i will not be able to have his children or anyones children –

& i think i could go my whole life without marrying a boy from the
village –

& i dont see why that is so bad –

after all my mother doesnt have a husband –

but perhaps that is the reason –

perhaps that is the thing she wont say to me –

that she doesnt want me to do the things she has done –

she doesnt want me to be always in this house in the forest –

she wants me to want more than that –

but is she allowed to want –

thats what i want to know –

because theres no use in a girl wanting but can a mother want –
can you want things if its for someone else –
any way whatever it is that my mother wants –
i end up in the sanctuary –
& perhaps thats not what any one wanted but its what we get –

no one is watching me & no one has given me chores to do so I creep away & go to a part of the sanctuary i havent been to before –

& that is the library where the books are kept theres no use me going there as i cant touch the books & theyre not for me theyre for learned men –

He is there in the library He doesnt hear me i hide just out side the door & look at Him i cant go in for then we will be alone there –

He looks at a book in the low morning sun bright on His hair His skin His very self gold & good & glowing –

He begins to read aloud a prayer one i have heard before but never in His voice His good gold glowing voice –

He says: ave maria gratia plena dominus –

Hes holding the book up now in a strange way He wasnt holding it before & i realise that from my place by the door i can see the book –

oh it is beautiful –

all edged in gold –

the centre red & blue & green such wonderful shapes & pictures such as i have never seen –

& also some black scratch marks that arent so interesting but He is moving His finger along the marks –

& as He moves His finger He says: tecum benedicta tu in mulieribus –

& i realise that the black scratch marks are some how the words He is saying though i dont know how He knows that –

He says: et benedictus frutas ventris tui –

He says: amen –

with out thinking i say: amen –

i clap my hand to my mouth but He doesnt look up He only smiles –

i stay there by the door hiding in the shadows in the dark –

& He in His patch of sun in the light He keeps reading –

He turns the page He holds it up for me it is even more beautiful –

He says the words His voice just as beautiful –

He says them for me –

there in church all of us –

    me & jennet issobel grissel marion agnes gilleis lizabet alizon jehan
hanna isidore oh & euphemia –

    all of us crane our necks to look up at our lord –

    he is wearing a loin cloth that is very small –

    more of a scrap really –

    not even enough to mop up a spill should you need to –

    should you spill some thing there in our lords presence & should he
whip off that loin cloth to help you clean up –

    should that happen –

    well the spill would mostly still be there i would say –

    so small is that loin cloth –

    & so much of his body there revealed to us in all its holiness & glory –

    the muscles on his belly lovingly carved each one –

    his legs crossed elegantly his hair long flowing beautiful –

    his arms muscled & strong –

    & we look at the knot that holds the loin cloth closed –

    & it is a very flimsy knot –

    barely covering a very muscular body –

& we think often of that body both there in church & later when we are back in our beds –

& by this of course i mean we all think often of the mortification of our lords flesh & all he sacrificed for us & his agony on the cross for our sins & how hard we must pray to earn his love –

of course that is what i mean –

i pray at the altar –

i pray for jennet issobel grissel –

i shift a little my knees on the stone floor & feel a rush a surge of blood as a thorn pricks my belly –

i pray for marion agnes gilleis lizabet alizon –

i shift again the floor really is very hard & cold & more pricks at my belly i lean a little & they dig into me further –

i pray for jehan hanna isidore euphemia the abbess father fleck my mother –

& i feel the thorns –

& the pain is hot a stab it burns –

& i pray harder & i shift my body over & over –

& a ring of roses blooms around my belly my blood seeping through my white dress –

& all of this all of this praying –

& all of this pricking –

is hope less –

because i cannot smell the incense burning all around me from the censers clouds of it thick swaying pulsing with my breath making my eyes cry i cannot smell it at all –

all i can smell –
all that fills my lungs –
all that fills me up right to the top overflowing –
is the smell of the rose petals crushed against my body –

why doesnt she leave –
    my mother i mean –
    why doesnt she leave her little house in the forest –
    we could do bigger tricks –
    better tricks –
    we could do things such as i heard of women like us doing –
    like eggs containing strange prophecies written on the insides of their
shells –
    like tapping on the walls that is secret messages from people who
have died –
    like a magical cow that can predict the weather based on where it shits –
    things that dont actually do any thing but seem powerful –
    we could promise the most elaborate curses –
    claim the most extravagant powers to kill or heal or prophesy –
    & then move on to the next town before any one notices that we cant
do any thing at all –
    but she doesnt –
    she stays there –
    in that house –
    by that village –

where every one knows her –
every one knows where she lives –
why does she stay –
thats what i dont understand –
who is she waiting for –

all of the girls say to the abbess –

thats jennet issobel grissel marion agnes gilleis lizabet alizon jehan hanna isidore euphemia oh & not me not me at all i dont say any thing now or ever i dont i swear on god & on the cross i dont i am not even there –

no i must be there for how else would i know what they say –

they say that shadowy forms of the fathers –

though not the actual fathers they are quick to make clear just their forms that cant really be the fathers only demons pretending to be them –

the shadowy forms of fathers come to them in the night –

moving around the corridors pushing open their doors lifting their bedcovers –

though shadowy forms of course not the actual fathers of course –

the abbess tells all of this to father fleck & he says my strange night dreaming all of our strange night dreamings are truly incubi sent by satan –

incubi are evil night spirits they suck the life & the holiness out of girls they have come to us in forms of the fathers & that is why the incubus comes to me in His form so that we will not be frightened but will let the incubi have their way & suck the life & the holiness from us –

which by the way i do not understand as why would we let the fathers suck our lives whether demons or the real fathers theyre our lives & we want to keep them for ourselves –

but the thing is that He –

or the incubi demon lifesucker pretending to be Him –

He comes only to me –

because my sisters have visitations too but for them it is not Him which i find a strange sort of relief for though He does not come to me really it is only in my dreams only in my imaginings still He does not come for my sisters even in their dreams which makes me feel that He does love me or He does feel my love for Him some how –

& which ever is the case demon or witchery or my own innumerable sins i still need to be exorcised again –

what ever it is is so strong within me –

my body twists turns burns –

every night i stitch back together the dresses i have ripped with my cursed exertions –

but my hands are tired & my stitches are loose & the demon is strong in me every night every day –

it is night & i am alone & i am sewing my dress –

it is day & i am with Him & i am ripping my dress –

there in my bed i come to myself & then i leave myself again & then i come to myself –

His hands steady tight on my wrists holding me here in this world not in that other in hell with demons in heaven with god i do not want them i want to be here with Him He holds me tight –

i look up at Him ready for His love His regard His warmth golden bright –

He looks away from me now –

He can not look at me –

He looks every where but at me –

i look down where my dress gathers my skin flushed my breasts bare a hundred stitches split –

i want to tell you a little about my mother –

when my mother goes walking in the forest mushrooms sprout up in her footsteps –

when rain lands on the top of my mothers head the raindrops sizzle –

when my mother bleeds it comes out thick like treacle –

tiny spiders hide beneath my mothers long finger nails –

all her teeth are black all her toe nails are gone all her bones crack –

i do not know what kind of thing my mother is i only know she is my mother & i suppose for that i must be glad –

one night my mother says to me –

by the way i am in my bed which is the floor by the stove it is not exactly soft or pleasant but i have a piece of sack between me & the floor & i can fall asleep to the sound of the fire crackling so that is pleasant enough or at least i am used to it –

i pretend that the sack of my bed is not sack but is actually the one soft thing in the house which is not my mother no thing soft about her –

the soft thing is a red ribbon its very soft and smooth or so i imagine i dont know my mother says i am not allowed to touch it so of course i am not allowed to have it for my bed even when my mother goes out i dont dare to touch it she would fine kill me if i did because she likes the strip of ribbon much more than she likes me it is kept high up on a shelf rolled up carefully like a long devils tongue & i am sure that one night when my mother thinks i am asleep i even hear her crying over that ribbon she loves it so much –

i would say i dont think i have ever loved a thing so much that i would cry over it but then i remember best rabbit i certainly do love him that much though he only makes me smile & never cry –

my mother never does a thing carefully except for rolling that ribbon up it must be very expensive but then you might be wondering why dont we sell it as its no use to us you cant eat a ribbon –

my mother says to me –

by the way she has some thing she keeps in a jar in a chest thats made of black berries left sitting in the dark & it stinks very bad & shes been drinking it & now she stinks of it –

my mother says to me: theyll always disappoint you girl they get old they dont stay true theyll disappoint you –

she rolls over on her straw mattress where theres a space beside her –

my mother says to me: dont ever be a wife girl –

which is a silly thing to say because how can a girl not be a wife you cant exactly be a husband can you –

the choice is only novice or wife or widow –

& a widow was once a wife so doesnt count –

my mothers voice is slow & sticky from the black berry some thing –

she says to me: they lose their hair they get thin they get sick they dont keep you warm at night they dont come round to see you any more –

& i dont reply i pretend i am asleep but i know what she means –

because its been a while & best rabbit is not looking so good –

not good at all in fact –

although i do my best to love him –

its true what she says though i know because best rabbit is still the best to me but he has got old & he has not lost his hair but i would say it is threadbare at best not thick grey lustrous fruitful like it used to be –

i do try not to stroke him too much though i am sad not to do it as i very much like it but i can see his skin through the worn out fur in places & by the way the skin is not looking so good either it barely covers his bones so i suppose he has also got thin like my mother says –

& as for keeping me warm well lately i have felt that i am the one keeping him warm & not the other way around –

& i wouldnt really mind that but its not the worst of it –

because perhaps the smell is not only my mother & the black berries she left sitting in the dark but also –

& i do not want to think of this –

perhaps the smell is best rabbit –

but either way it does not matter because in the morning my mother wakes with a head that aches & she finds me with best rabbit & throws him on the fire & he burns up to no thing & theres no use in crying is there because you cant unburn a fire & that is the end of that –

i leave the sanctuary & i crawl through the forest laden with crosses & it is not summer now –

the ground thick with leaves mud slugs bracken thorns all of it under my hands & knees as i crawl –

i slip on my own flowing blood –

hundreds of crosses hundreds hundreds –

will my penance be so much the lesser without just one of them –

surely i still suffer –

& i still repent –

with hundreds hundreds minus one –

one cross on my wrist is tied with string & i look around to see if god is watching & i dont think he is so i loosen the knot with my teeth & the cross falls into the leaf mulch & i am lighter i am lesser i am a tiny bit closer to the sky –

& i crawl a little bit further bleed a little bit more feel a little bit more repented & one cross around my neck is slippery with blood so the knot comes undone easily & the cross falls away & i feel a little bit lighter –

& i crawl a little bit further & another cross comes off –

in the day i eat mice & acorns & mushrooms –

at night i sleep under fallen trees & inside hollow logs & at the centre of stacks of bracken –

sleeping any where safe –

eating any thing safe –

nearly dead it feels like but not quite –

with every cross i take off & throw aside i feel lighter not just my body but my heart too –

& i get up off my knees & walk on my feet –

& as i rip off the final cross & throw it into the forest my shame burns away & in its place is anger –

anger against the people who did this to me & to my mother –

who was not beloved by many or even by me most of the time but she was still my mother –

my mother was killed as a witch because the people in the village heard that i was possessed by the devil & was exiled from the sanctuary –

or i was exiled from the sanctuary because my mother was killed as a witch –

how can i know –

who will ever tell me –

no one tells a girl any thing we do not need to know any thing we only need to clean cook pray smile lower our eyes lie back make babies die –

my body stops bleeding & starts healing –

my hands last of all they are so grazed & cut they heal slowly –

i catch small things to eat & i make fires to cook them –

i wash my skin & dress & cloak in the river as best i can –

sometimes i meet people who take pity on me & share their meals with me –

i pretend i cant speak so they wont ask me any thing –

but mostly i keep off the paths & go through the trees –

& when i make it home i am alive but i am wearing no crosses at all not even one & perhaps that means i am not holy not even one part but the forest behind me is perhaps a little more holy for all the crosses i left there or perhaps neither of us is holy at all –

& at home i do not find my mother as i knew i would not –

all i find is a scrap of ribbon all curled up in the corner behind the poisons –

& now that is all the mother i have –

i find the roses on the sanctuary steps –

    they are five in number & the most perfect roses i have ever seen –

    petals red as blood & soft as rabbit ears –

    i lift them i touch them i cant help it i stroke them down my cheek –

    velvet rabbit cloud kiss soft –

    a sudden pain & i start away with a gasp but the rose doesnt fall its stuck to me the thorn pressed deep into my thumb –

    i pull it out the blood beads i lift it to my lips suck my thumb into my mouth sweet copper salt –

    i swoon there on the steps –

    when i come awake i am still alone the roses spread around me –

    i tuck them into my belt under my dress –

    the petals stroke me –

    the thorns prick me –

    & i think this is a good thing –

    i think it will keep me good & holy because i will be reminded that His hands might be soft like the petals but they are really like the thorns & will bring me only pain –

    it is true that I do not do myself the violence necessary to resist my inclinations & through this laxity I fall into such great hardness of heart that none of the things of god any longer touch me more than as if I had been of bronze –

but see i am trying to be good i am trying to be free of Him –

though i know i can not be –

i bring up the fresh water so He & father fleck can both shave –

i put the bowl of water outside the room because i cant go in He is in there alone & we mustnt be alone together –

they do it like that the monks they face one another & shave one another not them selves –

there are no mirrors in the sanctuary mostly for the girls because we mustnt indulge sins like vanity & self love etcetera but apparently monks can also tend to love them selves as they cant have mirrors either –

i know after bringing up the water that i should go i have other chores & lingering is a sin probably most things i do are sins –

but He is in the room alone –

& i want to be in the room too –

i stand in the corridor my back to the wall –

& i am sure i can feel Him there on the other side of the wall –

i press my hand flat to the wall the stone is cold & damp & it smells like the bottom of a well but i press my palm against it & im sure –

i am sure –

that He is pressing His hand to the wall on the other side –

father fleck bustles along the echoing corridor in his black robes like a big black fly –

no i dont mean that lets say something more majestic a big black cat a lion a whale are they black i dont know –

he picks up the bowl of water & goes in to the room ignoring me & i put down my head & go to walk away –

but i dont walk away –

i am sorry god i am so full of sin my sins made me do it –

father fleck hasnt shut the door & the corridors do echo & i can hear every thing –

i hear the splash of the water the slick of the soap the rasp of the razor on the strop –

& i dont expect talking it is daytime there is no talking in the daytime only at matins prime terce sext etcetera & even then it is only father fleck talking & not us we only listen so perhaps i am in the habit of listening all of the time –

i hold my breath & lean in press my eye to the door hinge where a little light leaks through –

i see Him in His under shirt & i think my heart stops i cant breathe & my head turns into flapping white winged birds i clasp my hands tight nails digging in to keep my self from fainting –

there He stands in His under shirt as if He is not a devil among men as if He is not a tempter as if He is not sent here only to bewitch unsuspecting girls –

there He is as if He is a normal man –

He reaches for the soap –

but father fleck takes it from Him –

father fleck bows down & puts his hands to the bowl of water then lathers up the soap –

he stands & strokes the lather down His face –

water drips from His face & onto His under shirt the neck darkens His skin outlined –

father fleck runs the blade over the strop again the rasp of it –

the under shirt dampened i see the swell as He breathes in the dip as
He breathes out –

in the gloaming the sun thick as pollen the light slants low & i see a
drop of water caught in the hollow of His throat –

& my body aches for how much i want to lick that drop –

standing there in the corridor looking through the gap in the door
hinge i feel my knees shake my eyes blur i feel that my body is about to
turn into water & melt away –

i want –

i want –

He shakes His head the drop falls He steps forward presents Him self
to father flecks blade –

father fleck says to Him: turn your face to the light –

i close my eyes i can not look –

there at the door my breath held i close my eyes but i can not close my
ears –

i hear the scrape of the blade on His skin –

i hear the shush of feet shifting on the floor –

i hear the plink of the water in the bowl –

i hear my own heart go thud thud thud up my throat & into my jaw
thud thud –

then i hear a gasp –

a gasp & after it silence –

i wait –

i wait –

in the silence i wait –

& i cant wait any more –

i open my eyes & i peer through the gap in the door hinge –

i see father fleck with the blade in his hand –

i see Him with His face turned to the light & His gaze on father fleck

& a bead of blood a single bright bead of blood on His throat the blood red & sweet as a tiny plucked apple –

the blood swells & grows fat & then & then & then it over flows & drips down His soft sweet throat –

& He looks at father fleck –

& father fleck looks at Him –

& He lowers His head He looks at the floor –

& father fleck lifts his blade again –

grissel tells me a story she hears from some where about a man who wants a girl & intends to cast a spell to get her love –

he needs three hairs from her private parts –

he pays the girls brother to bring the three hairs to him wrapped in some thin cloth –

the brother tries but the girl wakes up & screams for their mother –

the mother knows witchery when she sees it & she beats the truth out of the brother –

when she learns his plan she decides to trick the man at his own wicked art –

she takes the thin cloth & goes to the shed where the young red heifer is –

she clips three hairs from the udders of the heifer & wraps the hairs in the thin cloth –

i am laughing now as i like that the man is being tricked serves him right –

the mother she gives the hairs in the thin cloth to the brother –

the brother gives them to the man –

the man casts his spell –

i dont know whether to laugh now as of course its funny him doing the spell on the heifers hairs but witchery is nothing to laugh at –

any way before long the love sick heifer appears at the mans door –
& there she stays –

nothing can be done she is in love with the man she follows him where ever he goes she is besotted theres no arguing with spells –

we laugh together grissel & i –

its funny about the man how silly he is –

we laugh about the poor love sick cow mooing at the mans window –

grissel & i moo at one another for a bit –

i love you moo i love moo –

any way grissel tells me the last part of the story –

the man is found to be a witch –

he is kept under ground & his finger nails ripped out & his thumbs crushed in the pilliwinks & his male part cut off & his legs crushed until the blood & marrow spout forth in great abundance & then he is burned alive –

oh well its not so funny at the end but i suppose witches must be punished its only fair & right –

i wonder though about that cow –

if she knew the man was dead –

& if that broke the spell –

or she loved him still –

i am told to bring in the cows so out i go –

    & i sing the bringing in the cows song –

    which doesnt have words only sounds that fly from my throat high &
lilting –

    & the cows like it i dont know why they do but they do –

    they turn towards me start to come down from the hills –

    they roam every where thats why you need a song to call them –

    they take a while they are slow cows they loll & roll as they walk bodies
swaying like they might tip –

    when they reach me their wet black noses come towards me their big
heads held low their warm bodies bump past me –

    they dont hurry but they like my song & they are pleased to see me –

    which is not some thing you can say for most people –

    & He must have been told also to bring in the cows –

    because after my song i turn & there He is as if He has always been
there –

    He & i there among the slow tide of cows –

    low gold sun catching His hair –

    a gust of wind & pollen blows around us –

    He nods to me & i lower my head –

because of course we can not speak to one another no men speaking to women allowed only father fleck & the abbess may speak to each other & then other wise its monks speak to monks & girls speak to girls & thats it –

but He hears me sing to the cows & i see Him nod & that is enough words for us –

on this late summer day –

breeze kissing our cheeks –

a strand of my hair comes loose & we are so close the tip of it touches Him –

pollenblow –

low gold sun –

if we married i think –

if i were not i & He were not He –

if we were different people entirely –

if then we could marry –

it would be bread & butter & milk & honey every day –

pollenfall –

gold gleam of it caught in my hair & in His hair –

we laugh we shake it off it clings to our hands –

we bat it off it clings to the hems of our clothing –

we shake our heads it catches in our eyes we see only gold –

we walk away leave a gleaming path behind us –

He pauses then in the shadows beneath the sanctuary wall where no one can see –

He lifts His hand to my cheek & touches it –

His hand comes away gold –

time stops –

we stop –

no thing will ever move back or forth from this moment –

but it does –

you know it does –

you know what is coming –

& now that i have told you every thing about it & about Him i can see what is coming too i can see yesterday & tomorrow –

though in that shadow beneath the sanctuary wall with His golden-streaked hand i do not know –

i do not know any of it –

He is shaved and tied to the stake –
    the fire is lit beneath Him –
    i am told to watch –
    i tell myself it is not real –

    He does not cry out even at the end –
    i look into His eyes until they turn black –
    i think i will die at the very moment He dies –
    but then He is dead & i am still alive –

    He smells like pork roasting –
    my stomach growls –
    i am sick on myself –

    that is all i want to say about that part –

there is another witch killing but i am not there for that one –

father fleck only tells me about it –

he comes to me after He has been burned & i can still taste my sick in my mouth & i cant see properly & every thing is too bright like there are three suns on us & all of them burning cold –

he comes to me then & tells me so holy the light of god in his eyes his faith so pure he gleams transparent like a man made of glass –

a man with no thing at all inside –

he tells me that my mother has died –

that my mother is dead –

that my mother is unholy & rotten & devilridden & dead –

that her neighbours who know her for years who buy charms & poisons from her & tell her things they didnt even want to say to themselves they turn on her –

she knows too much about them & even though she only knows those things because they told her still it is too much & they dont like it –

i have been at the sanctuary for four summers i think but i have lost track its so easy to lose track here it is always summer it feels always pollenblow low gold sun –

or at least it did –

with out me there to help my mother struggles alone & takes to
begging –

going house to house for a cup of milk or a scrap of bread –

& no one sends for me no one comes for me no one tells me that she
needs me –

so i dont help & neither does anyone else –

they dont want to help her she is inconvenient she is unquiet –

she screeches & scolds & stinks & is too old to work the land & is too
old to make babies so what is the use of her –

& even when she does have a baby meaning me she is old & that is
unnatural as she should not have been able to make a baby meaning me –

& where is her husband where did she get a baby is it even her baby
did she steal it is she a witch only a witch could make a baby with no man
and her so old too –

it is not that they are refusing to do good charity & help a poor woman –

it is that she does not deserve charity –

so they call her witch & try her in court & send her to die –

she dies for every thing she is & every thing they want her to be that
she isnt –

& all their secrets die with her & i bet they are glad of that most of all –

she died weeks ago & i hadnt known i hadnt felt it i was in the world
& she was not & i hadnt even known –

walking around & eating buttered bread & calling the cows & watching pollenblow & shrieking in bewitchment & feeling the devil pulse
cold inside me all of that –

all of that –

while my mother died alone –

& i felt nothing –

that day i first saw him –

    with the sixth hive calming the mad bees –

    he didnt calm them –

    did he –

    did he –

    i see it now –

    i was watching him & his beauty golden sunshine & now i know i can
hear the mad bees still –

    when he took the hive over the river to where the trees start –

    i heard the bees still buzzing frantic alarming in their madness –

    he ignored them he walked away from them –

    they were still throwing themselves against the inside of their hive –

    he never did calm them –

    he just moved them some where else so no one was bothered by them –

    he just walked away forgot about them –

    he never did calm them –

    they were just angry & alone in a different place –

that day i first saw him –
    in the rain with the daisies when i watched him from the window –
    the daisies werent saying yes –
    were they –
    they were too light too small for the rain –
    they were bowing under the weight of it –
    they were just trying not to break –

this is it –

    this is where it ends –

    all of it –

    all at once –

    every thing every one –

    men came to witness lined up around my bed an audience for a show their eyes bright glinting like coins –

    my body contorted twisted back bent heels to head shrieking my joints cracking whole body breaking –

    there in my bed i came to myself & then i left myself again & then i came to myself –

    pig grunts dog barks throat burning body burning –

    clothes ripped skin bare bloody bleeding –

    animals inside me demons –

    inside me –

    father fleck put two of his fingers in my mouth & stretched it wide & leaned his head down to mine & shouted into my mouth to fright out the devil –

    but nothing came out –

    father fleck put more fingers in three four both hands his finger tips to the back of my throat & then something did come out & i wished it was the devil but it wasnt i retched sick up sick all over father flecks hands all down my chin my throat burning –

grunts barks pig dog –

the devil in a fury inside me –

he beat me with great violence so that my face was swollen & my body all bruised with his blows –

he treated me in this way to make it uncomfortable for the demon to be inside my body so he would leave –

father fleck took the fingers out only when they asked me a question –

they said to me: what demon is in you –

& i barked like a dog –

they said to me: what witchment is this in you –

& i grunted like a pig –

they said to me: how did you do this to yourself –

& i retched animal sick hot –

the fingers back in i knew i must not bite even though i was not myself & i didnt know quite who i was i knew i must not bite father fleck or there would be consequences though i ached to bite him to the bone to break all my teeth for the sake of the harm of him it would be worth it –

the fever faded & for a moment i was myself & i heard the men –

the learned men the wise holy men gathered here to see me a girl alone in a bed clothes torn grunt & writhe & sweat –

they said things about me & their voices sounded sad & they said things as if i was not there with both my ears open as if i truly was a pig a dog that didnt know words & didnt know love & didnt know god –

they said but not to me: she is a witch –

they said but not to me: she must be cleansed –

they said but not to me: we have heard stories about her & about her mother theyre not good the whole blood of them theres no truth in them theyre just filth & rot thats what every one says & we thought she could be cleansed made holy she seems only a child but its a lie shes a devil inside –

i barking grunting swarm body shaking choking –

& i knew i knew what happened to witches they die they die & i did not want that i do not want to die not yet –

& i –

& i do not want –

& i do not want to tell you this part –

i could pretend i did not know what i was doing & i did not know what it meant but i did know –

as i knew not to bite father fleck –

we knew what we did –

what he & i did –

there in my bed i came to myself & then i left myself again & then i came to myself –

& they said to me: was it him –

& they said to me: did he possess you –

& they said to me: did he bewitch you –

& how else could i say it what else was it this thing that i felt for him this love this desire this burning how it possessed me how i was bewitched by it how i was reddened i was ridden i would be rid of it yet i wanted to be consumed by it i wanted it to enfold me so that i did not exist –

& my choice was condemning my self to death for my desire or condemning him to the same for his –

& if that was my choice there was only one thing i could choose & i dont think that is really a choice –

& they said to me again: did he possess you –

they said: did he bewitch you –

& i looked out of the window & the rain & the daisies & they nodded yes –

the rain fell –

the daisies nodded –
yes they said –

yes i said –

PART 3

1

Now She is Servant

Lux finished her story as she and Else emerged from the dark ocean of pines and into a grey dawn. Pink tinged the horizon, outlining the stronghold: solid-built and square, grey as a grandfather. The stronghold was so tall they had to tip their heads right back to see the top of it. Lux let her eyes drop down: a low wall, behind which she could hear the happy wet snorts of pigs in mud. Above the wall, the tops of fruit trees. Lux's belly clenched at the sight of the ripe fruit hanging there. It was hard to remember the last time she'd eaten anything other than what she'd found in the forest. A sudden breeze, and an apple fell from sight, landing with a thud.

She had expected a high wall, a gate, a drawbridge - a stronghold needed to be strongly held, after all. But, she supposed, all that would be on the other side, the city side. There was no danger from the forest, as no army could have marched through those close-set trees. As soon as they'd entered the shadows of the pines they would have scattered, lost in the eternal twilight, punctured by a hundred tiny needles.

All that stood between the pines and the pigs was an open-sided hut containing two men and two swords. The men were not looking at the pines. They were looking the other way, back towards the stronghold. What could possibly come out of the pines? A squirrel or two? A hare?

Nothing with teeth that could threaten strong men. Certainly not a person.

Lux and Else were almost upon the hut before the men heard them, and turned.

'Witchcraft,' one of the men said, his voice neither afraid nor joking, merely stating a fact.

'No,' said Lux, and she was afraid, and she was intimidated, and she had not intended to speak, but if telling her story to Else had shown her anything it was that there was power in words, and danger in accepting the wrong ones. If you didn't tell people what you were, they would decide for you. 'I am merely a God-fearing woman seeking honest work.'

'Where did you come from?' said the other man, the younger, rounder-faced one. He seemed amused by her sudden appearance. His skin was sickly pale, circles of pink high on his cheeks as if they'd been rouged. His jaw stuck out so that his lower teeth overlapped the upper ones.

Lux motioned behind her, to the blurred shadows of the pines.

'Can't have,' said the first man, the older one. His nose lurched to one side, many times broken and not set. His eyes were large and dark and slightly crossed. 'Can't no one get through there.'

'I am small,' said Lux, and she tried to make it so: holding her feet together, keeping her arms tight to her body, tucking in her chin so her eyes were chastely downcast. She was a girl, and small, and nothing more.

No reply from the men, so she pushed her luck further. She could always run back into the pines, if she needed to. If she was quick enough.

'And hungry, too,' she said. 'And willing to work. I am good in a kitchen.'

'Aye, and good in places other than that, I bet,' said the younger man. 'There's a toll, girl, to get through here.'

Lux held her breath. To get away from the sanctuary, away from the boys, from the hunt – and to end up in the shadows with men once more. How the world is just the same thing over and over and over.

'Wait,' said the older man. It seemed that he was looking at Else when he spoke, but when he came out of his hut, it was Lux that he approached. He took her chin in his hand, tipping her face up to look at it. 'That face,' he said. 'I've seen it...'

Lux kept her eyes cast down, her arms wrapped tight around her body. She knew that she was filthy and she stank, and hoped that would help. She heard a wet sound and realised the man's mouth had opened. She couldn't tell if it was into a smile or a grimace.

'I've never been here,' replied Lux, eyes down. 'I don't know you. I don't know anyone here.'

'Oh God,' said the man, his voice soft. 'Oh God, it's you. I thought...' He took a step back, though he kept hold of Lux's chin, holding her at arm's length. His hold now was gentle, the soft press of his thumb. 'You're the spit of your mother.'

Lux thought of her mother: the blackened teeth, the cracking bones, the long and yellowed fingernails. The hunched gait. The milky eyes. She was nothing like her mother.

But – how would she know? She'd only seen her own face reflected in a bucket of still water, and had barely been given peace to do that. So perhaps she was just like her mother after all. She cursed her own stupidity. Her mother must have been held at the stronghold before her drowning. She hadn't thought that she might be recognised.

The man seemed to be working through something, his eyes on Lux's face. Then he let go of her with a push of his thumb and went back to his hut. Lux glanced at the man, but he had his back to her now, standing at attention, looking up at the stronghold. It seemed she had been dismissed.

'Merik!' The younger man still faced Lux and Else and the pines. He put his hand on his sword. 'We can't let her past. She could be anyone.'

'Well, she's not, is she? I know exactly who she is.'

'Merik, shouldn't we –'

The older man laid his hand on the hilt of the younger man's sword, forcing him to lower it.

'Never mind *we*,' he said, his voice low and slow. 'I'll tell you about *we*. I plan to stand here nice and quiet and keep my back turned to the endless hours of nothing that's coming out of the pines, like I'm paid to do. And you'll do the same, boy, unless you want this sword through you.'

The younger man opened his mouth to protest, then thought better. He turned away.

Lux glanced up at the pair of broad male backs, and then down at herself. Or rather, at her arm, where she knew the red ribbon was tied under her clothes.

Quickly, before the men changed their minds, she and Else walked past the hut and opened the gate in the low wall to the kitchen garden. With each step Lux expected to feel the sharp tip of a sword pressed to her back, but it never came, and they closed the gate behind them with a sigh.

In the kitchen garden, a pebbled path led between well-tended vegetable beds many times larger than the ones Lux had worked with the other girls at the sanctuary. There the girls and the monks had subsisted on a few simple greens: peas and beans, kale and lettuce. Here grew every edible thing that Lux had ever seen, and many that she hadn't. She recognised leeks, spinach, black radish, bogbean, dock leaves; mint, chives, parsley; rhubarb, quince and elderberry. And as for the rest? They could be anything. She wanted to go and investigate - could they be useful, these plants? It didn't seem likely that anyone would let poisons grow beside things meant for eating - but she didn't yet know what was possible in this place.

Else paused to gather a handful of overripe apples from where they had fallen on the grass. She approached the pigpen, which was the size of the clearing around Lux's house. The pigs' house, in fact, was about the same size as her own, though without windows or a shingled roof. Also, it hadn't been burned to the ground, which was nice for the pigs. It seemed the pigs lived as well as - perhaps better than - many people whose houses she'd seen in the forest. In front of the house was a fenced-in patch of grass and mud across which the pigs grunted frantically to reach the apples in Else's hands. They peeled back their thin pink lips, plucking the apples with crooked yellow teeth. They crunched, making happy sounds deep in their throats. They must have been hungry; the apples were gone in one bite.

'We're here,' said Else, her voice a whisper. 'We made it to the stronghold.'

Lux leaned on the fence surrounding the pigpen. The wood was hard and a splinter jabbed into her. Even behind the shelter of the wall, the cold wind bit and clawed beneath her clothes. She pushed off from the fence.

'You can stay here with the pigs if you like,' she said. 'But I'm sick of sleeping outside. I want a soft bed. I want hot food.' And if no one was going to give it to her, she'd take it.

Getting into the kitchen was not as difficult as she'd feared. The door was not locked or barred. Why would it be? Anyone coming in from the kitchen garden must have also gone out that way. No one would have come from the pines. Lux simply walked in and began work. It was lucky for her that – judging from the pigs' hungry state – the stronghold currently lacked a swineherd. She could only hope it was also missing a kitchen girl.

It was chaos in the kitchen: the bustle of feet, the flap of aprons, the constant overlap of shouted orders. Every woman was dressed in dark skirts and a white apron, though most of them were only slightly white by this point in the day. A clean-ish apron had been abandoned on the table, so Lux picked it up and tied it around herself. In her dark skirts, Lux fitted in perfectly, as if she'd been working in the stronghold kitchen her whole life. No one noticed her. She could stand to be a little cleaner, but she scrubbed the dirt from her hands and hoped no one would pay attention to the rest.

There was flour, there was salt, there was yeast, there was a bowl of clean water. Lux began making bread. She stayed focused on this task, barely daring to look up. The familiar rhythms of work soon overtook her. It wasn't so different to the sanctuary kitchen. The smells of the kitchen were onions and fires and meat and sweat. She breathed it all in, belly twitching. She told herself she could eat soon, soon. But she couldn't take anything, as it might be missed, and then there would be trouble. For now, she had to make sure that anything she ate here was earned and not stolen.

She split the dough into three loaves, covered the bowls with a clean cloth and put them in an out-of-the-way corner.

She slipped back outside. Else had found a bucket of scraps and tossed it to the pigs, so now they made happy grunts every time she got near them.

'Pigs are simpler than people,' Else said with a smile, 'though not by so much as we'd like to think.'

'I made bread,' she said. 'Three loaves, and no one stopped me or questioned me. Stronghold, sanctuary – bread is the same everywhere. If I act like a kitchen girl, who'd ever know that I'm not? If you act like a swineherd, who'd ever know that you're not? We're women, and poor, and everyone will think we're too stupid to be up to anything else.'

'I'll start a garden,' said Else. 'With the poisons you brought. Somewhere hidden where no one will see.'

'Do you need me to help?' asked Lux. 'I can touch them, I've handled them since I was a child and they won't hurt me.'

'They won't hurt me either.'

Lux felt the cold wind bite at her again. She saw how Else didn't flinch in the chill. She saw Else's skin the white of eggshell, her eyes a silver gleam. Her pocked, twisted mouth. A face she now knew much better than her own. No, poisons wouldn't hurt her. Nothing would hurt her.

It had been long enough for the dough to rise. All was still chaos in the kitchen – organised chaos, true, but topsy-turvy enough that Lux could go around unremarked. The dough had risen beautifully; all Lux's hours in the sanctuary kitchen had not gone to waste. She slid the bread into the oven and tucked herself beside it to wait. The oven was warm and the heat felt good on her numb fingers. The grazes were starting to heal. She clasped her hands flat between her knees, as if she was praying, to stop herself from picking at the scabs where they itched. She'd done that before; lifted up the edge of the black-red coin that covered the deepest scratches until a red bead of blood pooled. She hadn't known what to do then – better to press the scab back down and hope it healed hidden underneath, or rip the whole thing off, seeing if it would do better open to the air? She pressed her hands together, keeping her blood inside. She thought about healing and waited for her bread to bake. It was so warm here by the oven.

Although Else hadn't admitted it, Lux was certain that she was a north witch. What must it have been like for her, growing up there? Everyone knew that witches needed babies for spellwork; if they couldn't get living ones, they'd dig up corpses from cemeteries. Witches couldn't make their own babies because they were barren, dead inside like a cave of snow; just mockeries of women. Because the devil loves dead babies, they have always held value for the wicked. Lux wondered whether now, when bodies could be found in abandoned houses and were left tied to drowning posts in the sea, they were still so valuable.

But perhaps her time in the north is what made Else so strong. Perhaps Lux would be different if she'd been born there. Perhaps her blood would run quick and black like the water in the north land. She'd find a place with a white sea that never rests, licking over the sand as black as night, the steady boom and suck of the waves. Steam billowing into the wild sea from a crevice in the folded rocks. The glaciers blue, floating out to sea, blue layered and layered. A wild land where the words a girl spoke would be heard, would be believed, where she could say – 'You!'

Lux snapped awake. A panting, red-faced woman shouted to her as she hefted a bowl of apples onto the table. Her hair, where some small curls escaped from her head covering and stuck to her temples, was golden as wheat. 'Make bread,' said the woman. 'Two loaves. Quick now.'

Taking up a cloth to protect her hands, Lux bowed to pull the loaves out of the oven and tipped them onto a wooden board. 'I've made three, my lady.' She held out the board. The woman did not reply. Lux chanced a look up; the woman was peering at Lux's face. Her words were wrong; she'd marked herself out as an intruder. *My lady* must have been coming on too strong; would *dame* or *miss* have been more proper? Lux was not used to speaking to people whose names she didn't know.

Again she held her feet together, kept her arms tight to her body, tucked in her chin so her eyes were chastely downcast. She was a girl, and small, and nothing more.

The woman picked up one of the loaves and held it to her nose. Whatever she smelled, it must have been good; she didn't hit Lux, and that was surely a success.

'Who are you, girl?'

'My name is Lux... my lady.' Perhaps calling her *my lady* was coming on too strong, but better too polite than not polite enough.

'You don't work here.' The woman's red face was settling pale, and her frantic breathing had slowed. With her wrist she pushed the damp curls from her forehead. Her hands were chapped, but the fingers were long and slender. Around her neck, on a leather lace, hung a walnut shell.

'I would like to work here, my lady,' said Lux. 'If it pleases you.'

'We'll see about that. How did you get in here?'

'My...' Lux thought of the broken-nosed man at the edge of the pines, of his thumb lifting her chin. She hoped that this woman hadn't known her mother, and wouldn't connect Lux to her. 'My... my father brought me. He was hoping there would be work for me here. I'm a good worker and I don't eat much.' That was true, but only because she hadn't had the opportunity to eat much. Given half a chance she would happily consume everything edible in this kitchen, and everything in the garden too. Including the pigs, from snout to tail.

The woman looked again at Lux, then down at the loaves she'd taken from the oven. 'Tear a piece of that bread.' Lux did so. 'Now eat it.'

Lux did so gladly, taking a small bite so she wasn't mistaken for one of the pigs, though she would have loved to cram the whole loaf in her mouth. She chewed and swallowed, then stood awaiting further commands.

'And another,' said the woman. Lux obeyed. The woman waited. Then she opened Lux's mouth with her hands and looked inside. Apparently satisfied that Lux really had eaten the bread, she said: 'You've not poisoned it, then.'

Lux put a slight note of surprise in her voice, though not too much. Always better to seem a little stupid. Or a lot stupid. It really depended on who you were talking to; as long as you seemed stupider than them, you'd be fine. 'No, my lady.'

'The lord is beset by poisoners. The lady does most excellent work in keeping him safe. We must be ever cautious.'

'I understand, my lady.' Was it disrespectful to the actual lady for Lux to call this woman *lady*? Probably. The wife of a lord would not be sweating and grumping around a kitchen. But it was too late to change now.

'Is there sickness in you?' asked the woman.

'No, my lady.'

'We'll see about that. I will keep the sickness from this place, black roses and fevers and all. I got rid of it and I'll not be letting it back in. First of all you can get those clothes off and scrub them with vinegar. Everything else you brought with you too, mind. It'll all need in vinegar. And mind you scrub hard.'

Lux glanced around the kitchen. Everyone was busy with their tasks, but they were still sneaking looks over to the newcomer; Lux wasn't invisible, and if she undressed here she'd be more visible still.

'Here, my lady?'

The woman gave a sigh of irritation and nodded towards the kitchen store cupboard. 'In there. You can have the last girl's clothes until yours are clean. They're on the bottom shelf. She died.'

Lux wanted to ask what the girl had died of, but didn't know if she wanted to hear the answer. She went into the cupboard and did as she was told, then stood waiting, wearing only her undershift, the rest of her clothes puddled on the floor. The pale-haired woman pushed Lux's arms up and held a candle close to her armpits. It was not so long since Lux had been with Ash, and she knew that her skin was free of the black roses then. She had felt nothing since: no rising fever, no weakness of body, no blood in her mouth. The woman tapped the skin around Lux's arms, checking to see if she winced or pulled away. But nothing hurt, and Lux stood still.

'What is this?' asked the woman, tugging at the red ribbon tied around Lux's upper arm.

'A good-luck charm,' invented Lux. 'Given to me by a ... a holy man. A priest. He blessed it. He said –' She grinned in the dark; she couldn't resist. 'He said that only the most pious would be able to see the words of God written on it.'

'Hmm,' said the woman. 'Yes, I see it.'

At the woman's instruction, Lux gathered her hair in her hands and lifted it, so that the woman could bring the candle close to check her throat. As she looked at Lux, Lux looked back. With the light so close, she could see a little brown mole on the woman's neck, in the soft spot just below her ear. Lux wondered if a man had ever exclaimed to see it, and kissed it.

Satisfied by what she found – or didn't find – the woman stepped back. Lux looked around for her new clothes. But it wasn't over yet. The woman lifted Lux's undershirt to her waist and pushed her knees wider. She lowered the candle, checking the place where Lux's legs met her body. Ashamed, Lux closed her eyes until the candle retreated. She could smell her own sweat, bitter with nerves. Finally she felt the woman step back.

'You call me Goodwife Ethelinda,' said the woman. 'Get yourself together now.' She looked away as Lux pulled on a dead woman's clothes.

As she lifted the fabric, the smell of vinegar clouded out. 'You made three loaves, so you may eat a little more of that one. You look like you haven't eaten in weeks, and I'll not have you fainting in my kitchen and getting blood on my clean things.'

'Yes, Goodwife Ethelinda.' Lux stumbled out of the cupboard, tore off a huge chunk of bread and ate it. It was the best bread she had ever eaten. Though likely anything was the best ever, if it was long enough since you had it last. She let the bread lie on her tongue before chewing and swallowing, then she reached for another piece.

She could do this. She knew how to be a kitchen girl. Bake the bread. Collect the eggs. Behead the fish. Chop the onions. Keep your head down. Don't take what's not for you. Don't want what you can't have.

This was it: she had all she wanted. Something to eat, somewhere to sleep. She waited for the feeling of her heart settling – and tried not to think about what it meant when her heart did no such thing.

Lux and Else took their places at the stronghold. The moon grew and shrank and winked out and returned again like the white of a cut nail. Night day night day night and the only thing that changed was the amount of light – of which there was a little more each day.

Lux learned the movements of the stronghold. She found her way around the gardens: a separate one for fruit, vegetables, dyes, bees, herbs. There was a different kitchen girl in charge of each one, but Lux filled in as best she could, helping everyone whether she was asked to or not.

She worked all day in the kitchen, and at night she slept in a truckle bed in the corner, near the fire where it was warm, bundled like a litter of puppies with the other kitchen girls: Hulda, Linden, Elen, Amity, Eolande and another Euphemia, though Lux could not be sure she was naming them correctly, bustling unfriendly red-faced aprons as they were. One of the girls – Eolande, she thought – had a foreign accent, and said she'd come here on a boat from far away. Her skin was darker than the other girls', though not as dark as Mister Gaunt's.

Lux waited for a moment to arrive like the one she remembered at the sanctuary. Sitting in a circle with her sisters, twisting the urine-soaked cloth in the garden, trying to laugh quietly so the abbess didn't hear as Alizon told them about her brothers' various pricks. It didn't have to be urine. It didn't have to be pricks. She just wanted a moment of light. But the kitchen was fast and hot and dark, and the other girls didn't talk to her, and no one laughed at all, and the moment never came. Still, she made the bread and cut the onions, and no one hurt her or looked at her too close, so that was fine enough.

Lux's sleep was no longer cold, but the night air was foul; the kitchen girls chewed garlic all day to keep themselves free of the sickness. While the black roses didn't seem to be catching here, Goodwife Ethelinda's worry about it certainly was. Anything that came into the stronghold from outside was washed with vinegar, and mixed with the chewed-garlic smell it fair made your eyes water. Even worse, one of the kitchen girls – Elen or Linden, though as they both had the same shiny chestnut hair which they both made equal fuss over, it was hard to tell them apart – had been told that a void in the stomach lets in pestilential humours. To combat this, she filled herself with boiled eggs and strong pickles at the first pang of hunger. Lux knew that when she had first emerged from the pines, she hadn't been the cleanest. But now, sleeping all night in the fug of garlic, eggs and vinegar, she realised that a little sweat was the least of anyone's concerns. She was just glad that the walnut hung around Goodwife Ethelinda's neck, which it turned out, was not just a strange bauble, but was full of quicksilver, and was believed by Goodwife Ethelinda to keep out the sickness, didn't stink.

Goodwife Ethelinda was needlessly worried about the sickness, in Lux's opinion. There were so many other ways to die: apoplexy, dropsy, mumps, winter fever. Bad food. Bad drink. Bad men. Lux had heard of people dead of stones falling from the sky, of stampeding cows, of tiny beasts bursting forth suddenly from their eyes. Was the sickness really the worst way to go? But Lux learned from listening to the other kitchen girls that Goodwife Ethelinda had lost her two brothers and both parents to the sickness, all quick after the other. So perhaps her worries did make a little sense. Besides, the garlic seemed to work, as none of the kitchen girls died. But how it stank. Perhaps it was good that none of them spoke to Lux; the dragonfire of their breath as they all said their evening prayers was probably enough to kill.

It soon emerged that Hulda, who was in charge of the bee garden and all its bright flowers, was the favourite, at least where Goodwife Ethelinda was concerned. All the other girls were slapped correct after even the smallest mistake, and spent most days with one or both cheeks reddened. Lux didn't go even one day without her face smarting. But not Hulda. No matter what she did, Goodwife Ethelinda contented herself with a tut and a sigh. It took many hours of Lux eavesdropping on the other girls' talk to find out why: before coming to the stronghold, Hulda had accused and given evidence against several witches in her village. It wasn't that Goodwife Ethelinda was afraid of Hulda and her accusations. She admired her. The other girls weren't afraid of Hulda either – or, not exactly *afraid*, but... aware.

Every morning Lux visited Else in her pigpen to bring her a cloth wrapped around some bread and cheese, and Else took her to their secret garden where she'd replanted all that Lux had taken from her mother's house. While they tended the plants, Else kept up a stready stream of whispers about the lord. At times it seemed she wasn't speaking to Lux as much as reminding herself, stoking the flames of her rage. Else spoke of how the lord calls women witches and sends them to drown. How he doesn't care how much pain and suffering happens in the world, as long as it doesn't happen to him. How he's a rat of a man, a worm of a man, a rotting corpse of a man. How he doesn't even deserve to be called a man.

Lux listened to Else's stories, though she wouldn't let them convince her. Else could have her revenge quest. Lux didn't intend to poison anyone – not by her own hand. It was different when she merely sold the plants and let others do with them what they wished.

Still, she loved to see the plants flourish. The garden was hidden behind the pigpen, in the murk and shadows, surrounded by nettles and pig shit. The spot might not be enticing for people, but the plants loved it. Lux had advised on what to plant: both the scraps she'd brought from the remains of her old poison garden, and some she'd found on their travels in the forest. Else followed her advice, and every poison she touched had thrived. The purple-flowered, mint-scented pennyroyal, which could be used to flavour food, drive away fleas, or cause a woman's blood to come if she wanted rid of a child inside her. The bloated, apple-scented mandrake, which if eaten could cause vomiting, pounding heart and eventually death – and alleviate pain, heal stomach ailments and loosen aching joints. The yellow-flowered, sticky-leaved henbane with its disgusting stench; just the smell of it could cause a stupor, but used correctly it could treat digestive spasms and sleeplessness. The hemlock, the foxglove, the cuckoo pint, the wolfsbane – Lux rejoiced to see it flourish.

All these poisons, she had realised from hearing the other girls talk about what they did and didn't grow in their respective gardens, were linked with witches and the devil. How silly it all was. A plant couldn't be either good or evil; it was what people did with them that mattered.

'I'm taking some of this mandrake,' said Lux to Else one day as they visited their garden. 'Just a little of the root. Eolande has been complaining of an ache in her belly for days and I'm going to slip a tiny piece in her food, to ease the pain and help her sleep.'

'If it will help her, just give her the root and tell her what it's for.'

'No, I...' Lux got to her knees beside Else in the nettles. 'I can't do that, I have to be cunning about it. It could be misunderstood.'

'Then don't help her at all,' said Else.

'I only want to help her because it helps me,' replied Lux. 'If she gets better then I don't have to listen to her complaining about her aches and pains etcetera.'

She did take the root, and she did sneak it to Eolande, and it did help her; the next morning, she awoke saying she felt fresher than she had in months, and Lux just smiled to herself, and was glad of the peace.

Only one thing made a crack in the hard-set surface of the new routine. Well, two – one was welcome, and the other, Lux wasn't so sure about.

A few Sundays after her arrival, a surprise. In the night, in the dark, a hand reached out and found Lux. Thinking it was a mistake – several girls in one bed was always an uncomfortable squeeze – Lux rolled over and tried to go back to sleep. But the hand found her again. Not an unpleasant hand, but a gentle one, both teasing and insistent.

Lux didn't know whose hand it was, and she didn't want to know; before long, she had reached out in return, and found that it was not just one girl reaching for another, but many reaching for many.

She thought then of Best Rabbit; his soft fur and the stink of him burning on the fire; of her lover at the sanctuary, and his golden gleam, and the way it had not saved him from burning too.

But there was no burning here. It was more like Ash, whose hands had met hers in the night, whose body had given her pleasure and taken it in return.

Just as Lux was making sense of this new development, another came, just before the season of fasting began. The lady's fear of the lord being killed by his many lurking enemies was always there, always kept to low burn; but now it flared high. It took a whole day of listening to the chattering kitchen girls for Lux to learn the cause of it. The lord hadn't died. The lady hadn't died. But someone had fallen very ill: the lord's food-taster.

It had happened soon after he swallowed the food, so the lord and lady hadn't eaten any, which was a blessing. The food-taster experienced a sudden expulsion from both ends, which made a terrible mess of the floor-rushes, and was combined with much crying-out. The kitchen girls took great pains to describe this, even though Lux knew none of them could have been there. Not only was there the vomiting and shitting to describe, there was also much eye-rolling and lamentation about how terrible it all was, how dangerous, who could it have been, which enemies of the lord could have infiltrated the stronghold, oh woe – all of which was really an excuse to talk about the vomiting and shitting again. The food-taster was dead within the day.

It was fortunate indeed that Lux had not been in the kitchen that day, being instead on errands in town with Goodwife Ethelinda from dawn until after the last meal. As the newcomer to the stronghold's kitchen, suspicion would have fallen on her – even though she had no apparent motive to harm the lord. She'd made sure never to mention him or show any curiosity about him. As far as anyone knew, she was only a kitchen girl – the newest and lowest one.

The other girls, however, showed much interest in the lord, and took no care to hide it. They'd been taken out of the kitchen one by one and questioned by a guard, but they said they'd all either giggled nervously or fallen to crying, and nothing was learned, but nothing could have been learned anyway, they said, as they couldn't imagine who would ever want to hurt the lord, least of all them, and even if someone wanted to hurt the lord then surely it would be impossible, he was too strong, too brave, too important.

'I heard,' said Hulda, her hair reeking of pollen after her day in the bee garden, 'that he has such knowledge, such power and such grace from God that he can tell simply by the way a woman throws her hair over her shoulder or interlaces her fingers whether she has known the devil.'

Hulda placed great weight on the word *known*, which made Lux wonder if it was Hulda who first reached out for her in the night. She didn't think so, but perhaps Hulda had more to her than Lux suspected.

'Well, I heard,' said Amity, her hands stained from the bright flowers in the dye garden, 'that he eats the heart of the bear at the Unmaking feast! He's been doing it for so many years that he has the strength of a bear. Several bears! Can you imagine? Many bears inside one man? He must be very strong. He could probably lift all of us at once.' She shivered then, in fear or in desire.

Linden, smelling sweet and rotten after her work in the fruit garden, added: 'He has a dozen horses, did you know? Sometimes he rides them all in one day, as he never tires even as they do. They are all white as the moon, and all wear fine silver chains. And,' she lowered her voice here, murmuring into Eolande's ear, so that Lux had to hold her breath to hear, 'he's bedded hundreds of girls like that, making them all scream with pleasure, and he wraps them in silver chains too.'

Eolande collapsed into giggles, then added: 'I heard he's massaged daily with scented oils over every part of him. That is how he smells so sweet. Never foul or stale, even after a day's hunt. He's not like other men.'

'And what would you know of other men?' asked Hulda, and that was the end of the storytelling, and everyone went back to their tasks in cowed silence.

I heard he sends women to die just because he can, thought Lux. I heard he has the heart of a rat. I heard – she thought back to what Else had told her as they tended their poisons – I heard he's rotting from the inside out, and if you were to look under his clothes you'd see nothing but decay, a writhe of worms and maggots, his whole body softening and caving inwards like old fruit.

Out loud, though, she said nothing. She just watched and listened; only a kitchen girl. A guard was stationed nearby after the food-taster's death, to watch the happenings and make sure that no food was tainted, though he seemed to spend most of his time and energy flirting with the kitchen girls.

Lux didn't know how anyone could be sure that the food-taster had even been poisoned. He might have breathed bad air, or caught a sickness from a dog or a horse, or have eaten too many rich foods and had his stomach turn inside out – Lux had heard of all such things happening.

She was fairly sure that none of the lord's food had been poisoned, at least not on the days she was present. All of his food, as well as the food meant for the others in the stronghold, from the high table down to the scraps for the dogs, went through this kitchen. Lux well knew the smells, textures and sights of all the common poisons, so she knew that none of them were in the kitchen. Sometimes, when no one was looking, she sneaked a pinch of food from the fanciest plates – the eel and wine stew, the poached eggs in custard sauce, the pears and quince in syrup. These delicacies were mean: for the lord, and Lux was just being sure. An unofficial taster, before the food got to the proper taster.

But that was not the only reason she tasted the food. It wasn't even the main reason. She tasted it because she wanted it.

Besides, she found herself less interested in the idea of the lord, and more curious about the lady. As she went about her kitchen chores, she imagined what it might be like in the lady's chambers. It would be comfortable in there, with soft things and pleasant smells, and a bed hung with red curtains, perhaps, and a wooden chest with a carved lid, and a screen painted with a picture of exotic animals suchlike as Lux had never seen, and layers of furs on the bed, and so many candles that even the deepest night would be day-bright. She imagined herself climbing the fancy stairs she'd never been allowed to climb, imagined herself walking along the stone halls she'd never been allowed to walk, through the door she'd never been allowed to open. They were just idle daydreams; kitchen girls were not invited into a lady's chambers.

January crept on, with its frosty mornings and long nights, and with it came the season of fasting. This was meant to bring them closer to God, but Lux felt no holier with an empty belly. In the stronghold it seemed they were fasting as much as they were not. Holy days, holy weeks, holy seasons. As a child she had been lucky to get any food at all; the idea of choosing not to eat food that was right in front of her wouldn't have occurred.

Fasting meant less food, but not no food at all. Meat was forbidden, but fish was allowed, and everything that lived on or around water was fish. Swans, geese, crabs, seals, beavers if they could be caught. In times of fasting, Lux helped to prepare lampreys in mustard sauce, pimpernels in a pie, and salted salmon. The kitchen girls only got the scraps, soaked up with barley bread and cheese, but Lux still felt like she spent every meal navigating her mouth around endless fish bones.

Fast times made for restless sleep and strange dreams. Some nights she dreamt of blue glaciers against a blue sky. Of black sand, and white steam billowing in the wild sea. But there was not much time for dreaming when there was bread to bake and vegetables to peel and pots to scrub out with sand. When there were important growing things to tend. When there were soft hands reaching out in the night.

Lux watched. She waited. She knew she wasn't really a kitchen girl, but she played her role as best she could. But then – the thought came suddenly to her. Were any of the kitchen girls *really* kitchen girls? Even Goodwife Ethelinda – the way she could hack apart a side of meat, knife thudding on the counter, blood staining her knuckles; then the next moment construct the most delicate sugared fancies, coloured pale and pretty as flower petals, so dainty that a single breath could topple them. The same two hands used to make both. Was anyone one thing only?

The only good thing about a fast, as far as Lux was concerned, was that eventually it had to end. And after a fast – a feast. Or, as Goodwife Ethelinda insisted on calling it, the Feast of the Presentation of Our Lord Jesus and the Feast of the Purification of the Blessed Virgin Mary. Lux didn't call it that; she didn't even have time to call it Candlemas. There was too much work to do. This was a time of light and purification, ritual cleansing and the start of spring. Other, smaller, feasts had been and gone in her time at the stronghold kitchen. Lux had trussed many chickens, brushed many pie crusts with many egg yolks, and chopped so many onions she could have roofed a house from the discarded papery skins. But all of that was nothing compared to the day of this feast.

Goodwife Ethelinda had all the kitchen girls running around from first light until last preparing foodstuffs, all of them in a sulk with their bottom lips petted. Lux peeled and chopped and stirred and washed. She plucked. She kneaded. She sweated so much she could have wrung out her chemise and filled a cup to the brim.

Hours before daylight, she was perched on a squat wooden stool, holding between her knees the body of one of a dozen geese needing to be plucked, her fingers numb with gripping and a snow of white feathers in a constant fall around her. From the grey pre-dawn through the pink beginnings of day to the firm yellow sun: a whole morning, just Lux and the geese. There was a moment somewhere in that long morning, with the feathers snowing and her fingers numbing and the kitchen turning through its familiar routine like an old carthorse roped to a stake, when Lux felt at peace. Felt that she belonged, that she could be still. But then the goose's flesh was bare, and it was time to let the feathers settle and do something else: there were many pie crusts to be brushed with yolk, and many chickens to be trussed, and the onions, always the onions.

Finally, a reprieve: Goodwife Ethelinda ordered Lux to go to the well to get more water. All the water, as much as she could carry, bucket after bucket, keep going until the well runs dry. Lux did not need to be told twice.

The air outside was cool and crisp, with a frost on the breeze. Lux stood in the doorway: the hectic, sweating kitchen at her back; the loose, icy garden at her front. And beyond it, the pines. She hefted her bucket and looked towards the well. Then she stopped. Glancing behind her, she saw that no one was watching. She turned from the well and went to the pigpen instead.

'Else?'

The pigs rootled towards her, snorting out white clouds and grunting in happy rhythm. When they saw that her hands were empty, they lost interest. Lux picked her way through the hard-frozen mud and ducked her head into the pigs' house.

'Else?'

But of course, Else wasn't in the pigs' house, but behind it. It was a bright day, and the cold sun cast the shadows black. In the depths of the poison garden, Else, dressed in a plain woollen dress with her hair covered, looked like a shadow herself.

She looked up, and saw Lux, and smiled. 'Our garden grows,' she said.

Stepping into the chilly shadows towards Else, Lux shivered and pulled her woollen cloak tighter. How did Else never feel the cold? She bent and toyed with a bead of nightshade. How she ached to thread a needle – even a pine needle, even a spiderweb-thread, anything she could find – and make herself a necklace. Those plump black pearls; the comfort of them around her throat.

Lux hesitated, then pulled her hand back. Frost still covered the ground every morning and the sun lay low in the sky. But nightshade berries ripened in late summer, not winter. 'The nightshade,' she said. 'And the henbane. The pennyroyal. They all bloom in summer. How did you...'

This should all be a mass of stalks and dozing plants – yet Else's garden pulsed with blossoming flowers and berries.

Else turned away, pulling a stray weed and tossing it over the roof of the pigs' house and into the pen for them to eat.

'We want the plants to grow,' she said.

'But plants don't care what we want – they only know life or death. Growing or waiting. So how did you make them flower when all of this should be under the ground?'

'There are more than just two choices.'

'There's dead,' said Lux, 'and there's alive. I don't see how there can be more than that.'

'I hope that you will. Someday. The line between death and life is not so clear as you think.'

Lux scuffed her toe on the frosty grass, liking the scrunching sound it made. Hidden behind the pigs' house, they couldn't hear any noises from the stronghold; all they could hear was the soft snuffles of the pigs as they rootled in the dirt. 'Could something from this garden have poisoned the lord's food-taster?'

'I suppose it could,' said Else lightly. 'Could something from it have saved him?'

'I can't say for sure, as I don't know what happened to him. But I'd have tried. And I suppose others must have tried too – the lord must have the wisest and most learned healers. The kitchen girls all say how strong he is. So they must be doing something right, and still all their skills and knowledge etcetera wasn't enough to save the food-taster. But I wonder...' Here Lux stepped among the nettles, taking care to keep the thick fabric of her skirt between the spiked leaves and her skin. 'I wonder which plants they used.'

'It doesn't sound like they used any plants at all,' said Else. 'The lady walks in the gardens every day. I hear her speak about the healers. She's careless when she walks past the pigs. She always stops to look at them. She likes their faces and says with their pink scalps and sparse pale hair they look like little old men.'

'She says all this to you?' Lux could taste the jealousy, sweet and bitter in her mouth. She had only seen the lady from a distance, and had heard little about her. Even the kitchen girls seemed scared to trade tales about her. She felt jealous of Else for getting to hear what the lady said, and jealous of the lady for being able to speak so freely.

'Of course not,' said Else. 'If she even knows I'm here, she clearly thinks I can't hear her. Or doesn't care if I do.'

'And what does the lady say?'

'That the lord's healers don't know how to heal.'

'If only they'd had a bezoar from a goat's stomach, or a cup of unicorn horn, or crushed amethyst or suchlike.' Lux stopped herself, and laughed. 'I've never seen those things. I don't even know if they're real. I've only heard of them. But they're healers; they should have everything, shouldn't they?'

'The lady said that all the healers do is bleed and purge. So many leeches they stuck on that poor food-taster. The sicker he grew, the more they bled and purged him. Finally he could barely open his eyes or make a sound. By the time he died all his insides were out.'

'They should have tried mandrake,' said Lux. 'If they didn't know what the poison was. A few of the berries, dried and crushed to a powder, mixed into liquid and swallowed all at once – or if they were quick, and got to him soon after he'd swallowed the poison, he could have eaten clay. If the poison was henbane, then mulberry leaves boiled in vinegar. Cabbage seeds mixed into butter will cause vomiting – but it doesn't seem that a lack of vomiting was a problem.'

Else toyed with a nettle leaf, apparently unaffected by its sting. 'Herbs can heal. But they can also harm. If you wanted them to.'

'The food-taster did nothing wrong. Why would I want to harm him?'

'Not him. Someone else. Someone who deserved it.'

Lux rolled a nightshade berry between her fingers, careful not to pluck it from its stem. 'Let's just say. Say I didn't have a poison garden. Then perhaps apple seeds – one or two will do nothing, but if you were to grind up a few handfuls and put them in, say, an apple tart – that would be something. It would begin with confusion and a spinning head, which might be put down to tiredness. Then the heart would begin to pound, then the body would fall into fits and finally the breath would stop. Or –' she grinned at Else, enjoying this chance to share all she'd learned from her mother – 'mushrooms. The red-capped sort that grow wild in shady forests. Dried, powdered and mixed into milk, it can lead to a deep and beautiful sleep – perhaps one from which you never wake. I've seen that peonies grow in the bee garden – they are valuable in easing childbirth pains or preventing bad dreams. But if the petals were to be mixed into a salad . . .'

'But you do have a poison garden,' murmured Else.

Lux smiled and stepped among the nettles, pushing them aside with her skirt-covered hands to see the plants beneath. The pigs had fallen silent, as if they were listening. 'In that case, foxglove will stop a heart, as will monkshood. They would be easy enough to slip into food or drink. Nightshade – that would be my choice. It's a beauty, and hard to resist if you don't know what it is. Those deep green leaves, the tiny purple flowers like hats for mice, the fruit as glossy and dark as a lake at night. Just a brush of the leaves can cause flushed cheeks and strange visions. Eating the berries means a quick death. And mixed with hemlock, mandrake and henbane – that would be my choice.' Lux swept her arms wide, rejoicing in the growing of the garden, the possibilities that lurked.

'Girl.' A woman's voice, high-spoken, clear as a frosty morning. 'Come here.'

Lux's heart stuttered. It was not a voice she recognised – though she did recognise the tone of someone used to being obeyed.

How much had this woman overheard? Would she think that Lux meant to actually poison someone – or that she already had? Lux felt her guts drop. There was only one person that voice could belong to. The lady.

'Now,' said the lady.

Lux glanced in horror at Else, but there was no help to be found: Else looked just as shocked as Lux felt. There was nothing to be done. Lux walked out of the poison garden and around the pigs' house.

She didn't dare look up from the ground. The lady's shoes were just visible beneath the fall of her skirts, the toes richly embroidered, and easily the most beautiful things Lux had ever seen. She saw the tendrils of vine leaves and delicate petals, all picked out in coloured thread. Then the lady took a step towards her, and Lux closed her eyes, not daring to look at all.

'What are you growing back there, girl?'

'N–'

'And don't say nothing. I am no fool.'

'Hemlock, my lady,' said Lux, her tongue feeling shrivelled in her mouth. 'And foxglove, and mandrake, and . . .' She had to say it, there was no way not to say it; it would be a sin to lie to the lady. 'And nightshade, my lady. But they're only for helping people, not –'

'Is that so?' said the lady, a smile in her voice. Lux dared to open her eyes. The cold winter sun had emerged, and it lit the lady from the ground up. 'Come, girl.'

A swish of skirts against the frosty grass, and Lux dared a glance up. Walking away, the lady was outlined against the sky, a black shape against the white clouds. She was small-boned, the sweep of her white neck as elegant as a bird's, her shoulders set. She moved with a sureness Lux had never before seen in a woman. Delicate, yet unbreakable.

All Lux could do was follow.

She thought of all the stories she'd heard about the lord. Bear heart; rat heart. Massages with scented oils; innards writhing and rotting like maggots. Making girls scream in pleasure; making girls scream in terror as they drowned.

But what about the lady? Lux had heard nothing. No one dared to tell tales about her.

Lux pulled herself from her thoughts. She was in a small wood-panelled anteroom, alone with the lady. Dark had come early. Outside the high window, stars. Lux's heart beat fast.

With one hand the lady held up a candle. With the other she reached her fingers to Lux's mouth. Lux, shocked, stepped back, but her heels hit the wall and she could go no further. The lady sighed and dropped her hand.

'If there is a remedy for poison hidden in your mouth, you have no use as a food-taster.'

'There is nothing in my mouth, my lady. I swear it.'

The candle flame guttered. From elsewhere in the stronghold, quick footsteps and a shriek of female laughter, quickly stifled.

'Well.' There was a lift in the lady's voice, as if she was smiling. 'I hope you'll forgive me if I don't take your word for it. Here in the stronghold we have the pines on one side, the sea on another, and the castle walls on another. We are protected from invasion. My wise lord knows that there is only one side that truly needs guarded: the side that faces the town, the side that feeds us. My lord is beset by poisoners, assassins and devils, and they are all trying to get to his mouth. My purpose in this world is to do what I can to battle against them.'

'Yes, my –' began Lux, but the lady had reached up her fingers and pressed them to Lux's lips, so she opened her mouth. The lady held the candle close and looked inside.

'Lift your tongue,' said the lady. Lux obeyed. The lady's fingers smelled of tallow and cinnamon.

'Now hold your tongue down,' said the lady. Lux obeyed. 'I could have you killed for that garden.' The lady spoke casually, as if the thought had only just occurred to her. 'But I will not. Instead I will give you the opportunity to atone. To be useful. You are a kitchen girl?'

Lux had the lady's fingers in her mouth, and could not answer – but to not answer would be disobedience. She held her breath, undecided. The lady's fingers moved gently inside Lux's mouth. Finally, she withdrew them. Lux resisted the urge to lick her dry lips.

'Yes, my lady.'

'Does it suit you?'

'Yes, my lady. I am very grateful for my work.'

'That is not what I asked. You say you are a kitchen girl. And yet I've never noticed any of them, have I? They are nothing but a muddle of red hands, swollen arms and the smell of onions. Is that what you are?'

'I –'

But the lady raised an eyebrow, and Lux stopped herself. 'I don't think that's what you are,' said the lady. 'You are not like them. You are more useful.'

Lux opened her mouth to protest that the kitchen girls *were* useful – who did the lady think prepared all her fine foods? Collected the eggs for her breakfast and plucked the chickens for her supper? Grew the plants and made the dyes for her clothes? Tended the bees who made her honey? The lady wouldn't be able to do a single one of these things. But she closed her mouth without saying anything.

Lux dared a glance up at the lady, and was relieved to see that she was smiling. It didn't reach her eyes, but it was better than nothing. Perhaps Lux wasn't about to be accused of poisoning anyone.

'You will be my lord's food-taster,' said the lady.

'But –' Lux bit back her words.

The lady raised an eyebrow in response. Lux held her mouth tight closed, cursing herself.

'Now,' said the lady, 'you will go back to the kitchen, and be sure to watch everything. I heard you in the garden. I know that you know which herbs will harm my lord, and which will merely flavour his meals. If he dies, so will you. Do you understand?'

Lux's mouth was too dry for words. She turned to go, but the lady was not finished.

'Have you parents?'

'I had a mother, my lady.'

'Don't give silly answers. Everyone has a mother at some point. You weren't raised by wolves, were you?'

There was a silence, which Lux didn't know whether she was supposed to fill.

'What about your father?'

'I never had one, my lady.'

'And your mother?' prompted the lady.

'She died.'

'So you are friendless in this world,' said the lady, her voice honey-sweet. 'All alone, no one but God to care what happens to you.'

Lux thought of Else. Her strong, cold hands slicing open a rabbit for their supper. The gleam of her wolf's eyes in the dark. Her smile when Lux had said she would go to the stronghold with her. Lux forced the words, the lie scraping: 'Yes, my lady. I am alone.'

'Well, not any longer,' said the lady, and for a moment she pressed Lux's hands between her own. Her hands were cool, like Else's. The lady smiled. The candle she held tilted, and a drop of wax dripped burning on Lux's skin. Lux tried not to flinch. 'I care,' said the lady. 'If you will be a friend to me, I will be a friend to you.'

'Yes, my lady.'

'I have heard stories about girls like you,' said the lady, her tone light. 'Filthy hovels, cold nights, biting hunger. It's always the same. Is that who you are, Lux? Just a filthy cold girl from a filthy cold hovel?'

No, thought Lux. 'Yes,' she said. 'My lady.'

'Would you like to be something else?' The lady didn't wait for an answer. 'I think you would.' She turned and dropped Lux's hands in dismissal. 'Now, girl, you think on that. Only I can make you something else.'

2

Now She is Sacrifice

Lux stood behind the lord's chair, her head still spinning. Her plain dress, heavy at the bottom with mud, had been cast aside, ready for the next kitchen girl. Now she wore dark green, marking her out as the lord's food-taster. She tried to still her restlessness; she'd never worn new clothing before, and it felt stiff on her body. Her scalp hurt from brushing, her face burned from washing, her eyes ached from looking. The great hall was the largest place she had ever been inside that wasn't a church. She tried to focus on her tasks, but her eyes kept betraying her. There was so much to see.

From huge cartwheels chained to the ceiling, many candles burned. Tapestries covered the walls, telling stories of ladies and lords, hounds and foxes, angels and the dead. The floor-rushes had been laid fresh that day, and their smell filled Lux's nose. Long tables stretched the room's full length, bracketed by wide benches, all of which were occupied. Every person in the room was a stranger to Lux; she'd never seen so many unfamiliar faces all at once, and she marvelled at the variety that was possible. High white foreheads, scar-dented cheeks, noses red and pulpy as tomatoes. Shoulders wide as doorways and hands tiny as flowers. Strangest of all was what lay on the table in front of the lord: a bear.

The bear's eyes were soft and dark, and Lux could just see the black of its gums between its parted jaws. She didn't want to look any closer than that, as the bear's head was on a pole, separated from the rest of its body, which had already been unmade, and lay across many platters on the table. The unmaking of the bear was the climax of a hunt which the lord was meant to lead – but considering how exhausted the hunters in the room looked, Lux guessed they'd done most of the work. Though she wasn't convinced it would be that much work to catch a tame bear. She flashed back to her desperate flight through the forest: the man on the white horse, the mummers with their ribbon-hung tree.

She closed her eyes and tried to focus. The hunt had passed; they were not after her. Thinking of the hunt made her think of Else, and all that she hadn't yet had a chance to tell her. Would she be pleased at Lux's new role? It did bring her closer to the lord, which Else might think would help her desire for revenge. But she'd realise it would also mean that Lux would be the first to be suspected.

She tried to focus, thinking of all the things she would tell Else. Her new duties consisted of three things. The first was to watch everything that happened in the kitchen: every ingredient that came in, every step of preparation. She'd already been in the kitchen all morning and was very nosy, so that part was done. The lord's previous food-taster had not done this; Lux had never seen him visit the kitchen, and perhaps this was his downfall. Lux wouldn't make the same mistake.

The second had to be kept secret from everyone except the lady, and that was to tend and monitor her garden, so there was a ready stock for the lord if he was to be somehow poisoned. No one could know about this, as healing was not women's work, but men's. The lord, however, had dismissed all his healers. Some had even been banished abroad for failing to save the food-taster.

The third was the one that thrilled and terrified Lux. She had to use a tiny spoon to taste a bite of everything the lord put on this plate. *Everything*. The chicken covered with egg yolks and sprinkled with spice. The wild boar with wafers. The stuffed peacock. The plums stewed in rosewater. Even the cups of sweetened wine (though she didn't need to use her spoon for that). No offal and frumenty for Lux; not today. That was the thrilling part. The terrifying part was that if the food was poisoned, Lux would die. Still, she'd made it this far. She was going to die sometime, just like everyone. At least she'd do it with the taste of rosewater plums in her mouth.

Lux had never seen the lord before, and she couldn't really see him now, despite the fact that she stood right behind him. There were so many candles above and around the lord that he seemed ringed in sun. To Lux, his body was nothing more than a black mass, his forearms and calves huge as pigs. The smell from him was of cloves and meat and incense – and underneath it, the faintest scent of rot. Could it be true, what Else had said about the lord? Or was what the kitchen girls said true instead?

He was draped in furs and velvet and gold, and wore a carved bull's head as armour to protect his skull and the back of his neck. The horns looked sharp enough to gore her. Beside him, the lady was as fine-boned as a songbird; the lord looked like he could swallow her in one bite. Her gown was as blue as a clear sky and her hair was roped in thick braids, looped to cover her ears and covered in round filigreed casings. Lux looked forward to her tasting duties; tallow and cinnamon still clung to her tongue, and she wasn't sure if she liked it.

She had been strictly informed that she must not look the lord or the lady in the face at any time, for any reason. She should keep her eyes on the ground or on the food she was about to taste. Lux was happy to agree to that; there behind the lord's chair, no one could see her anyway, so she could look wherever she pleased. She'd never been to a feast before, and didn't know what they entailed. All she'd ever seen was the platters going out of the kitchen overbalanced with food – and then coming back empty, licked clean by the dogs.

Surely the feast was about to begin. The food lay spread out in the centre of the tables. Everyone fidgeted on their benches. The servants filled the lord's and lady's cups with sweet wine. Lux held her little spoon, ready.

But not yet. Lux startled as the lord suddenly stood; she barely managed to step back out of the way of his chair.

'Behold!' boomed the lord, his voice so loud it made the tapestries flutter. There was something odd about his voice, as if he had something in his mouth. 'This Candlemas we give thanks for all we have been given. Behold all I have brought to you!' He spoke slowly, carefully sounding out each word. His voice was low and resonant, but he still sounded like he had something in his mouth. A small wooden ball, thought Lux. A halved plum. The head of a mouse. 'This meat I have hunted. These fruits I have grown. The Lord has provided all.'

Lux thought that probably when the lord said *Lord* he meant God, rather than himself, though it was quite hard to tell. She was fairly sure the lord had not hunted, for example, all the peacocks by himself - though even if he had, how hard could it be to catch a peacock, you'd be able to spot them from a mile off - but she wasn't about to argue with him.

'Lord!' said the lord. 'I speak for all gathered here. We give thanks for the feast you have prepared -' Lux had to bite back a snort at that; she didn't remember anyone, heavenly or not, helping her pluck those geese - 'and I ask that you forgive all those here for their sins and their trespasses. We ask for your light, Lord,' said the lord, and with a thump he sat back in his seat.

Lux shuffled forward, ready with her little spoon.

But no. First it was time for the Unmaking of the bear.

In the kitchen, the Unmaking had been explained to her by Hulda - imperiously - and Eolande - breathlessly - as they both rolled out enormous circles of dough for a pie crust. Lux couldn't tell what the kitchen girls thought of her new position. She was still to share a bed with them, and she was pleased that the soft hands in the night wouldn't change - not that anyone ever discussed that in daylight, of course.

The beginning stages of the Unmaking, it was explained, happened in the forest, where the bear was killed. First the bear was slit from front to back. Next the bear was skinned, with the skin used to protect the meat and collect the blood. The kidneys, small intestine, windpipe and blood were mixed with bread and fed to the hunting hounds, and relics were left at the kill site as a gift to the ravens.

Back at the stronghold, the body was brittled into pieces. And now, one by one, important men stepped forward and the lord handed them the appropriate bit of dead bear. The only parts missing were the offal and umbles - the parts that hadn't gone to the dogs, anyway - which were already in the kitchen, ready to be made into umble pie to feed the lowest status people at the stronghold. Lux, usually, didn't even get a piece of that pie, being about on the level of the pigs, and certainly below the dogs. It all seemed like a waste of time to her. Surely now they could eat?

But no. Frustratingly, still no one reached for a single chicken leg. The hall held its breath. Lux's belly made a complaint. She dared a glance at the food and her gaze landed instead on the table where the lord's hand rested, a bandage covering one of his fingertips. A little blood had leaked through.

A thought flashed through Lux of those hands closing around her throat. She suppressed a shiver and held her jaw tight. But still the thought persisted. Perhaps it was true, about the lord and his fine-chained horses, and his fine-chained girls.

As if feeling the weight of her gaze, the lord seemed to notice the blood on his finger, and moved his hands beneath the table.

Finally the lady reached out her delicate white hand, plucked up a candied fig, and placed it on her trencher. She licked a crystal of sugar from her forefinger and folded her hands back in her lap.

It was as if the clouds had burst after a long threat of rain. Everyone, all of a sudden, let out a great sigh and reached for the platters. Plates and cups and mouths filled. A trio of servants rushed forward and filled the lord's and lady's plates with food: a towering pile for the lord, careful morsels for the lady.

Finally, the moment for Lux and her little spoon had arrived. Her eyes gleamed with excitement. At the last moment she remembered herself, and pushed her gaze down to the floor as she stepped forward. But she had to focus on her tasting tasks. Meanwhile the lord scratched his balls and drank his wine, waiting to see if the new food-taster would begin exploding from either end. Lux knew she had to eat fast so that the lord didn't get too hungry waiting to see if she'd die, but it was hard not to draw it out. Who knew when she'd get to eat like this again? Perhaps the lord would leave a little on his plate, and Lux could sneak it away for Else before the trenchers were put down for the dogs.

She'd tasted a little of everything, and went to step back. But the lord grabbed her wrist and pulled her closer. His sleeve was as velvet as tongue. His skin felt hot and rough. Lux's bare wrist burned.

'Again,' he said.

Lux's hand shook, but she tasted everything again. It was still delicious. She still didn't die.

Without looking at her, the lord pushed her aside and turned to his trencher. Her little spoon clattered to the rushes, and she squatted to pick it up. Her blood surged, her head swam, and she decided to stay down there on the floor. No one would notice. She could savour the tastes still in her mouth and not have to worry about being caught looking where she wasn't meant to look. She shuffled back beside the lord's chair, ready for his next course. The priest had begun intoning the sermon, but she could hear it fine from down here.

Lux's head spun from sugar and sound and the thought of the lord's pointed horns, but as far as she could tell the priest was telling the traditional Candlemas story: Mary's cleansing so that she could go back to the church after Jesus' birth. She wondered if her mother had been cleansed after Lux's birth.

'Lord grant us light that we may see,' said the priest, 'and dark when the time comes to close our eyes.'

Servants stepped forward to refill the lord's trencher, but when Lux looked, she didn't think he'd actually eaten anything, just moved the food around. Still, she stepped forward, ready with her little spoon. Her mouth watered at the thought of the new tastes to come.

'Lord grant us a shadow that we may overcome,' said the priest, and though Lux knew she mustn't, she looked at the lord's face. Between his ornate bull's head and his plush velvet clothing, he looked like a carving made real: his eyes hectic and bright, his jaw set, his cheeks huge as a held breath. His black eyes gleamed – but he looked not at the priest or at the food, as everyone else did, but at the lady. The lord was the most powerful person in the room – in the stronghold – in the world, for all Lux knew – and his eyes were only on the lady. So what did that make her?

'Lord,' said the priest, and Lux did not know why, but at that moment the lord looked at her, right at her face, 'grant us light,' said the priest, and it was too late for Lux to look away and pretend she wasn't staring a hand's-breadth from the lord's face, 'for we need light more now than ever,' said the priest, and the lord's face lit up with something that Lux couldn't name, a recognition, a burning, and she forgot how to breathe as everyone joined in with the priest's words, 'in these times of darkness.'

Every day Lux ate a little of the lord's food, and the lord ate apparently even less of it, and the lord didn't die, and neither did Lux. She still hadn't visited Else at the pigpen – she was so busy with her new duties, and felt that the other girls were always watching her now, and would mark if she kept creeping off to the gardens. Then was Sunday, and like every Sunday that meant church. Lux was meant to be at the end of the line of kitchen girls trailing after Goodwife Ethelinda like ducklings: Hulda, Linden, Elen, Amity, Eolande and the other Euphemia. But she kept getting distracted. She'd followed them out of the stronghold and down the hill into the town, all fine, nothing to see except dirt and grass and the skirts of the girl in front. But as soon as they reached the town, she lost herself. She hadn't meant to fall behind, but there was so much to see; surely no one could be expected to keep their heads lowered and eyes on the ground among the chaos of the town. Besides, looking down meant all you'd know of the world was muddy streets rutted with cartwheel tracks and littered with fish bones, broken crockery and bits of rotten gristle even the dogs had rejected.

Look up and you could see the narrow strip of blue sky between the roofs of the houses; the way the buildings leaned in towards each other made Lux think of drunk people trying to kiss, but missing every time. Drag your eyes down a little and you see stalls selling combs and pins carved out of creamy white antler; blooms of purple cabbages piled so high they were about to tumble; strings of dried fish looped like garlands. The mist-eyed beggar with her handful of wildflowers. The cats licking bloody drips from the butcher's table. The swaying row of cows led by a boy no higher than Lux's hip. The whores in their yellow hoods. The smells of earth and meat and shit and flowers and fur and fires and the bodies of a hundred strangers.

Lux was distracted from her distraction by the group of children, twisting and turning with a long, bright ribbon they'd attached to a peg in the wall, and she didn't make it a habit to think about Ash or the mummers, but she thought about them then.

'Black roses, black roses, the devil paints them on. First you cough and then you sneeze and then you're good as –'

Lux felt a pinch on her elbow. 'Keep up,' said Goodwife Ethelinda. As they rounded a corner, she pushed Lux's chest so she stood with her back against the wall, in line with the rest of the townsfolk bracketing the narrow streets.

The air only held one sound now – no barking dogs, no rootling pigs, no cries of sellers touting their wares. The beating of drums and the high calls of hymns filled her head, and she realised the sound had been building for a long time beneath the other noise; it was only now the rest had fallen away that she could hear it. Suddenly the drums and song stopped. Lux's ears throbbed. In the silence, this new sound slowly emerged: the steady shuffle of feet and the unsteady snapping of whips.

She still couldn't see anything; she leaned forward and peered down the road. A staggering line of men approached, barefoot, all dressed in white robes, red crosses painted on their bare chests. In their right hands they held whips; on every seventh step they each shouted something, and snapped the whips hard over their shoulders so the spiked barbs bit their backs.

'What are... Why...' began Lux, but didn't know what she was trying to ask.

As the winding line of men approached, Lux smelled blood and milk.

'The flagellant parade,' whispered Goodwife Ethelinda. 'They give their lamentations and their tears to cleanse us all. Keep your hands down by your sides as they pass. Show some respect.'

The men came closer. Now Lux could hear what they said as they walked:

'I confess that I lusted for my neighbour's wife and had indecent thoughts of her. Let God take my sin, and make me be clean.' - a whip snap, and the man did not flinch.

'I confess that I took bread from my son's plate because I was hungry even though I knew that he was also hungry. Let God take my sin, and make me be clean.' - a whip smack, and the man kept walking.

As the men got closer, Lux kept her hands down by her sides, as Goodwife Ethelinda had said. She noticed, smugly, that Amity on her other side had raised her hands to cover her face. She hoped Goodwife Ethelinda had noticed, so she'd see that Lux was more obedient than the other girls, though even Lux knew this wasn't even close to being true. She didn't know how fully Goodwife Ethelinda had explained to the others about her new position; she'd hoped that the hands reaching for her in the night wouldn't change, but all that had stopped. The others seemed more careful around Lux, and often stopped talking when she came into the room. After slipping Eolande the mandrake and seeing how it relieved the ache in her belly, Lux had secretly healed several of the girls, and even Goodwife Ethelinda, when she heard them complaining of ailments. But she vowed to do that no longer. It was too easy to be misunderstood.

'I confess that I went to a witch for charms to help my wife through her childbearing, and I did not name the witch until my wife died. Let God take my sin, and make me be clean.' - a whip crack, and this man couldn't help it; he cried out, and a good thing he did, because it covered the sound when Lux cried out too, shocked at the spurt of hot liquid across her face. She looked down at her hands and realised she must have instinctively raised them, though too late to cover her face. The backs of her hands were smeared red with blood from the man's back.

She resisted the urge to lift her skirts and wipe her face clean; she couldn't go into the church in stained clothing. Instead she wiped the blood from her cheeks as best she could, then behind the curtain of her skirts she rubbed her hands on the wall of the house behind her, blinking hard to clear the blood from her eyes.

The flagellant parade passed, naming their sins and snapping their whips, and while their fronts were still white, red covered their backs and dripped down into the dirt behind them.

After them came a man leading his scolding wife in a branks, the metal cage over her head jerking and scraping her face every time he tugged the chain attached to it. The woman's front was spattered with vomit and flecks of blood. She tried to keep her head still, but her husband yanked the chain and she gagged again; the tongue-piece of the branks must be too long, and was poking the back of her throat. The sides of her mouth were cut and her gums torn, as when she vomited again, smears of red came too.

But the man wasn't a flagellant, and one scolding wife was meagre entertainment after the parade of confession and gore. The people were already turning away, but they turned faster when a woman in a yellow hood suddenly shrieked, falling to the ground and tearing off her clothes.

'He is upon me!' she cried. 'His wickedness is inside me!' Then she was saying something else, but Lux couldn't understand the words - they didn't seem to be words at all, but random thrashing of her tongue. The woman's skirts were up around her waist, with her cunt and arse bare for all the town to see. It was a shame, it really was; women couldn't help being more susceptible to possession. Women are, as Father Fleck used to tell them at the sanctuary, less intelligent, more suggestible, and have more entry points into their bodies. All those orifices ready for a devil to creep into.

Lux started to move towards the woman, forgetting the blood on her face, wanting to help. But Goodwife Ethelinda pulled on her wrist.

'Ignore her,' she said.

'But - Goodwife, she is possessed by something, shouldn't we fetch the priest to help her, shouldn't we cover her -'

'She's possessed,' said Goodwife Ethelinda, 'by nothing more than the desire to earn some coins. Prinked-up little baggage that she is. It's just an excuse to show off her wares.'

And sure enough, the woman had already ceased her wailing and writhing, and had straightened her clothing, and got to her feet, and was calmly leading a man down a nearby alley.

The bells began to ring. The townspeople gathered themselves and turned for the church.

Goodwife Ethelinda handed Lux an old kerchief. 'Wipe your face,' she said, her smile beatific. 'You must be clean for church.'

'Monstrous night!' shrieked the priest, 'and glorious light.' The church held so much echo, he had to pause after each word. 'I tell you first of night, and all that lurks within it. We have all heard the tales of long ago, of endless night, have we not?'

Lux had learned that these questions were not to be answered;

particularly not by a woman, and most definitely not by her. It was often said that women should always be silent in church, and church meant everywhere God sees, and that meant everywhere. Ideally a woman should make no sound at all. Lux thought of the vomit-spattered scold in her branks. Silence was definitely safest.

'It was a cursed time for us all,' went on the priest, 'when our day became night. Darkness came from the black land of the north, where resides the mouth of hell and all that is vomited out of it. A great fire burned and the land spewed forth from under the sea. Thick and palpable clouds overshadowed our land. Ash hid the sun. The crops withered in their fields. Sickness came for us. Darkness was upon the face of the land – but the spirit of God moved there still. And who brought the darkness to us?'

Lux had heard all this before, but tried not to let her mind wander. She kept her hands tucked under her thighs. Dry blood itched around her fingernails, and her palms smelled of stale milk.

'All those who give suck to the devil and his imps,' said the priest. 'Witches and devils and the practitioners of maleficium. They run their own ways, and give liking unto nothing but what is framed by themselves, and hammered on their anvil. They are rotten in their bones and their blood. They spread disease and rot to all good people. A witch is the very pestilence of the earth. All calamity is brought upon men by her. She torments good men and kills them at will. No man can be safe as long as she lives. God tells us: who so sheddeth man's blood, by man shall his blood be shed. We must root this evilness out. We must wash it clean.'

Lux fidgeted in her seat. Her hands had gone numb. The wood was hard, the air close and thick, heavy with perfume and other people's breath. She felt a sharp pressure on her hand; she flinched, but her hand stayed put. She glanced down to see Hulda pressing her knuckle bones hard into the back of Lux's hand.

Stop moving around, Hulda mouthed. *You're getting red on my skirt.*

'Women!' boomed the priest. 'I speak to you now. All wickedness is but little to the wickedness of a woman. What else is woman but an inescapable punishment, a necessary evil to be endured? There is filth to be cleansed. The milk of the mother is only pure if the mother herself is pure. Jesus is the purest of all, and everything that comes from his body will cleanse you. I ask all women to open their mouths only if Jesus wills it; only if Jesus asks to fill your body with his pureness. The milk of the mother comes too from Jesus, from his wounds that he bore for us, as a mother bears the pain of childbirth. Visit Jesus tonight as you pray, and kneel before him, and he will cleanse you. Jesus will suckle you as you suckle your children, and while he cleanses you, there is hope that you will not taint others.'

Lux wondered if God had held back her blood as a punishment. She could never be a woman the way the priest said. No childbirth. No milk. No cleansing. She could never have anything. She could never be anything.

But then – the lady had no children, as far as Lux knew. And she had power over everyone in the stronghold, except the lord, of course. That certainly counted as being something.

When the time came, Lux accepted the sacrament, her hands held behind her back to hide the blood.

All the walk home, the talk was of witches.

'They say,' said Amity, her lips scabbed where she bit them to make them red, 'that the north witches live on glass mountains.'

'How wide are they?' asked Elen, who darkened her pale eyelashes with ash from the fire when she thought no one was watching.

'How wide are the witches? They are normal width.' Amity spoke with authority, and Lux stifled a laugh.

'No, the mountains! Are they narrow as a broomstick? Do the witches straddle them with a leg on each side?'

'Elen, your mind is so dirty you belong with the pigs. In fact when we get back you can take the scraps to them.'

'It's not my turn!'

'That's what you get,' said Linden, whose turn it was. She and Elen both had shiny wood-brown hair of which they were very proud, and they both smelled of the boiled eggs and pickles they ate to be clear of pestilential voids in the stomach, so they were hard to tell apart. Lux wondered if it was Linden's or Elen's hands that used to reach for her in the night.

'The witches,' went on Amity in a long-suffering way, 'sit on their glass mountains and gaze out at the heaps of corpses spread across their lands, horses and riders who have died before reaching them, for they send mirages to trick the godly.'

'And,' added Hulda, 'they sit in their courtyards and sing evil songs to the many dying men there, who are unable to move further towards them as they have cut off the men's limbs with their swords of ice.'

'How can they have a mountain inside a courtyard?' When all the other girls turned to stare at Lux, she realised she'd spoken aloud. 'I mean,' went on Lux, even as she told herself not to, 'what use is it to see mountains and corpses that aren't really there? Why make a sword out of ice? What is his design through all of these things?'

'The Lord has his own designs,' said Hulda. 'We don't have to understand the designs of the Lord above, or the lord in the stronghold, do we?'

'What designs?' asked Lux. 'Does the lord have designs?'

'For you, perhaps,' said Amity, spreading her bitten lips in a smirk. One of the other girls – Lux couldn't tell who – made a horse's whinny, turning it into a soft moan of pleasure. The others laughed, but a sharp look from Hulda silenced them.

'Even if we tried to understand them,' said Hulda, 'it would be impossible. We are only girls. All we can do is observe the works of God. He made the seas rise up, didn't he, when we were only babies? He covered the land bridge between here and the north, once and for all, to protect us.'

'But doesn't the devil do things too?' murmured Elen. 'What does he want?'

'The devil has his own wicked purposes,' said Hulda, 'and we good people will never know the sense of them. Only the wicked look for sense in the devil's doings. If he wants you to see a mountain inside a court-yard, you will. And if –'

'Did we all see the nagging woman in the street getting her just pun-ishment?' called back Goodwife Ethelinda without breaking her stride. 'Do we all understand the natural result of women who speak when they don't need to?'

The kitchen girls knew better than to reply to that.

'And so,' went on Goodwife Ethelinda, 'we must only speak if needed. Does wicked gossip about wicked things seem like something that is needed? Or should we all close our mouths now and think of godly things? The purest woman is one who says nothing at all.'

Lux couldn't help thinking that Goodwife Ethelinda didn't really need to say that either, so by all rights it should be branks all round in the kitchen. Lux didn't know what Goodwife Ethelinda thought about her new position, if indeed she thought anything at all. She didn't treat Lux any differently; still ordered her around and forgot her name. But Lux felt secure under the lady's protection. She had a use now, and there was power in that.

Still, they all walked back to the stronghold in silence, and when they got there Lux wanted to sneak out to see Else at the pigpen, but she hadn't even had time to take off her cloak and hood when the lady sent for her.

She mustn't keep the lady waiting, so went immediately to her without washing her hands or brushing the dust from her hair. Lux was led not to the lady's chambers – a place she still had not been inside, though had often imagined – but to a room she'd never seen before. She was left out-side the door, which was made of black wood carved with figures.

Lux raised her fist to knock, then thought perhaps that was bad man-ners, so waited. The hall was lit by a single candle, and in the dimness she couldn't make out the carvings on the door. Her fingers touched them, trying to know them by their shape. Something bulbous – a face, perhaps – a series of spikes like a thorny branch.

The door swung open, revealing the lady, and Lux's hand was left grasping at air. She snatched it back before the lady saw the blood around her nails. She remembered about not looking into the lady's face, and cast her eyes down. That meant she was looking right at the carvings, and in the light from the room beyond, she could see them now. They showed men and women fornicating. Men drinking too much and vomiting up strings of sausages. Men and men fornicating. Babies roasted on spits surrounded by a trio of sagging, cackling old women. Women and animals fornicating. A combination of animals and women and men and something Lux couldn't identify fornicating. She stepped back from the door; her hands were already dirty, but this door seemed worse.

'We keep the sin on the outside,' said the lady, 'so the inside can be even holier.'

The lady pulled the door wider. The room beyond was twice the size of Lux's old house in the forest. The floor and ceiling gleamed black, the wood painted with some kind of tar. From eye height, the walls were lined by long, straight shelves, each of which held an elaborate golden box. Lux closed her eyes for a moment, dazzled. She had never seen gold before, except in church; she didn't know it was allowed outside church.

She opened her eyes and looked again. The boxes varied from the size of a mouse to the size of a calf. Some were plain, the gold smooth as a butter pat; some were studded all over with coloured jewels. Each had a glass window in the front so you could see inside. Most seemed only to contain a pillow, but a few had a thing on the pillow, an object a little like a dried mushroom or bit of chicken gristle. One – Lux quickly looked away from that one – seemed to hold three small teeth, such as the travelling women used to collect with their rusty dark pliers from the mouths of the village children.

'Do you know the day?' asked the lady. Lux snapped out of her distraction, and looked up at the lady, remembering too late that she was not supposed to look at her face. The gold reflected on the lady's skin, radiating a glow from her like an icon. Lux cast her eyes quickly down.

'Yes, my lady. It is Sunday, my lady.'

The lady raised her hand to one of the golden boxes, running her finger along the shining edge. Her voice, when she spoke, seemed wistful – but there was an odd bitterness to it. 'It is Saint Valentine's day. Some say that it is linked to desire and fertility, and that today is the best day for girls to go courting. Have you ever thought what it might be like to have a husband?'

Lux didn't know what the right answer was, so she said nothing. Had the lady really called her here to ask her about husbands? She realised then what she had never considered before: there were no children in the stronghold. The kitchen girls gossiped about Goodwife Ethelinda, and how she had no babies: Hulda said she must use something to stop them, which was against God; Linden, who always said stupid things, said she must birth babies and then kill them; Amity said they must fuck in a way that didn't cause children, and they all ended up collapsing into stifled giggles to think of Goodwife Ethelinda putting her husband's cock in strange places, both on her body and around the house. But Lux had never thought these things about the lord or lady, and now she felt her cheeks grow hot.

The lady waited expectantly, then must have concluded that Lux was simple, and sighed. She turned away from the golden boxes and towards Lux.

'My lord has asked something of you,' said the lady. 'Do you understand?'

'Yes, my lady,' said Lux. 'I will do what he asks.'

The lady laughed at that, a sudden joy forced out of her like a cough, unlike the high shivering sound that passed for her laugh in the great hall. 'What thoughts you have. Of course you will do what he says. That is the purpose of all of us beneath this roof. My lord wishes you to join the mummers.'

'But I'm a food-taster, my lady.'

'And before that you were a kitchen girl. Which do you prefer?'

'Food-taster, my lady.'

'I changed you from one thing to another. Now I will make you something else.' The lady held Lux's gaze, until Lux remembered herself and looked down. 'My lord sees something in you.'

'What –'

'You will only speak,' said the lady sharply, 'if I ask you a question. The purest woman is one who says nothing at all.'

The speaking of that phrase by the lady raised an obvious question about her purity, but Lux knew better than to ask it. She felt her heart beat harder. Hulda said the lord could tell by looking whether a girl had known the devil. What had he seen when he looked at her?

Lux pressed her hands hard into her thighs. She hadn't known the devil. It wasn't true what the boys had said about her in the forest, whatever story the girl from the sanctuary had told. She had to hold on to that: it wasn't true. The truth was that she had loved a man. He had seemed so much more than that at the sanctuary, not just to her but to all the girls. How they'd swooned in their trances and shrieked out their confessions. How they'd wandered unknowing among wolves disguised as lambs. They were just scared girls, alone in the world. But even though she'd loved him, Lux had sent him to burn – not a witch, but just a man. So she knew that it didn't matter if a story was true. It only mattered if people told it.

'The mummers have recently arrived at the stronghold,' continued the lady. 'The lord has commanded a special performance from them at the carnival feast before the beginning of Lent. A story of wicked and warning and God's justice. A story of a good man prevailing.'

Lux went to speak, then remembered herself.

The lady's voice, surprisingly, was soft; it seemed Lux's silence pleased her. 'The lord wishes you to be in it. You in particular.' She rested a hand on Lux's cheek. Her skin was the softest thing that Lux had ever felt;

softer even than Best Rabbit's fur. 'It's simply a role like any other. We women play them well, do we not?'

'Yes, my lady.'

'So you will play this one. My lord says you are well suited to it, and he is never wrong. It pleases him to see this story told, and it seems you're the one to tell it. My lord tells me ...' At this, the lady slid her hand to Lux's chin, using it to tilt her face this way and that, observing. 'He tells me you remind him of a person who died long ago. Do you understand?'

'N ... not really, my lady.'

The lady let go of Lux's face with a sigh. 'No matter. You needn't understand it. You need only do it. This will be in addition to your food-taster duties, which you are free to discuss, and your work on the garden, which you are not.'

Silence; Lux chanced a look up. The lady stood by one of the golden boxes.

'Come closer,' she said. Lux obeyed. 'This is a reliquary. Do you know what that is?'

'No, my lady.'

'All of the items in this room are reliquaries. They contain relics – the holy remains of saints. There is great power in even the tiniest parts: a fingernail, a tongue, a toe.' The lady touched Lux's hand as a command, and Lux stepped closer to the box. The lady's skin smelled of rose petals. Something inside Lux throbbed pleasantly. 'This one is the fingertip of Saint Melia. It is very holy and precious. Do you see it?'

'I can't see anything, my lady.'

'It's very small. You need to look harder.'

Lux looked harder. The cushion was very red and very empty. She thought then of the scrap of red ribbon she still wore tied around her upper arm; how she'd told Goodwife Ethelinda that only the most pious could see the words of God on it. 'Yes, my lady,' she said. 'I see it.'

'Good. There's a reason I asked you to come to me in this room. I need you to be able to see things even when others do not. Now go and watch the lord's meal being prepared.'

Before closing the door – being careful not to touch the carving of the man vomiting sausages – Lux glanced back. The lady stood alone in the middle of the golden boxes which were apparently full of tiny bits of dead people. She was very still. Perhaps, thought Lux, she was praying.

Lux shut the door as quietly as she could, leaving the lady alone in the empty, gleaming room.

It was early still; Lux was the first girl up. It wasn't her job to milk the cows, but she was going to do it anyway, as it was the only way she could think to get out to see Else.

Dew dampened her ankles and the pre-dawn sky was cold and blue. But the daisies would soon open, and Lux's breaths no longer chilled her throat. Spring was coming.

'Else,' she whispered into the pigs' house – but Else, sleepless, hunger-less, timeless, emerged instead from the poison garden.

'Lux!' she cried. Beneath her hood, Else's face was all shadows. She pulled Lux close in an embrace. Her skin was colder than the morning air. 'I was worried about you.'

'There is much to tell,' said Lux, leading Else to the milking shed.

She explained as best she could everything that had happened in the past weeks, about being the food-taster, about the Unmaking feast, about being in the mummers' play, about church and the men with whips and the woman in branks; but there was so much, and her words tangled around one another.

'And the lady said a strange thing to me,' said Lux, trying to slow her words so that Else could catch up. 'That the lord told her I reminded him of someone.'

They were about to enter the dusty warmth of the milking shed, but Else took hold of Lux's wrist, pulling her back.

'Who?'

'I don't know,' replied Lux. 'She didn't tell me. Only that it was a person who died. I think – Else, do you think it could be my mother? Do you think he saw her before she drowned? Do you think he sees her in me?'

Else let out a bitter laugh. 'I don't doubt he did see her.' Her grip on Lux's wrist tightened. 'Has he asked you about her?'

'He's never even spoken to me. He's only looked at me once.'

Else glanced around nervously before relaxing her hold and following Lux into the shed.

'We must be careful,' said Else.

'I am careful,' replied Lux. 'I do what I'm told. I watch in the kitchen. I taste the food. And now I do the mummers' play.'

Lux approached the tethered cow, murmuring nonsense words in a low voice, patting the cow's slow-heaving side. Behind her, Lux heard Else moving around the milking shed, picking things up and putting them down again. It seemed she wanted to say something, but couldn't settle on it.

Lux spat into her hands and wiped the udders with the warm spit to bring down the milk, letting the first few dusty squeezes spatter into the dirt.

'Tell me about the play,' said Else finally. 'Tell me what story is so important to him.'

'I don't know yet. The mummers will tell me. I'm to do the food-tasting for the lord, and tending the garden for the lady, and now the play for the mummers too. Though I suppose all of it is for the lord really.' She shunted her stool closer to the cow, so her forehead pressed against its warm side. Many a morning she'd dozed off like that, full of the smell of milk and hay and dust. She cupped the cow's teat in her palm and began to pull.

'So he has a story that matters to him,' said Else from somewhere behind Lux, and it was as if she was talking only to herself. 'That is something we can use. The lord has to die, but we must make sure there's a scapegoat. Harder if she's the food-taster, but easier then to put something into his –'

'Else,' said Lux, not looking up from her task. 'I can hear you.'

Lux shifted the bucket with her feet; she'd moved through the first teat, and it was soft and wrinkled. She moved on to the next.

'I wonder how easy it might be for you,' said Else, her voice light as if she really were only wondering, 'to put a thing in someone's food that shouldn't be there. If it could be done in such a way that suspicion would not fall on you. It would fall, surely, on one of the kitchen girls instead. You must have a least favourite among them.'

'It's not that simple,' said Lux.

'People die every day.'

That, at least, was true. People did die every day. There was a story going around the kitchen about one of the yellow-hooded women being attacked by dogs. The previous priest had died of inhaling bad airs. And once in town Lux had seen a man who'd been put in the stocks and had stones thrown at him until he died. For what? Likely not much.

'A dose,' said Else, 'that wouldn't harm you, but would harm someone else. Your tolerance for poisons is high. You could take just enough that you would sicken, but recover.'

This, also, was true. But – Lux leaned against the cow's dusty, breathing side. Did she want to kill the lord? Else said he sent women to die – that he'd sent her mother to die. But he wasn't the one who accused her of witchery. That was the people of the village, who wanted their secrets to drown with her. The lord hadn't wronged Lux. If anything, he'd helped her. Now she could eat delicious food every day. She could grow her garden. She could be in a play.

The lady, Lux amended. It was the lady who had made those things happen.

And besides, how did she know that Else's stories about the lord were any more true than the ones the kitchen girls told? The rat heart seemed just as unlikely as a bear heart. Could a man who rode girls to pleasure also send them to drown?

And there were more questions. With the lord dead, was it likely she'd be kept on as a food-taster? Was it certain that if she sickened just enough, she would be free from suspicion? How soon would the lady remarry? Would the new lord need her? If he didn't, where would she go? She had no one and nothing in this world, and Else wanted her to give up what little comfort she'd managed.

But she couldn't ask Else any of these things. So she said nothing about it, and carried on with her work. The smell of the milk spurting into the bucket reminded Lux of something.

'The men outside the church in town,' she said, 'hitting themselves with whips.'

'The flagellants.'

'There was a smell. And not just the smell of them – I don't suppose they bathe that often, and they'll have walked a long way, and probably don't get a chance to wipe their arses etcetera. But there was something else. I'm sure I smelled milk. And then I didn't know if it was because the priest was talking about milk, a poisoned mother cleansed by Christ, or something.'

'You weren't listening to the priest.' Else's tone was teasing.

'I *was* listening. I was just distracted because my hands had blood on them, and I could smell milk too.'

'It was the flagellants. They soak the lash in milk and then freeze it solid. Then as they walk, they shout out their confessions and whip themselves. As their blood starts to flow it softens the whip. The milk and blood mix.'

'Why?' asked Lux, but before Else could reply, she laughed and added: 'Why anything?'

Perhaps it was true, what the lady had said: things didn't need to be understood, they only needed to be done.

Else drew closer, resting her hand on the cow's broad side, her voice low. 'Tread carefully, Lux. You must play these new parts well. There's much we can do with them. We've come this far.'

I have, thought Lux. I have made my way into the stronghold, to the upper rooms, right to the lord's table. You have stayed out here with the pigs. And was that really what she'd agreed? Back in the forest, in the light of her burning house, is this what Lux had wanted? She'd thought Else could give her more. She let her head drop, breathing in hay and milk and the faint, sweet smell of shit. She almost slipped asleep there, with her hands keeping rhythm and Else pottering around behind her.

Although Else had never said she was a north witch, Lux had still believed it was true. Had hoped. But she thought now that she had been mistaken. Else didn't command anyone. She couldn't make anyone be anything. She didn't burn with power. But someone else at the stronghold did.

Lux snapped awake when Else spoke.

'When we first came here. The goodwife with the candle, checking your skin.'

'I remember,' said Lux. 'She was checking for black roses, to see if I had any signs of the sickness. But I didn't, so there was nothing to worry about.'

'That's not what she was checking for. She was checking for a teat to suckle the devil.'

Lux paused, her hands still circling the cow's deflated udders. She didn't know whether to laugh. But no, that wasn't true: she did know, and felt a chill.

'It's what the witch-hunters look for,' went on Else. 'A sure sign of guilt.'

Lux pulled, pulled, pulled to the slow beat of her heart. The last of the milk spurted into the bucket. 'But we don't have that. We don't have teats to suckle the devil, do we? So it's fine.'

'Today the teat is a sign of guilt. Tomorrow it's something else. Something we do have.'

'But no one thinks I'm a witch, Else. They think I'm a kitchen girl, and a food-taster, and a mummer in a play.'

'That is a lot of things for one person. It's witch work to heal poisons. If you can be all of those things at once, you can be a witch as well.'

Lux thought then of Hulda, sending women and men from her village to die, and getting no slaps in return. Things that were bad for some people could be good for others.

In the bucket of milk, a spot of red. Lux snatched her hand back from the cow's udder, but it was fine: no scratch, no injury. The froth settled, making the blood spread and spiral.

'Else,' said Lux.

In three steps Else was beside her. Together they stared into the bucket.

'Shall I tip out this milk and start again?' asked Lux. 'There won't be enough if I do that, and Goodwife Ethelinda will know something is wrong. Shall I scoop out the blood? I'll go to the kitchen for a ladle –'

Else picked up the pail by the handle and spun it around, right up over her head. Lux cried out, sure the whole lot would dump out onto the ground, but it didn't. Else put the bucket down, and when Lux peered in she saw that the surface of the milk was smooth and perfect. The blood was gone.

'Good as new,' said Else. 'White as white. No one would ever know it was otherwise.'

3

Now She is Whore

The next day's kitchen talk was of men. All the kitchen girls thought of was getting a husband; there was a much-lamented lack of men, as they were so apt to die in battles and fights and accidents. A woman could bleed every single month and still be strong, but men were flimsier. It seemed to Lux that the girls were fighting over bits of leftover gristle.

They spoke of the pedlar who brought spices. They spoke of the guards at the gate. They spoke of each other's brothers, whether they lived nearby or not. They even spoke of the man they'd seen in town leading his wife in a branks, which seemed particularly silly to Lux, as he obviously already had a wife. Some of the girls were of the opinion that the branks was a good sign, as it meant he was unhappy with his wife and might be available soon. Why they'd want a man like that, Lux didn't know; but then again, perhaps there was no such thing as a man who wasn't like that.

None of the men, in fact, seemed appealing to Lux. But she understood why the girls spoke of them with desire. She'd been hungry before, and knew she'd be hungry again; at those times, even a skinned rabbit, raw on the inside and burned on the outside, will fill you.

They spoke, most of all, of the lord. It seemed that the lord occasionally plucked kitchen girls he'd taken a shine to out of the kitchen and into his private rooms. When the girls returned, they never spoke of the task they'd been summoned to do, but they often had red marks on their throats or arms, which they didn't try to hide, but flaunted. When they told this, the kitchen girls cast sly glances at Lux. It didn't take her long to realise that they thought she was the lord's whore. She wanted to laugh at that; ludicrous to think that the lord would cast an eye at a scrawny whelp like her, when he had the lady in his bed. Besides, she'd never even seen the lord outside of the great hall, and had certainly never been alone with him. But she knew that trying to convince the other girls of that would only make her look more guilty, so she said nothing.

Finally, Amity spoke directly to Lux, though the tilt of her chin made it clear she found it distasteful. 'Did the lady tell you how many there would be?'

How many dinners for the lord? How many bits of dead saints in the gold boxes? How many more tedious men to discuss? Lux continued to say nothing. If the girls didn't want to speak to her, then she didn't want to speak to them.

Hulda joined in with a sigh. 'How many men, Lux. In the group of mummers. Are they all men or some women too? How old? What do they look like? Do they say nice things? How are their teeth? Are they taller than me?'

'I don't know,' said Lux. 'I haven't met them yet.' There was no need for Amity or Hulda - or for anyone - to know about her time in the forest.

'Then when? Goodwife Ethelinda told us we'd have to cover your kitchen work as you're going to be in the mummer show. Not that you do much of that anyway these days.'

Lux shrugged. 'Tomorrow, perhaps.'

Amity couldn't help herself. 'And will you tell us then? Will they come and visit you here? Will you tell us when they're coming so we can get ready?'

Lux said nothing. She tried to smile in a pure way, as if she was above it all. There were so few opportunities to have a hold over someone; she'd take whatever chances she could get.

There were thirteen mummers, and all but one taller than Hulda. They said a lot of things, though Lux didn't think those things were what the kitchen girls would consider *nice*. She recognised the lanky form of Mister Gaunt, as well as Posy and Pock, and a few others: the brown-haired woman with the scar, the man with the hair bristling from his nose. She hadn't seen Ash, though; there were new faces, and old ones missing. She guessed the mummers joined and left whenever it suited them. She'd wanted Ash to see her; to see how far she'd come from running scared through the pines; how far she'd come from being the maiden. Ah well. She met the mummers in the small wood-panelled anteroom where the lady had taken Lux to look inside her mouth. Every time she swallowed, she caught the taste of tallow and cinnamon.

'Little light!' Mister Gaunt called to her. 'You went through the pines? Brave girl.'

'I did go through the pines,' replied Lux with a grin. 'And you didn't.'

'Certainly not. It's the safe and easy way for us, thank you very much.'

The mummers circled round Lux, eyeing her curiously.

'Didn't think much of her when she was the maiden,' said the woman with the one white eye. 'Can she manage the stang?'

'We're not doing that any more. We've a new show now,' said Mister Gaunt. 'That was our last,' he added in an aside to Lux. 'Riding the stang. Not actually doing it – that would be too much. It scrapes off too much skin. We'd get through too many girls.'

Lux didn't know what riding a stang was, but she refused to ask. The day was still new and she'd not yet broken her fast; the lord would not be awake for a while yet, and she couldn't eat until he did. She was tired and hungry and not in the mood for games.

'I'll tell you then, shall I, little light?' said Mister Gaunt.

'Lux,' said Lux, because she might not know anything else they were talking about, but she did know her own name.

'You don't know the meaning of your name, is it? You've a lot to learn from us.' Mister Gaunt didn't have many teeth, and the ones he did have were all at the front, but he showed them now. 'You've heard of charivari? Rough music? How about a skimmington ride?'

Lux kept her face plain. The white-eyed woman grinned. 'She's never ridden a stang, then. Seems if we were to lift those skirts up high, her thighs would have not a mark on them.' Lux wouldn't flinch, she wouldn't press her legs together tighter. They meant her no harm, she was sure; they merely wanted to fright her. Perhaps because they'd seen her as a scared girl in the forest, they thought they knew all she was. Well, they didn't know she'd hunted with a wolf, she'd crawled for days on bloody knees, she'd watched a man burn and got hungry for the meat of him. Lux wasn't so easily scared as they thought.

'Leave off her, eh? We need her sweet to play this.'

'Do we?' said the woman. 'Seems we need her the opposite.'

'Fair enough,' said Mister Gaunt, and his smile made Lux more uncomfortable than his not-smile. 'This was all before your time. They don't make people ride the stang any more. A crueller world, it used to be. It was a just reward for all sorts. A widow who remarries too soon after her husband's death. A woman who has a baby with no man around. A weak, womanly husband who lets his wife beat him. Can't let that sort of thing go unpunished, can you? It's against the natural order. The stang we play – the one people like the best – is for women who've shown their secret parts to those they shouldn't.' He was getting into character now; Lux could see the mummer in him. He treated her like an audience of one, strutting around the tiny room, taking up more than his fair space. He flung out his hands like a priest, regardless of who they might hit.

'You see, little light, it's a useful show. A communal humiliation. The stang is a long, rough, unshaven pole of wood. The sinner's hands are tied behind her back. She straddles the stang like a –'

'Like a witch on a broomstick,' interrupted the white-eyed woman, picking dirt from her nails. 'Riding the wood all night.'

Mister Gaunt grinned. 'Except she doesn't climb on willingly. Her knees are tied beneath the stang and the pole is carried through the town. She's given a good bounce, up and down, up and down, nice and hard. Hard it is on the thighs and the secret place between – all that hard wood, over and over.'

Lux didn't mean to flinch, but she couldn't help it.

'Don't you worry, little light! We only play at it.'

'People like to see us play it,' said the white-eyed woman. 'Releases the tension. Like popping a blister. In every village there's a woman who talks too much, shows too much, knows too much. Always, as they say, "a troublesome and angry woman, who, by her brawling and wrangling amongst her neighbours, does break the public peace, and beget, cherish and increase public discord". Stick a branks on every woman in the world, and the second you take it off, she's working that mouth again, spitting blood between her words. There's not much you can do to shut a woman up,' went on the white-eyed woman, 'unless you're her husband or her father, so it's nice to see her – or a version of her – taken down a peg, being spat on by righteous women, being pissed on by righteous men, a smack or two across the teats, and a good old eyeful of that damage left by the stang. And she's fine afterwards, too. Couple of scars, but she'll live.'

'Is that –' Lux's voice wobbled, and she took a moment to steady it. 'Is that what I'm to do? Bruise my thighs and get spat on?'

'Ah! Not you, little light. We've got a brand-new story for you. Special-like, right from the lord's mouth. He was very specific. You're to play the witch.'

Lux felt her heart stutter. The lord with his bear hearts and his chain of girls. Did he remember her mother? Did he see her in Lux? What did he want from her really?

'Why me?' she asked, trying to keep her voice steady.

'You're refusing?'

'No, I – why this story?'

'Ah, we don't ask that, little light. We don't question the story. We only tell it.'

A thought settled on Lux, soft as snow: they need me. The lord asked for me to play the witch, not the white-eyed woman or the woman with the scar. Me. While the mummers stay here in the stronghold, they have food and a roof. No me, no play, no roof.

'Is the story true?' she asked.

'Ah now,' said Mister Gaunt with a grin. 'That depends on who you ask.'

Lux had learned from the last time she went to see Else, and this time she didn't check the pigs' house. She crept instead behind it, to the poison garden. She thought she'd find Else busy with the plants – but that's not what she found. Else sat in the middle of the garden, the nettles high around her, their tops almost covering her, their spiked leaves stroking her cheeks.

Careful to cover her exposed skin with her skirts, Lux pushed the nettles aside. Else flinched and tried to hide what was in her hand, but Lux had already seen: a tiny piece of red ribbon. Else had been stroking it with her fingers, gazing down at it, lost in thought. It looked just like the ribbon Lux wore around her arm, the last thing she had left of her mother. She could feel it still against her skin – but could Else have cut off a piece? When they were in the forest and Lux was sleeping, when they were walking through the pines in the endless dark, when –

But Else was on her feet and the ribbon was gone.

'Lux,' said Else, and her voice was steady. Her cheeks were pale as bone and her eyes gleamed in the morning light.

'I came to tell you that I learned about the play,' said Lux. 'The lord wishes it performed at the carnival feast before Lent.' She carefully pushed a nettle aside with her sleeve and toyed with a foxglove, its bright purple bells soft against her fingers. 'He was very specific about how the story should go, and I suppose I have to do it the way he wants it, as he's the one who provides the food and the roof and the beds. But I don't like it. There are parts I like, where I get to surprise everyone and reveal that I'm not who they thought I was. But at the end, she has to die – *I* have to die – and I don't like that. I think the story would be better if I got to escape at the end. It would be a surprise. Why does the witch always have to die? Couldn't she –'

'You play a witch.' Else's tone was sharp.

Lux flicked the foxglove bell away and wiped the dust on her skirts. She thought of all the other places she'd been; all the other costumes she'd tried on. All the other people she'd tried to be. 'I've been a novice, an accuser, a maiden, a kitchen girl, a food-taster. Why is this any different?'

'He wants you to play a witch,' said Else. She swayed her hands among the nettles' stinging leaves as if they were cool water. 'He wants everyone to hear a story about a rotting, devilfucking witch who tempts a good and innocent man. That's it, isn't it?' But she didn't pause long enough for Lux to reply. 'He wants everyone to see how good he is. How righteous and holy. Making her the evil one so that he's good. He can't let anyone's sympathies falter.' She clenched her fists, ripping up a handful of nettles. 'So he sends women to die. Then he must remind everyone that they're not really women at all, but witches.'

'Else,' said Lux, 'it's only a story.'

'You know better than anyone that there's no such thing as *only a story*. You can't be complacent around him. We came here to poison him.'

'*You* came here to poison him. So do it.'

'It's not that simple,' said Else.

'That's what you always say – nothing is ever simple. Well, what if it is? What if I could just be this? Is that so wrong?'

'In your play,' said Else, each word said carefully as if stepping over sharp stones. 'When you play the witch. Don't play it too well.'

'Why?'

'This attention. It wasn't our plan.'

'*Your* plan.'

'You were one of many kitchen girls. It was easy to go unnoticed. Now you're at the lord's table, you're in a play in front of everyone. There are too many eyes on you.'

'What other choice do I have?' asked Lux. 'Tell the lord no?' She saw a weed among the poisons and pulled it out, throwing it over the pigs' house the way Else did.

'Nothing good can come from the lord. Women suffered because of him. Women died. Your own mother died.'

'But do I have to suffer too, just because she did? Do I always have to be cold and hungry? Do I have to be pursued and cast out by priests with crosses, or boys in a forest, or men on horses? Do I always have to be a filthy girl in a hovel, scrubbing around in the nettles?'

'You're in the nettles now,' said Else calmly.

'But it's different! They're not hurting me. I'm warm, I'm fed – what's wrong with wanting that?'

Else bowed her head, and Lux again had the sense that she was holding back tears. She put her hands out, and without thinking Lux went to her.

But she hadn't been mindful of the nettles that clustered all around Else, and their spiked leaves brushed against her bare skin. She flinched back with a cry, her skin already pinching and reddening.

Else ripped up a handful of dock leaves and held them out to her. Lux took them, rubbing her stinging hands until the pain faded. But Else had turned back to her poisons, and didn't reach for her again.

That night, all the girls wanted to hear about the mummers. They lay in a tangle in the dark, whispering so that Goodwife Ethelinda wouldn't hear, as Lux told them as much as she could. About Pock, who had the same wheat-pale hair as Ash, but a fuller mouth and a looser way of speaking.

About Posy, who had Ash's golden-freckled cheeks, but hair red like autumn leaves. About the brown-haired woman with the scar across her cheek, the one with one eye perfectly white, the one who limped. About the man with hair bristling from his nose and an eye stitched shut. They weren't so interested in them, though; mostly in Pock and Posy.

'Is Pock a girl or a boy?' asked Hulda.

Lux thought of Ash, and replied with a smile, 'No.'

'It must be one or the other,' said Hulda, managing to make a whisper into a grumble.

Lux said nothing. If Hulda wanted to know, she could ask Pock herself.

'Sometimes,' said Elen, her whisper even quieter than the other girls', 'things aren't one thing or another.' She told, as all the others held their breath to hear her, about how her mother used to call dusk and dawn the time of the wolf: somewhere between light and dark, between day and night, between reason and superstition. A time when witches came out. A time when a person could slip in between.

Eolande added – eliciting many giggles – that in her home country, saying a girl had seen the wolf meant she had known a man for the first time.

Linden told a story she'd heard from her mother, about bodies who died and went to their graves – but came back. Revenants, she called them: people who could walk around, and talk and eat and pick things up, but yet were dead. Or perhaps not dead, and not alive, but a little of each.

Later, Lux woke in the first flickers of dawn and found that the bed was cold. Usually, no matter the season, the nights were hot and stinking, the press of bodies and garlic breath filling the air. Lux didn't know where the other kitchen girls were, and right then she didn't care. She stretched out her legs and arms as wide as she could. She dreamt of people who were neither one thing nor another, and how they were dangerous for that, and how she wanted them anyway; of slipping her hands beneath Ash's clothes in the night and being surprised at what she found there; of the north witches straddling their cold mountains until they melted; of the lady.

She slept and dreamt like that until the other girls returned and pressed back against her outstretched limbs, forcing her again to take up her given space, and no more.

The corridor where Lux waited smelled of beeswax and stale farts. All the other mummers were in the great hall, playing their parts while everyone feasted. The smell out here was probably better than in the great hall, which would reek of strong cheese and bacon fat; all the milk and meat that couldn't be preserved had to be eaten before sundown, before the Lenten fast began.

Lux tried to pay attention, ready for her cue, but her mind kept ribboning away from her. Her dress squeezed her lungs tight and the weight on her shoulders made it a struggle to keep her head up. Although she'd tried to dismiss Else's words, they repeated in her head.

Instead of worrying, she pulled up her veil, shifted the contraption on her shoulders, and crept closer to the door. She peered around, trying to see if Else was there, but the edges of the hall were cast in darkness. She tried to forget Else, and watched the play.

It began with a man, as all stories do. He was Mister Gaunt but also he wasn't because now he was the lord; he was all men and also a special and particular man better than all other men, and also he was a humble man. For much of the first part of the play, the man did many things for many people, all good and godly, and much of it in rhyme because he was clever. He made wise decisions that were fair and yet also strong. He married his wife and they both wore blue to show their piety. He hunted in the forest and fed the spoils to the people, never taking more than his fair share. He did God's work. He was a good man.

But then.

A woman.

Lux's heart was thudding and her belly burned hot and her teeth held tight the tip of her tongue. She pulled in a breath and held it. It was time for her to cast a spell.

Lux appeared in the silence of the great hall like a deep-winter snowfall, covered in white from head to foot. Upon her shoulders was balanced a metal ring of candles. When she was sure everyone was looking at her, she bowed her head and leaned to the lamp on the wall to light her first candle. She turned, allowing each candle to be lit, her head still bent. Finally, when she had spun a full circle, all in one movement she lifted her head and pulled her veil back from her face. Perhaps there was a collective gasp, or perhaps she just wanted there to be.

She knew her face, painted white as lilac petals, was lit heavenly in the glow of the candles. The white veil covered her hair, and her dress was a snowy expanse from her throat to her feet. Stones as smooth and white as eggshell circled her neck and hung from her ears. She looked like she had been carved from marble.

She kept her eyes piously raised, but from the silence she knew that everyone in the hall had stopped eating to stare at her. Slowly, slowly, she stepped towards the man, her dress trailing behind her like she was melting, leaving a part of herself behind with each step.

The music began then: a slow drum beat. Breathe in – beat – breathe out – beat. Lux approached in rhythm. The man was the size of three regular men, his chest and limbs padded with horsehair and wreathed in leather. He wore cunningly hidden wooden pattens under his feet, so he towered over everyone. And on his head, a set of golden bull's horns. Behind him, at the high table, sat the lord. Lux would have expected that compared to his horsehair-padded version the lord would look smaller, sillier – but instead he seemed to glow with an inner heat, the rage and satisfaction of him sparking a memory in Lux: an eclipse, a great black coin sliding across the afternoon sun, a thing she'd seen as a child and forgotten until this moment.

But still, Lux's eyes were drawn not to the lord in all his pomp and costuming, but to the lady. The gleam of her. The silent power. The lady had summoned her several times to the little wood-panelled room for news on how the garden grew, on what the girls in the kitchen said, on which men's gazes lingered too long; Lux found herself telling everything she'd ever known about poisons and cures, to try to extend those snatched moments, to stay longer in that room with the lady.

The drum beat got faster as Lux approached the man; by the time she reached her right hand out to clasp his, it was fast, fast, fast as a hunted rabbit's heart.

As she took the man's hand, Lux smiled a pale smile. A tambourine shiver; a high wordless song began from the female mummers. The witch was casting a spell.

The man was dazzled by the flames, so he didn't see what everyone else did: her left hand twisting strange, arm lifting up to her side, palm raised, middle finger tapping to thumb to make a circle through which the devil could look. That was how witchery was made.

The man was under her spell. Entranced, he began to lean down to her, but he couldn't: the ring of candles on her shoulders made a wall of flame around her. A witch can pass through fire without being harmed, but a good man cannot. Lux took a breath and blew it out again, one, two, three: she puffed out the trio of candles in front of her, leaving the rest still burning. At that moment, she glanced around the hall, and to her surprise saw the familiar dark hood, the frozen posture. She felt a flame leap inside her: Else had come to watch her. In the darkness, blinded by her own light, Lux couldn't see the expression on Else's face. She hoped it was one of pride and wonder; no one had ever looked at Lux like that before, and she liked to think Else could be the first.

Lux lifted her head reverently as if she was about to receive the sacrament from the man. He leaned down to her and, as she began slowly to turn, blew out all her candles one by one.

The act that happened then, Lux didn't really understand. It wasn't actually shown, because that would be sordid, so instead the man and the maiden disappeared out of the great hall, holding hands, and the mummers played a piece about how awful and sinful the secret thing was, so sinful we must never speak of it, oh no actually let's speak of it some more, just to say how sinful it is.

Lux could only guess what that thing was, because now she wasn't the flame-cast maiden twisting spells around the pious man; she was Lux, hiding in the corridor with Mister Gaunt, both of them breathing hard and getting ready for the next part of the story. The mummers moved around the great hall, leaping high and swaying low as the story required, their voices projecting up to the ceiling like the priest in church.

Mister Gaunt helped Lux to lift the metal ring from her shoulders. As she ducked out from under it, he held it steady to ensure that no wax dripped onto her dress. Breathing hard from their exertions, Lux and Mister Gaunt waited. It was almost time. Lux was forbidden from fumbling around in case her white dress got smuts and muck on it, so she lurked by the door while Mister Gaunt reached for the prop they needed for the next part of the play. Their eyes were still dazzled by Lux's candles, each blink lighting an afterglow, and it seemed that Mister Gaunt was having trouble finding things in the darkness. It was strange seeing him like that, this man who stood taller than any man she'd ever known, this man who she'd seen refuse to bow to a hunter on a white horse, on his knees scrabbling in the dusty shadows.

Lux waited, peering into the great hall, trying to find Else at the edges. But her eyes were drawn back to the lady. As she glanced at her, the lady's eyes caught hers: she was watching! Lux felt a thrill. The lady drew everyone's gaze to her; but the lady – she was looking at Lux.

'Where is it?' Mister Gaunt hissed. Lux looked over her shoulder at him. 'Your lip paint! It should be here.' He cast his hands around again, but couldn't find it. 'We need your mouth red to show what's happened. Red makes them think of the hunt. Of blood and a maiden's just-split cunt.' He sat back. 'Shit. If they'd let me keep that rhyme in, we'd be fine. Perhaps I should say it anyway. I'd like to see the lady's face when I do.'

Lux's insides lurched at that. She didn't want Mister Gaunt, or any man, thinking of the lady like that.

'If we changed the story,' she said. 'If the witch won at the end, then we wouldn't need –'

'Hush,' hissed Mister Gaunt. 'There'll be no more talk of that. The lord wants his story, and we must always appease our betters if we want food in our bellies and a roof over our heads. What don't you understand about that?'

'But –'

'You're no better than us, little light.' Mister Gaunt's tone softened. 'You tell your own story, do you? You never go along with what other people say? How bold you are.'

Then Lux had an idea. She reached for Mister Gaunt's hand and raised it to her mouth. He froze, caught between laughter and anger, unsure what she was planning. She brought his fingertip to her lips, and with her two sharpest teeth, she nipped his skin. He went to pull back but she grabbed his wrist with her other hand and squeezed, watching as the blood beaded. Just before it dripped, she lifted his finger and painted her lips with his blood. She immediately wanted to wipe it off, but resisted. She held her face straight so the blood would dry without cracking. She released his hand, and he watched his blood wend a thin line down and pool in his palm.

'Witch,' he murmured, as if he'd just found out a secret.

Not yet, thought Lux.

He shook his head, trying to wake himself from a daze. He rubbed his bleeding finger on his thigh, as if trying to rid himself of something.

There was a moment where he looked almost afraid, but then his face split into a grin. He ripped a scrap of fabric from his undershirt, wrapping it tight around his finger to stop the bleeding. 'Could have bit your own,' he said.

Lux motioned to the smear of blood now marring his clothes, and her own white dress. She had to stay pure – until she was not. From the sounds in the great hall, it was time for the next part of the play.

Lux stepped out, a column of pale ice, unflawed – but now with her lips wet and red. Her gaze now was not pious and skyward, but direct: she went around the great hall, looking right in the eyes of every person there. Most looked away, some smiled or looked uncomfortable, one or two leered and licked their lips.

Now that everyone had seen the maiden's red-painted lips, the focus was back on the man. He staggered around the hall, leaning his great bulk on first one person, then another. He was suffering, witch-struck: a great man made flimsy, his holiness pricked by the devil's thorns.

Finally, the man collapsed to the ground in front of the lord's table, his great bull's horns twisted to the side. At that moment, at the other end of the hall, Lux leapt on a table and began to spin, her bare feet stamping on the wood. Her white skirts lifted higher, higher – she grabbed for them and lifted them as she leapt off the table and onto the floor, flipping her dress over to reveal the black witches' rags beneath. The collective gasp was real now. She smeared the red of her lips across her chin and cheeks as if she'd just feasted on raw meat. A demon she was now, frantic and slavering, not a hint of the maiden she was before.

Perhaps all maidens hide witches in their skirts. Perhaps all milk has blood mixed into it. No one would ever know it was otherwise.

The rest of the mummers convened, joining Lux as she climbed back onto the table and strutted up and down it, swaying her black skirts, enjoying how the fabric swallowed the candlelight.

As the maiden, Lux did not speak. But as the witch, her tongue would not lay still: the true mark of a devil-ridden woman.

'Now I will tell you,' said Lux, said the witch, her voice a scrape and a shriek, 'what I shall do to this sad and stricken man. By my actions he should suffer incessantly, such as the man of him deserves. He was not a beast, but I shall make him so. For the lust of me, take away from him drink, food, sleep, the power that he might have relations with his wife, and the knowledge of the words of God. Take all this from him until he is a hollow man, left with a gap in him the exact shape of me.'

Lux had thought that her voice would shake; she'd never been allowed to speak so many words in front of so many people. But her voice rang clear, and she took pleasure in the echo of it between the walls and the roof and every person in the room.

She wanted to look again at the lady, to see if she was still looking at Lux. But she found it wasn't the lady's face that she sought out then, but Else's. What did Else think of her speech? Was she proud to hear her steady voice?

As the candlelight shifted and flickered, she caught glimpses of Else's face under the hood. She seemed – it was difficult to tell, but with growing concern Lux realised Else seemed not to be watching the show in wonder, not bored or annoyed by it all, not even glaring at the lord in hate. It was an expression she'd never seen on Else's face, and she couldn't identify it.

But she had words to say, and she couldn't stop now. Around her, the mummers swept the feasters' plates aside and laid down their own witches' feast: snails and sliding animals, slopping innards and slurries of mud. They pretended to defecate on the plates. They pretended to vomit in barrels. They pretended to spit in one another's mouths. Through it all, the witch preached.

'Then let him come to me and satisfy all my desire,' she shrieked to the sky, 'and when I am finished with him, let him be cast aside with none of his faculties returned. He will be a wrung-out cloth upon a midden, the mere wrinkled skin of a man, and I shall fill myself with his goodness, and I shall grow fat on it. My belly will fill with light taken from him, and he will live forever in the shadows. This is his punishment for what he has done to me: for making me love without loving me back. For staying pure and light though I tempted him from my darkness.'

*

Finally the man was absolved, the witch was purified, the child she'd had by him was taken by Jesus to heaven. Darkness was vanquished and light prevailed, shown by the reappearance of Lux's circle of candles, which now she wasn't wearing but was dying in the centre of. It was her end, her glory, finally cleansed, the devil burned out of her. It should have been a triumph.

But all of it was nothing to Lux. All of it passed like a dream, unreal, because all she could think of was Else's face.

As she collapsed fake-dead in the middle of the ring of light, she knew only one thing. In the light of the candles, she could see Else's face, watching Lux pretend to die.

Else, who travelled alone through the forest, who could see in the dark, who commanded a wolf. Else, who never went hungry and never needed to sleep. Else, who could never be hurt.

Else was crying.

4

Now She is Poisoner

L ux lay sleepless for what seemed like the whole night, but couldn't have been; she woke shivering to an empty bed, and outside it was still dark. In her mind was Else's face, streaked with tears.

By the time she'd taken off her costume and made it back to the kitchen, all the other girls were getting ready for bed, and she had had to join them or have her absence noted. She'd wondered if they'd be envious of her for being in the play, or scornful of her for seeking attention, but all they wanted to know was whether the glimpses they'd seen of the younger mummers' bodies promised something more. Lux's protests that she hadn't seen any more of the mummers than anyone else in the hall were met with disbelief; it seemed they really did think she was a whore, and had fucked every boy in the place, and wanted details.

Now, waking in this empty bed was a blessing: she could sneak out and speak to Else without anyone knowing.

She wrapped herself in the woollen blanket and latched the kitchen door behind her. It was pleasant to be outside, even in the cold and dark. When she'd first come to the stronghold, it had felt strange to her to be indoors for so much of the day. As a child she'd never been indoors during daylight; there was the fire to be made, the water to be fetched, the garden to be tended, the dinner to be caught, the villagers to be healed or poisoned as requested; after all that there was little sun left. At the sanctuary there was honey to be collected, herbs to be picked, clothing to be washed in the stream; admittedly there were also prayers – so many prayers – and they were done indoors. Lux didn't like the thought that her prayers floated up to the pointed roof of the church and got caught there like dandelion fluff, mixing with the prayers of all the other girls. Even if they managed to escape from there, how would her words be separated from the others? Far better, in her opinion, to pray under the sky, where her words could fly straight up and not snag on anything. She'd missed this: the outside, the night-time.

Under her feet, the grass was cool and damp. The sky was a heavy dark blue, the moon a bright eye. It blinked as a cloud passed. But Lux didn't need light to see. She made her way by memory to the pigpen.

A shriek of laughter.

Lux paused and listened.

The low murmur of voices, threading from the distance. As Lux turned and walked instead towards the sounds, they lowered and rose, joining steady in a chant, passing clear on the cold air.

'First blood, then flames, then a man gives his name. First blood, then flames, then a man gives his name.'

On the far side of the garden, the golden gleam of firelight. Shadows passed before it, making it blink in and out, and Lux thought again of the eclipse. Soon she was close enough to identify outlines: six figures in long dresses, circling a fire, their pale fronts gleaming in the light, their hands raised with palms pressed one to the next.

'Blood!' they chanted. 'Flames! Blood!'

Lux crept forward, barely daring to breathe – until she tripped over a lump of earth, landing hard on her knees. She gasped before she could stop herself.

A shriek, and one of the girls broke the circle and leapt towards her. 'We weren't!' she cried out. She slapped her hand to her mouth to pull the words back, but they hung there on the night air.

The fire crackled. Lux could hear a chorus of heavy breaths.

Finally, Lux spoke. 'Amity?'

There was a collective sigh of relief. One of the figures turned away from Lux and back to the fire. 'Don't panic, it's only Lux,' said Hulda.

'Lux!' breathed out Elen, lowering her hands from her mouth. 'You frightened us. We thought you were Goodwife Ethelinda come to scold us for being out of our beds. Why are you creeping around in the dark?'

'Why are *you*?' Lux's knees were scraped, and she was annoyed.

'We're getting husbands,' said Elen.

Lux looked around pointedly. 'They must be very small. Or have you already finished with them and thrown them on the fire?'

'Let's not tell her,' said Amity. 'She'll only be horrible.'

'I won't be horrible,' said Lux. 'Perhaps I want a husband too.'

A husband was the last thing she wanted, and she was sure the other girls knew it. Amity snorted and turned back to the fire – but she didn't stop Elen from holding out her hand and letting Lux into the circle.

In the firelight, the features of Hulda, Linden, Elen, Amity, Eolande and the other Euphemia twisted and moved, their shadows thrown high on the walls. Lux was warm now; she dropped her blanket.

'So how do you –' Lux began, but then Hulda bent and picked up a large jar from the ground. Inside it, one skinny black leech writhed.

'First you fill the leech with your blood,' said Hulda. 'You have to leave it on for a while.'

Hulda lifted the hem of Amity's dress to reveal a large black birth-mark on her calf. Lux found it strange that she'd never noticed it before, though they shared a bed and wash-water.

Then the birthmark moved, and Lux shuddered as she realised it was a leech. The other girls lifted their skirts to reveal leeches on all their calves.

'I brought a spare,' said Amity, 'in case one died.' She took the jar from Hulda and unscrewed the lid. With a spoon, she scooped out the leech and waited for Lux to lift her skirt.

Lux thought of things she'd heard happening, like eggs containing strange prophecies written on the insides of their shells. A magical cow that could predict the weather based on where it shat. Things that didn't help anyone, but didn't harm anyone either. But they *did* cause harm, just not the way it was meant; her mother had died for promising power when she had none.

Lux could go, now, and she could tell Goodwife Ethelinda that all the other girls were prophesying. How Goodwife Ethelinda would listen to her then! What special things she might be allowed to have! Lux might get new clothes to wear, and her own bed, and –

Then she thought of the sanctuary, of sitting in a circle and twisting a urine-soaked cloth while talking about pricks. She'd said it didn't have to be urine and didn't have to be pricks; all she'd wanted was to sit in a circle and have a moment of light. Well, here was a circle. Here was light.

Lux hesitated, watching the leech writhe. Then she lifted her skirt, and Amity put the leech on her.

'It has to get really fat,' said Elen. 'Fatter even than the lord.' This last part whispered with a glance behind, a giggle, a manic gleam.

'The lord's *dogs* are fat, you mean,' warned Hulda, and Elen quickly agreed: 'Because they're so well fed, the lord is such a masterful hunter, and generous too.'

Even there, alone in the safety of the dark, they didn't dare insult the lord. He was all-knowing, all-powerful; you never knew when he was listening. The heart of a bear – of several bears – could make a man strong indeed. But then – Lux thought of all she'd observed of the lord. The bloodied bandage on his finger. His scent of incense and rot. The way he glanced always at the lady, as if checking he was doing things correctly. There wasn't much of the bear about him. And was it really so impressive that he managed to hunt and catch a creature that had been raised in captivity? The bear probably sat calmly on its haunches and waited for someone to bring it a fish.

'Anyway,' said Hulda, 'yours looks pretty fat now.' She set a twig alight at the fire, then held the flame to the leech on Amity's leg. It writhed and twisted, then dropped to the grass. One of the other girls made a sound of disgust, but was silenced by a glare from Hulda.

Amity set a cooking pot on the fire. She scooped up the leech with a spoon and dropped it into the pot. It sizzled and writhed. The stink of burned blood filled Lux's nose.

All seven peered into the pot, the base of which was now smeared with Amity's blood. Lux didn't know what she was looking for, but she looked anyway.

'I see a shape,' said Amity. 'Do you see?'

'It's a huh!' said Hulda.

'It surely must be Hugh, the town crier,' said Eolande in a serious voice. 'The one with all the nose hairs.'

Elen let out a sudden high laugh.

'If you're not going to do it properly,' said Amity, 'I'll throw your leech to the pigs.'

'It's Henry, the mummer boy,' said Hulda, in a voice that didn't invite argument. 'The dark-eyed one.'

Amity seemed pleased with that, and Eolande lifted her skirt to go next.

'Why the leeches?' said Lux, trying to resist the urge to flick hers off her leg and pretend it had fallen. It didn't hurt, but she didn't like the thought of it there, sucking out parts of her. She thought then of the poor food-taster, turned inside out with all his blood gone.

Hulda furrowed her brow. 'To get the blood, idiot. Would you have us slice our palms open?'

'You could wait for your blood to come,' said Lux. 'Use that instead. Then you won't have to put the leech on you. And anyway, wouldn't the blood from there be more . . .' Lux didn't know the word *potent*, but that's what she meant. She'd heard many times at the sanctuary that a woman's blood made her unclean; and it must be true, because when the girls fasted for a long time, their blood stopped coming, showing that God had favoured them. A woman's blood could turn wine sour, could kill beehives, could turn crops barren. It was powerful.

She thought then of Father Fleck at the sanctuary. How he told the girls all this, never seeing how one thing went against the next. How could it be that a woman's blood, her ability to make life, was her only value? Father Fleck told them that the whore of Babylon would mount the beast and the abominations born of her lust would devour the world – and at the same time, Lux's inability to make anything be born from her was what made her dangerous. How could the ability to make life be a woman's only good thing and also her worst thing? Father Fleck hadn't told the girls that to cleanse them. He wanted only to shame them for things they couldn't help. A flame rose up in her then. She wished it would reach Father Fleck, and burn him.

'She can't,' said Amity. 'She doesn't get her blood.'

'No, I know not today, but if she waits until it's time then –'

'I won't be getting my blood,' said Hulda.

'Are you having a baby?' Lux asked.

Hulda rolled her eyes and pulled her shift tight against her belly to show its flatness. It wasn't just flat, it curved inwards, her bones the mouth of a shallow cave. 'Does it look like it? Anyway, I can't have a baby when I haven't got a husband, now can I?'

'No,' said Lux, though they'd all heard of women with a baby and no husband, and what became of them. 'Won't your husband be angry when you can't give him babies?'

'He won't know, will he? No man would think to ask about your blood before he married you. And it'll be too late when we're wed.'

'Yes,' said Lux, though a man could certainly get rid of a woman if he didn't want her any more. Just as a woman could get rid of his baby by him if she didn't want it any more. People died every day.

Lux thought of how she'd been sent to the sanctuary because of her lack of blood; how she'd tried so hard to keep it secret from the other girls, thinking they'd be suspicious of her. She wanted to tell Hulda then, about this thing they shared, but she hesitated. Hadn't Hulda sent women to the drowning posts? Women who couldn't have babies were unnatural, that's what the priests said: one step from witchery. Was that why Hulda had accused others – to take the suspicion off herself?

Well, Lux wouldn't tell anyone about Hulda. But she wouldn't tell Hulda about herself either.

Elen said something that Lux didn't catch, and Eolande made a sound of protest.

'I never said that!' said Eolande in an urgent hiss. 'I said I could *un*witch. I never said I could witch. That's wicked talk.'

'I only meant,' said Elen, but she spoke so quietly that Lux didn't hear what she meant.

That disagreement faded when they moved on to Hulda's leech, but another reared when Hulda said that Elen's and Eolande's blood both made a muh, which was clearly for Merik, the guard at the pine forest – which was all fine if it meant the younger one with the rosy cheeks and underbite, but not if it meant the older one with the much-broken nose and crossed eyes. From what Lux could tell, both men were called Merik, but apparently it mattered very much which Merik you got. Luckily, Hulda decided it meant the younger Merik, and the disagreement was over. Lux wondered how Elen and Eolande could both marry the same Merik, but perhaps that was a disagreement for another day.

Lux's blood looked to her like nothing at all, but it was decided it was an el, for the lord – not the actual lord, but the raw-boned mummer who was the lord in the play. Lux was amused to think of herself as Missus Gaunt, but didn't argue. Besides, she didn't know her letters, so she couldn't have argued even if she wanted to.

They made ready to go back to the kitchen, and Lux realised that if she went with them then she wouldn't get to see Else.

'I'll stay and kick out the fire,' she said. 'Make sure the leeches are all burned up.' The other girls traipsed away, pleased or irritated by the shapes of their blood, already thinking of the day's work. But Hulda lingered, eyes narrowed.

'I want to let the ashes cool and lay some grass on top in case anyone sees,' said Lux. 'I know the game with the leeches isn't witchery, but ...' She let it sit, watching Hulda's face.

'You're right,' said Hulda. 'It's not. The same as Goodwife Ethelinda's walnut full of quicksilver isn't witchery. And Amity throwing salt over her shoulder to unseat the devil. And you slipping something into Eolande's food to cure her bellyache.'

'I didn't –'

'It doesn't matter,' said Hulda. 'If it's not witchery.'

She turned to go back to the kitchen. Then she stopped.

'The mummers leave today,' said Hulda, without turning to look back; Hulda whose blood she'd decided was the face of the mummer Pock. 'You won't bring their meal. I will do it.'

'Yes,' said Lux, smiling, after a pause.

Lux wandered in the lessening dark to the pigpen. She was half in dreams, and she almost screamed when a hand closed around her arm.

'Else! You scared me.'

Else's hood had slipped back. Her eyes were wild and the scars around her mouth held tiny shadows. She didn't say anything; just gripped Lux's upper arms tight. It wasn't quite an embrace; more like Else wanted to pull Lux close but was stopping herself.

'*You* scared *me*,' said Else.

'How can I have scared you when you're the one hiding in the dark waiting to grab people?'

'There's nothing to be afraid of in the dark. The danger isn't out here. It's in there.' Else nodded towards the stronghold, a deeper dark against the night sky.

'You were at the play,' said Lux. 'Why were you crying?'

'I wasn't.'

'You were there, and you were crying.'

'It...' Else released Lux's arms and stepped back, turning away so Lux couldn't see her face. 'I saw how everyone believed it. It was the lord's story and everyone believed it. It made me think of a time I told a story, but no one believed it.'

Else reached into her cloak and pulled out a parcel. The parcel looked small and pale, wrapped in a scrap of fabric. Harmless. But Lux felt the pulse of it, the danger.

She held the parcel out to Lux. 'Put this in the lord's food. We've waited too long. I've put you in too much danger. I thought I was so clever, but other people can be clever too. I let you forget the wolf. Eating sugared figs, playing around in crowns of candles, flirting with fancy ladies. None of it's real. It never was.'

'Why can't it be real? My mother stayed in that house my whole life, even when she should have left. She could have lived if she'd left, but she didn't. I won't go the same way.'

'Your mother –' Here Else faltered. 'Your mother had her reasons for staying. But it's no different in the stronghold than in that house. You're still doing what everyone else tells you to do and being what they say you are. This is how you make things change.'

Lux looked at the parcel, but didn't take it. 'What is it?'

'It doesn't matter.'

'*What is it?*'

Else held her gaze. 'You know what it is. Nightshade, hemlock, mandrake, henbane. Just like you said.'

Lux caught the tip of her tongue between her teeth and pressed down, trying to quiet herself. 'When I said it, this isn't what I meant. I can't poison the lord. Would you have me die for this? Me, tied to a drowning post or sent to burn, all for your petty revenge?'

'He'll kill you if you don't. It's the only way. I would do it myself, but I...'

'But you don't want to die?'

'I'd die a hundred times for you, Lux. But you're the only one who can get close enough. I brought you here because I wanted the lord gone. For your safety. But I can't do it by myself. I need you.'

Lux felt something for Else then that she'd never felt for her before: scorn.

Else had no power. She needed Lux to do everything for her. She wasn't like the lady. Every time she saw the lady, she felt anew the power of her; the gleam, the burn. If the lady's bare skin ever touched the ground, it would burn black.

'I won't,' said Lux, and she pulled away from Else and let the parcel fall to the ground.

'Lux,' said a voice, far too close, and Lux's blood leapt. Hulda, standing two hands'-breadths away. Lux turned so that her blanket covered the ground where the parcel lay, telling herself that Hulda couldn't know by looking, she couldn't have heard anything, she couldn't know.

'What is it?' Lux kept her voice calm, as if wandering around at midnight and arguing with the swineherd was a perfectly normal thing to do. She looked up and saw that Else had already merged with the shadows; better, perhaps, if Hulda thought Lux was talking to herself.

'I forgot to tell you,' said Hulda, her face sly. 'When dawn comes, the lord wants you.'

Lux was up with the light. She washed and dressed and went to the lord in the relic room. Just as when she'd gone to the lady there, she hesitated outside the door. The smell of the lord filled her nostrils even through the thick wood: a heavy sweetness of cloves and incense, with a faint tang of rotting meat. She wondered which part of his body the smell came from. His mouth? His armpits? Or somewhere lower?

She reached out to the carvings on the door, all sex and death, but didn't dare touch them in case they stained her skin somehow and the lord saw. What if Else was right? What if the lord really did wish her harm?

'Enter,' boomed a voice from beyond the door, and Lux's blood leapt. But of course the lord knew she was there. The lord sees all.

She pushed open the door. Again she was struck by the heavy blackness of the tarry interior, the way it swallowed the light and gave nothing back.

The lord stood in the middle of the room, wide as a bear in his velvet and furs. Lux dipped her head to a bow. His boots were as big as dogs, his tree-trunk legs bulged, and his bull-wide shoulders were draped in velvet the colour of blood. Around his neck hung a rope of jewels, each the size of a robin's egg. Lux's mouth watered; she wanted to snatch a jewel from the rope and keep it for herself. Keep it under her pillow and when the other girls were asleep take it out and marvel at it, watch the way the moonlight changed its colours. Surely he wouldn't miss just one, when he clearly had so many. Lux knew that the relic room must still be the same size it was before, which was twice the size of the house where she'd lived with her mother – but now, with the lord in it, the room seemed the size of a cupboard. It didn't seem there was space for her to be in there too. She wondered if the ground shook when he walked. If fruit was shaken ripe from the trees to land at his feet. If he could reach to pluck birds down from the trees, and if he held a bird in each hand and bared his teeth and bit their little heads –

'Speak, girl,' said the lord, and Lux realised she was standing silent in the doorway, moony-eyed. She hoped she hadn't accidentally looked the lord in the face. She bent her head down until the bones in her neck cracked.

'Yes, my lord.'

'Is that all you have to say?'

Lux had no idea what she was meant to say. 'Yes, my lord?'

'It's clear to me that you are not the brightest girl. But even in the dark we can find useful things. I made the correct choice in selecting you as my food-taster, as I still live. And as long as I stay alive, you will stay alive.'

As Lux recalled, it was rather the lady who had chosen her. But perhaps the lord was not the brightest lord.

The first time she'd heard the lord speak, she'd thought he sounded like he had something in his mouth. Now that she was so close to him, she realised what that thing was: his tongue. It seemed too big for his mouth, and he was taking care to speak clearly around it. His voice was so deep it seemed to shiver the air around her.

'I will tell you,' said the lord, 'why I chose you to play my witch. The evil thing I sent back to hell. My tormentor, who cursed me with a wound that would not heal. You have the look of her. But I think there's more than that. I think you have a little of her power.'

'No, my lord! I have no power. I have nothing. I –'

'Quiet, girl. I think you can undo what she did.' The lord stepped closer. A single step and he'd crossed the whole world. The room was so small, so close, and he was so big, and Lux felt her gorge rise as the rot-spice smell of him filled her. He reached out a hand to touch Lux, then seemed to think better. She swallowed hard. 'Truth is a stranger to all women. So it's a good thing I'm not listening to you. I see the darkness in you, and I intend to use it.'

'But, my lord, I –'

'You are what I say you are. Now, a test. You will select something for me.'

This must be a trick, though Lux couldn't see how, or what the lord could gain from it. He surely had more important things to do than trick servant girls.

'Choose,' said the lord, and spread his hands.

Lux played her role as the dim girl, and stared blankly at the middle distance. The lord snorted in annoyance.

'Inside each of these pretty little boxes is a relic. Do you know what a relic is, girl?'

'Yes, my lord.'

'You will choose one of these relics. You will tell me whichever one speaks to you of the strongest power.'

Lux hesitated. If she selected the right one, she was a witch and could die for it. If she selected the wrong one, she would displease the lord and could die for it. She didn't want to do it. She wanted to run out of the room and back to the kitchen and she wanted to never be in a room alone with the lord again.

'Your life,' said the lord casually, 'is only as long as your use to me.'

Lux thought of her mother – her rot-toothed, pop-jointed, thick-blooded mother, who sprouted mushrooms in her footsteps and vomited black bile. Her mother who had kept them both alive with her stories. What would her mother do?

'Yes, my lord. The relics are ... very powerful. I was merely over-whelmed.' Lux swept her gaze along the rows of elaborate golden boxes lining the walls. The light caught on the glass windows, making them wink at her.

'Some, uh ... some more than others.' The lord stood in the middle of the room, hands on hips, watching her. 'I must – concentrate, my lord.'

How was she supposed to choose? She was no witch. She had no power, no darkness in her. And even if she was a witch, how would she know which bit of dead flesh held the most magic? The lord couldn't believe they were really all from saints. Lux had met several pedlars in the forest who made their living by paring bits of corpses and selling them as holy objects. They hadn't called them relics, though, but some-thing much ruder.

She ran her fingertips over the boxes, pretending to consider them each in turn, but really looking at the lord over her shoulder. Now that he wasn't paying attention, she was free to observe him a little. She'd stood by his table many times, but after that first time, she had avoided looking at him. The intimacy of his body in this small room was overwhelming: he was the size of a bull, and his smell was so strong it felt like fingers forced into her nostrils. She heard a clacking and realised the lord was restless behind her, the rings on each of his fingers knocking together as he fidgeted. The difference between the lord at table and the lord now was that he was without his carved bull's head armour. Bare, the back of his neck was surprisingly narrow. Lux felt a strange urge to reach up and touch the back of his head to check for a soft spot, like on a baby.

It surely wasn't appropriate for them to be alone together. But the lord had wanted it, and lords got what they wanted.

Despite what her eyes had told her when she'd been here with the lady, she'd thought that the boxes must all have something in them; that the objects were very small. After all, no one would take an elaborate golden box and cover it with gems and place a silken pillow inside – and then leave the pillow empty. But now that she had the time to look closely, she saw that quite a few of the boxes were indeed empty.

'This one, my lord,' said Lux, resting her hand on the nearest box that contained something she could see. The box was a simpler one, plain gold without adornments, and the thing inside looked like a piece of inexpertly dried bacon.

The lord narrowed his eyes. 'You are sure, girl?'

'Yes, my lord.' Too late now if she'd somehow chosen wrong.

'But of course it would be this one. A strip flayed from the leg of Saint Jarrow.'

'It is very powerful,' Lux agreed. 'I see many things in it. It speaks darkly to me.'

At that, the lord seemed to flinch back from her. Lux felt her heart stutter. Could he be afraid of her? The lord, a giant wrapped in costly cloth, who had more power in his earlobe than she could ever dream of wielding? And she made him flinch. Perhaps she did have a little power. Or perhaps she'd gone too far.

But the lord had already forgotten her; he was busy opening the box and taking out the little bit of meat. He held it reverently.

'I've sent away all the healers,' he said. 'Useless, all of them. I saw what they did to my food-taster. He died puking and shitting and bleeding all over the place. He was barely even a man by the end of it. I refuse to die like that. Do you hear me?'

'Yes, my lord,' whispered Lux, although he didn't seem to be listening to her anyway.

'You will heal me instead. Whatever curse that devil-bitch put on me, you'll know it. You'll undo it.'

Lux felt hope spark in her, a single candle flame in the dark. If all he had was a stubborn wound, she could heal it. Or at least, she could try. A daub of honey to clean the wound. A poultice of comfrey and garlic to draw out any rot. Spider webs or egg white to seal it, tied on with sage leaves. If there was pain, then a little mandrake root.

But Else wanted her to kill the lord, not heal him. Lux didn't know how she could both heal and kill the same man.

'You'll heal me, won't you, girl?' There was a wet sound as the lord swallowed. Lux had never been so aware of another person's body before. She wished the room was big enough that she could take a step back.

The lord took the snuffer from the wall and went around the room, killing all the flames except for one – the one beside Lux. She was dazzled by its gleam at the corner of her eye, and couldn't see anything beyond it. She felt the lord as a looming presence, unlit, filling the room.

'I am the light,' said the lord from the gloom and the dust, holding the flesh of a dead stranger in his hand. 'I am the light, and I will defeat the dark.'

Lux flinched as the lord bent down and laid his hand along her jaw, his thumb against her lower lip. The gold of his rings felt hot as a brand. For one awful moment, she thought he was going to force open her mouth and make her eat the relic.

'Show me that tongue, girl. Show me what saves my life.'

Lux closed her eyes and parted her jaws. She waited for the press of the lord's thumb, forcing its way into her mouth. She waited for the wrinkle of the ancient dead on her tongue.

But after a moment, his hand was gone, and he was gone, and she was alone. The breeze from his billowing furs as he left blew out the final candle.

Lux stayed for as long as she dared. She could taste the lord on her tongue. She could feel him inside her. But there, keeping company with shadows, nothing could get to her. In the dark, she was safe. For now.

When she got back to the kitchen she stole a clove of garlic and chewed it whole, to get the taste of him out of her mouth.

The next day, all the kitchen girls got their blood – except Hulda, which the other girls knew about, and Lux, which they didn't. Eolande and Elen both wore pouches of sweet herbs at their waists to cover the smell, Linden and Euphemia begged off milking the cows, and Hulda and Amity whispered about it at night – how strange it was that they'd all begun at once. It had never happened before. Perhaps it was a portent, coming the day after their spell with the leeches. Perhaps it meant they were all due husbands. Lux didn't know about that; it seemed to her it just meant they'd all waste more time soaking rags in cold water.

Later, when all the other girls had gone out on errands and they were alone in the kitchen, Hulda put the loaves into the oven and said suddenly to Lux: 'I'm not going to accuse you of anything.'

'All right,' said Lux, not sure what else to say.

'I know what everyone says about me. That I sent all those people to be killed.'

You did, thought Lux, but said nothing.

'It's not as simple as that.' Hulda's voice grew thick, the words coming harsh. 'I was accused first. Because I didn't get my blood. Everyone knew, the way everyone always knows everything. They wouldn't listen when I said I didn't know why it hadn't come. But then they stopped accusing me because I said one of the old women in the village had bewitched me. I said she reprimanded me after I hit her pig which had eaten some of my mother's soap, and that's why my blood hadn't come. And another woman, one nobody liked because she was pretty and her husband died and she wouldn't take another, I said her cat had bitten me on the throat. And another, I would give only bent pins when she asked to borrow some, and she cursed me for it.' Such small things, thought Lux. Small concerns in a small place. 'My blood still didn't come,' went on Hulda, 'and they were still suspicious of me, but as long as I kept saying names then they listened to me. Every name I said was someone who had already got themselves under suspicion. All I did was nudge it a little. There was a man who somehow won every wager he placed. A woman who took no husband of her own but glanced too long at those belonging to others. A couple who always tripped over the words of the prayers in church. No one defended them and no one was sad to see them go.' Hulda lifted her hands to her face and rubbed at her eyes. 'It's the only time anyone ever listened to me.'

Lux felt a rush of emotion. Was that what had happened to her mother? Was her accuser a powerless girl, finally being listened to?

Lux waited a moment, then spoke carefully. 'I'm listening to you.'

'I wish I hadn't done it.' Hulda's voice was barely louder than breath. 'Don't tell anyone.'

'I won't,' said Lux. She reached out and took Hulda's hand. For a moment they stood there, the kitchen quiet around them, flour on their palms mixing together. Lux didn't dare look at it too closely, but it seemed that whatever was between her and Hulda had just changed. Then Hulda took her hand from Lux's and shook her head as if she had cobwebs in her hair, and they never spoke of it again.

Lux kept busy avoiding Else. She didn't want to see the little parcel or hear about the danger of the lord. But she often caught Else's hooded figure out of the corner of her eye: flitting between the shadows in the great hall, ghosting through the corridors as Lux fetched things for the lady. Once she woke in the night and was sure that Else had been leaning over her as she slept. Was Else keeping her safe – or trying to hurt her?

5

Now She is Wolf

L ux had become so used to going where she was summoned and doing what she was told when she got there, she thought nothing of it when she was called to the lady's chamber. She'd never been there, other than when she dreamt of it.

The chamber was not at all like her dreams, but she was sure she would dream of it from now on. Lux was used to cramped and smoky rooms, but the lady's chamber was more like a church: high, bright and still. The dark wooden furniture gleamed and warm tapestries covered the walls, each showing swans in flight, so you could follow the flock from one part of the room and right around back to where it started. In one corner a low fire ticked and muttered. To one side of the room, raised on three steps, was a carved wooden bed; to the other side a large wooden tub steamed with hot water. Both were draped with heavy red curtains; the bed closed, the bath open.

In the middle of the room stood the lady in a blue gown, with her golden hair looped up and covered in filigree casings. She glowed.

'You will help me with my bath,' said the lady.

'Yes, my lady,' said Lux automatically.

'Both my handmaids got themselves with child within a month, the little idiots. I was sent another to draw my bath, but I do not like her face.'

'Yes, my lady,' said Lux. But she stood in the doorway, confused. The water had already been heated and poured into the tub. From the sweet scent of the room, herbs had already been brought up from the kitchen and added to the water. What other use could she have?

'Close the door,' said the lady. Lux did so.

Then she stood there with her empty hands useless by her sides, no idea what she was supposed to do. The lady, thankfully, didn't seem annoyed. 'I cannot very well bathe in this heavy gown. You will help me.' She smiled at Lux and waited for her to approach.

Lux's hands shook as she began unfastening the lady's gown. There seemed to be endless laces, all tied too tight, and bits of unnecessary fabric and layers and pieces that attached in strange ways and she was so close to the lady that she could smell the scent of her hair and why was it so hot in here? Why hadn't she thought to chew some mint leaves and fasten a herbal posy to her waist? She and the lady were the same height, and she was aware that she was inhaling the lady's exhaled breath, which smelled of cinnamon and summer. She tried to hold focus – but lost it again when she noticed what was under the lady's skirts. Although the outer dress was a sober plain blue, the inside of the skirt was heavily embroidered. Everything stitched out in the gold thread was wild: wildflowers, wild animals, wild men. Lux couldn't help running her finger over the intricate stitches. She thought of her dress at the mummers' show: maiden above, witch underneath.

The lady stood there in only her chemise, and Lux stepped back to allow her to get into her bath. But the lady didn't move. Should Lux do something else? Add more herbs to the water? Pull the curtain back more?

'Go on,' said the lady.

Lux felt like an idiot. Of course – her hair. She would want Lux to wash it. 'Forgive me, my lady.' She removed the filigree cages and unfastened the ribbons holding the braids.

'Oh, much better,' said the lady, shaking her head to loosen the braids.

Her hair tumbled down in soft waves, glinting in the candlelight, which was so much softer and steadier than the rushlight Lux was used to. 'Do you know, with that hair and those cages, I can barely hear a word anyone says? I sit beside my husband during all those feasts, and all I can hear is my own heartbeat.'

'Did you hear –' Lux couldn't believe her own boldness – but she wanted to know the answer, so she asked. 'Did you hear the mummers' play, my lady?'

The lady smiled. 'I did. My lord has told me that story many times, but I had never seen it played before.' Then she sighed. 'The story pleases my lord. He tells it often. He likes to have everyone hear it. He likes to have authority over many. But I –' The lady ran her fingers through her hair, making it gleam in the soft light. 'I am happy with influencing only a few. The ones that matter.'

Lux cast her eyes to the ground to stop herself staring at the lady standing there in her chemise.

'Go on, Lux,' said the lady.

It took Lux a while to realise that the lady meant for her to lift her chemise. This was something new: Lux and her mother and the sanctuary girls and the kitchen girls and everyone else she'd ever known washed in their underclothes; she'd never known anyone to bathe in only their skin. But, after all, ladies were different.

She lifted the chemise up and off the lady, then clutched it to herself, feeling the warmth from the fabric. The lady stood in the middle of the room, entirely unclothed. Her skin was like the inside of a shell. As if in a dream, she ran her hands up her own hips, her breasts, through her hair. She did not seem shamed; she was enjoying herself. She let out a breath as if she'd been holding it for a long time, then she stepped towards the bath.

The lady reached out a hand for Lux to steady her as she climbed into the water. Lux pushed away her spinning thoughts and took the lady's weight, entranced by the candlelight glowing on all that bare skin. As the lady settled into the water, her golden hair spread out around her and the heat brought rose petals to her cheeks. Lux wasn't sure she'd ever seen anything more beautiful. To stop herself staring, she looked around the room – and saw another intriguing sight.

On a carved wooden stand, splayed open, its colours enticingly bright: a book. As far as Lux could tell, it was similar to the last book she'd seen: in the sanctuary library, the low morning sun catching the pages all edged in gold. The pictures red, blue, green, between the harsh black marks of words that she couldn't understand. Then she had been standing in the shadows, while in a patch of sun, pure, praying, reading, was the man she – but she couldn't let herself think of that. She felt a pulse of desire and a pull of loss, both at the same time.

'Whatever is the matter?' asked the lady.

Lux realised she must have been staring blankly, and blurted out: 'You have a book, my lady.'

'I do.'

'But they're for . . .'

'For what?'

'For – learned men, my lady. And you are not . . .'

'Not a man?' Lux almost glanced at the lady's body in the bath, as if to check, but stopped herself. In response, the lady raised her arm up out of the water, letting droplets cascade off it.

'You will wash my hair,' said the lady.

'Yes, my lady,' said Lux, and she did so. Oh, it was a wonder to feel the hot water against her skin, even if she was only immersed to the elbows. Since arriving at the stronghold, Lux had not been able to soak in water. As a child, her mother had washed her in the river in the summer months, and at the sanctuary they had weekly baths. Here she had stand-up washes at dawn from a basin of cold water, just like the other kitchen girls, but there was no time to wallow in a tub, never mind to heat all that water, and the river in town was filthy. What would it be like to have hot baths any time you wanted them, and not have to make them yourself?

What would it be like if Lux lived here, in the lady's chambers, and could laze around naked in steaming water, and toss aside her fork and use her hands to scoop up delicacies that would fill her whole mouth, and sleep in a bed so vast and so soft with the lady beside –

'It's true,' said the lady, 'that I am not a man. But my husband is, and he likes things that cost a lot of money. He likes to wage wars and revel in the spoils.'

'And what do you like?' The words were out of Lux's mouth before she knew what was happening. '– my lady,' she added weakly.

'I like stories,' said the lady. 'Each person is stuffed full to bursting with them, fat as pigs ready for a feast. The littlest prick and all those stories will simply explode out, shrieking like fat in a fire, and anyone nearby can hear it all. My handmaids come from all over, and they bring many tales with them. Would you like to hear one?'

'Yes, my lady,' said Lux. She continued scooping up water in the jug and carefully rinsing the lady's hair.

'This is about an old woman living alone in a hovel in the forest. People came to her for cures for their sickness. How they feared it coming back, as bad as it had been before. Many people came, lined up at her door, so close their clothing touched, so close you could feel another person's cough on the back of your neck. The old woman gave them herbs and tinctures, but they did nothing. All the people died. The more people came to her, the more died. And, ah, this woman –' The lady sighed, relaxing back into the water. 'They were right to be suspicious of the woman. No husband, and yet a baby, suddenly, even though she was old. Strange indeed.'

Lux didn't say anything, because it wasn't a question. Without thinking, she reached to her throat for the comfort of her nightshade pearls – but of course, nothing was there.

'So many stories in this place! How they spread like sickness,' went on the lady, her voice silken. 'I heard this from one of my handmaids. She heard it from someone else she knew, who likely heard it from someone else. It's about a girl at a sanctuary. A charity case, very poor, plucked from a hovel in the forest. The parents of other, better-born girls pay extra to allow the less fortunate to be cleansed alongside them at the sanctuary. Helping the poor is good for one's soul, and a place at a sanctuary stops a girl from becoming a whore. You'd think such a girl would be full of grace and thanks for such a thing, would you not? For someone valuing her soul and not only what's between her legs. You'd think that girl would work ever so hard on keeping both places clean, and would never let them become befilthed.'

Lux's blood began to pulse in her ears and she felt her head spin. But the lady had asked her a question, so she had to answer. 'Yes, my lady.'

'The saddest part of the story is that the poor girl thought nothing of her own soul. Instead she lay with a monk at the sanctuary – a young man, very handsome by all accounts. To cover up her sin, the girl accused the monk of bewitching her. Such a performance she made of it: shriek-ing all night as if possessed by demons, so the good men of the sanctuary had to perform exorcisms to calm her, filthying their hands on what leaked out of her. But someone had to pay for the story she'd told. The monk had been accused of witchery, and that could not go unpunished. He was burned and his ashes sent up to God. Wasn't that the only thing that could be done to him?'

Lux's hand forgot to lift the jug. Her tongue felt swollen in her mouth.

The lady laughed, a sound like silver bells. 'I see you've learned when to stay quiet. A useful skill for any girl.'

Suddenly the lady stood up. For a moment Lux was lost in the patter-ing sound of the water falling from the lady's body, of the soft rise and fall of the lady's breath. Then she remembered herself and set to drying the lady.

'I will dry myself by the fire,' said the lady, stepping out of the bath. But as Lux went to follow her to the fire, the lady took her wrist. 'You may bathe now.'

'No, my lady, I –'

'You will bathe now.'

The lady undressed Lux, which was much quicker than Lux undressing the lady. The lady's hands were still wet. She stripped Lux right to her skin. For the first time, she was ashamed of her shabby clothes, her meagre body, her rough hands. She stepped into the water and let it cover her.

The lady, smiling, still bare, stepped over to the fire and bent to it, combing her fingers through her hair. After a while, she began humming a song. It seemed familiar to Lux - a lullaby, perhaps. But she couldn't relax. She couldn't unfasten her arms from around her knees. She saw that the herbs were shaking in the water, and realised she was shivering. What did the lady mean by telling her that story? Was it meant to display her hold over Lux - that she knew much more about Lux than Lux could ever know about her? Strange that someone so powerful would feel the need to prove it. To cover her unease, she scooped up some water and splashed her face.

She wiped the water from her eyes, and jolted to find that the lady was now kneeling beside the tub. She was wearing a clean chemise which clung to her damp skin.

'I want to tell you something,' said the lady, her voice soft. 'Words are a woman's weapons.' Lux, whose words had never done any good at all, said nothing. 'A knife has both a sharp end and a safe end. Even a blade brought out to be used against us can be grasped instead by the handle. The threat remains, but it points elsewhere.' The lady took hold of Lux's chin, lifting it so Lux met her gaze. 'An accusation is the same thing, little poisoner, only turned around. Not everyone can win, you see. Someone must always pay. All we can do is make sure it's not us.'

The water was growing cold, and Lux's shivers were getting worse.

A knock at the chamber door. Both women jumped. Lux began to stand.

But the lady pressed down on Lux's shoulder. She gave a sly smile. 'Stay.'

And before Lux could reply, the lady had closed the curtains around the tub and left her alone there in the cooling water.

It wasn't entirely dark: the candlelight from the room filtered through the red fabric, casting Lux in a pink glow. She hoped that the lady would send the knocking servant away soon, so that she could get out. Her skin was all gooseflesh and she had to clench her teeth to stop them from chattering. Her shivers made tiny ripples in the water.

But she felt a deeper chill when she heard the voice of the lord.

'There are too many women now,' he declared as he shut the door behind him. His voice seemed to vibrate the air. There was a wet sound that must have been him kissing some part of the lady. It went on a little too long for Lux's liking.

The lady murmured, 'And too few men?'

The lord carried on talking as if she hadn't spoken. 'They flutter around me, these low-birth servants, day and night, chattering like geese. They should be married off so they can make soup and babies, or they'll all become witches and whores.' His footsteps strode around the room – then twin thumps. Removing and dropping his shoes, perhaps?

Slowly, Lux moved in the tub so that her back met one rounded side, then pressed her feet against the other side so she was braced. Her knees made islands. If she tensed with her back and legs, she could lessen her shivering.

'Women only have a few good years,' went on the lord, 'while their flesh is still ripe and soft-furred like fruit. Soon they will bruise and grow overripe.'

'What a shame so many men were killed in your wars, my love, or fell to sickness. Now there are insufficient to marry off so many women. The men should have eaten the best parts of the bear. Should have been stronger, like you.'

The lord coughed, deep and wet; afterwards, it took him a moment to catch his breath. Now his voice dropped low – a tone of threat or seduction. He spoke to the lady, but Lux couldn't make out the words.

She heard the shush of cloth against cloth, and a powerful smell reached her. She tried hard not to flinch from the invasion in her nose; it would only jostle the water and make a sound. The lord's usual scent was of spice with a faintness of rot; this was almost entirely rot. The only explanation Lux could imagine was that the lord and lady had brought a leper into the chamber as an act of charity or abasement before God. It didn't seem likely, but what did Lux know of what lords and ladies did?

'A woman's desires are not like a man's,' said the lord, his voice grown bitter. 'They are wolfish, bloody, starved and ravenous. They have vicious dogs' souls. A woman's desires can drag a man through hell, and how he suffers for it.'

The lady murmured, and if she was saying words then Lux couldn't understand them. She seemed to be cooing wordlessly, as if to soothe an animal.

Lux heard the sounds of shifting bodies – hesitant, though, not moving in violence or desire. She was freezing, frightened, confused – but also curious.

She chanced the tiniest glance through the curtains. She didn't dare move much in case the water made a sound. Through her peephole she saw a sight she couldn't understand, and would be hard pressed to explain.

The lord stood beside the bed, one leg bare from the knee down, and at first Lux thought he had a thick pad of moss, a handspan length, wrapped around his calf for some reason. Then he shifted his leg, the smell intensified, and she realised the blackish-green mark was a wound, long suppurating. It had eaten away his calf almost to the bone, and it smelled like death.

The lady knelt before him, but she was not showing respect and he was not blessing her: in her hand she held a knife, and as Lux watched she sliced away some of the rot from the wound. The lord sucked air through his teeth; it must have been agony. Lux was amazed the lord could walk without flinching. Then she noticed the plain gold box she'd selected from the relic room, sitting on the ground beside the lady.

'The witch-girl said it was very powerful,' said the lord, and if Lux didn't know better she'd say he was close to tears.

From the golden box the lady reverently lifted the scrap of old flesh, then laid it on the open wound.

'Yes, my love,' she said. 'I'm sure this will be the one.' With one hand she held his knee, as if to steady him, and with the other she set the knife aside and reached for a needle and thread. The lord gritted his teeth and gripped the bedpost, letting out a single, childlike cry of pain as the lady stitched the relic to his leg.

'I must be what the people need,' he said, and it seemed he was speaking to himself rather than to the lady. 'They want me to win wars, so I win wars. They want me to rid the land of the witches, so I rid the land of the witches. They want food and drink and mummer shows, so I give them that. And still. Still...'

Lux watched, motionless with horror, as the lady wiped away the flowing blood and wrapped the lord's leg in fresh bandages. That sparked a memory: the bandage on the lord's finger the first time she'd attended his table. The empty box that should have contained the fingertip of Saint Melia. The lady telling her that even the smallest part of a saint could hold great power. How many of those boxes in the relic room were empty now? How long had the lord been doing this? How much of his body was not his own?

She closed the gap in the curtains, trying to stay silent as she heard the lord's clothing and jewellery drop piece by piece to the floor. She stayed silent as she heard the wet smack of bodies coupling. She stayed silent as the water grew freezing and her shivers uncontrollable.

It was embarrassing to be present for this intimate moment, but Lux tried to think of it as medicinal. Women, after all, do suffer superfluities of lust, and for married women this is fine as she may lie with her husband and be cleansed by his fluids, which wash out her womb and stop it from wandering or going sour. But unmarried girls have no such luck. Lux had heard the other girls talk about midwives you could hire who would anoint their fingers with oil and then massage your birth passage until relief was had. It wasn't as cleansing as a man's vital fluids, but it could keep a naturally lustful girl from madness.

She closed her eyes and thought of hands reaching for her in the night, the soft tangle of the kitchen girls in their shared bed. Of Ash under the twisting stars. Of the sanctuary, and her pricking belt of thorns. Of a place with a white sea that never rests, licking over the sand as black as night. Of a woman with light and dark together in one.

The room was quiet for a long time before Lux dared to move. It seemed that the lord and lady had completed their coupling and fallen asleep. It was true that the lady had told Lux to stay there, but surely she hadn't meant her to be there all night and freeze to death – if only because the lady would get a nasty morning shock seeing a corpse floating in her bath.

Lux tweaked back the curtain around the tub. The curtains around the bed were closed, but no sound emerged. She held in a gasp at the sight of a huge black dog hunched in the middle of the room – but breathed out when she realised it was only the lord's furs. Jewels winked among the folds of discarded clothing. Lux carefully climbed out of the water and reached for a cloth to dry herself. She rubbed vigorously, trying to get some feeling back into her numb limbs.

The ends of her hair were still dripping, but drying it by the fire was not an option: she would have to go to bed with it wet and hope she didn't catch cold. All she had to do was get dressed and sneak out. But her clothes were nowhere to be seen. Lux began poking around the room, peering under benches and drawers where her clothes might have been kicked.

With a bare toe, she poked at a loaf-sized object. From its crinkle and give she realised what it was: a horsehair pad. There were several of them in the pile, from loaf-sized up to pillow-sized, each stitched with a ribbon to tie them onto something. Ladies and lords certainly did have some strange things.

She froze as the curtains around the bed parted. There was nowhere to hide.

And then an old man clambered awkwardly from the bed, and Lux didn't know him, a man ancient and hunched and scrawny, his bones protruding, his body scarred and bandaged in odd places.

And then the old man turned to look at her, and it was the lord.

Lux tasted blood and knew she had bitten her tongue. The lord didn't seem sure whether to cover his body - so small and weak without his pads and furs - or launch himself towards her. It was the only time she ever saw him doubt - and even in that moment, Lux knew there would be consequences of this moment, and she knew they wouldn't be good.

She wanted to say: I didn't see anything.

She wanted to say: I won't tell anyone.

She wanted to say: the relics won't work, but I know what will.

She said none of these things, but knew that even her silence wouldn't keep her safe. Not now. She'd seen him weak, and small, and crying out like a child. He would stand for none of it. She knew in that moment all that Else had said was true: the lord was a danger to her, and he would see her die. She bowed her head and started to back away -

But the door slammed open: Else, looking like a shadow made flesh in her black hood, eyes bright in the candle's gleam.

Lux knew what Else saw: her standing bare and shocked, wet hair plastered to her shoulders, trying to cover herself; and the lord, naked, angry, his prick dangling.

Else threw back her hood and roared, a wordless sound, stretching her mouth so wide the pocks around it ripped open and began to bleed.

She leapt at the lord, and his eyes widened and he stepped back, tripping over his discarded furs and landing on his back with a thud, and the look on his face was abject terror, and his mouth was opening and closing as if trying to speak, and his hands were up in surrender, and there was a shriek from the tumble of bed that could only be the lady, and Else grasped for something, anything, and her hand closed on the lady's discarded knife still marked with blood from the lord's leg.

Lux ran towards Else and tried to grab the knife, and for a moment it seemed that she might win. But Else's eyes were wide and her teeth were bared and Lux heard a howl, too animal to have come from Else, and she lifted the knife high over her head –

And then – hot breath – black fur – jaws snap – sharp teeth – red tongue – screams, cries – spatter of blood – hot-metal smell of new meat – bitter reek of fear. Everything so fast, all at once.

'I'm sorry,' said someone, and Else wasn't there, and the wolf wasn't there, and Lux was holding the knife, and the lord's chest was a mass of red.

The lord looked down at the open wound and the blood pooling out. The blood spilled over and flowed down the hollows between his ribs. The lord tried to reach up to cover the wound but his hand fluttered and lay back down. He looked curiously at the hand as if the struggle was something he had observed that had nothing to do with him.

'No,' he said softly, and it sounded like a question.

'I'm sorry,' someone was still saying, 'I'm sorry, I'm sorry.'

And the lady shouted for the guards, but already the sound of running footsteps, and the door crashed open again, and a dozen armed guards swarmed in, and Lux threw the knife away from her but it was too late, they all saw her, stood there naked with blood caked and dripping up her wrists, and she backed up until she hit the wall, and before them all the lord gasped out his last breaths, and the lady bent over him, sobbing and lamenting, pressing her poor husband's limp hand to her heart, rising to her knees with her eyes gleaming bright and her finger pointing straight at Lux, and 'Witch!' she cried, and the guards seized Lux's arms and dragged her from the room, and someone was still saying I'm sorry, and it was only when the guard put the black hood on Lux that she real-ised that the person speaking was her.

Lux didn't know how long she was in the cell. There was no light, no food, no water. The room was tiny and low-ceilinged, and she couldn't fully stand, sit, or lie down, but only hunch over with her knees and back pressed cold against the walls. When the thirst became unbearable, she licked the drips from the damp walls. Like this, she stayed alive. She won-dered if Else was in a similar cell, and where it was, and whether the wolf was in there too. She tried tapping on each wall in turn and waited for a response, but nothing came.

So this was it, she supposed. She'd thought that witches had power, that witches had strength. That the air around a witch must shimmer with menace and mastery.

And yet here she was, accused of witchery, and she had nothing.

She thought then of the people in the village, watching their families and neighbours choke to death on their own blood, powerless against the sickness, desperate for someone to blame. And of Hulda, and of other girls like her, raising her voice in a cry of *witch!* because it was the only way it could be heard.

There, alone in her cell, Lux realised that power did not just sit around waiting to be found. Power could only be taken – and only from people who had less of it than you did. Women already had so little, and poor women least of all; they were easiest to take from. So what does a woman do if she is already poor, already powerless? She finds a poorer woman and blames her.

The lady had seemed so commanding to Lux. But it ended at these walls. The lord was helpless against his own body, and the rot of his sin, and his fear of the dead woman who had cursed him. He and the lady – they both took from others, but had no power over themselves.

And that, Lux knew, was all she had wanted. Not power over others. Only over herself.

But it didn't matter what she wanted, as she couldn't have it anyway. There's no use in a girl wanting.

Days passed. Weeks, perhaps; it was hard to tell. But she didn't die, so it couldn't have been months.

The lady came for her. She took her out of the cell and into a room with a bench and some water and food. Lux fell on it, not caring if it was poisoned, not caring if it was a trick. She couldn't lift her head or stand up straight. When she'd wolfed the food she stood, swaying, by the wall, leaning on it so she wouldn't faint. She had been dressed in a white slip with no sleeves and no stockings, and she was ashamed of her bare skin, at the dried blood on her arms where they'd scraped on the walls, at the filth on her legs from her own shit and piss. The lady sat neatly on the bench, her hands clasped.

'I don't hate you, little murderer,' said the lady, her voice soft. She reached forward and tucked a strand of filthy hair behind Lux's ear. 'But I cannot forgive you. Tonight you will drown.'

'It wasn't me.' Lux's throat ached and she could only whisper. She coughed painfully. 'My lady.'

'No?'

'It was the wolf, my lady.'

'What wolf?'

'It – it came into the chamber, my lady. Suddenly. And then it attacked the lord and was gone.'

The lady said nothing; just gazed steadily at her.

'If anyone is a wolf,' said the lady, 'I'd say it was you. More beast than girl, I'm sure anyone would agree. Are you going to persist with this story?'

Lux realised how ridiculous it sounded. How would a wolf have got into the stronghold? How would it have got right up to the lady's chamber without anyone seeing it? How did it disappear from a locked room? If Lux didn't want to drown, there was only one other creature to blame for this.

'I am innocent, my lady.' The words caught in Lux's throat. Was she really innocent? All the poisons she'd sold, the lover she'd sent to burn, the blood still under her nails from the lord's heart. Worst of all, what she was about to say.

'It was – it was Else.'

'Else? As in – someone else?' asked the lady.

'No! Else is the swineherd. She will be out with the pigs. Send some-one to find her, my lady. I wished the lord no harm. I tried to help him. I chose the relic for him, to heal him. I tasted his food every –'

'Enough lies,' said the lady.

'She was there, when you first saw me. In the poison garden? I was talking to Else then.'

The lady sighed, as if tired of indulging a child. 'You were alone, as you have been every other time I've seen you. Goodwife Ethelinda tends the pigs.'

'Goodwife Ethelinda! She will speak for me. She'll tell you how I always did my duties. I was a kitchen girl when told to be, and I was a food-taster when told to be. I came to you in your bath when you told me to, and I stayed in it when you –'

'And were you truly those things?'

No, thought Lux. 'Yes,' she said.

'I don't think so. I think you were only pretending. And I think that underneath it you are something else entirely. A witch.' Lux didn't get a chance to speak before the lady continued. 'But here is a strange thing. None of the kitchen girls will speak against you. They have all been given opportunity and promised immunity whatever they say about you. One girl accused several witches in her village before coming here. And yet with you: silence.'

'Because I am not a witch.'

Lux felt a warmth inside her. Hulda hadn't accused her. None of the girls had. They could have, but they didn't.

The lady waved her hand to silence Lux. She had said her piece, and anything Lux had to offer was of no consequence. 'You see you haven't been tortured? That is my doing. I said you had confessed to me, and that was good enough. Be glad of that.'

Lux would have laughed, but then she would have started crying. '*Glad?*' she said.

'Don't forget your place. Don't forget what you are. I could have had you stripped, shaved, beaten. I've seen the witches going to the drowning posts. Have you seen them?'

'No,' said Lux.

'They're tied to posts and left there. If they're witches, they'll go to the north land where they belong. If they're innocent, they'll float to the south land.'

'Have any women washed up in the south?'

The lady was clearly tiring of the conversation. 'They die as innocents and go to God. You're going to the drowning post anyway. Would you like to go there still with all your teeth? Your fingernails? Your eyes? I could have taken them from you.' She put her finger to Lux's chin and tipped it up to see her face. 'I still could.'

'You could,' said Lux, staring right back.

'And yet I haven't.'

And the lady called for the guards, and Lux was put back in her cell, and that was the end of that.

Lux spent the rest of her time in the dark planning what she was going to say as they led her to the boats. She was going to say that she was not a witch, not like they said. She had not consorted with the devil. She had not compromised her soul.

What is a witch, anyway? I ask you: have you wished anybody harm? Have you grasped for a tiny bit of power when you had none? Have you been scorned and cast out? Then you too are a witch.

All of this she would say. All of this they would hear.

And how they would cower before her.

But as it happened, they came to her and took her away, and she said all that she had planned, every word of it, and it was as if their ears were stuffed with wax, and no one listened to a word she spoke, and they chattered and laughed among themselves as if she wasn't even there, and they put her in the boat and rowed her out to the drowning post, and they tied her to it and they rowed away, and the whole time she spoke, and it was as if she had said nothing at all.

Then the sound of the oars receded. Only silence. She was alone.

And in the silence, a voice.

Else.

They must be tied to neighbouring posts. The water was only at Lux's hips, but she knew the tide would rise, and she knew she would drown. Even if she got free, what then? She couldn't swim, and if she could, both the north and south lands were too far away. She'd drown either here or struggling to reach shore.

Else stayed with her. Else whispered and murmured and sang to her. Just as Lux had told Else her story as they travelled through the pines, now, as the waters rose and death crept closer, Else told Lux her story.

PART 4

PART 4
Else's Story

I will tell you about my mother first because that is where I began

My mother was primal darkness

My mother was concentrated gloom

My mother filled every available space and some that were unavailable

My mother had a thrawn left ring finger because she was once beset by thieves in the forest

And they broke her finger to get her wedding ring which was the only thing of value she had

But as they made off into the dark she laughed

And called after them that they were the lowest of idiots because the ring was base metal and had no value

And the only thing she had that was worth a thing was her cunt and they hadn't thought to take that

My father on the other hand was blunt and protective like a cudgel

Which is fine until it's coming down on your head

They told me that our only protection against starving was the fear we could inspire in our better-off neighbours

Who left parcels of food in exchange for our poppets and herbs to kill or cure

Though we never did ask what they did with those things after they
took them from us

I just know we were powerless wielding power

And I liked that

Our house was deep in the trees and trees bordered it on three sides

Casting it in shadow all the time except at high summer

When the sun overhead warmed us all day

And in deep winter when the lights shifted and glimmered overhead

It seemed a waste to me that even when that light came all it showed
was the same house I'd always been in and the same trees that had always
hemmed me in

But I was small and feared what lay past the trees

The wind whistled through the gaps in the walls and every night I lay
in bed thinking of nothing

Praying of nothing

And in through the walls came the wind and stiffened my nipples and
watered my eyes

When no one was looking I liked to walk all the way round the house
with my left hand dragging on the mossy logs of the walls

And there round the back of the house under the eaves where it was
darkest there was a secret home for woodlice

And I couldn't see anything at all it was horrible back there

Stinking and damp and whispering

But if I kept going if I kept my left hand on the wall and kept walking
then I would eventually come back around

It's a child's faith that safety will always be there when you need it

Years passed like that

And nothing would ever change

Until it did

I can't say that I knew the darkness was coming

But I did know that something was

That morning when I milked the cow it came out creamy and frothing but when I looked closer I saw it was threaded with blood

But instead of tipping it all out and wasting it

I took a spoon and stirred it until all the blood was mixed in and you couldn't see it

That night the sky flamed bright like the devil's eyes

Not green and purple like the winter lights but red and orange like the sky was on fire

People cried and screamed

And said that god was angry at all of us for our sins

No one cried over their own sins

It was all about other people's sins

And whatever sins they hadn't fancied committing

It turned out were the exact worst sins that made god the angriest

My mother didn't cry or scream

She drank and spat and laughed and dragged a log round the front of the house so she could sit and watch the world burn

My father I don't remember seeing

I think he was busy burning something himself

The next day dawn didn't come and the sky was all ash clouds

Black as growing soil

But nothing would ever grow in that soil

It would be the end of lots of people

Including eventually me

But I will get to that

Over the following months the ash didn't go

It stayed there in the sky except the parts that fell sticky and clinging on all the plants and houses and people

Everything on the earth was covered in it

Every moment stayed not quite day and not quite night as the light never really came and never really went

The black mist and the black rain sat heavy on the land

As the ash and the soot and the sand congealed like black honey over everything

The harvest didn't grow the way it was meant

The animals didn't birth the way they were meant

The food stores didn't get filled up again like they were meant

Things were bad after that

But bad for others meant good for us

Meant more food for us

Meant more poppets and poisons

The more afraid people are the better for those who understand fear

I stayed there at the house in the woods

I helped to make the poppets and poisons

I thought that would keep me safe

Or I didn't care much for being safe because I didn't know there was any other way to be

The fire had come

The ash had fallen

The food had dwindled

My father had disappeared and returned and disappeared again

My mother had screeched and hit and prophesied

And still there I was

No longer a child

Food in my belly

Fire still lit

The loss of my father no loss at all

My left hand on the mossy walls

Going round into the darkest place and coming out the other side

How dull it was to be safe

Instead I wanted

I wanted

In the end it all comes back to this:
    The blue pool

I hear on the night air the thudding hooves of his horse and I don't wait
for him to get closer or to speak to me instead I stand up and raise my
arms the water sluicing off my woman's body under the moonlight and
he stops his horse which is as huge as a house and snorting clouds up to
the stars and he looks at me and I swear his mouth drops open I see
myself there an uncovered golden power arisen from the blue pool in the
night I see myself through his eyes as if I am a figure in stained glass in a
church window I see myself as if I am a creature from an old story pure
beautiful magical from another world I see myself all wreathed in gold
like a halo all the precious things on my body catch the moonlight and
light up my face like a circlet of lit candles as I step out of the pool and
the water falls away from me like I'm the virgin mother dropping her
blue cloak and I see that I am perfection and it's no wonder he wants me
but he can't have me I think as I smile up at this strange man on his
strange horse because there is nothing I need from him and even if I did
need something I'd take it and give nothing in return and he climbs off
his horse and even there on the ground he is twice the size of me and no

wonder his horse must be so huge so that he can be on it and not break it and he drops to his knee there in front of me and I don't feel ashamed I don't feel vulnerable or unsure even though I stand there clad in only my skin wearing the stolen jewellery of a hundred dead strangers and now there is a man on one knee in front of me on the black sand with the blue pool lit holy behind us and I reach out my hand and I place it on the man's head and in my mind I say a blessing for him and I think that everything is going to be good and I have had to go into the darkness under the eaves with the woodlice but I kept going and now I have emerged into the light but I brought some of the darkness with me and I am all the more holy for it there in the place where dark and light mix and I in the centre of it all

I left home three full years after the fire in the sky

It seemed like a sign of something that my mother and I were still alive

Other people had starved or got the sickness

Other people had lost their homes and husbands and animals and babies

But we had lost nothing yet

Except my father

But we couldn't blame the sky for him wandering off

And anyway I wasn't a girl any more by the time those years had passed but a woman with breasts and blood

A woman ready to be given to a man and filled with child

Which would have been fine except I was a wild thing in the woods making poppets and poisons

And no man from the town would dare to link himself to that in the sight of god and man under the high screaming white roof of the church

Though the man from the town would happily lie with her in a clearing as the north lights pulsed overhead

And I remember wondering then why if man is superior is woman made weaker by being with him

Why if man is superior is woman not grown stronger and better each time she lies with him

Why if woman is so filthy and man is so clean is she not made cleaner by being with him

Or has every woman filth enough to cover two

Anyway that meant it was no churched man for me

No babe for me

Just a good slow fuck under the sky

And that was all fine with me

Because everyone else was sickening and dying and I was not

So god must have been fine with me and mine and all we did

I heard a lot of talk from the people of the town

The ones who were still alive which seemed fewer and fewer

But we didn't care as long as there were still enough to want to kill or love one another

And trade us food for the things we grew that helped with killing or loving

The people said that there were many reasons for the ash in the sky and the sickness in people's blood

Actually I can't remember now if I heard all of these things from the people of the town

Or whether these are things I heard later when I travelled around

Because as it happened I ended up seeing a lot more of the world than the same house I'd always been in and the same trees that had always hemmed me in

But I will get to that

First the reasons we were told for the sickness

They said it was strangers in our land

It was jews and moors

It was reptiles and snakes released from under the ground by earthquakes

It was poisoned air which was also released from under the ground

It was sailors who had been travelling and brought invisible horrors home

It was sea serpents with their forked tongues and sulphur breath

It was the sea itself

It was something from elsewhere

It was someone who was elsething

I should have wondered then how much I was elsething

But I didn't

I didn't wonder anything at all except what was on the other side of the trees

There I was in the doorway looking up at how the sky was still ash and the ground was still ash and the house was still ash and it had been ash for so long that I couldn't really remember what it was like when things weren't ash

And as if made from ash himself a pedlar came right up to me

And nodded the morning

And opened his coat

And the coat was lined with ribbons and I stared at their colours

And I was hungry so very hungry

Hungry not just in my stomach but in my eyes and my mouth and between my legs

Staring at those ribbons all colours all bright all spilling from the innards of his coat

I was so hungry for the colours of those ribbons

Red of berries that grow in the woods for feeding to those you hate

Pink of a freshly slaughtered sheep's heart

Blue of the sky in summer when it never gets dark

Murky green of old bruises almost healed

White of the mucus part of an egg

Pale yellow of new onions chopped open

Deep brown of the last days of a woman bleeding

Black of closed eyes in the darkest part of night

I reached for the ribbons

But he closed his coat

So I kept reaching and took his hand instead

I had nothing to give but myself

The pedlar had good teeth and good calves

But mostly I remember his hair

It was dark and soft and curly so I could reach out and pull a strand straight

And when I let go it took its shape again

And it made me think he could be like that too

That he'd never let anyone change him

That he'd always be nothing but himself

It's hard to remember more than that or I can't bear to

I like to think I felt a tug in my blood for him

For the promise I imagined in him

The dark-curled pedlar hesitated then reached into his coat and pulled out a length of red ribbon

It was very soft and smooth

Like a devil's tongue rolled up tight

He put it in the doorway where my heels had stood

And I took a step towards him

The ribbon was a fair payment to my mother I'd say

A girl like me was worth half a ribbon at most

The ribbon was easily the most valuable thing that had ever been in our house

A lot more valuable than my mother's cunt though at the time I should have learned from her and wondered at the value of my own cunt and the trouble that owning a cunt could get a person into

But I didn't

I just smiled at the pedlar and let him lead me away

I didn't look back at the crouching toad of home

If the rain came before my mother did the ribbon would bleed all
over the doorway

I wondered if the red would go back into the house

Or outwards along the path I'd left by

Following at my heels

But I didn't look back

So I don't know

In the end it all comes back to this:

The blue pool
The gold girl

I allow the man to put his cloak around me and while he does it he glances away coy-like which I know is only for the look of it for he has already seen me bare and anyway I don't think I need a cloak at all I feel fine there in the night with the blue water drying on me and the black sand under me I feel like I am where I was always meant to be but the cloak is soft and I like that and he's still looking at me like I'm made of light a special sacred thing emerging and it's only then that I realise who he is I have seen him in church in the town in the south just past the pine woods not that I was at church but I was passing on the way to rent a room with my dark-curled pedlar and I saw the man then in his furs and his finery strut through the town like he owned it which I suppose he did and I saw how no one ever turned their back to him and I resolve then that I will turn my back to him because I can and that makes me smile and he thinks I'm smiling at him so he gives me a piece of black bread and salty cheese and I take it and I eat it and he watches me as I eat it the way a fox watches a chicken through a fence except there wasn't a fence there was nothing at all to keep him from me which I don't think about at the time I just eat the bread and cheese and the man starts to ask me questions polite and steady sort of questions and I answer them true because I don't see why not I don't think this man is a threat to me or to anyone I know he is very big and important but at that moment in that place I feel important too and he offers me many things that will be delicious to eat and sensual to wear and enjoyable to watch and all I have to do is go back to the south land and be his mistress and lie with him and while I do like fine to lie with a man and I think it could be fine indeed to lie with a man while the stars shine bright and a horse kicks black sand and gold lights me up like candlelight still I don't think I want to lie with this man not here in the north land and not following him to the south land either but I do want all the things he offers and I think well why can't I have them look at all the other things I've had like love and the moon and the sand and the pool and all I need to do is take it for my own I can do anything I can be anyone the world is delicious I want I want

Oh

    Oh

    I never thought I'd know such love

    Little light I can't even tell you

    My voice doesn't have enough colours to describe the wonders of my next few summers

    Even the winters were bright then and never got cold

    The spring and autumn smelled like summer too

    I swear summer came earlier in those times and even in the rain we weren't cold

    In the darkest parts of the year it was still summer to me

    I can't tell you how many years passed like this

    Every day was shimmer meadowsweet

    Much happened in the world but none of it happened to us

    I had such wanderings with my pedlar and our ribbons

    Those ribbons coloured like death

    Like berries and fresh hearts

    Like a cat's night-blinking eyes

    They were how and why we had our wanderings

    Up and down and across the lands

Trading ribbons for things we needed and even some things we didn't

And my pedlar loved me

Every time he kissed me he took my face gently in his hands and stroked my cheek with his thumb

Oh he loved me

Slow or quick or with a churchlike kiss

Though we never went anywhere near a church

In part because my pedlar was not a Christian

In part because I felt no need of god when I had him

But still god let me live when others did not

So I knew he was fine with me and I carried right on going

Criss-crossing the land like ribbons on a maypole

We wove circlets from the year's last lavender and danced with strangers under the midnight sun

We fed foxes with licks of salt from our palms

We rampaged in glory through the trackless woods

We fell asleep under a sky like a dark wolf pelt with little white teeth of stars

For a while we travelled with a pardoner who sold documents to grant freedom from sins the buyer had committed

These pardons could be had cheaper in times of strife when it seems sins were not worth so much

Or people didn't care so much about having committed them

For a while we had as our companion a soothsayer who predicted doom or glory in your future

Depending on what he thought you wanted to hear

He asked me many times if I wanted to know what was ahead for me

Every time I said no and smiled and shared instead what little food we had for the night

I didn't think I needed to hear it

I believed that my future was mine to decide

But even if I had known what was coming I couldn't have done anything about it

We circled round the country and then began steadily north

By then people had noticed that the sea was rising and there was talk that the land bridge between south and north might flood and disappear

And he was curious to explore the north land before that happened

I loved his curiosity and the way that he loved my curiosity in return

As that was a thing that no one had ever praised in me before

He was curious and he was bold and if he wanted to go to a place or do a thing then he would just do it

And it never seemed to come to his mind that he might not be able to

He had come from so far away and travelled so much already

And all this adventure we did with our own two bodies

Ladies and lords have horses and carriages but all we had was our feet and they took us where we needed

Although slower and with more stops

But we had ribbons

And we had time

We heard whispers and rumours about the sickness and how it spread and what it was doing

And how all of it was caused by the fire in the sky and the poison vapours and the ash

And how all of it came from the north

The south land was suffering

The farms and homes abandoned

The animals unfed and unmilked and left to die in their pens

The crops from last year rotting in the fields as none lived to harvest it

The crops from this year never growing or coming up stunted and pale

The babies born too soon and too small and never taking a single breath

The merchants all banned in case they brought sickness from afar

The port set on fire and all boats turned away

The relics of saints paraded through the streets to cleanse the people

The awe and fear towards a god who was angry and could not be appeased

The rage and malaise stacking up like dry tinder in everyone's hearts

Just looking for a spark

And none of it touched us

None of it

We were seeing all that the holy folk prophesied come true

We felt the lonely dread of passing through a village with every door wide open and only darkness inside

Or every door nailed shut from the outside and marked with a cross

We passed through town after town and saw no one alive

No fires and no smoke and starving dogs fighting over the corpse of a child

We saw cows dying for want of milking and crops rotting in the fields

There was nobody even in the churches

No one left alive to speak the mass and no one to hear it

And still we thought it couldn't touch us

But then my pedlar with his coat full of bright ribbons

My dark-haired man who'd always be the same no matter what happened

He bloomed with black roses

He coughed up black blood

He tried to walk and he staggered and righted himself and fell finally to his knees

I did not know how long he had been weakening

For he hid his black roses from me

He did not want me to see him weaken

It could be that he had been hiding it from me for weeks

Hoping it would go

Hoping we would be fine

But we weren't fine

I paid for a room a filthy sad thing in a filthy sad town

A tiny space barely the span of my arms in a low apologetic house

Shutters hanging and shingles slipping and walls streaked with birdlime

But it was the best I could manage and being off the main street I thought we would be safer

We were so close to the land bridge

If he could get a little better I could take him across

He always seemed better when we were on the move

People did get better sometimes

I had heard of it happening

Even from the deepest depths of the sickness they could be lifted

And it wasn't only the richest or poorest or holiest or wickedest who got better

It was some people

It was some times

But not this person and not this time

I tried to hide him for as long as I could because I knew if anyone saw his sickness they would board us up in that room and leave us there to wait us out until the sickness got us or we starved

They may even have burned the building to the ground with us in it

I had seen it happen and no matter that the houses squatted so close that a fire would surely take the next house and the next too

Such was everyone's fear of getting the sickness

Almost everyone who sickened soon died

Most didn't make it two Sundays from when the black roses first bloomed on them

So when the black roses came for me I didn't tell him

He was not much aware of things by then anyway so he wouldn't have noticed

And I barely had time to worry about it myself
I was so focused on trying to heal him
I did not want to die but more than that I did not want him to die
I resolved that I would not let that happen
Not this Sunday and not next Sunday and not any day holy or unholy
But it turned out I was wrong about that

In the end it all comes back to this:
   The blue pool
   The gold girl
   The bold man

I like it there with the world laid out before me and I want to wallow in it a little let the black sand sift through my fingers let the stars spin above me and I feel dreamlike and slow like I'm in the hungry gap just before the harvest when last year's stores are down to the last grains but it's not ready to cut down the new ones so everyone is half starved and woozy except now it's like that but in a good way I feel like my body could split into parts and float right up to the sky and I don't mind that the man is there he can be there or not there it's all the same to me it seems then that things don't have to change because of a man's presence and when he pulls me up onto his horse behind him I think that is a good thing for the night is cool now that I am out of the water and his body against my skin is warm and I leave behind the pile of rich clothes I took from the people in the pit but I grab up my coat and all its ribbons and bundle it onto my lap and as the horse trots along the man is talking at me saying he is here in the north to negotiate something or another and how fortunate for him that he's found something extra a little treat for himself to celebrate a job well done and I really don't care what he's saying I stop listening fast and instead I think about soft words pretty words dream slow sleep words that my dark-curled pedlar had said to me or that I had heard from others and collected the sort of words that feel smooth or sweet-spiced on my tongue like furled tousled river-run plash cloudburst coracle loam swathe shimmer meadowsweet I make myself swoon on words and delicious they are in my mouth and the tide is up as we cross the land bridge and the sea covers it but only shallowly so that the horse plashes knee-high but I am above it all and I luxuriate in myself high up on a fancy horse and if I was on my own two feet they would be wet and dragging now but they're not I am high and dry and drunk on words just me and the sky and I can have it all I can have everything

I woke in the gloaming in a plague pit

Though I didn't know at first it was a plague pit

All I knew was that the light was golden and everything stank and there were teeth on my wrist

Without thinking I kicked out at the thing biting me

I felt rough fur against my feet

The biting thing squealed and fell back and I saw it was a wolf

The wolf considered me and seemed to think about trying again

But I raised my foot in a warning and it backed off

From the sounds it had started to drag off someone else instead and that person didn't or couldn't fight back

And that's when I realised how bad things were for me

Even though as it happened I was the some person some times who got better

I turned my head and I was face-to-face with my lover

But that wasn't his face

He didn't have a face any more

It was just some meat

But above the meat was hair

Dark and soft and curly hair

And I knew him by that

I reached out and pulled a strand straight and when I let go it took its shape again but he didn't

He didn't

He would never again

I wanted to take a lock to remember him by but I had nothing sharp to cut it

So I didn't

I slid off his coat with all the ribbons inside and I put it on

I wasn't pleased that the filth on my body would then go on the ribbons but there wasn't much else I could do in the circumstance

I turned away from the black hair of my pedlar and I climbed out of the pit

The stink and rot of it

I try not to think about it

The give of flesh as I stepped on it

The twist of my foot as a body rolled under it

Reaching out to climb higher and realising I had taken hold of a cold dead hand

But holding it anyway and letting it lift me free

When I stood on the edge of the pit and looked down I didn't see bodies piled there

I saw gold

The dropping sun gleamed on the wrists and necks and fingers of the dead and cast them haloed

And I knew it couldn't be real gold or the gravediggers would have taken it themselves

They would be afraid of the sickness but greed is stronger than fear

Still I thought if it had tricked me for a moment then it could trick others

Even just for long enough to trade for something to eat

If I ate fast

Though probably not long enough to trade for somewhere to sleep
So I took what I needed from people who no longer needed it
And I said a prayer for each one
For all that would do
And by the time I set off it was full dark and I was still filthy and dead
but I was clothed in fabrics and adornments such as I had never seen or
felt before
And I didn't look like a queen and never would
But at least I looked like something more than I was

The land bridge stretched between the south and north lands
It was a high strip of hard-packed dirt with the sea licking along both
sides
It took a full day to walk across and was the width of three carts
I didn't have a cart
Only my own feet and the splendours I carried on my body
I saw no one as I passed which was good as a woman travelling alone
is a strange thing
And a woman alone with splendours is dangerous and disgusting and
surely devil-ridden
People by then were suspicious of the north land and did not want to
go there in fear of the sickness
And in time the sea did rise up and swallow the land bridge
Whether it was god angry at the north and punishing them
Or god pleased with the north and protecting them
I don't know
I only knew I had to keep moving
While the sea whispered and taunted on either side of me
I listened to it
The whole way I let the sea speak to me
And I liked what it said

*

I made it across the land bridge and to the north and I wasn't dead

Or at least no more dead than I had been before

The north land was the most beautiful thing I had ever seen

It made me realise that I'd never understood the word beauty before because pretty isn't beauty

I was always told that a pretty girl is beautiful but I realised pretty is soft and sweet and silent and probably has high tits and a tight cunt and that's why it's good to call a girl pretty

But not beautiful

Beauty is dangerous

Beauty has power

Beauty has violence

I saw red honeyed lava belching into the sea through a crevice in the black rock and billowing white steam as it met the raging silver sea and the salt tide scoured and purged and swallowed the black sand and spat it back over and over

I heard the boom of the swell as the sea's tongue licked deep into the caves and the shivery retreat under ancient hollow rocks

I felt the moonlight striking full and pure on my face and my shoulders

On all the open parts of me

And the light didn't care that I was filthy and that I stank and that my skin was black with the rotted blood of many strangers

The light loved me and painted me gleaming without judgement

I knew the pearly everlasting there

I knew light

I knew god

I dropped to my knees there on the black sand under the white moon

And before me was a blue pool of water

As if waiting to baptise me in my new knowledge

I shed all the clothes I had stolen from dead people

That didn't fit me anyway and shouldn't have been on my skin

Those clothes weren't meant for an elsething wild whore from the woods

The false gold I kept on as I liked how it gleamed in the night

I washed myself clean there in the pool

I saw my own body as if for the first time

I listened to the stories it told

On the fingers of my left hand the white crescents at the base were dark with blood underneath

So someone had stepped on my hand or caught it in something

The skin under my arms and between my legs had been clotted black

But it washed off and underneath I found my skin was white and smooth and unmarked

So in that pit among the dead when I knew nothing of it I had healed and my black roses had gone

Beneath my breasts were long uneven stains like the marks some babies are born with

But I had not been born with one and had never had one before

The stains were red and purple and yellow

So the ribbons inside my coat had become damp and the dye had leached out and stained my skin

On my wrist were still dints where the wolf's teeth had bit but they didn't bleed and they wouldn't scar

So the wolf had only nipped me hard enough to wake me but not hard enough to hurt me

And then I heard

On the night air

Thudding hooves

In the end it all comes back to this:
  The blue pool
  The gold girl
  The bold man
  The red stain

I'm drunk on words and the sky and the sound of the horse plashing through the tide so by the time we arrive at the empty shore of the south land I almost forget the man is there so when he lifts me off the horse and pushes his cloak down off my shoulders I put out my left hand and take hard hold of his wrist to stop him because I don't want to lie with him whether he's carried me across the water on his horse or not I don't care the answer is still no and I start to tell him as much and now would be the perfect time for me to turn away from him and go on about my life but it doesn't work out that way the world is not shimmer meadowsweet not at all as it happens and I learn that lesson right then because my hand is small and his hand is big and as it turns out all that really matters in this world is what a man wants because you either give it to him or he takes it and gives nothing in return I keep hold of his wrist but it doesn't make any difference when he grabs a squeezing handful of my breast and with the other hand he snatches at my coat which I still have a hold of and he sees the flash of a stain under my breast that has been left by the ribbon and he scratches at the stain and a little comes off under his thumbnail and he looks at it for a moment considering as if he has just realised something he looks at my coat and it's old and tattered and it stinks of my body and of death and he looks inside the coat and he sees the rows of bright ribbons in there and I suppose he knows then that's what I am and that's what I do and that's why I was there alone bathing in a pool at midnight because only the sort of woman who opens her coat up and sells what people can see inside would be out alone and as if trying to make sure of a thing he is not yet sure of he twists his arm a little so that he can see my left hand which is still holding his wrist and he looks at my marrying finger but that is the one finger I didn't put a ring on after I climbed out of the plague pit as I thought it was bad luck I thought it meant I'd never marry and who I thought I was going to marry I don't know because my dark-curled pedlar was dead I had thought for a moment just one single moment that I didn't always have to be a wild thing in the woods making poppets and poisons if I didn't want to be but I see now that we are what other people say we are and we can never change that and he knows from my coat and from my hand and from what is and isn't there that I am not married and I sell the bright soft things inside my clothes and he laughs a little like he is relieved or disappointed it's hard to tell he says I know what you are and that's the last thing he says to me during all that happens next he doesn't speak another word so it spins round and round in my head the whole time I know what you are I know what you are I know what you are

I can't recall quite when I decided

It's always hard to find the exact place that a thing began to grow

The exact moment that the rot sets in

Just a slow grow until something in me was so sick that it all spewed out of me

I survived that night

The man rode off on his horse like nothing had happened

I didn't die there in the dirt like he wanted

Instead I waited for the tide to drop again and I crawled back over the land bridge to the north

I thought it would be safer there

I thought there was a reason he had taken me back to the south land before throwing me to the ground

For several months I lived beside the cold water

With blue glaciers drifting by on their way out to sea

I met three blue-eyed women who were kind to me

They set my jaw straight and helped it heal

And every night they told me stories of their land and its history and things that had happened and things that could never happen

And I should have stayed there

I should have stayed there

I ate so much I got fat

Though only in the belly and it took me longer than it should have to know what that meant

My blood had stopped coming but I thought it was because he had damaged me inside

I told the three women what he did

They did not judge me or mock me or blame me

They believed the story I told them

And that made me bold

And eventually that made me dead

Because after that I told everyone who would listen

And I crossed to the south in a boat because by then the land bridge was flooded by the sea's sudden rise

And I went to the town where I'd first seen him and I told everyone there too

Everyone who would listen and everyone who wouldn't

And none of them believed my story but I didn't notice as I was so caught up in my righteous telling of it

And I knew it was true so I never thought that anyone would think otherwise

I made my way to where he lived and I got as close as I could and I told everyone going in or out of the stronghold

Most of them didn't listen but unfortunately one of them did

A man hired to heal the lord and then fired when he could not

That man knew what I didn't and what everyone else didn't

That the lord was secretly ailing with a rot in his leg

The left leg the one I had put my blood on

And it all began on the night I cursed him

And so he knew there was something true in my story even if he didn't believe all of it

By then I was hugely bloated in the belly with what he'd left in me

I felt it as a great white mass like a moon made of writhing maggots
If for a moment you'd thought the thing inside me would save me
You are very much wrong
A childless woman is missing her motherness
She can still be made whole if she marries and gets with child
But a witch swelled and brooding is the opposite of mother
Unmother
Unholy
Unhuman

When the men on horses came for me and took me inside the stronghold
At first I was glad
I thought this was my justice
That notion lasted not long
I should have known
But I was stupid and I thought I could be more than I was
I thought I could be something not yet defined
Could be whatever and whoever and wherever I wanted
None of which is true for a woman of any kind and most particularly
one who is born in a rotting damp house and grows up selling poisons
and rutting with men in the woods
I do not know what a woman like that is but certainly none of the fol-
lowing which are the only available options
Maiden
Wife
Nun
Widow
And I could not be any of these even if I wanted to
But there is one other option for a woman and it is the worst of all
Witch
Witch
Witch

We must remember that a woman can never act alone

All that a woman says and knows and does must be at the command of a man

And if there is no man around and still a woman says and knows and does

Then the man commanding her

Must be the devil

When I realised what was happening I tried to run away

The men chasing me and laughing like I was an animal at the hunt

And not even one they needed for food but one they chased for sport

They didn't think I'd dare run into the pine woods but I did

And was soon lost in the shadows

I felt like I wandered for days

The pine trees grew as thick as the fur on a wolf's back

It was dark there even in the middle of the day and always silent

My feet were pricked constantly with needles and my shoes grew useless and sodden with blood

It was all the same for miles and miles and I must have got turned around

Because eventually when I stumbled out half crazed and blinded by the day

I was exactly where I had gone in

The man in the guard hut had dark eyes slightly crossed and a nose that lurched as if it had been broken once

I fought him

More wolf than woman

Smashed my elbow to his bent nose and broke it again

He swore at me through his blood

Said there was no use fighting or running off because if I went into the pine woods again I'd only have to come out in the end

And there he'd be waiting

*

The lord asked me to heal him
    But I would not
    The lord tried to force me to heal him
    But I would not
    The truth is I couldn't
    But even if I could
    I still wouldn't
    I knew he could take everything from me
    But he could not take that
    Denying him was the only power I had left
    But I didn't know it was no power at all
    Still there was only one thing left that he could do to me
    Only one thing left that he could take
    They held me in an underground place so god could not see
    It was a long time to get my confession
    By the end of it all of my fingers were broken and I couldn't sign an x
for my name
    So they signed it for me

On the route to the trial they led me through the town
    They told me with humiliation comes transcendence
    First they shaved my hair off so I couldn't hide charms or poppets in
there
    I was happy to see it go
    I could still feel the grind of it between my teeth and taste it down my
throat
    I hoped it would never grow back
    And it turned out it didn't but not for the reason I thought
    Then the branks went on
    And none too gently
    My skin already splitting and bleeding at the corners
    My lips ripped against the rough metal edges

The branks held my mouth open and I felt my tongue roll free

Fat and flopping like a slug

But I couldn't speak

I could only open and close my throat to make a strange sort of gagging sound like a cow does when she's birthing a calf

It seemed that the purpose of this was so that everyone we passed could show their holiness in front of god and their disgust for all those who go against god

By spitting into my mouth

With humiliation

Comes transcendence

I couldn't spit it back out so my choice was to swallow it or let it drool down my chin

Such are the choices a woman is given

Who is no longer even a woman but a witch

Which is both more and less than a woman

My learning went on forever

But I don't know that I actually learned a thing at all

Despite everyone's best efforts

Or at least I didn't learn the things they tried to teach me

Humiliation

Transcendence

Finally I made it to my trial

My tongue by then was swollen and spongy

My gums stained metallic

My back tooth broken and jagged

My mouth tasted of a hundred strangers

I'm still waiting for my transcendence

In the end it all comes back to this:
  The blue pool
  The gold girl
  The bold man
  The red stain
  The word no

I say to him no I don't want to no and I stand up and I take a step away from him and in that moment I actually let myself believe that it matters what I say that he will listen that anyone would listen and I know that's the worst part that I really do believe it I can blame the spell cast on me by the moon and the pool and the gold but really it's no one's fault but my own what kind of stupid girl would ever get on a man's horse like that what kind of stupid girl would ever believe that a man would listen to her what kind of stupid girl would think she can have what she wants I know you don't have to tell me I'm stupid I've suffered enough for it and I suffer for it right then because his fist is fast and hard as a thrown stone and I feel the bone of my jaw crack and see white sparks in my eyes I fall to my knees gasping like a landed fish all the breath gone out of me so shocked I don't know what to do and I couldn't speak even if I knew what to say and I still haven't managed to take a breath when his fist comes again just to make sure right on the bone under my eye and at least that one doesn't crack and all I can do is blink fast but at least I can still see he has not burst my eye and as I kneel there trying to breathe with my jaw hanging wrong he takes the gold coloured things from my neck and my wrists and my ankles and my fingers and I'd happily tell him they're not real gold only base metal and that the night is tricking him but I can't speak and I wouldn't tell him anyway I don't care he can have the gold he can have it he can leave me there ungilded I found that gold and I can find more I've already died once how bad can it be I remember thinking that and it hurts me now to say how stupid I was how I thought I had seen the world but I had seen nothing at all and he takes my hair which is uncovered now falling long down my back covering my body he twists it into a silken rope wraps it once around my throat wraps it once around my mouth wraps it once around my eyes he ties it there tight I can't see I can't breathe and the hair grinds between my teeth and tickles into my throat I want to gag I want to vomit on him but I know I'd only be vomiting on myself I can never hurt him I can only hurt myself

Before my trial I was washed and dressed in clean clothing
   For which I was pathetically grateful and cried much
   Though I knew that crying was a sign of my guilt
   As was not crying
   But then I cried more because they did not remove the branks that
held my mouth open
   And as they washed and dressed me I was knocked and bumped
   Rough metal jaw clamped tight bones grinding
   All I could do was scream inside myself because my bones had not
healed properly from when he hit me
   I could feel them scrape from the inside
   The pain flashing white behind my eyes
   So there I sat
   My mouth open
   My tongue lolling like a cow
   Trying not to choke or drool like a baby
   The weight of the branks for all those days of the trial grew so heavy I
could barely keep my head up
   I had to use my hands to hold it or my neck would buckle and fall
   The weight of all that scraping metal on my head

Reminded me of the weight of all that stolen false gold on my body

I stopped struggling then

Which I suppose was the point

I had tried to get away from my own body by giving it to the devil

I had tried to be more than my body

I had tried to be more than a woman

More than a wife

More than I was

Now the branks would bring me back to myself

Back to my body and the pains of it and the weight of it and the look of it and the knowledge of it

People from various towns I visited with my dark-haired pedlar had been found

They testified to the evil I left in my wake

Though at the time I didn't recall any evil as we left

Just them going about their day with new bright pretty ribbons in their hair

They said that their rooster wouldn't stop crowing and all the chickens' eggs had bloody yolks

They said that a catch of fish was all dead before it was pulled out of the water and when they cut the fish open the guts inside were already rotting and all the bones were black

They said that their children were taken over with shivers and fits and spat up pins and cried my name out in their sleep and screamed that the unholy spirit of me sat on their chests and stopped their breath

I had never heard any of this before

These were all new stories to me

All I could think was if only I really did have power like that

If only

The things I would do

But I don't and I never did and I never will

And then he stood up and said some things he'd made up and every-one listened to him and believed him

And I sat there with my mouth held open

Unable to speak a word

I had to listen to him just like everyone else

He said I had reached for him with my left hand and that was a sure sign as that is the devil's hand

I thought it was enough that I pushed him away no matter which hand I used

But it seems not

He stood there

Gigantic

Unbreakable

His voice shaking the walls

And who can disbelieve a voice that loud

He said that the witch

That is me apparently

The witch tried to seduce him in carnal knowledge but he would not yield to her as he was a good man

The witch tried to entice him with trickery and wiles but realising that would not work took him by force

The witch having only one force available to her which is the wicked-ness given to her in her pact with the devil

The witch tried to make him into a beast

Tried to make him into a hollow man left with a gap in him the exact shape of her

The witch took him and used him most horribly to satisfy all her desires and when finished with him cast him aside like a wrung-out cloth upon a midden

The witch grew fat with all she took from him and filled her belly with light taken from him

I was by then in a colossal somnolent vertigo with the effort of keeping my head up with the heavy branks upon it

My head swaying

My eyes unfocused

My back screaming

I wouldn't cry

I wouldn't fall

I would just be

Although it was just being that got me here in the first place

The second-best of his evidence was his leg which he revealed with much pomp

Everyone gasped and moaned at the decay of it

The wound unclean and unhealing that he said had been cursed by my blood that night under the moon

Cursed witchlike and wicked with words said unholy

So that it never might heal

The best of all his evidence was the great white maggoty swell of my belly

For a woman can only conceive if both man and woman spend and here was proof beyond doubt

That I had known him

And that I had liked it

We both had rot growing in our bodies from one another

I did feel a power in me then

I had wondered why if man is superior is woman made weaker by being with him

When surely every man should make her better

And yet this man had used force on me and it had made his body turn against him

It had made him weaker

That was something at least

He said that he did meet me there at the pool and he did get me down
on my knees

But only to pray

He only wanted to pray

And the devil pushed me the rest of the way down

And what was I doing there anyway out in the world alone

Without the protection or guidance of a man

Only a shameful woman would roam for vain amusements

Any woman alone is a whore

He called out then

Tilted back his head to the roof and spoke to god

Which I thought was a bit dramatic and I would have laughed if I
didn't have a broken face wrapped in metal

He asked of me then without looking at me

Why did I hate goodness

Why did I hate god

Why did I hate life

Why did I hate light

And at that I closed my eyes and thought of arriving in the north land
with the blood of my dark-curled pedlar still on my hands

Thought of the sunlight striking full and gold on my face

Thought of the light not caring that I was filthy and that I stank

Thought of the light loving me and gilding without judgement

But then seeing that my eyes were closed they came over and prised
them open

So that all I could see was him

I don't hate god or light

I only hate him

But the bones of my jaw scraped and my tongue flopped uselessly
and no one would have listened anyway

The judge said that his unsealing wound was not natural

For it didn't have a natural cause which was shown by no natural remedies working on it

And if it was not natural then it was unnatural and caused by the devil through me

Before the trial began I thought there was a chance I could be found innocent

I had heard it happened as much as not

But no

Not for me

Not in this time

Not in this place

Not with this man

I am what they say

I am not innocent the way they want a woman to be

I am not pure white clean a maiden fair covered always ankle to hair

I did lay a curse and I did mean it true

I am not a bitter rotting evilspitting devilfucking elsething

But those are the only choices

Guilty

Innocent

There is nothing in between

A woman must be entirely blameless if she doesn't want any blame

A woman must never fuck if she doesn't want to be always fucked

A woman must do nothing if she doesn't want to be punished for everything

One drop of blood taints a whole pail of milk

In the end it all comes back to this:
    The blue pool
    The gold girl
    The bold man
    The red stain
    The word no
    The hard ground

I cry when he fucks me not at first but eventually I cry and I want to wait until he's gone so he doesn't see but he's taking so long and I can feel the blood coming out of me making me wet there and that makes him do it more he is taking so long and while he fucks me the seas rise and swallow the land while he fucks me mountains fall and rise again while he fucks me generations of people die out while he fucks me the day of judgement comes but god doesn't see us even though I shout to him and while he fucks me the world burns out and remakes itself again but still the first woman tempts the first man with fruit and curses them both forever but her more so than him and she carries that stain forward into her daughters and their daughters and their daughters and their daughters and the stain of woman puddles where they pause and marks what they touch and has a metal meat stink and that raw bleeding visible mark of being a woman is worse than a cut worse than a burn worse than a scar because scars heal and fade eventually but this never will this never will this never will and that's when I cry hot snot dripping pig-like sobs the tears trickle salty in my mouth I cry wah-wah-wah like a baby feeling sorry for itself I wait for him to mash his hand to my face to shut me up I must look repulsive like this it must be putting him off surely he'll hit me any moment surely he'll want to shut me up but he doesn't do anything he doesn't even look at me his eyes are closed his teeth are clenched it's like he's not there or he is there but I'm not I'm just a hole in the ground well then why doesn't he fuck a hole in the ground they don't bleed

My prison was an underground room twice the length of my body
   The ceiling low so I could only stoop or sit or lie
   The walls scooped from the earth still rough and muddy
   At least the branks was off my head and I had shoes on my feet
   These were the things I was glad of by then
   I had no idea how good life had been in ribbons
   At the top of one wall there was a small opening lined with something
smooth and hard which I spent a long time exploring
   It was the size of my eye and when I poked my finger in it I found it
tilted upwards and went on a long way
   It smelled of fresh air so it must have gone all the way up to above-
ground but no light ever came down it
   The holy women told me there needed to be salvation to atone for my
sin which was vast and tarry and black and had dripped and stained
everything and so would need a big sacrifice to balance all that out
   It was all for my own good
   It was all for my own transcendence
   A woman's sin is passed on and on and on
   So the child in me was already tainted

But I knew though no one told me that still the lord thought I would love it

This thing half-him inside me

The gall of him to think I could ever love something that had him in it

He would wait until it was born and then he would use it to make me heal him

Which was a thing he was still sure I could do

More fool him because I knew it wasn't a baby anyway

It was a maggot-white mass of filth and the sooner it was out of me the better

And even if it was a baby

What use is a baby

What use is a child for that matter

I have no lands to farm

No beasts to tend

No home to clean

No need of extra hands

What good is it to me whether the baby is here under the ground or out there under the sky

They tried to tell me about Lilith who is a thing with a woman's face and breasts and a long scaly tail like a fish or a serpent

Lilith the symbol of unconstrained desire and uncontrolled birth

Lilith who is carved into benches in churches as a warning for women and I told them to stop as I was tired of listening and I had given up so much that I felt it only fair that at least in return I should be allowed to be rude

And that was true as they stopped talking to me then

So I told them to take the thing when it came out of me as I did not want it

I tried to sound penitent rather than disgusted and I don't know that I managed it but it didn't matter by then

They smiled in a way that seemed to me pitying and regretful and very very holy

And then they came with a needle and a length of black thread

And they stitched my mouth shut

Leaving only a space at one side for water and some small food to pass in

I don't remember it hurting

I don't remember anything really hurting after I'd gone underground

This punishment was not because of what I did but because I told

If I had kept my mouth shut like a good woman then I would still know the sun

Though knowing that was not much use to me at that point

I had no candles or fire and the dark sat velvet-heavy on me

I realised I had never before known true darkness

Always a candle through the keyhole

Always the distant gleam of stars

Always the moon under mist

This was a heavy ancient dark

I couldn't tell whether my eyes were open or closed

And it didn't seem to matter so I kept them closed to go with my stitched mouth

If I could have closed up all the leaky parts of me then none of this would have happened as the devil wouldn't have got into me in the first place

The holy women didn't speak to me and of course I couldn't have replied anyway

Once a day they brought water and food and they tended to my stitches

One woman in particular wiped away the blood and put on a salve and reminded me not to try to open my mouth

Not to try to speak or cry out no matter what

Because it would only hurt me

And she rested her hand on my hand when she said this and it seemed like a long time since someone had touched me without wanting to hurt me

And I was grateful for that

I was grateful

My fingers though were never splinted so they healed twisted and were no use at all

I thought of my mother's thrawn left ring finger and how she liked to tell how she'd got it

What would I tell about how I'd got this

What would I tell about the scars around my mouth from the needle and thread

When the thing inside me was out of me what would I tell about how I'd got that

Would I be able to tell anyone about it anyway

I imagined that when I emerged from my prison I would have hair as white as bone and a face wrinkled like an apple

Though I can't say I hated it there under the earth hidden from god

It was damp and dark and always smelled of my own shit

But it certainly wasn't the worst place I had been

I was alone for so long I felt like I was always in a dream or in a trance or I was bewitched

Smells and sounds were overwhelming and seemed to slip inside my body like there were no boundaries and I couldn't get them out

I knew my own body like I never had before

I felt the slow creep of my blood

The stretch and shrink of my lungs

The flap at the back of my throat contracting each time I swallowed

Time used to mean something but it didn't any more

I didn't think it passed any more

It didn't pass around me or through me

I felt a desperate need for light

And for an end

And for my mother

Which I did not expect

When I blinked I saw a silvery gleam on the insides of my eyelids as if my eyes now made their own light

I sang to myself in the dark and I heard the words and felt the clear sound of it though I knew my mouth couldn't open

Down there in the dark I saw a pile of hundreds of oyster shells each with a tiny baby inside lying in its own tiny bath of blood

I saw a row of purposeful rabbits marching across an icy lake each holding a human heart up above its head

I saw the tips of spades poke through the ceiling as someone dug down from the surface and I raised my hands to stop a mass of earth from falling on me

I saw the walls recede away from me so that if I ran for days I still wouldn't reach the end of my prison

I saw my own self and then I merged with it so I didn't know which was real

I don't know when I was asleep and when I was awake

I dreamt that the devil came to me

He kissed me all over and held my body and his breath was sweet and I breathed him in

He fucked me gently with his long cold prick and it felt strange and good and I felt myself pulse around him

And he pushed it deeper and made a sound like he liked what I was doing

And I liked that he liked it

Afterwards he took his prick off and set it aside and lay down with me

His body was warm and covered me soft

He fed me milk from his body and I fell asleep like that

Although I was already asleep and dreaming

Down there in the earth I was dead and buried

But also I was unborn and waiting

Ready to emerge

In the end it all comes back to this:

The blue pool
The gold girl
The bold man
The red stain
The word no
The hard ground
The curse

I lie there and watch my blood mix with the dirt he gets off me and wipes my blood off his prick then stands and brushes the dirt from his knees he gets ready to leave and I'm sure any moment now he'll start whistling a tune and there on the ground I lie bare and open I don't take my eyes off him and I say to him my voice low and still I say you will regret this I say you do not know who I am and you do not know what I can do and you will regret this more than you have ever regretted anything and he laughs and says nothing because he doesn't need to he knows I am nothing he knows I can do nothing and it could be he's right and I am nothing but nothing is a void a black pit an endless fall let's see how you like nothing if that's what you want I try to get up but I can't so I put my hands down to my cunt and scoop palmfuls of my blood then with all my strength I flip my body a sad fish gasping for breath I flip my body and reach for him but all I can reach is his left leg so I grab it and wipe my blood down from his knee to his foot my dark blood clotting my dark blood staining my dark blood tarry and sticky and tart he shakes me off like he touched something rotting and I reach my red hands up and I curse him I curse him with the quaking sickness the sea sickness the land sickness and all the sickness that god or the devil ever ordained I curse the sickness into his mind and memory and liver and lungs mixed up together I curse his words and thoughts and memory I curse him with sickness into his flesh and bone I hate him I hate him I have never known before what it was to hate I want him to die I would give anything to make him die but I am on the ground bare and bleeding and he is already walking away as my red hands reach for him I shout after him until I know he can't hear me any more I curse him hard I curse him forever I mean the curse I mean it with everything I am and I feel the power in that moment I feel my heart splitting I feel toads spilling from my mouth I feel the devil rise up in me and in that moment I know I am a witch

I didn't have a way to mark the days or weeks but I know they passed

Because while I might not have known time the thing inside me some-how did

And I felt that I had already died but it couldn't be true because the thing inside me lived

Finally it was time for it to come out

On all fours I breathed and heaved

For hours I strained and squirmed in silence until I was sure that all my insides had come out

I felt the thick sausagey tumble slipping out onto the floor leaving me hollow and new

But when I felt my body with my hands I found the meat of me had stayed inside and instead I became more

More meat

More flesh

More animal

I felt fur prickle and sprout along my shoulders and back

I felt my teeth stretch long and sharp inside my closed jaws

I felt the roof of my mouth turn black and grow ridges

I felt wolf

I felt wolf

I was wolf

The holy women came with candles but my eyes could not handle light and I had to look away

The pain took me out of myself

Out of my body

I pinched my hand to bring myself back but I couldn't tell whether it was my hand or that of the woman holding me

I knew there was pain and I could see blood but I didn't know if it was happening to me or to someone else

Someone was in my body but I don't know if it was me

I heard someone screaming far away but I knew it couldn't be me although my throat burned with it

I thought I had known pain before but it was nothing beside this

Pain so that I didn't understand how I was still alive

And it seemed then that I wasn't

Something came out of me I couldn't see what

I knew it was alive because I could hear it

The holy women took it away in a huddle and the sound of it lessened to silence

When they came back their hands were empty

The holy women told me the thing that came out of me had a huge head and twisted limbs and a black tongue and a full set of teeth gnashing constantly

The holy women said the thing that came out of me was the devil's child and it looked like meat boiled in a pot and stank like rot and although it was alive it shouldn't have been

The holy women said that while a woman carries a babe her monthly blood was food for it and after the babe comes out that blood becomes milk for it but my blood was thick tarry black bad blood and so that is why the thing came out of me like that because I had poisoned it with myself

But I didn't believe them I didn't believe them at all and I will tell you why

The opening in the wall the size of my eye

The one that tilted up and went right to aboveground but through which no light ever came

Just as the child came out of me

Just as her body became a separate thing to my body

Just as I fell back on the ground exhausted and turned my face away from the candle because it was unbearably bright to me

Just then a beam of bright white morning light came through that hole in the wall

Just then the sun was at the only place it could ever shine down on that piece of ground and reach down to this prison

Just then my child was bathed in light

Just then the light chose her

And I saw her

My little light

And even though it tugged at my stitches I smiled

And whatever they try to tell me I know what is true

That I birthed a girl and there was nothing wrong with her

And I begged them to bring the girl back to me

I told them that I only wanted to see her

But I did not want to see her

I wanted to kill her

I wanted to make her safe so the lord could never get to her

And I had never done a good thing before but this would be the first and the last

And god heard me then because one holy woman knew what I was planning

And she came to me and said that they'd told the lord the baby had died

But she had found a guard who pitied me and felt bad for what he'd done to me

A man with crossed eyes and a much-broken nose
And together they'd smuggled the baby out and left it at my mother's
door
And I didn't know if it was true
But I believed her story
I had to believe her because it was the only hope I had left
To my mother would go a baby
All that was left of the girl who was once her baby
I thought of the house deep in the woods with the trees bordering it
on three sides and cast in shadow all the time
I thought of the same house I'd always been in and the same trees that
had always hemmed me in
I thought of walking all the way around the house with my left hand
dragging around under the eaves where it was darkest
If I'd kept my hand on the wall I'd have eventually come back around
to safety
Or there never really was any safety

I wanted my dark-curled pedlar
I wanted my blue pool alone under the sky
I wanted to hold the thing that came out of me
But I didn't get any of that
I got the darkest place and nothing else
I thought of the journey my child had taken
The journey we all take at the start and at the end
Through the known world to a brand-new land
I thought of how scared she must be
Pulled from the deep warm dark
The safe waters of my body
That fed and warmed and grew her
That was her entire world
But she never saw me

She never knew me
I hoped one day she would
But I died there in the dark
With my face to the wall
And my mouth stitched shut
And no one to know I had gone
And my last thought was
I have already died once
What's one more

PART 5

1

Lux coughed awake on a spit of cold sand. She didn't know how she'd got out of the water. Perhaps she hadn't. Perhaps she was dead.

If they're innocent, she thought, *they'll float to the south land. If they're witches, they'll go to the north land where they belong.*

Well, here was the north land. And here she was.

Above her, stars wheeled. Below her, the sea breathed in and out. Behind her, the land stretched into darkness. Beside her, Else tended a fire. It must have been burning for a while, as the sticks had burned black, and Lux could feel the heat in her cheeks.

Her hood was gone. By the time Else had finished her story, the water was up to her chest – but now her skin and white dress were dry. She lay there for a while, catching her breath. Then she turned to Else, reaching out her hand and, very gently, touching the scars around her mouth.

'Little light,' she said.

'Yes,' said Else.

'I'm your child then, aren't I? I was born there underground?'

'Yes.'

'And it was the lord at that blue pool.'

'Yes,' said Else again.

'I'm glad the wolf got him.'

Else looked calmly at Lux for a moment before replying: 'I knew she would.'

'What happened after you died?' asked Lux.

'My body was burned. My baby was sent to my mother.'

'Why did the holy women help you, when they could have killed me, or given me to the lord like he wanted?'

'They thought no child should be used as a bargain.'

'But they were told –'

'Lux, people are not like bees in a hive. We don't all do and think the same things. One person believes all witches must be killed before they destroy the world. The next believes only God has that power, and even with the devil's help no woman can summon a storm. Another believes that no child should suffer for what her mother did.'

'The lord is my father then,' said Lux, and she felt something rise up in her throat. She scooped up a handful of sand and let it sift back down. In the light of the fire and the full moon, she could see well. Everything was so wide and clear, the land stretching out behind her, the sea stretching out before her. She felt dizzy.

'I had a lot of time to think down in that hole,' said Else finally. 'I kept coming back to this: I want to give my girl a choice. We can say it was the lord. We can say it was my dark-haired pedlar. We can say it was that gentle devil who came to me in my underground cell. She looks unlike all of them. I would know, as I've spent many hours looking at her face. She looks quite a lot like me, but mostly like herself. I'll be half of her. The other half – she can choose.'

Lux thought then of her mother – her *grandmother*. She'd kept Else's red ribbon all those years. How she must have worried and wearied. It couldn't have been easy – her only living child, suddenly gone one day, ran off with a pedlar – and then years later, a grandchild she never asked for, one she could ill afford. She could have thrown the baby Lux into the nettles and left her there, and no one would have ever known. But she hadn't.

And Else – she could have left Lux in that house to be taken by the boys, or in the forest to starve or be killed by robbers, or in the water to drown.

But here Lux was. Alive. Loved.

'You didn't come back right away,' said Lux. 'When you . . . died. Why did you come back when I was at the house? Not when I was on my knees crawling through the forest. Not when I was being exorcised at the sanctuary. Not when my grandmother died. Why then and not before?'

'You took the ribbon.'

'She kept it,' said Lux. 'All those years. Kept it clean and whole when everything else she owned was sold or ruined. It was the most precious thing she had.'

'I don't think that's true.' Else looked at the ground and swallowed hard. 'There was something more precious. She sent you away to the sanctuary and stayed in that house alone. You were all she had, but she sent you away. To keep you safe.'

'She stayed in that house because she didn't believe that you were really dead, and she wanted you to be able to find her if you came back. She wanted to keep you safe. But even she wasn't safe in her house, not in the end.'

'No. She wasn't.'

'Perhaps they put me on the same post where she was drowned.'

'Perhaps they did.'

It was night, and this land was strange, and Lux knew that she should be afraid. But being there with Else, she found that she wasn't.

'This is the north land, isn't it? How did we get here?'

'I don't know – as you passed out, I did too. A fisherman? The wolf? Witchery? The ghosts of other women who were drowned? A heavenly miracle from up on high, the likes of which we've never seen before and never will see again?'

Lux thought then of her time at the sanctuary – the early-morning prayers, her aching body, the brief moment of rest on the misericord. Her tired hand feeling the carving on the side, the woman who was half-fish, who could swim away, could go anywhere she wanted.

'Or I'm a fish-woman and I saved myself,' said Lux with a smile. 'If you can be a revenant –'

'A what?'

'It's a story one of the girls at the stronghold told me. Bodies who died and went to their graves, then came back. People who could walk around, and talk and eat and suchlike, but yet were dead. Or not dead, and not alive, but a little of each.'

'I've never heard of a revenant,' said Else, 'I didn't know they existed.' The light from the fire lit up her shining eyes – shining not because she was a north witch, but because she had spent so long there in the dark.

'Perhaps they didn't exist. But here you are, and now they do.'

Lux had tried living in the dark: selling her poisons, moving through the forest in the dead of night, lying in the snow with a stranger as the sky pulsed purple and green. And what had that got her? The choice only between being a victim or a maiden.

She had tried living in the light: baking bread at the stronghold, tasting delicacies, mass every Sunday. And what had that got her? The choice between being a servant, a sacrifice, a whore, a poisoner, a wolf.

There was only one more thing to try.

'I want to find the north witches,' said Lux.

They walked together, the path narrow and winding, wide enough for a single horse. Not that they had a horse, unfortunately. To both sides of the road, strange green humps covered the landscape. Lux had investigated them with the stamp of her heel, only to find her foot sinking into the mossy ground. She quickly retreated back to the path.

In the first pale glimmers of dawn they saw a house. At first they didn't realise it was a house, as it was carved right into the side of a small hill with only a black-timbered front visible. But Else spotted the thread of smoke issuing from a slit in the hill, and they looked closer.

A dim light burned in one window, but there was no other sign of life. A blanket hung over the open door. It looked warm. Lux's bones ached with cold.

Quick as a fox, she ran into the yard and tugged the blanket down off the door. She wrapped it around her shoulders, closing her eyes and pressing her face into the folds. It smelled of woodsmoke and new bread.

The breath caught in her throat as she heard a low growl. She opened her eyes to a wolf. No – not a wolf. The light was still pale and shadowed, but as she focused she saw it was a dog. It was tall and rangy, its short fur all-over black except for a bib of white down its front. Its lower legs were skinny as chicken bones, but its upper legs were thickly muscled. A hunting dog, similar to the ones the lord kept. And it was growling at Lux and Else, hackles raised.

'Who's there?' The voice from inside the house was breathless, and so faint Lux could barely hear it. The accent seemed strange to her, the words soft and slushy. Lux couldn't take her eyes off the dog, sure it was about to leap for her throat. The silence stretched, and the dog's growls grew louder.

'No one,' called Else. 'It's no one. We're leaving now.' She tugged at Lux's hand – but Lux still held the blanket.

'Rún,' said the voice, and it must have been the dog's name, or a coded command, because it lowered its hackles and slunk into the house. Not far, though: it lay down with its head on its paws just inside the door, watching.

Lux knew she should let go of the blanket and hang it back up on the door. She was scared, but she was also cold. Lux kept her eyes on the dog – but couldn't help looking behind it, into the room beyond.

The house was small and low-roofed, panelled with wood. To one side a platform bed was built into the wall, topped with a rumpled mass of blankets and furs. To the other side, the fire in the hearth was just embers. The house looked empty – so who had spoken? Lux narrowed her eyes against the gloom – and felt her heart jolt as she realised someone was in the bed, hidden in shadow. As she had been staring into the house, a woman had been staring right back at her.

Lux's heart leapt rabbit-fast. Perhaps this was one of the north witches. Perhaps she would teach Lux all she knew. She held herself still, trying to feel the crackle of power.

'I . . . was putting the blanket back up on the door,' said Lux.

The woman regarded Lux from her pile of furs. She could imagine what the woman saw: a filthy, shivering girl, wearing only a tattered shift, her hair like bracken and her eyes hollow. Why didn't she jump out of bed and snatch her blanket back? Lux could take it and run. Did she trust her dog would give chase?

The woman looked at her for a long time. It was clear that she wasn't convinced, but eventually she sighed and closed her eyes. 'Take it,' she said, her voice a whisper. 'I won't need it soon.'

Lux told herself to take the blanket off, but could only clutch it tighter.

'Only first,' said the woman, her eyes still closed. 'Water. Please.' It seemed that the woman had to fight for every breath, and her sentences could only last the length of a gasp.

Lux hesitated – then stepped into the house.

It smelled of ashes and wood and something faintly, sweetly bad. Scattered across the floor were some pale-looking vegetables, a wooden trencher, a spoon. It looked like an abandoned attempt at a meal. Lux picked up a cup half full of water and brought it to the woman in the bed.

She held out the cup of water, but the woman didn't reach for it. Her hand twitched on the blanket, then settled back down. Lux stepped closer to the woman, bringing the cup to her lips. The woman could barely lift her head, and drank haltingly.

She was possibly the oldest person Lux had ever seen. Her face was wrinkled and sunken like a forgotten piece of fruit. Her white hair, half-blown dandelion fluff, lay sparse on her head. But her long eyelashes and small hands clutching the blanket reminded Lux of a child. She seemed to exist between worlds: as if she'd only recently been born, and as if she was standing on the threshold of death.

Lux was careful to tilt the cup slowly so that the water didn't spill. Then the cup was empty, and the woman lay back down.

Was this a north witch? The creature Lux had spent so long fearing and desiring? So untamed they burned the earth where they stood. So unholy the very seas rose up against them. So wild they could see in the dark. She peered at the woman, trying to see the black glitter of power and threat.

'Go now,' the woman said, her voice a little stronger.

She knew she should go. She already had the blanket.

'Your fire is almost out,' said Lux, and she went out of the door to find the firewood.

Else was in the garden, poking through the vegetable patch. 'I saw an onion. There's a leek. Some sad-looking cabbage.'

'You're never hungry.'

'Not for me. If you make potage for her, you could share it. And, Lux –' Else led her deeper into the garden. 'There are herbs here too.'

Lux used her foot to part the leaves. 'I see garlic, bishopwort, worm-wood. That will help, at least a little.'

'With what?'

'To heal her. If I heal her then perhaps she'll teach me the secret of her power. She must be very powerful, don't you think? A north witch. Not everyone here can be a north witch, but some must be, and perhaps she's one. Why else is she alone here?'

Lux noticed a bucket propped against the front wall, and wondered if there was a well. Around the other side of the house she found just that, along with a horse tied to a hitching post. It was small but sturdy, and a pleasing sandy colour. The horse stopped ripping up grass and stared at Lux as she passed. She took the opportunity to run her hand along its flank and check its eyes: it seemed healthy enough.

Lux drew water from the well, and as she lifted it full she couldn't help but drink from it. The water was sweet and cool. She filled the horse's empty trough, and it immediately dipped its head to drink. Lux refilled the bucket.

She came back round the house with the full bucket and an armful of cut wood.

'Lux,' said Else, who hadn't moved from her place. 'Wait.'

'What is it?'

'You think this woman is powerful because she's alone.'

'A woman alone must be powerful.'

'Lux –' Else stepped closer, her voice low. 'Think of it another way. She's not powerful because she's alone. She's alone because she's old and sick and dying.'

Lux hesitated. The water and the wood were heavy, and she wanted to set them down. 'If that's true, then all the more reason to heal her.'

'I think it's too late for that.'

'Then we can ease her burden, can't we?'

Else didn't argue with that.

Back in the house, the woman was sitting up in bed with her eyes open. They were the bright blue of a summer sea.

'What's your name?' said the woman.

'Lux.'

'And who is that?'

Lux glanced over her shoulder at Else in the threshold. She realised that no one, in the forest or at the stronghold, had ever acknowledged Else. Could Else be right about the woman? She was close to death, and that's why Else was real to her.

'That's Else. My mother.'

'Lux. Else. I am Saga. And my man there. Is Rún.'

At the sound of his name, the dog began thumping his tail on the floor without lifting his head from his paws.

'He guards you well,' said Else.

'You needn't fear him,' said Saga. 'He has strong teeth. But prefers to use them. Only on rabbits.'

Together, the three women ate. At some point, Rún had slipped out of the house and caught himself something for his meal; he slunk back in soon after, licking his lips, then lay in front of the roaring fire and set to work cleaning his paws.

'Do people –' Lux swallowed a spoonful of potage. 'Do people here – fishermen, I mean – do they save the women on the drowning stakes? If they pass them in their boats and no one from the south shore can see?'

'They may. I don't know. Plenty of boats go by. Not always watched. By those on either shore.' Saga's voice came easier now that she had taken Lux's concoction of herbs, but she still fought for her breaths. She looked as fragile as a bird in her mass of furs, and even though the fire burned hot, she never seemed to get warm. Lux's hand had touched Saga's when she handed her the bowl, and her skin was as soft as petals, but very cold. 'Is that how. You got here? From the posts?'

Lux didn't know whether to tell Saga the truth.

She fixed Lux with her bright eyes. 'Bad business. The drowning posts.' She held Lux's gaze. 'I don't care. What others say you are.'

Lux thought then of a place she'd seen endless times, but only ever inside her head. The white sea that never rests, licking over the sand as black as night. The steam billowing into the wild sea from a crevice in the folded rocks. Light and dark together in one woman, every word she spoke burning with power –

'Is there a place,' she said carefully, 'with a white sea and black sand and huge blue glaciers? And steam billowing from the earth even on the coldest days? I think a volcano erupted there in the years before I was born. Else told me that in the south it was blamed for the sickness. Then when it came back, the witches were blamed.'

'Witches,' murmured Saga. 'Are only in the south land. They send them to the posts. But they come no further.' She smiled at Lux. 'Usually.'

'No,' said Lux, and again she felt the freezing waves lapping at her thighs; again she felt the bite of the wolf's jaws on the lord's throat. 'No, that's not true. The witches are in the north, that's what we were told, that's the truth of it. That's why people get sent to the drowning posts, so that God will save them if they're good, and they'll go to the north land if they're - if they belong there. And there's a place, a black and white place, and that's where the north witches come from.'

Saga said nothing. She looked at Lux with a new expression, one that Lux found hard to identify. She didn't know if anyone had ever looked at her like that before. It wasn't disdain or disgust or curiosity or teasing or confession or regret. It was - Lux couldn't bear it, and looked away.

'Is there?' asked Lux, and she felt the words catch in her throat. 'Please. Is there a place like that?'

'North,' said Saga, her voice soft. 'You'll find it north. Take my horse.'

'We're not taking anything,' cut in Else.

'Because we're not leaving you,' said Lux with a smile, and got up to refill Saga's bowl.

It was a long night, that first and final night with Saga, and filled with stories. At first, Else tried to stop Saga, worrying it would tire her, fearing the steady gasps as she spoke. But Saga waved her away and kept talking. In the warm dark of the little house, Saga painted pictures and made music with words. It was, Lux thought, like the lady had said: each person is stuffed full to bursting with stories, ready to explode. Saga had given them shelter and food and warmth just when they needed it; if Lux could give Saga anything in return, she would send her more sweetly off to wherever she was going next - and until then she would hear her stories, and know their worth.

Saga spoke of going into the mossy green hills and being offered meat and fruit and sugared things with the queen of fairyland, who was heavily clothed in lemon-coloured linen, and the king of fairyland, who had a broad face and a booming laugh; but of not eating those things, because she knew it was all a trick, and if she did she would have to stay there for-ever under the earth, like a bright mushroom, somewhere between the living and the dead – and this story, it soon became clear, was not just a story, but a guide to the different mushrooms that grew in the north land, and their uses in eating, and in healing, and in bringing on visions.

She spoke of a beautiful girl and an audacious wolf, both kept captive by a wicked lord, chained to opposite walls of a low prison which lay beneath a grate in the floor of the lord's room. The lord's intent was for the wolf to tear the girl apart for his amusement – but as he watched, the wild beast crawled fawning to the girl's feet and lay his head on her lap. In a rage the lord sent them both to be hanged, but they escaped and ran away together, and had many children, and were happy together. But the woman outlived the wolf, as they do, and she honoured him by making his white fur into a mantle, over which her long red hair flowed like heart's blood – and this story was really about the connection between animals and people, and how we can use it and how we must respect it, and how what we see of someone may not be who they truly are.

She spoke of a king who grew very rich but let his people starve, and who daily had gold dust blown over his naked body, and then swam from one side of a black lake to the other, letting the gold dust wash off him as tribute to the dragon living in a cave in the deep and hidden depths of the lake; as soon as the king left the water the people waded in with their buckets and their sieves to collect as much of the gold dust as they could, not because they didn't fear the dragon, but because they feared starving to death more – and this story was really about lords, and their people, and each one's responsibility to the other.

There were more stories inside Saga than inside all the books in the sanctuary – more than inside all the sanctuaries in the world, perhaps. Her stories crossed such lands and such great spans of time that she couldn't have experienced them all. But then – what did Lux know? Per-haps Saga was as old as all her stories.

And she spoke, finally, of her most important story. The one that burned in her with a white light. The purpose she had served over all her years: how she had lived here in this house alone, far from others, and yet had known many hundreds of people. How she had seen the arrival of dozens of babies into this world, and eased the passing of many people out of it. How she had prevented children that were not wanted, and brought on ones that were. How she had soothed pain, healed wounds, taken away cares simply by hearing them spoken aloud and sharing their weight. How she had known things, and kept them safe. How she was, now, passing some of them on.

'I will remember,' said Lux to Saga. 'I will remember it all.'

Saga smiled and closed her eyes. From her seat by the fire, Lux looked again at Saga, searching for the north witch in her. The untamed power, the unholiness, the wildness. She couldn't see it.

She looked again and tried to see what Else had seen: an old woman, alone and abandoned, about to die. But that was not what Saga was either.

When she looked at Saga, Lux did not see a north witch. She did not see a lonely woman. She saw something more important and more powerful: a woman who was entirely herself.

Saga died just before dawn. Lux must have fallen asleep by the embers; she woke to the sound of Rún whining, the soft pad of his paws as he crossed from the hearth to leap up on the bed to lie alongside Saga. By the time Lux had sat up, Else had joined Rún on the bed beside Saga. Without a word, Lux climbed up too, stretching her body out between Rún and the wall, putting her arm around Rún and Saga, her hand meeting Else's as she did the same. They held hands and lay like that until the light came.

'We could stay,' murmured Else. 'We could live in this house, and we could grow cures and poisons, and sell them to the people here. We could be what Saga was. Women alone, and powerful in our way.'

And in that moment, Lux was tempted. It would be so easy. Everything was laid out for her, ready. The water in the well. The plants in the garden. The people who needed her. Just like the red dress of the maiden, the white veil and black rags of the witch. Ready for her to wear.

'If we stayed,' said Lux, 'then we would be just as we were before. That house in the forest, surrounded by nettles to hide what grew there. A woman always on the outskirts, waiting for her usefulness to end and everyone to turn on her.'

'That wouldn't happen here. They didn't turn on Saga. They don't use the drowning posts. It's different.'

'That wasn't who you were, and it's not who I am either.'

'Then who are you?'

Else's question hung in the still-dark room, and Lux did not answer.

Lux and Else laid Saga to rest together. Sometime in the night it had snowed, and the ground was too hard to dig; they laid Saga out in her blanket among her herbs and poisons, so that her body could help them grow.

Lux hadn't been there when her grandmother had died. She'd died alone, and afraid, and abandoned. Saga had died in a warm bed, with a full belly, in company; Lux and Else had given her that. And it didn't undo what had happened to her grandmother. It didn't make it better. But it was the best that Lux could do.

It was a rich pink dawn, and in the distance Lux could just see the line of the water that led to the south land, lit like a layer of flower petals by the sky. The snow caught the light and reflected it back, casting a rosy glow across the world. But they weren't going back there. They were going forward.

Together, she and Else climbed onto the horse, set the dog walking at their side, and took the road north to find the witches.

2

Lux and Else set off, wrapped in Saga's furs, packs rattling with the remnants of Saga's food and the herbs from her garden, Rún padding along beside them as they rode Saga's horse – which Lux had named My Lady, just because she could.

The rain had chased away the snow. The path was black earth, loamy and thick, and My Lady made steady progress. Frost cracked in the ruts. The further they travelled from the sea, the higher the hills loomed, the silver-grey rocks painted with green, so it was not at all difficult to imagine the fairy queen in her lemon-coloured linen waiting underground. All of Saga's stories felt so real here, and Lux treasured her new knowledge.

The weather was always a surprise. Lux had grown used to the shelter she found in the shadows under the trees, the constant light of the sanctuary and the stronghold. But here, nothing could be predicted. One moment was blinding spindrift and the push of wind; the next blue sky and gentle sun stroking her cheeks; then a low sea mist rolling over the land, so she could only see one step ahead. Here they were never too far from the sea. If it wasn't visible at the corner of her eye, she knew it was just beyond that hill, or the next, or the next.

At times Lux felt again as she had when they'd first washed up on the shore of the north land: dizzy, porous, like there was too much for her lungs to breathe and too much for her eyes to see. One slow morning, riding through the growing dawn, she finally realised what it was: the sky.

She had gone from the house in the forest under a canopy of trees, to the sanctuary with its high roofs and massed buildings, to the pines where it was dark as night, to the stronghold kitchen, to the town where the buildings kissed and blocked out the sky. She had never seen so much sky.

She wasn't sure if she was imagining it, but it seemed to her that Else had begun to ... flicker. Just a little. There were moments when she thought Else was right beside her, but then when she looked, she wasn't there. But then she'd blink, and there Else would be, as if she'd never gone anywhere.

Finally they reached the edge of the town. The buildings were squat and severe and sharp-edged, made of blackened wood that loomed up in the gloaming. As they clopped through the streets, road-dusty and travel-sore, things seemed strange. Where was everyone?

Then, cutting through the silence, a burst of music. They followed the sound.

Suddenly, shockingly, the buildings ended. A clearing opened up. In the centre of the clearing stretched a silver birch, wrapped round with col-oured ribbons. Torches burned all around. At the edges of the clearing, what looked like the whole town stood, watching thirteen people dressed in wild costumes, playing instruments and performing acrobatic feats. As Lux watched, the mood changed: the music slowed, fell almost holy, and eleven of the thirteen moved to the side, keeping the slow rhythm. Onstage stepped a man dressed as a priest. After him crawled a girl on her knees, wearing a black dress and laden with dozens of wooden crosses.

Lux didn't recognise the girl. But she instantly knew the man. He was the tallest person that Lux had ever seen, with the darkest skin she had ever seen. He was as thin as a skeleton: if he lay on his side during rain, a tiny puddle would form in the hollow of his cheek.

The mummers had come to the north land. And they were telling a story she knew.

*

The girl was covered in crosses, made of all kinds of wood: dark, light, new, old, smooth, rough; tied on with rope and string and ribbon. They were tied around her waist, her thighs, her arms, her chest, her belly, her neck, so tight her breath came short and fast like a dog. The crosses were so heavy she could barely lift her head, so she faced the ground as she crawled on her knees towards the man dressed as a priest.

The others came forward, all in white, heads held high. The priest spread his hands to the pale sky and cried out, voice echoing: 'Thus I banish you home, wicked girl! This is a holy place full of holy men – yet you thought only of other holes! There are other girls here, holy girls, and their holes are holier than yours!'

The girl on her knees crawled to the priest and pulled at his clothing, begging him to cleanse her. He cast her violently aside and she fell to the stage, crying, lamenting, repenting, but still also looking pretty. The girl offered to suck the priest's parts if he'd let her stay – to suck all the parts of all the priests. Much time was spent on her telling about all the other things she'd sucked, both on priests and on her fellow girls. But it was all to no use: the girl was banished, and crawled offstage as the white chorus sang of her sin and repentance.

After that there were many things, some of which Lux recognised, and some of which she didn't. There were barefoot men with red crosses painted on their chests, whipping themselves and crying out their sins – both real and imagined – as others threw red liquid onto the crowd as mock blood. There was a devil with his carved wooden prick the size of a tree branch, a fiend with smoke and flames issuing from his rear end, and a crowning of flowers. There was the girl again, free of her crosses now, but hunched and cackling, a thick-blooded witch, sending praises to Satan on his throne of bones, asking him to help her garden of poisons grow so that she could kill all the men, every single man, and perhaps some boy babies too.

And in the final scene there was a woman, beautiful and innocent, dressed all in blue with her hair tied up in a huge golden cage, crying out in desperation as the witch-girl plunged a knife into her good, strong, blameless husband's heart. So that was the end of that.

After the show, Lux parted ways with Else, who tied My Lady to a post and went to explore the stalls and entertainments. She flickered like a candle flame, moving invisibly between the people, who didn't seem to see her at all.

Lux was intrigued by her surroundings. Many things were similar to the frost fair: roasting mushrooms and skewered meat, a woman reading palms, children singing songs for coins. But there were new and wonderful things too: the scent of unfamiliar herbs, figures carved from wood and decorated with petals and moss, a pure white fox stealing a lick of salt from a woman's palm, golden tokens to give to the sea-goddess so she wouldn't drown you in a storm, a line of cats parading through the crowd led by a child with a length of bright ribbon.

But Lux felt strange and hollow, visions of the mummers' show caught behind her eyelids. The shadows called to her. She walked into them, Rún padding close at her heels.

At the edge of the town, she found the tall man, still dressed as a priest, drinking a cup of ale, singing quietly to himself, watching as the lowering sun threw blood and honey across the sky. She waited in the shadows for a moment, listening to him sing. She didn't know the song, and it didn't seem to have any words – or nothing she recognised as words.

'Do you sing to hold off the dark,' she called over, 'or to draw it in quicker?'

Mister Gaunt twisted his lanky body to peer behind him. It took him a moment to focus his eyes. Lux stepped forward, Rún close behind. The expression on Mister Gaunt's face was complex: shock, joy, contentment, or something between them. His hands twitched out as if he wanted to grasp Lux and check she was real. He waited until she had come and sat down beside him before answering. He shifted a little closer so their shoulders almost touched.

'Neither,' he said. 'I merely sing in the dark. It comes whether I like it or not. And speaking of things that come whether I like it or not, what brings this little light to the north land?'

'I'm travelling,' said Lux.

'By yourself?'

Lux smiled. 'Not exactly.' She rested a hand on Rún's head.

'I heard a story about you,' said Mister Gaunt, and though he tried to keep his voice light, there was a tension in it like a plucked string. 'I heard you drowned.'

'Not completely.'

'Well,' said Mister Gaunt. 'Well, I'm glad.' He opened his mouth as if to add more, but seemed at a loss.

The silence stretched. Then Lux tipped back her head and laughed, sending the sound up to the darkening sky. 'There's a thing I never thought I'd see. Mister Gaunt, wordless.'

Mister Gaunt lifted his cup of ale and took a sip, then another.

'*Mister Gaunt*,' he said thoughtfully. 'So that's what they call me. I shall count myself lucky, as I got off lightly indeed – I have been called much worse.'

But Lux wasn't listening. Her thoughts, suddenly, were too loud. She might not be the fastest thinker, but she got there eventually.

'How did you get to the north land?' she asked. 'On a boat?'

'Easier than swimming from south to north. I don't like to get my feet wet.'

'Did you –' Lux lowered her voice so no one overheard, though she knew no one was there. 'Did you take me off the drowning post?'

'Oh, no!' Mister Gaunt leaned back as if shocked. 'Such poor mummers as we wouldn't dream of such things. It would be punishable by death to help a witch. Not to mention the burning of our tragic souls in hellfire for all eternity.' Mister Gaunt pressed his palms together and raised his eyes heavenward. 'I look out for myself alone and stay well out of trouble. I intend to keep myself pure for that good light. Pure as a nun and a monk praying alone, bare to the skin, in the same innocent state as they were born, that's me.'

Lux nodded slowly. She knew it wasn't wise, but she couldn't help being disappointed. She thought of the misericord: the woman who was half-fish, who could swim away, could go anywhere she wanted. Lux hadn't saved herself after all. 'Thank you,' she said, and her voice came out low.

Mister Gaunt dropped his head, almost touching his forehead to the ground in a dramatic bow. 'At your eternal, innocent service.'

He swayed upright and disappeared into the shadows; Lux assumed their conversation was over, but then he reappeared with a cup of mead and two bowls: one containing a rich, salted fish soup, the other something soft and white with a spoon in it. Lux lifted the spoon and tasted it: it was sweet and creamy. She spoke between mouthfuls.

'I enjoyed your show.'

'It's a story I heard,' said Mister Gaunt, and perhaps Lux was imagining it, but it seemed that he chose his words carefully. 'In the north land, they like to hear about the wild things that the south folk do. Scary stories to remind them why they stay up in the nice north land. Just as the south folk love to tell about the north witches and their terrors, to remind them of their nice south land.'

'My mother – my grandmother used to tell me those stories.'

'Yet it didn't keep you in your nice south land.'

'It seems that stories don't always do what we want them to.'

Mister Gaunt gave a bitter laugh, gazing off across the darkened land.

'Do yours?' asked Lux.

'Ah, little light. I have many stories that I can't tell on a stage. Stories that people don't want to listen to.' Mister Gaunt bent his long back and hung his head, clutching his cup of ale with both hands.

'I'll listen,' said Lux.

Mister Gaunt turned and looked at her. Something bright gleamed in his eye. Lux realised this was the first time they had looked one another in the eye. The first time that they had been on the same level. He handed her his cup.

'You'll need a drink for this one.'

Lux tipped back the cup and swallowed as Mister Gaunt began his story, the heat of his breath sending each word up to the sky in a puff of smoke.

'There was a woman,' began Mister Gaunt, and Lux couldn't help it: as he spoke, she saw his words as a show, the people and events happening before her eyes. 'A woman always clothed in blue to show her purity. A woman flighty and small-boned as a bird, with a sharp gleaming eye. We'll call her . . . Thrall.'

And a scent filled Lux then, tallow and cinnamon and strange skin; the mothwing-touch of delicate fingers in her mouth.

'Thrall had three husbands,' went on Mister Gaunt. 'She was many things, but most of all she was clever: she married up each time, climbing the social ladder. She was widowed by all three.

'The first husband was rich and cruel. He had a bad heart and demanded only the most expensive doctors. They fed him tinctures of gold, crushed pearls, syrup made of sugar and violets. When he died, so they say, it was discovered that he actually had no heart at all. Later it was found, shivering in its final beats, among the gold in his treasure chest. It's said that in the next world, lovers will have to weigh their hearts to see if they're unbalanced. I would be keen to see how the mistress Thrall fares then.'

Lux could hear the final shiver of the heart, could taste the violet sugar syrup, could see the gleam of the gold, as vivid as if it was unfolding before her.

'The second husband – he was the pretty one. He wore embroidered clothing and crushed a handful of fresh rose petals between his hands every hour to smell always sweet. His cloak was so heavy with its stitching and jewels that the cords tying it closed had to be held by two servants, lest it fall and choke him. I did say he was the pretty one, but he was not the clever one. When his wife suggested he join a foolishly waged and badly fought war, he readily agreed. He died there, but at least when his heart stopped beating, it was beneath his ribs where it belonged.

'The third husband – and here is where the fool comes in. The fool wasn't Thrall's husband; fools are the wisest of all men, and the last thing she wanted was a wise husband. The third husband was sickening. He had received a wound years ago and it had never healed. But he hid the rot of him: bulked his failing body with horsehair pads, scented it with spice and posies. He grew mistrustful, sure someone was out to harm him, and he wore layered fussy armour and picked at his food, sure an assassin was waiting to slit his throat from behind or dose him with poison. He feared dying like that: alone and cowardly.

'As a distraction the third husband got himself a fool. Right strange this fool was, tall as a bear but narrow as a bone, kept as a sort of human pet. He was a learned fool, having travelled far, paying his way with gabbles and acrobatics, and learning much in each new place. A fool is allowed into places that others aren't, and allowed to see things that others may not.

'Thrall, though, had a problem. You might have seen by now what her problem is. Three husbands – and no living child.

'She'd had babies by the first and second husbands. But there are so many things in this world that can carry off a child. She lost one to dropsy, one to tissick, one to purples, one to rising of the lights, one to a fall, one to head mould shot, one to the bloody flux, and the last was planet-struck. So in the end she had none. But she knew, if she tried, she could get another.

'By her third husband, though – nothing. Not a whisper. Not a whisk. They lay together every night, but her blood came every month without fail. (This, too, was a thing that the fool knew, for fools know everything you suspect they might, and much more besides.) It couldn't be the third husband's fault. If a couple is not blessed with children, the fault is always with the woman. And if God does not send a woman such a blessing – well, then she must be serving another, wickeder master. The third husband knew this, and was growing suspicious of Thrall.

'One year without a child could be bad luck. Two years – her goodwill among the people is wearing even thinner. Three years without a child, and a woman was a cursed thing indeed. Thrall had no one to confess to. Except...

'She knew no one listened to a fool. He was little better than an animal. And if an animal talked, who would believe a word it said? So she told the fool her story. She said she'd tried charms and prayers and precious gems and everything that anyone suggested, no matter where it lay between religion and magic. None of it worked.

'The longer she had the third husband, the more suspicion against her would grow. She needed to get rid of him. She asked the fool to help her kill him, but he was not such a fool as that. As soon as he could, he left. I heard he joined a mummer troupe.

'Anyway, the third husband died a few years later, so she got her way after all. Some little bit of a kitchen girl stabbed him in the heart.'

By the time Mister Gaunt had finished his story, Lux's food was finished and the sky was full black. Her head spun and she realised she'd forgotten to breathe, so caught up in the story. She took a minute to blink away the colours; to swallow down the taste of tallow and violets.

'What will she do now?' Lux asked.

'Who? The kitchen girl?'

'Thrall.'

'She will marry again,' said Mister Gaunt. 'Hope for a child.'

'And if a child doesn't come?'

'Then there's not much she can do.'

How the world is just the same thing over and over and over. Unless we choose something else.

'I heard,' said Mister Gaunt, 'that she wasn't just a kitchen girl. There are other stories. I heard she was a food-taster, or a whore, or a poisoner, or a mummer, or a witch.'

'And which was she?'

'That's not for me to say.'

'And you?' asked Lux.

Mister Gaunt sighed. 'Today, a priest. Tomorrow, a bear. Then Death. We'll see where we are and what stories the people want.'

'And yet you don't tell the one story you know is true.' Lux set her empty bowls aside. 'You're not free. You travel where you like, and you can live the way you like – but you can't say what's real. You just tell the stories you're made to tell – the ones that rich and powerful people want told.'

'No one made me tell you about Thrall.'

'You're afraid of her! You can't even use her name. You tell the story about her only to me, in private, in the dark, on the edge of town. The story you tell onstage is the one she wants.'

Mister Gaunt didn't reply to that.

'A convenient end, wasn't it?' said Lux. 'For the kitchen girl to rid her of her problem.'

Mister Gaunt took a long time to reply, and Lux wondered if he'd fallen asleep. But when he spoke, his voice was strong. 'Perhaps things aren't quite as they appear. Why did she think that a girl who knew poisons was so valuable? Why was the kitchen girl there in Thrall's chamber? Why was there a knife?'

'So she planned it. For the kitchen girl to kill him. With poison, perhaps, but then the knife was there, and ...'

'Ah, little light. Don't take it to heart. It's just a story. Soon people will tell another.'

Lux shivered; the night was cold, and the fires were far. 'Then here is a story for you. A new one, one that you haven't heard before.'

There in the cold night, Lux told Mister Gaunt her story, beginning to end. She told him about a woman who ran away with a pedlar, and went on adventures, and had her future stolen. About the house in the forest with its poisons outside and its warm fire inside. About the bee-loud sanctuary, the girls there thinking always of God, but being controlled by those who thought themselves godly but were only men. About the stronghold, with its intrigues and rot hidden under layers of velvet and fur, and the people who really keep it all running. About the north land, harsh and beautiful, home to fire and ice, home to so many stories that play out and die and get lost forever – and now, also, home to her.

When she'd finished speaking, Mister Gaunt sat for what seemed like a long time. 'Can we tell it?' he asked finally. 'Not Thrall's version. Yours.'

That was Lux's reason for telling him, but she just smiled and nodded. Let him think it was his idea. Lux had been forced to play out a lie, to play Else as the witch. And now, instead, there would be something true. It didn't undo what had happened. It didn't make it better. But it was the best that she could do.

'My arse,' she said, getting awkwardly to her feet, 'is numb.'

'My balls, too,' said Mister Gaunt, following with a sigh.

'Your balls are needed,' called a voice from the shadows. 'The ladies of the town want to meet the priest.' A figure emerged.

Hair cut short, pale like wheat. A spray of golden dots across a long nose and high cheeks. A small mouth with full lips, swollen like a flower. A pointed chin that Lux still wanted to take in her hand and turn towards her so she could suck those lips into her mouth, bite into them a little, to see if they tasted like rose petals.

'Ash,' said Lux.

Mister Gaunt turned wordlessly towards the market square, where the celebrations were in full swing. There was dancing, drinking, eating, laughing. At every doorway torches burned. In the cold air, the plumes of everyone's breath lifted to the sky. But Lux and Ash walked away from it all, into the night. The moon was bright and full above them, lighting the world in silver gleaming.

Ash was not quite as Lux remembered. But then, she imagined she was not quite as Ash remembered either. They were both older. Quieter. Lux thought of all she'd seen since they last met below the north lights, all that she didn't want to tell Ash, and wondered what secrets Ash was keeping.

'You weren't at the stronghold,' said Lux.

'You know the mummers. We come and go. As long as we number thirteen, it doesn't matter so much which of us make up that number.'

'So where were you?'

'I was otherwise engaged,' said Ash.

Lux laughed. 'To who?'

She could see now where they were going: not far ahead of them, white smoke billowed from the ground. Her heart leapt as she wondered if this was the place she'd been ... but no, she realised as they got closer; it wasn't at all like she'd dreamt.

She looked around for Ash, and realised that Ash had been walking oddly, hands held low, and hadn't reached out to touch Lux. Now, Ash paused, and waited for Lux to stop too. She saw Ash's hands in the moon-light. Ash's hand.

'What –' Lux took a moment to catch her breath. She wanted to reach out for the space where Ash's right hand used to be, but stopped herself. 'What happened?'

'Stole,' said Ash simply, and started walking again. She understood. Ash had stolen, and been caught, and had a hand taken as punishment. Ash was not the first person this had happened to, and wouldn't be the last. 'Still,' said Ash, voice falsely cheery, 'makes me fit in better with the others. We're all outcasts in some way. Can't join the mummers other-wise. Abject people, all of us. Traitors, criminals, scapegoats. And I can do the shows just as well with one hand. I can do –' and here Ash winked, and Lux recognised the charm and strange that had so enticed her before, and still did now – 'I can do everything just as well with one hand.'

She reached out as they walked and took Ash's left hand. She felt the callouses, the soft centre of the palm; tilting Ash's hand to the moonlight, she saw a blood bruise under the thumbnail. Those good, strong hands. She could cry from the waste of it, the unfairness. She wondered what Ash had stolen – but it didn't matter. Ash had only done what needed to be done to survive. Like Lux and her poisons. The lord and his relics. The mummers and their stories.

Lux saw now where Ash was taking her. Scattered around the path lay a dozen small blue pools, bright like jewels under the huge sky, each one a different shade. Steam billowed from them: some in fast and endless clouds, some a few scattered puffs. Ash avoided the billowing ones, as they were clearly too hot, and led Lux instead to a gently steaming one.

'Thought you'd like it,' said Ash, suddenly shy.

But Lux was not interested in shyness now. She pulled off her clothes, then Ash's too. Together they eased into the water. They floated, bodies warming and soothed.

Lux reached for Ash, and Ash came to her, and it was just as it had been that night out in the snowy forest, the lights twisting and throbbing above them. Ash, always the same, always new.

Afterwards, they basked in silence. It was companionable, comfortable. Lux stretched out, settling into the water, the sky, her body.

There in the steaming water, under the starry sky, Lux saw a blue pool. A gold girl. A bold man. A red stain –

She gasped awake, and it was only her, and the pool, and the sky, and Ash beside her. There was no sound of hooves. There was no lord.

'He's dead, you know,' said Lux. 'The lord. I was there.'

'I heard,' replied Ash.

'Do you think it'll stop now?' Lux couldn't help it; she glanced around again, out into the night, sure she heard the distant thrum of hooves.

'No,' said Ash simply.

Lux started to argue, then stopped. She knew Ash was right. The lord was gone. But the lady was still there. The priests were still there. The others who had made accusations and given evidence were all still there. There would always be another lord.

'Why don't you come with us?' said Ash. 'We're moving on in the morning. On to the next town, and then the next, and back around. You could be the maiden. I heard you made a great witch too.'

Lux could do that. It would be so easy to put on that red dress, those black rags, that crown of burning candles.

She climbed out of the pool and shook herself like a dog, drops of water pattering to the earth. She began putting her clothes back on. After a moment, Ash followed.

Lux's clothing was damp, and she was cold, but she hoped that the heat of her skin from the water would see her back to the town, and to her horse and her dog, and to Else. They would keep going north until she found what she needed.

The lord had found Else in a blue pool, and he had wanted to hurt her. Lux had gone into a pool with someone who only wanted her to feel good. And it didn't undo what had happened to Else. It didn't make it better. But it was the best that Lux could do.

Ash and Lux stood apart, dressed now. The same as before, but also new.

'Perhaps I'll see you again,' said Lux.

'Perhaps you will,' Ash replied with a smile, and kissed her, very gently, at the corner of her mouth.

3

Lux and Else travelled through many small villages and past scattered homes. Sometimes they passed other travellers on the path. They traded some words, or they didn't. Most nights, they were allowed into a stranger's home and could share their meal; for this, Lux traded her knowledge of plants, herbs and mushrooms, some learned from her grandmother, some from Saga.

She met people warm and full of stories, their children crawling over her lap and making toys out of fabric scraps and leaves so that they could play with Rún. She met people quiet, content with the flicker of the fire and the gentle comfort of a full belly after their meal. She met people who whispered to her about a problem they had, which only a stranger passing through could fix with the proper subtlety, and which thankfully Lux could indeed fix with the things she'd taken from Saga's garden. In many ways, the people were the same as those in the south land, but in others they were different. No one was suspicious of her knowledge. No one told her what she was, or what they thought she should be.

On the nights there could be no roof over their heads, Lux found a cave or a nest of bracken. She made sure Rún and My Lady were warm, settling themselves as animals do. Else sat, present and watching for danger, or flickering out to wherever was on the other side of the veil. And Lux – she didn't go somewhere else, but she became something else. She curled up beside Rún like pups in a nest and slept all night, never cold, never afraid. And when she woke, it was to strange memories: soft fur, sharp ears, her tongue pressed to the black ridged roof of a mouth grown large, arched like a cathedral ceiling, teeth and claws licked clean.

They travelled for many days and nights. Lux had never been so far in her life. She didn't even know there *was* this far. So much world. So many strangers. So many stories. And yet – never the one she most wanted to hear. In every home, Lux found a way to ask about the north witches. But all she heard was confusion, pity, even scorn. Witches were only in the south. Witches were only an excuse. Witches were a story, nothing more.

Lux shrugged it all off. She got back on her horse and kept going north.

When they'd washed up in the north land, winter hadn't quite let go. There were still late snows, and most of the flowers still slept. As they crossed the land, they brought spring with them. The snow shifted to rain, and bright green shoots appeared. Soon every patch of earth was fretted with tiny flowers. Rivers that were iced over now melted and burst in eager torrents, chattering as they went. Birds wheeled and shimmered overhead. Slowly, the dark retreated and the light grew longer.

Lux knew the place the moment she saw it. They had travelled half a day past the last town. The light was fading, but Lux didn't need to see sharply to know this place. She'd seen it before, many nights, with her eyes closed.

A white sea that never rests, licking over the sand as black as night, the steady boom and suck of the waves. Steam billowing into the wild sea from a crevice in the folded rocks. The glaciers blue, floating out to sea.

Lux stopped My Lady and looked around. Above them, spread across the tops of the hills, myriad lights suddenly flared up.

'Bonfires,' said Else. 'I heard about this. For the summer equinox, when the light and the dark are exactly balanced.'

But where were the witches? Lux had thought she'd be able to feel them. That their power would thrum through her blood even from a distance. But she couldn't see anyone.

Lux thought then of when Else had first come to her and led her through the night forest. Else had said there was goodness in the dark, and Lux hadn't believed her. She'd craved the light. But then she'd trav-elled with Else, and she'd met the mummers who found safety in the dark, and she'd finally been able to tell her story in the gloom of the pine forest. There was beauty in the dark, and safety and wonder. The dark was not bad, was not evil or secretive; the dark just was.

Then she'd gone to the stronghold and lived only in the day, and been always lit by dozens of candles. But what scheming and secrets were hid-den in the light of that place. The light was not good, was not pure or cleansing; the light just was. Without one, there can't be the other.

'The bonfires will burn through the night,' said Else, answering Lux's thoughts, 'and be extinguished at dawn. Light in the dark.'

'And dark in the light.'

Else came to Lux and held out the curl of ribbon.

'I'm ready,' she said.

They stood together, looking down into the grave Lux had dug at the mouth of the cave, where the red ribbon lay on the earth. Else had faded to shadows now; if Lux didn't look directly at her, it was like she wasn't there at all.

'I don't know if I can do this alone,' said Lux.

'You don't have to be alone.'

Without thinking, Lux reached out and felt Rún's soft head, as he stood there beside her, as he was always beside her.

'You're more than where you came from,' said Else. 'I wanted to give my girl a choice. The lord. The pedlar. A devil in a cell. But there are more places than that to come from. There are more places than that to go.'

A thought had been growing in Lux for a long time. She was afraid to let it out, to look too closely at it in case the clean gleam of it was just base metal.

'Your wolf,' said Lux. 'The one you said was hungry. The one who scared away the boys and killed the lord and got food when we needed it. Do you think that Rún could do all that?'

'I think,' said Else slowly, 'that a dog is just a wolf who sleeps inside.'

That was all the permission Lux needed.

'I'm the wolf.'

'Yes,' said Else. 'You always were.'

Lux turned to Else, and she was full colour, solid flesh, no scars around her mouth, and her eyes clear. Then she was gone, and Lux covered over the scrap of red ribbon, the last of Else, and laid her mother to rest.

Lux stood there at her mother's grave at the midpoint of the year: equinox, light and dark exactly balanced. She was between the dog and the wolf, between tame and wild, between life and death.

She began the long climb up the hill to where the bonfires burned. The higher she got, the darker the earth grew, until her feet were climbing firm on land burned black. The wind picked up her hair, tangling it into a wild nest. The fires caught in her eyes, making them gleam. Her breath came hard and her heart throbbed in her fingertips like the crackle of a storm.

Below her, a white sea that never rests, blue glaciers cast up glassy and gleaming on a shore of black sand. Steam billowing into the wild sea from a crevice in the folded rocks.

Finally she reached the crest of the hill. There she stood, between the fires.

Light and dark together in one woman.

A woman neither one thing nor another.

Fire inside and power in every word she spoke.

No need for power over others as she has power over herself.

Perhaps it was true that there were no north witches before.

But, now, here she was.

Acknowledgements

Editorial: Elizabeth Foley & Mikaela Pedlow
Copy-editor: Katherine Fry
Proofreader: Alex Milner
Cover designer: Kris Potter
Illustrator: Lea Yunk
Production: Konrad Kirkham
Marketing: Sophie Painter & Katrina Northern
Publicity: Bethan Jones & Mia Quibell-Smith

Thank You:
Cath Summerhayes for always being there.
Liz Foley for making me a better writer.
Susie Francis for hours of rambling story chat.
Alex Kahler for being unofficial dramaturg.
Heather Parry for the daily check-ins.
Camilla Grudova and Heather Palmer for being sounding boards.
Rachael Stephen for plot embryos and existentialism.
Hetta Howes for medievalism.
Elaine Thomson for poisons and plants.
Hawthornden, particularly Hamish, Ruth for the puddings, and Mary and Debbie for the lunch hampers. Thanks also to everyone who sent postcards and letters to me there, especially Jenn Ashworth.

Villa Sarkia in Finland, particularly Shawn for the lake swims, sauna confession and horror movie nights.

AIR Literature Västra Götaland residency in Sweden, particularly Gunilla, Helgi for nightly Hannibal and wine, and Susan for a new perspective.

Everyone who listened to me ramble on about witches and the Middle Ages ('it's a bit more complicated than that') in the past six years.

All the many, many family and friends in our baby-raising village.

And Annie, always.

Kirsty Logan is a professional daydreamer. Her first story collection, *The Rental Heart & Other Fairytales*, won the Scott Prize, the Polari First Book Prize and the Saboteur Award. Her first novel, *The Gracekeepers*, won a Lambda Literary Award and was selected for the Radio 2 Book Club and the Waterstones Book Club. *A Portable Shelter* won the Gavin Wallace Fellowship and was published as a limited edition illustrated hardback which sold out on pre-order. *Things We Say in the Dark*, a collection of feminist horror stories, was optioned for TV. Her short fiction and poetry have been translated into Japanese, Spanish, Italian and Chinese, adapted for stage, recorded for radio and podcasts, exhibited in galleries, and distributed from a vintage Wurlitzer cigarette machine. She lives in Glasgow with her family.